The Serpent's Tail

Martin Dillon has won international acclaim for his non-fiction books about Ireland, notably *The Shankill Butchers*, *The Dirty War* and *The Enemy Within*. The filmscript of his first novel won a European Script Fund award in 1993. After a spell as a newspaper journalist, Martin Dillon spent eighteen years working for the BBC in Northern Ireland. He was on the *Timewatch* team in England when in 1992 he left the BBC to pursue his writing career. As well as seven works of non-fiction, he has written two plays for television and radio, and since leaving the BBC has written and produced documentaries for Channel Four, the BBC and RTE. He lives in France with his wife Kathy and their two children, Crawford and Nadia.

Other books by Martin Dillon

The Serpent's Tail

a novel by
MARTIN DILLON

RICHARD COHEN BOOKS · London

British Library Cataloguing in Publication Data:
A catalogue record for this book is available from the British Library

Copyright © 1995 by Martin Dillon

ISBN 1 86066 007 X (Pbk)
ISBN 1 86066 006 1 (cased)

First published in Great Britain in 1995 by
Richard Cohen Books
7 Manchester Square
London WIM 5RE

3 5 7 9 8 6 4 2

Typeset in Linotron Baskerville by
Rowland Phototypesetting Ltd,
Bury St Edmunds, Suffolk

Printed in Great Britain by
Clays Ltd, St Ives plc

1

It was a cold and dismal Monday morning in winter. Mist hung low over the Divis Mountain, and West Belfast was quiet.

Ursula Carlin opened her door, left it slightly ajar and made a last-minute tour of her living-room to make sure she was ready to leave the house as soon as the laundry was collected.

A faint knocking on the front door alerted her to the presence of the laundry girl.

'How's Danny?' asked the young Englishwoman as Ursula bent to lift the bag of washing.

Before she could reply, Ursula saw a blue car screeching to a halt at the side of the laundry van. The driver of the van reached to his left, as if to retrieve something, but was fumbling in panic. From the car appeared two armed men, their faces hidden by balaclava masks. One of the gunmen rushed to the side of the van and fired two bursts from an automatic weapon. Ursula and the laundry girl were frozen to the spot as the body of the driver jerked backwards and forwards with the impact of the bullets. The second gunman was at the other side of the van firing one long burst into the roof of the van above the front passenger cabin.

Everything ended as quickly as it had begun.

Suddenly the gunmen turned towards Ursula, who could only stare at them and grab the laundry girl, her instinct telling her that this young woman was in danger because she was English. But the girl's demeanour changed abruptly, and Ursula was flung against the door as the girl ran through the house towards the back door.

'Get down! Get down! . . . Get outa the fuckin' way!' yelled the gunmen, motioning to Ursula to allow them a clear line of fire at their next target.

She couldn't find the means to scream. She fell sideways into the hallway and lay there as the men jumped over her and ran through the house. Moments later they returned, paused briefly to look down at her, then rushed to their car. It sped off, the tyres leaving a trail of smoke as they burned the tarmac.

Major Tim Johnston's broad shoulders filled the doorway of the Ops Room. People who were shouting orders and listening to radio messages turned to look at him.

'Who's got the latest update?'

A young intelligence collator rushed forward with a single sheet of paper. The SAS major took it from him and glared at the others in the room. The hubbub resumed.

'Christ!' said Johnston as he made his way to a group of radio operators. 'What have we got?' he asked in a more measured tone which nevertheless suggested he was resigned to bad news.

One of the operators removed his headset and stood up, his head barely reaching the major's shoulders. 'The laundry's been compromised, sir.'

Johnston was clearly irritated by the reply. 'For God's sake, man, give me the latest.'

'There's at least one down in the van, sir, and we've lost contact with Lieutenant Horton. The latest we have says she's running.'

'Has she used her radio?'

'Not yet, sir . . . She's in hostile territory and on foot.'

'Stay on her frequency,' said Johnston.

Then he turned, crossed the room and approached a soldier who was studying a map of West Belfast. The soldier was in fatigues, and wore no insignia to denote regimental allegiance.

'How bad is it, Ron?'

'It's bad, sir. The RUC say a housewife saw Jane escape and the sapper driving the van is dead. The others . . . your

8

guess is as good as mine. I think we have to assume the worst and concentrate on Jane.'

'OK,' said Johnston, moving closer to the map. 'Get a heli over that area. Put some of our people on the ground and, when we've got a fix, get her out. The IRA'll be after her and I don't want her falling into their hands. Keep the RUC out of this – the less they know the better. I don't want their forensic people examining the van. Have it moved to our base. And fast.'

Tim Johnston walked to a desk where four men were using secure phone lines to communicate with military intelligence operatives at British Army HQ.

'Get on to the Psy Ops people at the Information Policy Unit. Tell them we need damage limitation in the media and to get their story out before the IRA has a field day with this one. The official line must be that this was a surveillance operation . . . tell them to stress that.'

He turned to Sergeant Ron Dawson. 'Keep an eye on things,' he said. 'I've the unenviable task of breaking the news to Five.'

'Good luck, sir.'

'Luck won't get me out of this one.'

Four months later, Richard Milner, one of MI5's most talented officers, was on his way to meet Major Johnston at Palace Barracks.

He was on board a helicopter, accompanied by two armed soldiers who had developed a capacity for staring ahead and resisting any temptation to speak. They were in fatigues with no insignia and were armed with short-barrelled sub-machine-guns which were not British Army issue. Milner had arrived from London over a week before, but this would be his first meeting with the SAS major.

Seconds before the helicopter touched down, the soldiers leapt from it and were waiting for Milner when he carefully stepped on to the ground. Taking his arm, they hurried him from the down draught of the rotary blades which sent dust into his eyes, ears and nose.

Darkness made it impossible to comprehend the sheer size of the base at Palace Barracks. A jeep was waiting for him, its engine already running and a driver in place. The journey through the camp was conducted in silence. His two escorts sat beside him and the driver, who appeared to ignore the right of any other vehicle or person to use the same route.

A large concrete structure loomed into view as the jeep screeched to a halt. Milner's escorts jumped out and told him to follow, leading him towards a massive bunker with a metal doorway and no windows. A single arc-light illuminated the entrance, where remote-controlled cameras were positioned to scrutinise visitors.

'This compound is out of bounds to the regulars,' said one of the soldiers. The other pressed an intercom button on the metal door and announced, 'He's here.'

After a few seconds the door swung open to reveal two men in combat gear, similar in style to that of the soldiers who had accompanied him.

'Just follow those guys, sir. They'll take you to the major,' said one of his escorts. Then he and his partner disappeared into the darkness of the camp.

At thirty-five, Richard Milner had over ten years' experience in MI5, but his bright blue eyes and slim build gave him a youthfulness that was disarming.

After graduating from Cambridge with a First in Classics, he had been introduced to the world of intelligence by a family friend. Unlike many of his contemporaries, who revelled in the new radicalism of the 1960s, Richard had spent those years learning the intricacies of counter-espionage. Based at MI5 headquarters in Curzon Street, London, where considerable resources were devoted to tracking foreign diplomats, he learned how to analyse information collected through electronic surveillance. His private life was occupied mainly with listening to music and drinking fine wines in the sanctuary of his large apartment in Holland Park.

One crisp spring morning in 1974, Richard had been summoned to a meeting with his superiors who had casually suggested he might consider a new post in Northern Ireland. Richard had frozen in his chair. Nothing in his career had prepared him for this. He was told his role would be to liaise with military intelligence and oversee a top-secret operation already in the planning stage.

'The first thing you must do is to find out why one of our major operations has recently been penetrated by the IRA,' his controller had told him.

There had followed a two-week briefing from senior operatives with Northern Ireland experience, and an intensive examination of MI5's involvement in the conflict. He was informed that, unknown to the government and often the generals too, military intelligence had been running several covert units along with MI5 and the police Special Branch.

'Don't place too much trust in the indigenous security apparatus in Ulster,' one of his briefing agents had said. 'Be careful about Special Branch rank and file – only deal with the man at the top. It's your job to find out how this operation has been penetrated by the IRA, shore up what's left and provide the right analytical skills, to keep us protected, and to make sure there's a blanket of secrecy round the next one. Your co-partner in all of this is an SAS major, Tim Johnston, and you can be sure he's on the level. His file is on your desk . . . Read it as if he were a target because you must know his weaknesses and strengths. Remember, though, that officially the SAS are not in Northern Ireland and there is no Major Johnston.'

On the morning of his departure for Belfast, Milner was asked to sign a document which stated that he was accepting a post as a 'liaison officer', appointed to improve communications between military intelligence and MI5. It was intended to be a bland brief should anyone at ministerial level decide at a future date that they wanted to know why Milner had been sent to Northern Ireland. Two electronics experts were assigned to him under the guise of 'collators', with the task of providing electronic security and secretly recording telephone traffic between himself and the major.

Twenty-four hours before his departure, he had immersed himself in the file on Major Johnston, which contained a detailed military history and assessments of his personal characteristics. It was an impeccable record, with commendations for operations carried out in Cyprus and Oman.

A character description written by one of the MI5 collators included the fact that the major was forty years old, and commented on his experience of undercover work. 'He is a dedicated soldier who can be relied on to undertake secret operations with no political fallout. He has a tendency to be arrogant and dismissive of authority, which relates to his experience of working independently and rarely has a bearing on his professional duties. His personal life has been somewhat messy with a failed marriage and a series of affairs with military personnel. He operates best when he is permitted freedom to develop his potential.'

Richard was fascinated by the military citations in the file, especially an account of how the major had wiped out an EOKA cell during the emergency in Cyprus. Assisted by an SAS sergeant, he had attacked a terrorist hide-out in hilly terrain under cover of darkness, leaving six dead. The killing had taken place at close quarters and his partner had been shot dead in the first exchange of fire. Johnston was wounded when a bullet struck the base of his neck and exited through his upper jaw, yet he had managed to return to base on foot and was later awarded the Distinguished Service Order.

There was, however, a missing ingredient in the file: the SAS major's tour of duty in Northern Ireland was not listed.

Stormont Castle, on the outskirts of Belfast, was the seat of the Ministers sent from London to run Northern Ireland and was situated within sight of the impressive parliament buildings where Protestant Unionist governments had held power for their own people. Richard Milner had been allocated a suite in the castle containing a bedroom, a dining-room, an office and a small ante-room which he had immediately recognised as an ideal den where he could listen to the record collection he had brought with him from London.

His electronics experts had used a device to 'sweep' his quarters to make sure they were not bugged, and on his instructions planted miniature recording devices in his dining-room.

Major Johnston lived within the secrecy of a secure compound at Palace Barracks near the town of Holywood on the coast road out of Belfast. It was not far from Stormont, enabling Richard to hold meetings with the major at short notice. Radio communications between them would be conducted through special lines fitted with scramblers.

Secure telephone lines linked the suite with London HQ and Palace Barracks, and a sophisticated trip alarm and miniaturised cameras were fixed to inner doors to detect any unauthorised entry.

One of the first discoveries which had brightened Milner's arrival was a well-stocked wine cellar and an excellent chef, who welcomed the opportunity to indulge his creativity.

After five days spent reading briefing documents about the security apparatus and the personal characteristics of senior figures within it, Milner had made his first sortie from the confines of Stormont to visit the headquarters of the Royal Ulster Constabulary. He travelled in the back of a heavily armoured jeep with members of the uniformed Special Patrol Group sitting on either side of him.

Inside the office of the head of the RUC Special Branch, a large, dour man sat behind his desk, shuffled papers and made no effort to offer a civilised handshake.

'You're one of the "London calling" crowd,' he said, his gaze not leaving the documents.

Richard Milner picked up a chair, placed it within a foot of the desk and stared at the Special Branch chief, who lifted an official memo and scrutinised it before looking at his visitor.

'I knew you were coming, and this memo tells me who you are.' The piece of paper was dismissively flung to one side.

The Special Branch chief's large hands, ruddy complexion and broad shoulders were those of a man from a rural background who did not take kindly to strangers.

'You know who I am,' said Richard, 'and I know you're Commander Stanley Davidson, so let's define exactly what my role is here.'

Richard waited for a reaction. Instinct warned the big policeman that the slim figure in front of him was no pushover.

'London's told you what I'm about. Is that correct?' Richard folded his arms across his chest.

Davidson mumbled and nodded his head to indicate he'd been briefed.

'My role stops at your desk,' said Richard, 'and I expect your co-operation. It's clear you're not happy about my being on your patch, but I'm afraid that's your problem, commander.'

Stanley Davidson moved uncomfortably in his chair, his face and hands twitching as he tried to control his anger.

'No doubt you're aware that London expects full co-operation,' Richard added, 'and they're going to know if I get any less than that. There are to be no leaks at this end.'

Davidson raised his hand in protest but Richard ignored him.

'We may not like each other's perspectives, but that's of little consequence. I expect you to provide me with a list of your best field operatives and their agents within the IRA, and I want it tomorrow.'

Richard rose and quickly left the room, the door swinging behind him.

The following morning a special courier arrived with a large file and a handwritten note from Commander Davidson which assured Milner of Davidson's utmost co-operation and support. It also named two of Special Branch's best officers, Bill Green and John Bradford, and identified their agents as Stephen Kirkpatrick and Michael McDonnell.

That's a job well done, thought Richard, and put the personal note into a small paper shredder on his desk.

The file comprised career details and photographs of the Special Branch officers and their agents.

Forty-eight hours later, Milner was relaxing in his den at the castle listening to a scratchy recording of Teresa Berganza singing 'Una Voce Poca Fa' from Rossini's *Barber of Seville*. Suddenly his tranquillity was disrupted by one of his aides, who gingerly entered the room.

'Sorry to disturb you, sir. Major Johnston's been in touch. He says there's a helicopter waiting for you at his end . . . at your pleasure, of course."

'Tell him on this occasion he can take precedence over Rossini,' said Richard Milner, smiling.

The aide looked confused. 'Is that a code, sir?'

Richard laughed. 'Don't be silly, man. Just tell him to send the transport.'

As Richard entered the large concrete building in the Palace Barracks compound, the steel door slammed shut behind him and his new escorts walked either side of him along a winding, half-lit corridor, down a steep flight of concrete stairs and into a wider passageway with rooms on either side.

Christ, this is like Hitler's bunker, thought Richard.

One doorway was marked 'Mess' and another 'Target Room'. Milner was so busy observing the signs on doors that he failed to notice he was fast approaching the end of the corridor and a door with a remote-controlled camera above it.

'This is the Ops Room, sir,' said one of the guides, keeping a restraining hand on Richard's left arm. 'Just press the intercom. The major's expecting you.'

Before he could act, the door swung open and a tall, heavily built man dressed in fatigues held out his hand and smiled.

'Tim Johnston at your service.'

Richard winced as his hand was held and shaken in a vice-like grip.

'Sorry to phone you so late. I really thought the sooner we met the better,' said Johnston, leading his visitor to a large oak table covered with stacked documents. 'I hope I didn't interrupt you.'

Richard gave a thin smile. 'The only person who can answer that is Rossini.'

'*The Barber of Seville*, perhaps,' remarked the major, with a twinkle in his eye. 'I do my homework on people who are going to work with me, Richard. No doubt you have done the same thing.'

Richard laughed, and the tension eased. He was impressed by this first encounter with Johnston.

The major was well over six foot, brown-haired, blue-eyed, with the muscular physique of a rugby number 8, and the rugged features of a man who'd lived hard. A woollen cravat hid the scar of the bullet which had almost taken his life in Cyprus; a small jagged wound on his right upper jaw was the only visible evidence. The son of a general, Tim Johnston had trained at Sandhurst and chosen the SAS because it was a regiment which suited his desire for total self-reliance.

'If I may be excused just a moment . . .' Johnston walked towards an ante-room, leaving Richard to take in the atmosphere of the Operations Room.

The banks of typewriters, radios and teleprinters were silent but a wall of photographs of IRA volunteers, each one named and identified by rank, spoke for itself. Closer scrutiny revealed that the names were ordered in a hierarchy and comprised the intelligence structure of the Provisional IRA in Belfast. At the top of the pyramid was a hand-drawn outline of a face and, underneath, the name 'Brendan' written in large capitals. Another wall contained maps of Northern Ireland counties, and one had Belfast districts marked in green and orange to denote Catholic and Protestant zones.

Richard's gaze was drawn towards a photographic display with the heading 'Military Reaction Force' and, beneath it, the word 'Agents'. Among the photos, Richard recognised the four soldiers who had been his escorts earlier that evening. He was about to turn away when he noticed an arrow pointing sideways to a group of four photographs: head-and-shoulders shots of Special Branch operatives Bill Green and John

Bradford, and further arrows indicating two young men with their names written in block capitals – 'MICHAEL MCDONNELL' and 'STEPHEN KIRKPATRICK'. They were similar to the pictures he had received from the Special Branch chief.

Milner was so engrossed in examining them that he failed to hear the major re-entering the room.

'I'm ahead of you, Richard,' said the Major. 'Davidson told me you'd requested them . . . but I had them first.'

'The bastard,' said Richard, his gaze fixed on the wall display. 'He didn't tell me you'd been in touch.'

'He's a wily old bird,' replied the major as he placed a large tray on the oak table.

Richard looked round and was pleasantly surprised by what he saw. On the tray was a bottle of wine and two Waterford crystal goblets.

'I hope you don't mind,' said the major. 'I believe you enjoy a good wine, so I liberated this bottle from the officers' mess at HQ.'

Richard smiled and approached the table. 'Good heavens, a '70 Haut Brion . . . I never thought such things existed in a bunker.'

The first glass of wine led to an exchange of pleasantries about life in London; by the second glass they were settled into an appreciation of each other's company.

It was then that Johnston's face assumed a look of concern. 'I think it's time I explained our recent disaster. It should help you to grasp what we're up against.'

He put down his glass of wine and strolled across to the wall of IRA photographs, then pointed to the blank facial image with the name 'Brendan' underneath it.

'This is our target. This bastard is dangerous and cunning. This is the guy who has just blown our operations in Belfast.'

'Why is the face a blank? Don't you have a photograph of him?'

'No, I don't need one. I know how he thinks and operates. That's more important.' The major returned to the table.

'Tim, I must find out if we can proceed with the next stage, so I need to know the damage.'

Major Johnston swallowed a large mouthful of wine, as if to lubricate his vocal cords for a lengthy explanation. 'It's like this. I set up the Military Reaction Force under classified orders using some of my own people and a mixture of agents we'd recruited from within the IRA and the loyalist paramilitaries. It was based very much on our operations in Cyprus and elsewhere, but it was a lot more sophisticated than previous campaigns.

'Only the generals and military intelligence knew about this one. My task was to create counter-gangs, train people to behave like the IRA and carry out assassinations which we could blame on the enemy. My people operated with IRA weapons. The intention was to draw the Provisional IRA and the Official IRA into a feud, and carry out sectarian killings to encourage a war between the IRA and the loyalists.'

Johnston drank some more wine. 'I thought this approach was too crude. So I decided to look for a more sophisticated way of getting at the Provisionals, because they were emerging as the greatest threat. Then some of our intelligence people suggested that we set up a bogus laundry service, but using the facilities of a bona fide laundry in Belfast. The idea was to provide a cheap service, to get us into the Andersonstown area, where we knew the Provisionals had their best men. Then we'd spread the service to other republican districts. When we collected washing, the stuff from the homes of people on our suspect lists was separated from the rest and forensically tested before being returned to the owners.'

'I don't quite understand what you're getting at,' said Richard.

The major smiled. 'When a gun is fired, it leaves traces of lead on clothing. When explosives are handled, the same thing happens. We couldn't pull everybody in . . . but we suspected that certain people were shooters or bombers and one way of proving it was to find out if their clothing contained the evidence. In that way we could target them and pass on intelligence to the forces on the ground.'

'Ingenious.' Richard allowed the major to pour more wine into his glass.

'That's not all,' said Johnston. 'We built a special compartment into the roof of the laundry van to allow two of our men to lie face down. At the front of the van, above the windscreen, was the laundry sign with small slits in it which allowed our hidden operatives to take notes and secretly photograph people on our suspect lists.'

Richard nodded. 'OK. Fine. But what exactly went wrong?'

The major detected his unease with the lengthy explanation of the MRF's history and reached for a file on the table. He opened it and placed it in front of Richard. The first photograph showed the laundry van, with bullet holes and a mass of bloodstains inside the cabin. The second was a close-up of the roof interior which was riddled like a sieve.

'The Provisionals knew we had two people in that roof compartment.' Johnston removed two other photographs from the file, one of a young man and the other a pretty, slimly built young woman. '*He* was taken out by the bastards. *She* escaped, and we recovered her in the nick of time. Another two minutes and she'd have been in their hands.'

'Why were the operatives in the laundry service not armed?'

'The driver was, but he couldn't get to his concealed weapon fast enough. The two men in the roof were always told never to react if the van was attacked because we believed that no one would know they were there.'

'What about your lieutenant, Jane Horton?'

'We couldn't take the risk of arming her because she was in such close contact with the public. She had a miniature radio, and that saved her life when she escaped.'

'What did you do when you heard what had happened?'

'I closed everything down and pulled everyone in. Then I discovered that two of our terrorist agents were missing. You must understand that, in using terrorist agents, the secret is to allow them to operate like terrorists, otherwise they can't provide us with information. That means they are out of contact with us for several days at a time. Our routine was to train them, then have them with us for a few days, then allow them out again, and so on. This was like a rest home. They came here to relax, as well as be debriefed.'

'How could you ever be sure you could trust them? Forgive me if that's a naïve question.'

The major smiled. 'It's a strange question coming from an MI5 man.'

Richard laughed. 'Russian agents and IRA gunmen are hardly in the same category, are they?'

'But isn't it all about judgement?'

Richard nodded in agreement.

'We compromise them, blackmail them until they are more frightened of the IRA than they are of us. We know their weaknesses and strengths.'

'That doesn't explain how your operation was penetrated.'

'There's the answer.' Major Johnston walked across the room and placed the palm of his hand on the 'Brendan' image. 'This man got to two of our young agents in the IRA – Wright and McKee. They were ideal . . . from Republican families . . . In fact McKee's uncle is one of the leaders of the IRA's Belfast Brigade. That's how close we got.'

'And where are they now?'

The major laughed and slapped the image. 'You'll have to ask that bastard.'

'I'm asking *you*.'

Johnston half apologised. 'Forgive me. I tend to think that you know what I know. Our agents were uncovered by IRA counter-intelligence – that's Provo-speak for internal security. I can only conclude that our agents gave themselves away because of loose talk, their routine or simply because the IRA are good at what they do. From what we know, they were abducted from their homes by armed men and they haven't been seen since. That happened days before our operation was hit. So they were probably interrogated, perhaps tortured, and revealed everything they knew about the MRF and my operations.'

The major tugged at his cravat. 'Don't ever underestimate the enemy – those bastards are good. They hit us before we had time to realise that two of our people were in their custody. We may never know what happened to our two young agents. They'll possibly turn up in black plastic bags on a border road. There's no way the IRA would have kept them in Belfast knowing that we would mount a search operation to find them. Perhaps we'll never find them.'

He returned to his chair, and Richard paused for reflection.

'Have you tied up the loose ends and are we back in business?'

Richard's question hung in the air until Johnston smiled.

'That's why you're here, Richard. I've got everything in place to move once you give the go-ahead.'

'Yes, but what's the risk of failure?'

'I would say the chances of success are much better.'

Richard laughed. 'That's all very well, Tim.' A solemn expression spread across his face and he added, 'But there is no room for error with this one. There's too much at stake, and we need the right handlers and agents.'

'Of course. We learned a lot from the recent fiasco.'

'Yes, but the plan we're about to undertake demands more than tight security. It will require total commitment. We pull this one off and the IRA are finished. If we fail and this ever gets out, it could bring down the government, and believe me there are people out there who have an interest in doing just that. This time the agents selected will have to know we mean business. They'll need to know that their lives are in our hands. It's up to you and the Special Branch handlers to put the frighteners on them. I need to be certain that their psychological profiles accord with our plan.'

'You can be sure I will deliver.'

'Good. Now, if you've another bottle of the same wine, Tim, I think I could be persuaded to drink to success.'

'Persuasion is one of my stronger points,' said the major, chuckling as he walked towards the ante-room. 'But don't ask me to elaborate on that one.'

2

Stephen Kirkpatrick eased his right leg from under the bed-clothes and placed it on the bare floorboards. Slowly, rhythmically, he tapped out the sound of footsteps.

'I know what you're at!' shouted his mother from the kitchen below.

Stephen smiled, and quickly removed his six-foot bulk from the bed. 'I'm up!' he yelled.

He pulled on a pair of faded denims, and walked into the bathroom where a full-length mirror confronted him with his shaggy appearance. He ran his fingers through his thick black hair, and arranged it in a style he hoped would persuade his mother to believe he'd brushed it. After a cursory cleaning of his teeth, he went out to a tiny landing which linked three bedrooms and led to the ground floor. It was not a house where anyone was likely to be confused about the layout.

On his way through their tiny living-room, Stephen caught a glimpse of his mother in the kitchen, tending a pan of boiling water.

'There's an egg in this for you. By now it's probably as hard as your hearing,' she remarked.

Stephen ignored her, sat down at the dining-table and tucked into a bowl of cornflakes while his mother kept her eyes firmly fixed on the cooker.

'You're almost nineteen years of age and you're still usin' that ploy in the mornings. If y' were in bed earlier, y'd not be lyin' there half the day.'

Stephen looked at the greasy face of a clock which showed 10.30. Experience had taught him that his mother, when agitated, was best ignored.

Mary Anne Kirkpatrick was a formidable woman in her mid-forties, and her large frame disguised her weight, which was only a chocolate cake off twelve stones. Her dark hair, large brown eyes and strong features resembled what the Irish called 'the Spanish Galway look'. She often said, much to Stephen's displeasure, that she was descended from one of the sailors of the ill-fated Armada wrecked off the west coast of Ireland. He dismissed the claim because he took after his mother, and the idea of a sailor, a Spanish one at that, in his lineage did not appeal to him.

Stephen's mother drew her strength and resilience from years spent on a factory floor. Her husband had died penniless when Stephen was five years old, and she was left to support her young son and his two elder sisters. Mary Kirkpatrick was shaped by the rigours of working-class life, and the grief of losing her man in the formative years of motherhood. She was kind, but rarely expressed a physical affection for her children. Stephen often wondered if all the love she possessed had followed his father to his grave. He loved her but resented her tendency to treat him like a child.

'I suppose you were out last night with that waster, Michael McDonnell? When your two sisters were your age, they weren't runnin' around half the night.'

Stephen suppressed an urge to reply that perhaps his sisters might not have married so young if they'd had a bit more freedom at home.

As Mary Kirkpatrick flattened her plumpness into a tiny wooden chair, he was aware of the heat in her breath and the venom in her voice.

She moved aside a large milk jug which was obscuring her view of her son. 'That fella's a . . .' Her voice tailed off as she searched for a suitable word to describe Michael, her son's best friend.

Before she could return to the charge, her attention was diverted by a slight movement. Stephen was much too busy munching cornflakes to hear a minor disturbance behind him. His sisters were standing at the entrance to the kitchen and had been there for several minutes listening to their mother's anger. They gleefully motioned to her to continue the tirade but she didn't need encouragement.

'And what's more . . . She pointed her finger at her son, until it rested on the top of the egg in front of him. 'You and that Michael McDonnell are runnin' around like layabouts. It beats me how the two of y' are always flush with money. I could see through it if you both had a job . . . But oh no, you'd rather lie in your bed all day.'

Stephen's sisters kissed him affectionately on the cheek.

'And what's the problem with our wee brother?' asked Sheila.

'Is our little brother gettin' a hard time from his mammy?' asked Deirdre.

He knew to expect his sisters to indulge themselves at his expense. Mary could not resist smiling, even though she realised that Deirdre was determined to trivialise the situation; Sheila, who had more experience of her mother's short temper, would try to humour her.

Stephen kept his gaze fixed on the table. He pushed aside the cornflakes bowl and began to remove the top of the egg untidily with a small spoon.

'Look at him,' said Mary Kirkpatrick. 'He can't even get off his arse t' fetch a knife t' cut the egg properly.' She was frustrated by his refusal to respond and by the diversion created by her daughters, who were leaning against their brother like two buttresses.

Sheila and Deirdre, both married with children, loved their brother and constantly sought his affection. Deirdre was closest to him because they were separated by only two years and had shared their childhood dreams and troubles. She was good-looking and vivacious, her dark features resembling Stephen's to the extent that when they were younger they were taken for twins. Underlying her lively manner was a penchant for sarcasm, which Mary said was inherited from her grandfather.

Sheila was a pretty blonde who did not look her twenty-four years; in fact she could easily claim to be a teenager. Stephen often teased her by calling her 'Barbie Kirkpatrick'. It was a description which left her embarrassed but secretly pleased.

'So what's the problem?' asked Sheila.

'He lies in bed all day to stop himself gettin' wrinkles,' said Deirdre.

Mary Kirkpatrick slammed the palms of her large hands on the table and reopened hostilities. 'He's been runnin' around with Michael McDonnell, whose only interest in life is girls and bars.' She ran her right hand across the table in front of her in an agitated fashion and continued her train of thought. 'We all know Michael's a chancer, but can I get that int' his thick skull?' she said, pointing at her son.

He reached for a slice of cold toast, as Mary continued her verbal assault.

'Sure it's true he's got Stephen int' trouble in the past and I'd like t' know where they're gettin' all the money for clothes and drink.'

Mary's audience were inclined to think she had talked herself out but she was not a woman short of words. Deirdre was keen to add to Stephen's discomfort but found it difficult to create room for her contribution. She heaved a sigh of boredom, which earned her a stern rebuke.

'You can have yer say in a minute,' said Mary angrily. She leaned back in her chair with her tongue well sharpened. 'And what's more –'

'Y' mean there's more?'

Deirdre's interjection was ignored. 'There's that lovely little girl round the corner and he never sees her because he's with McDonnell all the time.'

If there was one thing Stephen couldn't tolerate, it was any reference to Bernadette Kane, his girlfriend. His sisters knew that but only Sheila sensed his physical distress and reckoned it would quickly be translated into a bitter exchange with their mother. She held him tight in the hope their closeness would discourage him from being drawn into his mother's web.

'Our Stephen could get off with any girl he wanted in Belfast. You're just hell bent on gettin' him hitched. He's not

25

ready for marriage, and anyway there are plenty of fish in the sea,' said Sheila, springing to his defence.

Deirdre was not to be outdone. 'I hope they're not all as slippery as Bernadette Kane.' She laughed loudly, but no one followed her example. She continued, 'Michael's an arrogant little bugger but the one good thing is that he keeps you away from the clutches of that girlfriend of yours.'

Mary stared at her daughter, her eyes narrowed in anger. 'You and your sister are married,' she said, 'and what's more you don't live in this house, so don't give me advice. Nobody's goin' t' pull the wool over my eyes. You two don't see what's goin' on, and I have a bad feelin' about this. He and that Michael fella are hidin' somethin' from me and believe me it'll end in tears . . .'

Mary's voice faded into a whisper as she finished an almost inaudible sentence and her eyes moistened. She rose from the table and walked towards the kitchen door. Suddenly she turned, and it was clear from her posture that she was about to deliver her last thoughts on the matter. She spoke slowly and deliberately.

'Mark my words, he'll rue the day he was ever associated with that fella McDonnell.'

There was silence as Mary left the kitchen, lifted a coat from a chair in the living-room and went out of the house.

Sheila broke the silence first, her voice carrying the authority of her seniority. 'Look, Stephen, Mummy's very worried and we know that you and Michael should be careful. She's right when she says the two of y' are layabouts, and what is there to yer lives?'

'I don't know what you're all concerned about,' said Deirdre. 'Our Stephen's never done a decent day's work in his life, so why change the habits of a lifetime? As for that wee squirt Michael –'

'You weren't sayin' that when you were eighteen,' put in Sheila. 'C'mon, you really fancied him.'

'Aye, right, somebody must have been feedin' my guide dog at the time.'

There was an embarrassed pause, and again Deirdre sprang

to her own defence. 'All right, I admit it, but that was before I knew what a little shit he really was. Anyway he was too young for me.'

Sheila had not finished dispensing advice to Stephen. 'You're livin' in a dangerous area in dangerous times. You and Michael know that only cats have nine lives. I don't know what you're up to, but don't break Mum's heart a second time.'

Stephen rose quickly from his chair and strode to the other side of the table, muttering, 'There's somewhere I've got to go.'

Sheila laughed. 'It must be somewhere important – You're lookin' so elegant.'

Stephen smiled. 'I'm off to see Jimmy the Natural.'

'Jimmy who?' asked Sheila.

'That's Deirdre's name for Jimmy next door.'

'Y' don't mean that dirty auld fella! He's a nutter,' said Sheila.

Stephen ignored the comment, blew each of them a kiss and hurried from the room.

Sheila turned to her sister. 'Maybe Mummy's been right all along about Stephen and Michael. Maybe there's somethin' goin' on that none of us knows about. I'll tell y' one thing: I don't know what you think . . . but if it's anything like before I want nothin' t' do with it.'

'There you go again – puttin' the boot in. They're only young lads.'

'Young lads? Let's not forget that they were old enough to rob that shop leavin' the old man needin' three stitches. You seem to think our Stephen's a saint.'

Deirdre banged her cup on the table. 'Just hold on there, Sheila.'

Sheila was unimpressed by the outburst and shook her head.

'I know our Stephen's no saint,' continued Deirdre. 'And maybe he is easily led by Jack the lad, but half the young fellas in this neighbourhood wanted t' join the junior IRA and our Stephen was no different. Maybe if Daddy had been alive he would have had somebody to look up to, and wouldn't have needed to join the Fianna.'

Mary Kirkpatrick suddenly entered the room. 'What's goin' on here? I could hear the two of you in the street.'

They looked at each other, embarrassed.

'I hope it's not the usual row about husbands,' said Mary, taking off her coat.

'No,' they said in unison.

'I've enough problems.' Their mother scrutinised them both.

'Maybe I should get a taxi home,' said Deirdre, glancing at Sheila, who laughed.

'Don't be silly . . . get yer coat. My eldest will be out of school in half an hour . . . We've left your groceries on the kitchen table, Mummy, and I've put your meat in the fridge. If Peter doesn't have a game on Saturday, I'll have the car so I'll bring the wee ones over to see you. What about you, Deirdre, do you want me to pick you up?'

'I'll see what Brian's doin' . . . we might be going over to his mum's. I think it's her birthday on Saturday. I'll let you know.'

'Give me a ring during the week,' Sheila told her mother, 'and let me have yer grocery list.'

Stephen rang the bell and waited for Jimmy Carson to open his front door. There was a three-minute delay while his friend pulled aside the lace curtains on the window and confirmed the identity of his visitor. The garden was overgrown and the front gate rusted on decaying hinges. Stephen expected some busybody neighbour to monitor his movements, but there was no sign of life apart from a mongrel dog which was deciding whether a small privet hedge merited his urine. As the door opened slowly, Jimmy peered out and waved to him to come in and close the door quickly.

'There's more snoops in this street than fleas on Charlie Brown,' said Jimmy.

Stephen walked into the small cluttered living-room and

settled into a dusty armchair. Announcing that he was about to make a pot of strong tea, Jimmy slouched towards the kitchen, and began to conduct a dialogue at a distance. Stephen glanced across towards a pile of old newspapers in a corner of the living-room, and asked his friend why he kept them.

There was a moment of hesitation, as Jimmy struck a match to light the cooker, and replied with the satisfaction of a man pleased that anyone wished to make such an enquiry.

'I cut them int' bundles of four-by four-inch squares, punch a hole through them, put a length of string through the hole and hang them in the privy. In other words, I wipe my arse with the news and that's the best place for it. There's been many a politician who's seen my back passage.'

It was a typical piece of Carson humour, spoken without desire for applause, and Stephen had to fight hard to suppress laughter. The old man's comment was intended to be received with serious appreciation.

An undernourished mongrel appeared from the kitchen, displaying the trepidation of an animal abused.

'I see you've got yerself a dog.'

'I found the poor wee thing hangin' round the back alley two days ago,' Jimmy called out from the kitchen. 'Even dumb animals find it difficult t' survive in this shit-heap of a district.'

The dog tentatively allowed Stephen to stroke its head but crouched in a position which suggested that it expected to be battered at any moment.

Jimmy loved animals, particularly his elderly tabby cat, Billy.

'Why did you call your cat Billy?' Stephen had asked. 'It's not exactly a good Irish name.'

Jimmy had replied, 'Well, hasn't he got a bloody great orange stripe down his back like one of those fellas walking along the Shankill Road on the twelfth of July? . . . All struttin' for King William of Orange and the Battle of the Boyne . . . That's the way my Billy walks. Mind you, if that stripe of his had been yellow I'd still have called him Billy – maybe even William.'

Today, half hoping his friend would deliver another humorous riposte, Stephen remarked, 'That dog should make you a good companion. It'll keep an eye on the house, and hold the fort when you're out shopping.'

Jimmy rose to the occasion. 'Oh, he's friendly, all right,' he called out. 'Mind you, when he first arrived he stuck his nose up Billy's arse. Well, Jesus, you wouldn't believe it, but didn't I discover that he's blind in one eye and he was only tryin' t' be friendly? He was simply sniffin' the wrong end. As for him holdin' the fort – he can't hold his own water. He's been pissin' all over the house since he arrived. I thought Billy was bad but that fella has three kidneys, I swear t' God.'

He entered with the tea and poured it into two large cups browned by constant usage and lack of detergent. Then he walked across to a small cupboard beside the window and withdrew a biscuit tin decorated with a faded image of Dublin's O'Connell Street. The tin was offered to Stephen, who removed the lid.

'Get yer gnashers into them,' said Jimmy, with a half-smile. 'If y' can't tackle them you'll need a dentist's drill.'

'Thanks,' said Stephen as a cup of steaming tea with a suggestion of milk was placed on a stool beside him.

'You'll have t' do with the milk that's in it because Billy needs the rest of the bottle. He's the kinda cat that must have liked his mother's milk.'

The mention of mother's milk sent Stephen's thoughts racing to a story he'd heard his mother tell his sister Sheila. When Sheila had her first-born christened Derek, her mother had insisted it was a Protestant name. Mary Kirkpatrick had said that both her daughters were born in the Jubilee wing of the City Hospital.

'Even at that time,' Mary had told Sheila, 'the Jubilee had Catholic and Protestant women and some of them had milk and others didn't. If y' had too much milk, y' donated some of it to other mothers. Now that meant that some Catholic women who were without didn't know whether their babies were bein' fed Catholic or Protestant milk. Now when I was in there with you, Sheila, I had t' borrow some milk – which maybe explains why you've named yer son Derek.'

Stephen looked at Jimmy and thought that, if only his mother could swap stories with the old man, life would be a lot better for everyone.

Jimmy sat on a rickety pine chair, the biscuit tin in his lap, the mug of tea in his left hand.

'See that biscuit tin.'

Stephen stared at it, waiting for some rational explanation for its presence.

'That was O'Connell Street in Dublin at a time when real men were prepared t' die for Ireland – not these sons of Fianna Failure who call themselves Provos. Have y' ever heard of an army called Provo? Mind you, Provo would make a great name for that dog there.'

The dog may well have been more intelligent than Jimmy imagined because when he pointed at it, and suggested the name, it ran into the kitchen.

Jimmy swapped his tongue for his stomach and concentrated on his tea and biscuits, allowing his visitor time to observe him at length. His spectacle lenses were so strong that they doubled the size of his pupils. His thinning grey hair was combed over his forehead. His hands, which had once built walls, resembled the gnarled tops of blackthorn sticks; and his upper torso still bore signs of a man who, in his youth, must have been a formidable adversary in a bar brawl. The shirt and pullover, which Stephen had bought for him two weeks earlier, were his only claim to elegance. His trousers were dirty and heavily patched and his toes protruded from the tops of his slippers.

Jimmy had been a republican activist in the late 1930s but had become disenchanted. He detested the Provisional IRA for advocating violence and the British soldiers who patrolled the streets of his city. When he talked about the Provisionals he described them as 'wide boys' or 'the soldiers of someone else's destiny'. In recent months he'd acquired a distaste for the British monarchy, calling them 'spongers'. The obsession began after Prince Charles had visited Northern Ireland for a brief stopover, much like British politicians in times of crisis. After the royal visit Jimmy declared that all monarchies were doomed because of an earlier history of incest and, in the case of Henry VIII, 'the dreaded syphilis'. He denounced the Church of England, observing that only the English could give their allegiance to a church which was set up because Henry wanted 't' screw Anne Boleyn'.

Stephen was convinced that Jimmy's growing cynicism, even paranoia, about many aspects of society was partly due to his reclusive lifestyle. He was ostracised by neighbours because he seemed different, and was liable to say the most outrageous things about the most dangerous people, namely the IRA. Nevertheless there were times when he was lucid, thoughtful and capable of keen insights. He often remarked that many people considered him 'a nutcase', yet, he said, 'They can't see that the people's heroes of the IRA were all temporarily abnormal.'

The IRA was never far from the old man's thoughts after members of the Fianna, the IRA's junior wing, had smashed his windows two years earlier when he refused to contribute to a door-to-door collection.

Mary Kirkpatrick didn't encourage her son's attachment to their eccentric neighbour, warning him not to visit Jimmy because others might think he shared the old man's opinions of the IRA.

'There's somebody out there.' Jimmy was agitated.

Stephen moved to the window, gently pulled aside the faded lace curtains and saw Michael McDonnell standing beside the garden gate straightening his tie. He watched as Michael ran his fingers through his fair hair, lifting it back from his forehead.

Jimmy was first to the door when the bell rang, but Michael brushed him aside and sauntered into the living-room.

'I thought I'd find y' here,' he said, pointing at Stephen, who suddenly felt uncomfortable.

Mumbling inaudibly, Michael searched for a clean chair on which to place himself and his expensively tailored suit.

Jimmy was uneasy as he entered the room and observed the disgust displayed by the new arrival.

Stephen did not wait for the old man to be hurt. He leaped from his chair, ushering his friend into the front garden.

'Just a minute, son,' said Jimmy, beckoning to Stephen to return to the hallway.

Happy to be away from the house, Michael removed his friend's grip on his arm and walked to the garden gate. As soon as Stephen stepped inside the hallway, Jimmy pulled him into the living-room.

'Listen,' he began, and looked unwaveringly into Stephen's eyes. 'Watch yourself because that fella will drag y' down. I've seen the type of him before. You two have no friends among the soldiers of destiny.'

Stephen gently extricated himself from the old man's grasp. In an attempt to humour him, he said, 'I hope the dog will soon learn t' sniff the right end of the cat.'

The joke fell flat. Jimmy closed the door and retreated into his seclusion.

'How the fuck can you drink tea in there?'

Stephen ignored Michael's question, opened the front door of his home and quietly led the way to his bedroom. Michael sat on the edge of the bed and Stephen reclined on the floor, his back against a pine dressing-table.

Michael constantly rubbed his hands together, a clear sign that he was about to unburden himself of a problem, one which Stephen knew only too well would be lack of money.

'I'm stony broke.'

There was nothing new in the admission. Stephen frequently loaned him money in the certain knowledge it would not be repaid; he accepted that reality because he was his closest friend and constant companion. They shared a similar history, the same schools, bouts of truancy, the loss of their fathers – and secrets which only the two of them knew. They were inextricably bonded, tolerant of each other's character traits and weaknesses.

Stephen was well aware that everyone else in his life, especially his mother and his girlfriend Bernadette, disapproved of Michael. Bernadette resented the closeness and his reluctance to divulge to her the minutiae of his life with Michael, yet she was the only other person with whom he discussed personal matters. However, with Bernadette there were certain subjects which had to remain closed. At least, he felt, she had his promise that when they saved up enough money he would escape with her to America.

Bernadette worked as a typist in a law firm, and every month she set aside part of her earnings and deposited it, along with money that Stephen occasionally gave her, in a joint account in a local building society.

'I suppose you've given all yer money to Bernadette,' Michael grunted.

Detecting animosity in the remark, Stephen did not reply, but Michael was not easily deflected.

'What is it you always say . . . ? Oh yes . . . you're savin' for a rainy day. For God's sake, you rarely see the girl, and anyway she's not worth the effort.'

The comment, and the mockery with which it was delivered, spurred Stephen to abandon his otherwise calm demeanour. He raised himself from the floor and stood over his friend, towering over him and by sheer size making him look like a child. Michael had a reputation for being a terrier in a brawl, but Stephen felt his reputation was at stake and had to risk asserting himself.

'Cut the crap. Bernadette's none of your fuckin' business.'

Michael got the message; his manner softened, though his apparent compliance was motivated by his desire for a hand-out.

'Look, I shouldn't have said that about Bernadette.'

'Just fuckin' keep her out of this. She's not one of your runabouts.'

Michael laughed. He was proud of his track record with young women, and the prospect of a long-term relationship didn't interest him. Michael often wondered what Bernadette's attraction was for his friend. He suspected that she was a mother-figure, a safe haven, a girl who made no demands, who was prepared to wait for the day she would be married. It was embarrassing every time he was in their company because she clung to Stephen like a limpet. Michael knew she disapproved of him and he enjoyed her discomfort when he was in her presence.

'I could let you have a fiver.'

Michael was in no position to decline, the offer, though it was much less than he'd hoped for. 'OK.'

While Stephen rummaged in his jeans for the money, Michael rose from the bed and patted him on the back.

'We've a meetin' tomorrow afternoon with our friends. Be at the Kennedy Way roundabout at two-thirty. They'll pick us up in a blue Vauxhall Cavalier.'

'Why the fuck didn't y' ask me before you fixed up a meetin'? You bloody well know I take Bernadette for a walk on Sundays. Do these bastards never rest? I was hopin' t' take Jimmy's dog with us and go up in the Glen.'

Michael grabbed the five-pound note, opened the bedroom door, then suddenly turned in the doorway. 'Thanks for the fiver. We'll have more of that tomorrow . . . Just make sure you're there on time. You know our friends . . . like I know our friends. They don't like t' be kept waitin' – not in this area.'

Sunday was important to Mary Kirkpatrick too. She made her weekly pilgrimage to St Peter's pro-cathedral in the Lower Falls where she'd worshipped from childhood. It required a bus journey which took her past many of the streets that marked events in her youth; she needed this regular dose of nostalgia to remind herself where she'd come from.

After she married, she had lived for the first fifteen years in a tiny house near St Peter's. There were two bedrooms, a toilet in the yard, and a tin bath which they filled for the family once a week. She and her husband, Sean, had been happy in those years just after the war. Neither had been able to find work that paid for much more than the basic essentials, but until Sean's early death they were contented; they loved each other deeply. Mary reared her three children in that small house and only moved to Andersonstown because council housing offered more space for a developing family.

The Lower Falls held her most cherished memories of her husband, her aunts, uncles and grandparents, who were once held tight in a caring community. People were bound together because they shared a similar plight, they lived in close proximity to each other, and the church was a focal point in their lives. Andersonstown was the antithesis of that environment. It was a big open estate which brought together people from areas where the same sense of belonging and intimacy did not exist. It also heralded a modern world with the emphasis on material possessions to the exclusion of communal dialogue and imagery.

Stephen usually accompanied his mother to St Peter's and it was the part of each week when she had him exclusively in her company. It was the only day he was willing to get out of bed early, to make the journey to eight o'clock Mass.

He too had fond memories of the tiny dusty streets surrounding St Peter's. He was seven years old when the family left for Andersonstown, where he had to make new friends; it was there he first saw Michael, who was also making the transition from the Lower Falls to a new home. In the early years, Stephen was a devout child who attended Mass every morning and made a weekly visit to the confessional. On reflection, he felt that his attachment to Catholicism then was conditioned as much by the family's proximity to the church itself as his mother's insistence that he and his sisters followed her example. They had lived in the shadows of the twin spires of St Peter's which dominated everything and everyone. Even in the back alleys where the cats scrapped through the decaying rubbish, the spires were visible. Now, in his nineteenth year, he was still overcome by their darkened splendour and awesome dimensions.

Stephen had once asked his father why the church needed tall spires, and he had explained that it was to make sure the Protestants of West Belfast knew there were Catholics in that part of the city. According to his father, Catholics built real churches, and the spires gave the poor a sense of importance; a feeling that they belonged to an organisation which could afford such a massive structure.

These days Stephen enjoyed pleasing his mother by making the weekly trip with her, and it didn't bother him that on Sundays he heard the same stories about her antecedents, and her memories of times past. For her part, she was glad he went to church; she said God would find a way of strengthening his faith. As for Michael, he derided Stephen's church-going – and the whole concept of organised religion. In any case, he reserved Saturday nights and the early hours of Sunday for drinking and girls, and rarely saw daylight until the bars opened at 11.30 on Sunday morning.

'Are you comin' in or are y' goin' t' stand there all day?' asked Mary Kirkpatrick, who was about to enter the church and was agitated by her son's insistence on standing in the street, his eyes fixed on the spires.

'You go ahead. I'll be in soon,' said Stephen, looking up at the bell-towers with their slated roofs and the spires, each topped by a metal cross.

The spires were a refuge for pigeons as well as a solace to people. When he was five years old, he watched for days while a hawk circled overhead and gradually reduced the pigeon population. Two years passed while he waited for the hawk to return. Then one autumn morning it arrived and the carnage began again. For three days, feathers fluttered down on the bell-towers and settled on the church porch.

The priests of the parish shared a pair of binoculars to observe the killing spree more thoroughly. No one else got as close as they to seeing the way in which the hawk was capable of clinically disposing of its victims.

Then someone decided enough was enough and took revenge. One damp morning, Stephen went to Mass and saw the lifeless body of the hawk on the front steps of the church. Lying there, the bird looked no more fearsome than the dull grey pigeons. In death it looked innocent, devoid of the savagery which characterised its life above the spires.

Stephen had wanted to bend down and examine it, to find a reason for its death, but his mother dragged him from the carcass with the comment 'It's got its come-uppance.'

No one explained why the hawk had apparently plummeted to its death. He wondered if someone had killed it for defiling the church with pigeon feathers. Sean Kirkpatrick, a man not given to exaggeration, told his son that people did not wish to live with the constant killing. The pigeons belonged in the spires and the hawk was an outsider. He refused to elaborate on how the hawk met its fate, but Stephen's grandmother was heard to remark that there were plenty of guns in the parish to deal with hawks. In childhood, Stephen rejected the idea that the hawk was killed for murdering the pigeons, since people showed no respect or affection for the pigeons when the hawk was not there.

'I suppose you're still lookin' for a hawk!'

Mary Kirkpatrick was standing at the church entrance, her arms folded across her chest, her eyes fixed on her son. Then her gaze swiftly moved from him to the street beyond. Stephen looked round and saw a British Army patrol snaking its way towards the church. Realising that his scrutiny of the spires might encourage the soldiers to think he was acting suspiciously or signalling to a sniper, he hurried into the church, taking his mother by the arm as he made for a pew close to the rear entrance. She refused to be directed and persuaded him to move nearer to the altar, where she felt he might pay more attention to the service.

Unlike services later in the day, early Mass was a brief event because there were too few people present for the celebrant to feel that a sermon would find willing ears. Most of the congregation were elderly ladies who sat behind the marble pillars which rose high into the nave. They whistled aloud their prayers in a patois that only they understood, and a sermon would not have penetrated the dullness of their hearing. They bowed their heads before and during the elevation of the host and presented their furrowed tongues for communion.

The celebrant was Father John O'Connor, a balding curate who reserved his brusqueness for young altar boys who failed to pour a sufficient quantity of wine into his chalice. Stephen regarded the Sunday Mass as a pure piece of theatre, and harboured a sneaking respect for the eccentric ways of the priest. He was determined that if, in a moment of madness, he decided to go to confession he would choose Father O'Connor.

The journey home was his mother's opportunity to remind him of the history of his birthplace. She was animated after Mass, as though she had fulfilled her duty and could address the world with increased energy. On the bus journey, she rarely stopped to draw breath as she identified her favourite streets and the people who once lived there.

She was unaware that in that Catholic republican area much of the symbolism was both British and military: many streets bore the names Crimea, Balaclava, Omar, Servia, Bosnia.

Back home, Stephen enjoyed a breakfast of bacon, two eggs, potato bread and soda bread. Then he went next door to have a cup of tea with Jimmy Carson.

Having asked the night before if he could take the dog for a walk, he discovered that the old man had made a lead from plaited lengths of rope which he proceeded to put round his dog's neck with the warning that it should not be pulled tight. Stephen assured him he would take care of his new-found friend.

'By the way, what have y' decided t' call him?' he asked.

'Provo,' declared Jimmy with a mischievous grin.

'What? How the hell can I shout for him round here with a name like that?'

'Would you attack anybody with a name like Provo? Maybe I should get it tattooed on his arse . . . Then put a patch on that bad eye of his and he could resemble some of that lot who're always collectin' at my door.'

As he walked the dog into the street, Stephen was uneasy because Provo was reluctant to leave the house and three tugs on the rope were required to get him to move. He stole a glance towards the front window of his own house and was thankful that his mother was not there to see him. He was sure that she would have had plenty to say. As it was, she did not approve of Jimmy, so she would have been especially indignant at the sight of her son holding a scruffy, half-fed mongrel with a rope for a lead.

Stephen hurried along Pearse Row wondering which of his neighbours was observing the dog. He now knew how Jimmy felt every time he appeared in the street. Fortunately it was quiet and Provo quickly realised the value of being able to stretch his legs. The walk to Bernadette's home took five minutes and the dog didn't waste a second. He sniffed every hedge, and twice left his mark on the hub-caps of cars, walking away with his scrawny tail in the air.

Bernadette, whose family home was grander than those in Pearse Row, lived beside Casement Park, a large Gaelic football ground. The garden was surrounded by a high, manicured hedge; access to the house was through a brightly painted wrought-iron gate. Stephen hesitated before opening the gate, and for a few seconds considered tethering Provo there, to avoid any embarrassment should Mrs Kane be the first to welcome him. But Bernadette was standing in the porch waiting for him and saw him arrive.

While he was deciding what to do with the dog, Bernadette motioned to him to remain at the gate. Within two minutes she was walking down the driveway dressed in a pullover, jeans, a short sheepskin jacket and cowboy boots. Bernadette was not the prettiest girl in the neighbourhood but she was attractive and her slim figure was enhanced by her casual clothes. She knew how to dress to make the best of herself, and her long black hair was left free to find its own shape. She applied make-up sparingly to features which exuded warmth rather than beauty: deep brown eyes and a wide mouth which, when she smiled, exposed perfect white teeth.

She kissed him, and he responded, but in doing so he pulled the dog's lead tight and Provo yelped. They both knelt down and petted him to reassure him that he was not in mortal danger.

'So this is the beautiful dog you told me about on the phone,' said Bernadette as she stroked Provo's head.

'I really meant that he . . . well . . . he has a lovely temperament,' Stephen explained, embarrassed.

'Oh, I'm only joking,' added Bernadette, patting him in the same manner in which she'd soothed Provo.

Stephen heard the front door open and decided that the question of Provo's pedigree was not one he wished to discuss with Mrs Kane. He ushered Bernadette into the street, dragging a reluctant Provo, who was eager to make the Kane family garden a place of remembrance. His back leg was still raised as he was unceremoniously removed from the scene.

How much liquid is Jimmy giving this dog, thought Stephen, but reckoned the animal's toilet habits were an issue he wouldn't bring to Bernadette's attention.

She spoke very little as they made for the Glen Road at the edge of the city limits. When they reached the river bridge which marked Colin Glen, they turned into the wood, and Provo was released to find his own pleasure.

At first the dog was terrified to find he was separated from his protectors but soon realised that the two humans were following him. Suddenly the wood became a world of excitement. Like an animated rag doll with four legs, he frolicked in the undergrowth and pretended to hunt among the trees and bushes. Stretching his spindly legs, he undertook strenuous leaps over tree stumps and patches of bracken. Bernadette laughed so much at the dog, she failed to notice that Stephen was depositing a small box in the right-hand pocket of her jacket. As they walked along the glen, Stephen pointed out little bends in the river where he had camped with friends in his youth. He was twelve years old when he discovered Colin Glen and its secrets, and seven years on he still felt the same way about the place. It was far removed from the barricades, the riots and the sheer energy of a city in conflict.

Bernadette knew all his reminiscences about the glen and was willing to hear them every Sunday; she was happy to have her boyfriend detached from the clutter of his life, particularly from Michael's influence. In Colin Glen she recognised all that was innocent and youthful about Stephen. Their time in the glen was not taken up with the brooding she'd observed in him in recent months. She had known him for two years and, although at first her mother disapproved of their relationship, Mrs Kane had grown to like him. Neighbours whispered that Stephen and Michael had an unsavoury past but her mother was not one to give herself to gossip. She and her husband shied away from the politics and the personal details of other people's lives.

The couple reached a curve in the river and a little bank where they always sat.

'Stephen, I know I'm not supposed t' ask you . . . but I'm frightened . . . You keep giving me a lot of money and I worry about where it comes from.'

Stephen bristled. 'Has my mother been talkin' to you?'

'Of course not, love. I'm just concerned.'

'We've been through all this before. You know Michael and m'self have been sellin' a lot of Paddy O'Reilly's seconds up at the Knox Corner Market every Saturday. It's a load of old shite – pullovers and things from his factory – but it gets it off his hands because he can't sell it to the big stores. Apart from that he gives us a few quid on the side for keepin' our mouths shut because he can offset it as damaged stock.'

'Y' must be sellin' a helluva lot of pullovers t' clear five hundred quid.'

'Well, to tell y' the truth, love, Michael and me did a treble in the bookies last week and if Yellow River hadn't taken a dive I'd have been givin' y' a helluva lot more.'

'I know, Stephen but yer mammy says –'

'You know what she's like. I don't know what she hates more – me havin' a bet or workin' in the market. Sometimes I think she'd only be happy if I was Father bloody Kirkpatrick.'

'Don't you even think of being a priest,' said Bernadette, laughing.

Stephen looked at her and the anger faded from his face. He drew her closer and kissed her.

'You'll just have t' trust me, love. I know it's hard but, believe me, some day we'll both be off this island and then I'll explain everything that happened in the past. If you keep puttin' pressure on me, I'll have to walk away, for your sake as much as mine.'

Bernadette placed his hands round the back of her neck. 'OK, I'll believe you if that's what y' want t' to tell me. But please, Stephen, if it's anything dangerous, for God's sake be careful. I don't want t' lose you.'

He unclasped her hands from round his neck, held her face and looked into her eyes. 'Look, the IRA can get stuffed as far as I'm concerned.'

She was reassured, and smiled. 'OK, just leave it.'

He began kissing her again, running his tongue round the corners of her lips, and felt desire for her growing within him. He knew her religious commitment was such that she was not prepared to have sex before marriage nor to allow him to fondle her.

Secretly she would have loved him to do all those things but she did not relish the prospect of revealing the details of the experience in the confessional. Their loving was simple and sexually frustrating, but they had dreams and the anticipation of enjoying sex when they were committed to each other for life.

Provo sat at their feet and demanded attention by yelping or sadly placing his head on Bernadette's boots. Eventually the lovers gave way to his demands, took him on a long, rambling trek through the glen and by midday were back at Bernadette's home.

At the front gate, Stephen kissed her goodbye. 'I've left a wee present in yer pocket.'

He waited for a moment while she removed the small box and took out of it a gold chain with a gold heart suspended from it.

'That'll remind you of me when I'm not around or away working.'

With tears in her eyes, she carefully fastened the chain round her neck and gave him a brief kiss. Then, as Stephen walked away, Provo by his side, she opened the tiny gold heart; inside was a photograph of him.

Back at Jimmy's house, the old man thanked Stephen for looking after his dog. It was obvious that he had advice to offer.

'See that fella, Michael. He's far too domesticated for my likin'. Y' see that's the problem with this civilisation. We've lost our connection with the natural order . . . the umbilical cord of the mind. Now, you take animals in zoos – they pace up and down because they're domesticated, just like that fella, Michael. He's always pacin' up and down and he's always agitated.'

Stephen saw the connection. Jimmy was like a poker player on a roll, anxious to maintain the momentum of his thoughts.

'This civilisation is Al Caponian.'

It was several seconds before Stephen grasped the meaning of 'Caponian'. Then he asked, 'Where y' gettin' all this stuff about Al Capone?'

Jimmy walked across his living-room and lifted a small frayed book from under the pile of newspapers. It had the appearance of being well handled. Jimmy pointed to the title – *Don't Lie to the Children* by François Bouan.

'Bought it years ago in a second-hand shop. Very bright man, this Bouan. He's a French philosopher, y' know.'

Stephen had never heard of the author and declined an offer to borrow the book.

'This Bouan fella says we're all accomplices and victims. Now, if y' think about it, he's right. Take the soldiers of destiny in this area. We let them do what they want and we become the victims . . . Al Caponian, eh?'

Stephen decided enough was enough and was worried that Jimmy was about to deliver the complete text of the Bouan philosophy. 'I've got t' get home . . . things t' do.' He opened the front door and decided to distract his friend from his preoccupation.

'If I've any time tomorrow,' said Stephen, pointing to the

overgrown garden, 'I'll borrow my mother's clippers and cut down those nettles.'

'Don't you touch those nettles,' said Jimmy, angrily. 'Those nettles are a paradox. Some people say I have those nettles t' keep people out and some people think they're there t' keep me in.'

'I suppose that's another gem from that guy, Bouan.'

'Oh no, that's me,' replied Jimmy, 'but I'll tell y' what Bouan said about nettles . . .

'What Bouan says is this . . . Have you ever noticed that nettles always grow around the outside of buildings? What he says is that this is nature's way of teachin' the young about the outside world. Before we had our great urban development and weedkillers, if a wee child wandered too far out of the house the nettles stung its wee hands and legs because a wee child would be the right height t' touch the top leaves of the nettles. The minute it did that it went cryin' to its mummy and wouldn't go past the nettles again. This was nature's way of protectin' the young from the dangers of the outside world.'

'Aye, right, Jimmy,' said Stephen, trying to suppress a yawn.

'I'll tell y' another thing I bet y' don't know,' said Jimmy, a determined look on his face, 'just t' prove I'm not talkin' a load of auld shite . . . If y' close yer hand round the base of a nettle plant and run yer hand upwards to the top of the stem, y' won't get stung. Now in my book that's like you and yer friend, Michael. *You* don't know enough t' know that y' know damn all, and while *you're* always touchin' the top of the nettle *he'll* be grabbin' the base.'

3

John Bradford pushed a file marked 'Classified' across his desk and invited Bill Green to examine it. Bradford leaned against the back of his chair while his colleague took a pair of reading glasses from the inside pocket of his tweed jacket and began scanning the contents of the file.

A few minutes of silence elapsed until Green exclaimed, 'Fuck me, I knew the little bastards were takin' us for a ride.'

'Read on,' said Bradford, smiling. 'That's only the tip of the iceberg.'

He opened a filing cabinet beside his desk and, with one hand, removed two whiskey glasses and placed them in front of him. The movement was repeated and a half-bottle of Bush-mills Black Bush appeared from the cabinet. He held the bottle in the palm of his right hand and, with the dexterity of a practised drinker, unscrewed the top with his thumb. Two large measures of the liqueur whiskey were dispensed. Then he paused for a moment to observe Green, whose face was red with fury.

Green reached for a glass. 'It'll take more than a Black Bush to calm me down.'

Slamming the file shut, he replaced his spectacles in his jacket pocket and turned to the whiskey. The glass was emptied in one gulp.

'I'll have those two bastards!' he shouted, banging the glass on the desk.

Bradford eased his body forward. 'It's a fuckin' disgrace that I'm in here on a Sunday. It's the only day of the week my wife and daughter expect t' see me, and here I am dealing with this shit.'

Green was in no mood for a conversational diversion and the whiskey increased his anger. He pointed to the classified file. 'Those two have been feedin' us fliers and takin' the money.'

Bradford was the measured thinker in a partnership which extended over two decades. With a quiet, reflective temperament, he relied on analysis rather than emotion. Life was the RUC Special Branch; his waking hours were monopolised by his job. Yet his frequent complaints that he was deprived of a social life and time for family rang hollow. Colleagues regarded him as a dedicated professional, a driven man. He had joined Special Branch from CID, where he had excelled at running agents within the criminal fraternity in Belfast. He cared little for the inherited Unionist politics of his Protestant tradition and defined his role as protector of the state. It didn't matter whether his targets were Catholic or Protestant paramilitaries.

From 1970, he had been assigned to recruiting agents who could provide intelligence on the activities of the Provisional IRA. It was a dirty business. His wife, Sandra, did not share his enthusiasm for the Branch. Her days were spent worrying whether her husband would return each night to their house in a suburb of Lisburn, twelve miles from Belfast. It was a relatively safe area with a heavy security screen because of the presence of British Army headquarters on the edge of the town. Nevertheless, total security was not possible in a terrorist war, and their house was a mini-fortress with bullet-proof windows, a sophisticated alarm system and a loaded pistol which remained at Bradford's bedside. Their home was one of six detached dwellings in a cul-de-sac which enabled the Bradfords to observe everyone who entered it. Sandra regarded strangers with suspicion; she had become so nervous of the occupants of all cars entering the cul-de-sac that she had grown dependent on tranquillisers.

Rebecca, their nine-year-old daughter, was an affectionate child, but prone to tears at the slightest provocation. When she began bedwetting, the family doctor diagnosed the problem as a symptom of the child's vulnerability to stress and strongly recommended that John spend more time at home. The child was old enough to be aware of the seriousness of the threat and was frightened to sleep alone. Even her school friends were vetted. She had also been ordered never to discuss with friends anything that pertained to her father's work.

John Bradford's partner, Bill Green, was unmarried. His existence was dominated not only by his work but by an obsessive preoccupation with concocting new methods of running agents. Green was devious, callous and self-interested. Senior officers tolerated him because of his knowledge of fieldwork but avoided any social contact. Heavy drinking, irrational moods and an unscrupulous attitude to agents did not detract from his reputation as someone who would undertake the most unpleasant tasks. Other staff wondered how a cool, intelligent man like John Bradford could find time for a person they regarded as a thug and a malcontent. Yet Bill Green's introverted nature was understood by his partner, who treated him with sensitivity and kindness.

The cold and damp of dark alleyways, and the excitement danger brings to those who make it a profession, were factors which united them. They shared a deep conviction that in moments of danger each would deliver the goods; a certainty that each would provide the necessary back-up for the other, and an acceptance that theirs was a murky world in which partnership and trust were vital for survival. Bradford had the edge over Green, with four years' seniority in the force, and Green deferred to his experience.

The half-bottle of whiskey was empty and Bradford looked at his watch. 'It's time to go.'

Green reached into his jacket and withdrew a .45 pistol from a holster under his left armpit. Gripping the butt in the palm of his right hand, he held the barrel upwards and used his thumb to press the release button, ejecting the magazine into his left hand. A quick glance confirmed that it was fully loaded; he slammed the magazine back into the pistol and returned the weapon to the holster.

'Better be safe than sorry,' he remarked as Bradford performed a similar exercise with his .9mm Browning. 'Is the other piece in the car?'

'It's in the boot under a blanket and ready for use.' Bradford opened the top drawer in his desk, withdrew a pair of black leather gloves and threw them to his partner. 'Stick those on and don't forget the plan.'

'Not likely. We're gonna put these guys where the crows won't shit on them, otherwise somebody up above is goin' t' ask why we spent so much money on a fuckin' fiasco.'

'No fuckin' messin', Bill. This has t' work, so don't go off half cock.'

At 1.45 p.m. they left their base at police headquarters. John Bradford was at the wheel of a blue Vauxhall Cavalier, one of many vehicles they used in the course of their duties. There was a workshop at HQ where Special Branch cars were regularly resprayed and registration numbers altered. In some cars, the registration plate acted as a two-way mirror, which enabled a watcher to lie in the boot and film the movements of suspects.

Bradford pointed to the clock on the dashboard. 'We're forty-five minutes off our rendezvous.'

Before meeting an agent they allowed themselves time to make two passes of a rendezvous point – a technique to ensure they were not being set up. Agents were recruited because they were vulnerable, but that also made them susceptible to inducements from terrorists.

The IRA's internal security apparatus was devoted to rooting out informers. IRA volunteers, those on the fringes of the organisation and people who drank in bars frequented by republican activists were generally on the unemployed social register and not expected to have a surplus of cash. Anyone who suddenly started spending as if he'd had a windfall was reported to the IRA. Barmen were often the eyes and ears of the IRA. But most agents were reluctant to have their payments made into a secret bank account, preferring to see a quantity of hard cash which most of them had never touched in their lives. Bradford privately feared that some day one of his informers would be exposed by the IRA, recruited as a double agent and used to set up his handlers with the result that a rendezvous point would be transformed by the IRA into a trap.

Although Bradford and his partner were armed, their car was not bullet-proof. IRA watchers could recognise a bullet-proof vehicle at several hundred yards. The tell-tale signs were the type of glass in the windows and the low-slung car body which rested below the tyre rims because of the extra weight. Young IRA 'scouts' in republican districts were skilled at detecting undercover military or police vehicles and identifying anyone who betrayed signs of fear, discomfort or a tendency to scrutinise others. They had lists of residents' vehicles, and a car not on those lists was regarded as a potential threat. Word was passed via two-way radios to IRA active service units, armed and ready for action at a moment's notice. Any suspect vehicle was observed at other points on its journey, sometimes photographed, occasionally stopped or fired on. Bradford used a different car each time he entered a republican district.

Today's meeting was at the Kennedy Way roundabout which linked the edge of the Catholic Andersonstown with the M1 motorway. It was not the normal venue, more a convenient one for what they planned.

Five hundred yards along the motorway was an expanse of wasteland once known as Bog Meadows. Alongside it was Milltown Cemetery, the main Catholic burial ground in the city. It held the monuments to IRA dead, many of them young men who had given their lives to a conflict they scarcely understood. Rising above the cemetery was the breathtaking beauty of the encircling mountains which would have quietened any other place. Conflict had transformed this beauty: Divis and Black mountains now overlooked a cauldron.

At 2.20 p.m. Bradford and Green made their second pass of the rendezvous point and reckoned they were safe to make a final approach.

Michael McDonnell waved excitedly when he saw the Vauxhall Cavalier approach the roundabout.

'Look at that silly bastard,' said Green.

Bradford drove the car alongside the pavement.

After the pick-up, the car climbed steeply towards Divis Mountain and the tiny hamlet of Hannastown. As they approached Hannastown, Stephen gazed at the passing fields and began to feel that something bad was about to happen. This was the first time they had met at the edge of Andersonstown. He'd expressed his worries to Michael, pointing out that a safer meeting place would have been somewhere neutral on the other side of the city, particularly East Belfast; somewhere few Catholics lived and there was no risk that he and Michael would be recognised.

Green's voice interrupted Stephen's thoughts. 'Are none of the likely lads listening t' me? I just said it was good t' see y' both again.'

Michael could not resist the temptation to reply insolently, 'Let's hope, Mr Green, that you've some money for us lads.'

Green was in no mood for that kind of humour. He detested the young men in the back seat, especially Michael. 'Don't fuck with me, you arrogant little shit.'

'The problem with our Mr Green here is that he's no sense of humour,' said Michael.

Stephen nudged his friend, to try to dissuade him from seeking confrontation, but Michael was buoyant.

'Cut the crap,' Bradford warned, glancing in the rear-view mirror at Michael. 'If I let Bill loose on you, even yer mother'll have difficulty decidin' you're hers.'

Michael laughed half-heartedly but he knew the message was clear: he was stepping too far out of line.

Stephen habitually avoided verbal clashes with the two Special Branch officers. He left it to his friend to do most of the talking and negotiating about money. He was wary of them both; they were powerful people who gave the impression they could make anything happen, just as he would expect of Special Branch officers.

On the outskirts of Hannastown, Bradford drove the car off the main road into a leafy lane, where he brought the vehicle to a stop.

'This is the spot.'

He pointed to a grassy embankment which obscured the landscape beyond.

'It's an ideal vantage point.'

The lane was quiet and there was no evidence of habitation in the immediate vicinity. Bradford kept the car engine running and turned to face the two young men.

'Just follow Bill.'

Bill Green was standing upright, flexing his hands and arms. Michael mimicked him to annoy him, while Stephen stood waiting for further orders.

Green strode to the back of the vehicle, opened the boot, and removed an Armalite rifle from underneath a blanket. He clicked a magazine into the weapon and attached a large telescopic sight.

Stephen froze with fear when he saw him emerge from the rear of the car with the gun.

'Don't worry, it's not your time . . . yet,' said Green, and laughed, running a gloved hand along the gun barrel.

He crouched, motioned to the young men to do likewise and, edging forward to a slight elevation, beckoned them to follow. When Stephen reached the indicated spot, he faintly heard people cheering. The sound was deadened by the raised bank but it seemed to be coming from a point below their position.

Green motioned to him to peer over the bank cautiously, without betraying his presence. Stephen lay against the slope and gently parted two large tufts of grass.

Below him, at a distance of 200 metres, was a large crowd of men, women and children watching a Gaelic football match. The high position offered a panoramic view of a pitch, a rough field with posts at either end. It was a typical rural event. To the left of the pitch was a small wooden hut.

Michael did not wait for an invitation to view the proceedings, but he was too hasty in his approach and was unceremoniously dragged back from the rim of the bank by one of Green's leather-clad hands.

'I said t' be fuckin' careful,' whispered Green through

clenched teeth, moving upwards until his body was flush with the curve of the embankment. Resting against the slope, he raised the rifle barrel and placed it on top of the bank. Slowly and meticulously, he began to adjust the telescopic sight until he found a target.

Stephen looked at Michael, who was preoccupied with Green's manipulation of the rifle. Instinctively, Stephen went to move his hands downwards with the intention of pushing himself from the scene but his action was instantly halted by Bradford's pistol butt, which was shoved against his right temple.

'Stay where you are. This is for your benefit.' Bradford spoke menacingly as his partner's right index finger steadily closed on the trigger of the Armalite.

Stephen shut his eyes, Michael put his fingers in his ears, and three rounds were discharged from the rifle in quick succession.

Within seconds women were screaming and running for cover; fathers dragged their children from the edge of the football pitch and some of the younger men began racing about wildly searching for the source of the gunfire.

Bradford seized Stephen's right leg and dragged him towards the car while the other two slowly edged backwards, keeping low to the ground. A few yards away from the car, Stephen was getting to his feet when Green pushed the rifle towards him, forcing him to grasp hold of it. He tried to hand it back but Green refused to take it from him.

'I'll bet your buddy isn't frightened to hold a gun,' said Bradford, and Michael eagerly reached forward and seized the rifle, grinning broadly.

The instant he handled it, Green roughly removed it from him, walked to the boot of the car and wrapped it in heavy-duty plastic. He slammed the boot shut and returned to the front passenger seat.

The car was already in motion as Michael and Stephen got in and shut the rear door.

From the moment the gun was fired until they left the scene it was a mere two and a half minutes, not long enough for those at the football match to determine the exact location of the gunman or to summon assistance.

Bradford drove towards Belfast but appeared to be in no great hurry. Hannastown and the football field were so far outside Belfast that it would be a considerable time before security forces would arrive at the scene of the shooting.

Stephen couldn't prevent his hands from shaking. 'For Christ's sake, what was that about? Those were innocent people . . .'

No one appeared to hear the question and Green laughed loudly as though enjoying a private joke.

'What's so fuckin' funny, Mr Green?' asked Michael.

Green glanced across at his partner and shrugged, indicating there were more serious matters to be addressed.

Bradford was watching the young men in his rear mirror and addressed them both. 'You lads handled that weapon. That means yer fingerprints are on it. My friend Bill knows better because he was wearin' gloves . . . Now there was a very good reason for that precaution – that rifle in the boot has just been used in a murder bid but Bill here's a crack shot and he deliberately put three rounds into that little hut up there. Y' see, we're not the murderin' type . . . not at all like the bastards we're after. The spent cartridges and bullets will be found by our forensic people. The rifling on the bullets will confirm they were fired from one weapon – but where's the weapon? I think it's time for my friend Bill to give you the good news.'

Green took the opportunity to put further pressure on the young men behind him. He leaned over the back of his seat and grinned at Michael. 'Now, lads, what happens is this. We bury the rifle somewhere near the scene of the shootin'. We tell CID we've had a tip-off where it's buried, and when those boys examine it for fingerprints . . . guess what? *Your* prints will be on it. They'll then test-fire the weapon . . . and guess what? They'll match the bullets against the ones found in the hut.' Green paused for emphasis. 'Now you guys might say, "How does that lead them to us?" Well, it's very simple: we'll tell them. We'll say we've had a tip-off from one of our touts that you guys were the shooters. They'll fingerprint the two of y' and . . . guess what? Won't your prints be on the rifle? That'll get each of y' twenty years.'

Stephen was terrified and couldn't speak; but Michael refused to be intimidated by what he heard.

'So fuckin' what? We'll tell them all about you and yer partner and how y' set us up.' He laughed.

Green leered back at him. 'So you think y're a smart little shit. Who'd believe what *you* say?'

Michael was undaunted, and tried another approach. 'Who's goin' t' believe that Catholics like us are goin' t' kill their own people?'

Bradford was prepared for that line of argument and crisply delivered the *coup de grâce*. 'One of those Gaelic footballers was a prominent member of the Irish National Liberation Army and you know how much the Provos hate those boys. We'll leak it to the Crown Prosecutor that the motive for the murder bid was a feud between the Provos and the INLA . . .

'Now, when you appear before the court, yer lawyer will probably tell y' that you haven't got a shit's chance of gettin' off. He'll tell you both t' plead guilty t' get a better deal, maybe fifteen years instead of twenty, and you'll take it because the evidence is stacked against you – that's the way it cuts with lawyers. It'll be all over the papers that yer sentence was for the attempted murder of a leadin' member of the INLA. And when the both of you are inside, the INLA prisoners will want yer balls and the Provos . . . oh, those bastards'll definitely do the job because they'll know that you're not two of theirs. They'll believe you were probably workin' for the Brits who sold y' out. You see, the Provos believe the Brits are capable of almost anything. So from here on in, lads, we own yer balls.'

Stephen, recognising the terrible logic, swallowed hard. 'So what is it y' want from us?'

Easing some of the tension in the back of the car, Bradford began to speak quietly, gently. 'This is a business relationship.

You deliver the product and we pay for it, provided it's a quality product.'

'You've been fuckin' us around,' said Green, looking directly at Michael. 'And you've given us names and addresses that you've taken from phone directories. You fuckers tagged innocent people. That's embarrassin' for us. We ordered a search of one address and it turned out to be a seventy-five-year-old woman and her mentally retarded brother. That's a fuckin' end to it! You lads get yerselves out and about in the bars and clubs of Andytown . . .' Green paused, staring hard at each of them in turn.

Then he went on, 'We want t' know who associates with known Provos. We want t' know when a leadin' Provo has a piss. We want t' hear what you hear. You, Michael, my little shit, you've no problem pickin' up women – so next week you'll pick up a little package at the Central Post Office. It'll contain pics and photofits of people we want. You two study those pics and let us know if any of those people appear in the haunts where you two lurk. Burn the contents of the package after you've memorised the pics. McDonnell, you can use yer phone t' ring us because yer mother is out during the day.'

In a subservient tone, Michael asked, 'How can I possibly be expected to conduct a heavy social life without funds?'

Bradford released his left hand from the steering wheel, reached inside his jacket, removed a bulky envelope and tossed it over his shoulder into Stephen's lap.

'Kirkpatrick, make sure you get yer share of that.'

'If it was up t' me, they'd work for fuck-all,' said Green, spitting out the words.

At Kennedy Way roundabout Bradford ordered the young men to get out of the car. Green leaned out of the window as the vehicle moved off.

'Remember it's dangerous t' fuck with us,' he said, glaring at Michael.

When the car reached the motorway, Bradford said quietly, 'Never leave agents so terrified that they've nothin' t' lose. Always spread some largesse. Keep them frightened but keep them afloat. The day I suspect that they're prepared t' fuck us, I'll sell them out to the Provos.'

Walking towards Andersonstown, neither young man spoke for several minutes until Michael broke the silence by rubbing his hands.

'We're back in business.'

'I swear to God, Michael, one of these days you'll get us killed. I told you not t' give them that bogus list. I don't like this fuckin' game and I'm not goin' t' cheat on innocent people.'

'We've got the money, haven't we?' said Michael.

Stephen grabbed his arm and moved him to the edge of the pavement. 'Let's put it this way. If there's an articulated lorry, and its comin' down this road, why walk in front of it when y' can stay on the pavement. I don't want t' be in this business but I've no fuckin' choice, so let me tell you one last time that while I'm in it I'm avoidin' articulated lorries.'

4

Stephen opened the swing doors of the Crow's Foot and braced himself for the swirl of cigarette smoke which was sucked past him into the street.

The din of hurried conversations, the clinking of pint glasses, the dimmed lighting and shabby figures confirmed for him that this was a likely place to find Michael. For mid-afternoon it was an eerie atmosphere, not uncommon to West Belfast. In the early years of the Troubles, it had been an illegal drinking club, and legality had not transformed its appearance. There were no windows in the brick walls, which were covered with Sinn Fein posters and a large Irish tricolour flag.

A loud cheer from the far end of the room drew him towards a group of men who were pointing at a television set. In their midst was a shock of fair hair bobbing above the others. Michael was leaping up and down on a bar stool, pointing to the horse which had just passed the winning post in the 3.30 at Kempton Park.

'He's done it, the little beauty! That's the fuckin' treble!' yelled Michael.

'You're a jammy wee bastard,' shouted one of the other men.

'It's nothin' t' do with luck,' replied Michael. 'It's knowin' form. Y' can't pull two trebles in a month and call it luck.'

I know what I'd call it, thought Stephen, staying at a distance from the scene: a load of bullshit. He'd never known his friend to make a successful bet, much less pick three winners in a row.

'How the hell do y' do it?' asked a large red-faced man who was balancing a cigarette on his bottom lip.

Stephen moved closer to the group, while Michael sat down and drew the big man towards him in a conspiratorial manner.

'It's like this,' whispered Michael, as the others, straining to hear him, formed a canopy. 'I've a mate who works at Downpatrick racecourse and he's the best tipster y' could ever meet.'

'Who the hell is he?' asked a little man, whose head miraculously appeared between Michael's left arm and his body.

'Now, if I told you that, you'd tell all yer friends, the money would pour in, the bookies would get jittery, the odds would rise and where would I be?'

'No, he wouldn't!' shouted the others.

'Yes, he fuckin' would, so the drinks are on me.'

The offer of free drinks unloosed the human knot around Michael.

'I'll have a large vodka and it's on you,' said Stephen, patting his friend on the shoulder and gently drawing him away from the bar.

The others were busy taking advantage of Michael's largesse and failed to notice him being escorted to a quiet table in a corner of the lounge.

Michael temporarily detached himself from his friend and waved reassuringly to his companions.

'What the fuck are y' doin'?' asked Stephen when they sat down. 'You wouldn't know a horse's arse from its head.'

'I know that, so keep yer voice down.'

'You're throwin' money around like there was no tomorrow, and in a place like this . . . For Christ's sake have some sense.'

Michael ignored him and waved his hands in the air until he caught the attention of Martin, the barman.

'Two large vodkas an' Coke.'

He turned towards Stephen with a self-satisfied grin. 'Just watch how quickly that bastard serves me and I'll bet y' he doesn't ask the waitress to bring the drinks.'

'Hey presto,' said Martin, as he placed the glasses of vodka on the table with a flourish and deftly added a measure of Coke to each.

Michael slipped him a large tip as though he were his personal valet. 'Martin, after the next round, cut off the flow to those guys . . . Gotta keep some money for the bookies.'

He laughed, and Martin nodded. 'Whatever else they might say about you, Michael . . . you're an officer and a gentleman.'

'I'll bet he says that to all the boys,' Stephen remarked, as Martin strode towards the bar, his right hand digging the note deep into a trouser pocket.

'I know what you're gonna say,' whispered Michael, leaning forward, his glass raised to his lips. 'You're gonna say I'm throwin' money around and drawin' attention to myself. Well . . . that's exactly what I'm tryin' to do.'

'You're off yer fuckin' rocker! You know the score.'

Michael waved his right index finger at his friend and put it to his lips, indicating that he didn't approve of either the conversation or raised voices.

'OK,' said Stephen, dropping his voice and smiling. 'You couldn't predict midnight, never mind a winner. Any horse you'd pick would probably walk with a lisp.'

'You mean a list,' replied Michael, who didn't appreciate the joke.

'OK, a list of its losses and a lisp.'

'You're in great form, Kirkpatrick. It must be funny cigarettes or Bernadette's opened up . . . if you know what I mean.'

Stephen looked angry at the mention of Bernadette and it was clear to both that tempers were likely to flare. A public slanging match would be dangerous; they were known as friends who never engaged in open quarrels or personal invective. Stephen eased the tension by demanding another large vodka from his friend's winnings and Michael responded by summoning a waitress whom he wished to impress.

Another double measure and Michael lost some of the sparkle in his eyes. 'Listen, Stephen, *you* might know I'm no gambler but *they* don't . . . That's what matters. I watched the first two races from Kempton on the telly at home and then came in here with the names of the winners. I arrived a minute before the end of the last race, and when I saw the horse just passin' the winnin' post I said that was my third horse in the treble. It doesn't always work because if there's a photo finish and I pick the wrong one it doesn't have the same impact on these wankers. When it does, they expect me t' be the big spender and that gives me the chance t' get in there and be one of the boys. It also gives me an excuse t' throw money around . . . Good thinkin', eh?'

'Why should they believe you?'

Michael lit a cigarette, took a large draw on it and smiled. 'Because they fuckin' want to. Those guys are bettin' and losin' every day. They're happy if anybody beats the bookie . . . Free drink helps a plan come together. The big fella with the blue nose who was on my right, he borrowed five quid from me last week. His son's a leadin' Provo and if he thought I was dodgy would he be in my company or tappin' me for money? See what I mean?'

He bent forward until his face hovered over Stephen's glass. 'What if somebody discovers that Bernadette has a lot of money she can't account for?'

'Let's get a bottle and get t' hell outa here,' said Stephen, downing his drink.

'Don't be so fuckin' ungrateful.'

'Keep yer voice down.'

'What pisses me off about you is that I'm in here doin' all the work – gettin' into that kind of company and pickin' up scraps of information that keeps us in pocket money.'

Stephen nodded apologetically, worried that his reluctance to be impressed might further excite Michael.

'And what's more . . . one of those guys today was talkin' about somebody our friends are interested in.'

'Look . . . I was only –'

'Who plays the idiot and spends all his dough?' Michael pointed at himself. 'Me!'

'OK, I'm sorry . . . I know you're doin' yer best for us. I must admit it's a fuckin' good ploy – good thinking . . . It's just that this whole fuckin' business gets me down sometimes

61

. . . bein' nice to these assholes in the hope they'll blurt out somethin'.'

'Forget it. You've covered my ass often enough.'

Stephen patted him on the shoulder and they raised their glasses in salute to each other.

'Let's get a bottle and get to hell's gates outa here,' said Stephen.

'My place it is,' Michael announced loudly. 'And what about a wee bet on the way?'

He winked at his earlier companions, who were eagerly waving, expecting another round. 'This is the leftover from the last treble,' he loudly remarked, taking out three bank-notes and handing them to the waitress. 'Those are for the lads over there and here's something for yerself.'

He slipped another note between two buttons of her blouse and whispered in her ear.

'What did y' say to her?' asked Stephen as they breathed the fresh air of the street.

'The kinda thing you'd never say to Bernadette,' replied Michael with a mischievous grin.

On the way home they bought a bottle of vodka, two large Cokes and four cans of Newcastle Brown, Michael's favourite. Their journey took them close to Casement Park.

'It always reminds me of my dad,' remarked Stephen.

He'd spent many Sunday afternoons there on his father's shoulders watching Gaelic football and hurling matches. On wintry days he used to bury his tiny hands under the collar of his father's overcoat and his face into his mop of black hair. There was only one stand, with surrounding grassed terraces exposed to the wind that raced upwards from the city. His father had liked to watch the game from the hill at the roadside end of the ground which offered a panoramic view of South Belfast. Sean Kirkpatrick had wanted his son to share his enthusiasm for Gaelic games but Stephen almost dreaded those biting cold Sunday afternoons.

'Do y' remember how they used t' play "The Boys of the Old Brigade" and "Sean South" during the intervals?'

'The only thing I remember', said Michael, grinning, 'was those bloody awful toilets in a concrete bunker.'

'I remember my dad unzipping my fly and holdin' me up because the floors were covered in piss. There was a terrible smell and all I saw were the stained marble urinals.'

Michael looked momentarily puzzled, then laughed. 'Yea, every time I visit the loo in the Crow's Foot I think of those urinals in Casement.'

'Why's that?'

'The writing on the urinals. It was years before I could read it properly – 'Twyfords of Byford and Lynas'. Those boys hit on a great idea when they made those things because everywhere I've pissed since, including the Crow's, there's the same brand name.'

Seeing the gates of Casement Park were open, Stephen went into the ground and waved to his friend to follow. As they reached the top of the roadside terrace, Michael pointed to the far end of the ground.

'My father stood on that hill the last time he took me here.' There was a look of sadness in his eyes which deprived him of his typical cockiness. 'My dad used t' sing all the republican songs while he downed a half-bottle of whiskey. It kept him warm but did nothin' for me.'

Intrigued by this unusual outburst, Stephen watched Michael staring ahead at the vacant end of the park.

'When I think about it, he wasn't such a bad guy. I never really knew him. He was dyin' of cancer when he took me here so maybe the drink was t' kill the pain. He used t' say things t' me like, "Life's short, so enjoy yerself while y' can" and "Don't ever let the bastards grind y' down." But he lost his job in the factory when he got ill, y' know. Bastards.'

An army helicopter appeared over the end of the ground and startled them.

'Let's get t' fuck outa here,' said Michael, angered by the interruption. 'You can't find peace anywhere in this city, even from the Brits.'

Stephen laughed. 'At least they're payin' our drinks bill.'

*

Raglan Place was a cul-de-sac of ten houses with small, untidy gardens to the front and rear. The McDonnells' garden at number 8 was the only one that appeared ever to have been tended. It was grassed, and had a small privet hedge and a trailing rose which bore signs of neglect. The other gardens were either concreted or overgrown and covered in dog turds. The rose-pink curtains of number 8 were garish against the stippled white walls which characterised all the houses. The tell-tale sign that Rose McDonnell was a tidy woman was a gleaming brass knocker and a letterbox rubbed to a perfect sheen.

'The kids round here wreck everything,' said Michael, pointing to broken planks in the wooden gate and fence. 'My mother loved that fence because it kept the dogs and the kids out. The little bastards kicked the shit out of it.'

As he opened the door, he turned to deliver a parting shot at his neighbours. 'That's the trouble with hugging the altar rails. Too many fuckin' kids, cats and dogs. When they're not stonin' the Brits, they're stonin' each other.'

Stephen hesitated as Michael waved him towards the living-room.

'She's at work.' Michael went off to fetch two glasses.

Stephen felt uncomfortable in this house; it seemed to exude sadness and little warmth. In the living-room there was an old armchair covered in a faded flowery fabric, a rocking-chair which was a family heirloom and a fake-leather sofa with a worn wood surround. A large television set had been given pride of place in an uncluttered corner. On a dark oak sideboard were numerous photographs of Michael as a baby and a large silver-framed portrait of his father.

The diminutive Mrs McDonnell did not feature in the picture collection. As long as Stephen could remember, she had worn her hair in a bun. She was a mousey woman, kind, gentle, but somewhat withdrawn. She resembled women in an era when the death of a husband confined them to an existence in which the drabness of their clothing confirmed their unrelenting acceptance of widowhood. Mrs McDonnell indulged her son, refusing to recognise his excesses of temperament and lifestyle. She had once defended him to a relative, explaining that he was highly excitable because he had never accepted his father's death. The absence of a father-figure, she believed, was hard on Michael at a time when Belfast was in turmoil. 'Just look at all those so-called men out there,' she had said, 'running around with guns. For God's sake, they're treated like heroes, so what can y' expect from the children?' She worked part-time for a local butcher, and avidly watched the news on television. The news enabled her to converse with people who came into the shop; everyone was knowledgeable about the latest bombing, shooting or riot.

Michael handed Stephen a large cup and apologised for the lack of glasses. 'My mum thinks that if there are no glasses in the house I won't drink. Bloody eejit.'

The two of them went upstairs to Michael's room. Stephen insisted on pouring his vodka himself, fearing that Michael was in the kind of mood where the Coke would become redundant. The bedroom was comfortable, with a deep-pile white carpet, a single bed and a large stereo system, all of which confirmed Michael's tendency to spoil himself. An adjacent room was his personal wardrobe, enabling him to make his bedroom a little den where he could entertain friends or any girls who were not apprehensive about his reputation.

'I'm sorry about the hassle in the bar,' said Stephen quietly, lounging on the bed as Michael sat down on the floor and filled a cup to the brim.

Michael raised his glass in salute to them both. '*Slainte!*'

'Look, Michael, I'm a born worrier and you're happy-go-lucky. I mean you're in it for the money, whereas –'

'What fuckin' world are you livin' in?' shouted Michael, raising himself slightly from the floor and then reclining backwards to sip the vodka. 'You must be outa yer fuckin' head.' He waved a finger at Stephen. 'D' you think I like this? Don't ever take me for stupid. Happy-go-lucky . . .'

He threw back his head with a wicked laugh.

'Your fuckin' problem, Stevie, is that y' see yerself as the only victim here and me as an asshole.'

Stephen wished he'd poured a larger measure of vodka but was reluctant to reach for the bottle.

'Those bastards', continued Michael, 'Bradford and that sidekick of his, had us by the balls from the start.'

'Is it all right if I have another drink?' Stephen hoped his request would ease the tension between them.

'Help yerself,' Michael replied gruffly. 'Just remember, when you're playin' Babes in the Wood on a Sunday with Bernadette, it's me who's in the bars pickin' up the information that pays for that vodka.'

Stephen gently drew the bottle towards him and held it in mid-air, equidistant from both of them. 'Y' can keep yer fuckin' vodka, if that's the way you're gonna be.'

He made the remark with such childlike annoyance that Michael began laughing and Stephen responded by smiling and tipping the bottle towards his cup. Michael tapped the edge of his cup against the underside of the bottle and Stephen gave him another measure.

'Here, why don't we go see Jimmy?'

'That nutter?' Michael looked up from his cup.

'OK, what about a trip to Donegal? I could take Bernadette.'

'Fuck off. I'd rather take Jimmy Carson.' Michael sniggered. 'And anyway he'd get on like a house on fire with that other eejit, Jimmy the Natural.'

Stephen giggled, falling backwards on the bed and spilling half the contents of his cup.

'Remember the last time we were in Donegal?' he suddenly asked.

'I'm not likely to forget it.'

They sat in silence, smiling inwardly, knowing they shared a memory which neither felt the need to explain.

Three years earlier, they had hitchhiked to the wild and rugged coastline of the north-west of Ireland and stayed in a tiny thatched cottage on an outcrop two miles beyond Killybegs. The cottage was a holiday home owned by Michael's uncle, who'd been persuaded to let the boys use it. It was mid-summer and a gentle wind rolled off the sea and moved the hillsides of heather in a rhythmic kaleidoscope of colour. Tiny fields hewn from the rocky, barren soil dotted the landscape like disjointed pieces of a tapestry in which there was order only for the beholder who appreciated controlled complexity. It was a land exclusively for sheep, and people who understood that the winters were unrelenting in their harshness. This was where Europe crumbled into the Atlantic; the last outpost, where the winds and rain reached out from North America, carrying the salt air which stunted growth.

The road from Killybegs to the cottage was narrow and the tarmac worn into ruts and pitted with holes. For Michael, at sixteen, it was his first experience of the countryside; for Stephen it was Colin Glen on a grander scale. They spent the first two days living on a diet of baked beans, toast and canned beer and exploring the turfed hillsides. Michael was anxious to find other signs of habitation, and when it was obvious they were alone he became bored and wanted to return to Belfast. He complained that he couldn't bear the remoteness of the cottage; he said the land, in parts, looked like a golf course with sheep, and he couldn't stand the silence.

Yet Stephen loved the tranquillity, the coarseness and the colours of the landscape. It was an opportunity to escape the drabness of Belfast, the sounds and the images of conflict. He was intrigued by the bleached white wood strewn between the turf ditches; he felt an inner attachment, as though the ground held layers containing something of his past, perhaps a distant memory, a suggestion that he had been there before. He couldn't find the words to explain it and reckoned that, if he could, Michael would dismiss it as 'loopy'. Years later he would regret that he ever left Donegal because it was the one place where he felt free and his mind was uncluttered. Stephen hoped that one day he would be on that ocean heading for America, like so many people before him. Perhaps the land held that message for him; and maybe the thoughts of a lost generation that had walked on the same soil and looked westward with the same longing.

They soon discovered a tiny pub where the owner did not question the age of his customers but intimated by gestures that under-age drinkers were welcome in a back room.

One evening after they had downed several pints of Guinness, the landlord spotted Stephen moving unsteadily in the general direction of the toilets and insisted he leave the premises.

It was midnight when they set foot on the road out of the town, singing snatches of Irish songs and shouting obscenities. After a loud rendering of the first verse of 'The Cliffs of Dooneen', they realised that a country road on a starless night was no place for a drunken ramble. There were several tumbles into the hedgerows before they clasped each other's hands, hoping to remain in the centre of the road, equidistant from the ditches on each side.

Suddenly Stephen stopped and steadied Michael, as though impelled by an unknown force.

'Do y' hear anything?' he asked.

'Yeah, the wind behind me from that Guinness,' answered Michael, and patted his friend on the back.

'I'll swear I heard footsteps.'

'It's only those wickets,' said Michael, with a loud belch.

'Wickets? . . . Whadya mean, wickets?'

'Wickets . . . wickets . . . Y' know, those wee things that sing at night.'

'Wickets? Ya thicko, y' mean crickets. If there's crickets in Donegal, they'd need to be dressed in thermal underwear and snow boots.'

A bright light appeared a foot from Stephen's face, forcing him to blink and step backwards.

Michael lost his grip on his friend and fell to the ground, swearing profusely and scrambling for a foothold.

Stephen focused on the light, which came from a torch. It pointed upwards against a man's chin, revealing a smiling face, wild eyes and a woolly hat which reached to the eyebrows. In seconds the light was switched off, and running feet signalled the disappearance of the apparition.

'What the fuck was that?' said Stephen, forgetting that Michael was still crawling blindly in the roadway.

'Just get me home. I feel sick,' pleaded Michael as he got to his feet.

Stephen woke him early the next morning and asked what he remembered of the trip home. His reply suggested he had consigned the events on the road to alcoholic amnesia. Stephen pressed him for the tiniest recollection and delivered a detailed recapitulation of the previous night's incidents including the songs they sang until the arrival of the 'apparition'.

'You're doin' my head in,' said Michael, adding that on two occasions when Stephen went to the toilet in the pub he had persuaded the landlord to pour him 'a sneaky whiskey'.

'That explains why you were so pissed, ya sneaky bastard.'

'Hold on a minute,' said Michael, his right hand trying to stem the rumblings of a severe headache. 'I remember something about wickets – and here, look at this.'

He opened wide his hands and counted the cuts and bruises.

'There's still a thorn in that one.' He pointed to his right index finger.

'D' you remember a light and some wacko in a woolly hat with a torch under his chin?'

'Are y' sure you weren't on the whiskey?' replied Michael, trying bravely to smile.

Stephen wandered aimlessly in and out of the cottage for the rest of the day while Michael rested his hangover. It was ten o'clock at night before conversation returned to their lives, and Michael began by scouring the cottage for discarded cigarette butts. He was like an addict looking for a fix and his behaviour so annoyed Stephen that they began exchanging insults. Michael complained about the silence, that there was no radio, nowhere to buy cigarettes and if they had any sense they would go home. Stephen was launching into an attack on Michael's decadent habits when his friend screamed, reached for an empty milk bottle and blundered towards the front door.

'He's out there!' shouted Michael as he flung open the door

and disappeared into the darkness. He returned swearing and waving the milk bottle in the air.

'What the hell's with you?' asked Stephen, who saw an element of humour in his friend's deranged behaviour.

'That light,' said Michael, breathing heavily, 'that fuckin' light you talked about . . . The wacko . . . the one with the torch and the woolly hat . . . Jesus, he was at the window. Could be a fuckin' axe murderer.'

He rushed back to the door, bolted it, returned and placed the milk bottle on the table and lit up the remnants of a cigarette.

'Did you ever see that film . . . the one with yer man . . . what's his name? . . . they're up in the wilds on this river?'

'Yeah . . . *Tales of the Riverbank*.'

'Fuck you.'

Michael spent the night sleeping on a couch with the milk bottle beside him and the kitchen table wedged against the front door.

Michael now was sitting in a wicker chair asleep, his head on his chest and an empty vodka bottle at his feet. Stephen wondered if his friend's slumber had been activated by the reference to Donegal or by over-indulgence.

Without disturbing him, he quietly left the room, having no desire to explain Michael's condition to Mrs McDonnell.

On the journey home he visited Jimmy Carson; the longer he remained away from home, he thought, the more time he would have to sober up.

'Sit down and rest yer weary limbs,' said Jimmy, and Stephen carefully picked his way through the cluttered living-room.

As Jimmy left the room to make tea, he mumbled, 'Y' look as if y' need a cup of tea y' could stand in.'

Provo was excited by Stephen's presence and quickly established a resting place at his feet.

'Hey, do y' want this tea or not?'

Stephen opened his eyes and found Jimmy standing over

him disapprovingly, holding out a mug of boiling tea. He grasped the mug in the palm of his right hand and raised it to his lips.

'Y' smell like the back end of a brewery,' said Jimmy.

The tea had a strong, sickly taste and Stephen was unable to put it aside while the old man watched him from the folds of a shabby armchair.

'Y' must take it in moderation.'

'What, the tea?'

'Everything,' replied Jimmy with a solemn nod of his head.

I'd rather have vodka, thought Stephen.

Jimmy looked pensive.

'Is anything wrong?'

The old man shuffled to the window and looked through the lace curtains at the house opposite.

'I let Provo out this morning and that auld bitch across the way was over here complainin' that he'd shat in her garden. I told her that if her garden didn't look like a council pavement he wouldn't have bothered.'

Jimmy was referring to Bridget Jones, a widow who lived at number 18 and spent hours standing at her front door exchanging gossip with neighbours or anyone willing to listen. She reserved her most spurious allegations and venom for Jimmy, who she claimed was bringing down the tone of the street. His misfortune was that his house was in her direct line of vision, and recently she'd bought venetian blinds for the front windows to shut out what she described as 'an obscenity'. Jimmy's house offended her sensibilities with its overgrown garden, windows rarely washed, curtains held together by dust, and a front door like the entrance to a shed.

Jimmy settled back into his armchair, adjusted his spectacles – which were held together with a rubber band – and poured himself a cup of tea.

'I just asked her what was her problem, and that was the wrong tack. François Bouan says y' never begin by asking people what their problems are because that's all they'll focus on. Y' must say, "Good day, can I help you?" It's easy to see he never lived in Belfast.'

Stephen could have pointed out that it was daft to ask Mrs Jones about anything, particularly her problems. She'd begin by detailing her medical history and describing every pill she'd ever taken. She was especially adept at discussing gynaecological matters and how she overcame the menopause. Moreover, she would finish by defining her major problem as Jimmy Carson.

'I suppose she was ramblin' on about her hystericalectomy,' Stephen suggested, a smile creasing his lips.

Jimmy was in no mood for jokes; his mind was on the single track of what he saw as the relevant points in the episode.

'She said Provo was eatin' her flowers and I told her that's probably why he was shittin'. She points this finger at me.' Jimmy stood up and pointed at Stephen. 'That finger could have filled a dyke. Bouan says people who make threats are contaminated by greed or envy . . . Here, let me show y' what he said . . .' He reached for *Don't Lie to the Children*.

Stephen was only interested in the developing story and successfully steered the old man away from his favourite book of quotations.

'What sorta threat did she make?'

Jimmy's spectacles were at a 45-degree angle to his forehead and his arms were folded in a gesture of defiance.

'She said I didn't feed my dog. That was below the belt. You know I feed my animals better than myself. Look at Billy . . .'

The cat was lying on a pile of old newspapers, his front and back legs hanging over each end. One eye opened enquiringly when he heard his name.

'His balls are so big he's cuttin' a furrow down the middle of that rug, and Provo . . . sure's he's a head as big as a bull's . . .'

Stephen closed his eyes, convinced that if he couldn't see Jimmy he wouldn't be tempted to laugh.

'So I says to her, "Look at that mangy auld cat of yours . . . he looks as if you've been knittin' his food." You know the one I mean, don't you?'

Stephen opened his eyes and pretended he was concentrating on the cat in question; it was clear he was playing for time. Jimmy considered any lapse in concentration a dangerous sign and began fidgeting with the ragged edges of his pullover.

'Aye, I know the cat,' said Stephen with a vagueness which was not lost on his host.

'The grey one.' Jimmy used his hands to draw its form. 'The one with a tail like a poker . . . just think of a gradient, maybe one in three . . . long legs at the back, short ones at the front, a snout like a screwdriver and a ribcage like an accordion.'

Stephen could no longer control his urge to laugh. There was no mistaking the grey cat with the hungry look which frequently sat on the window-sill outside his mother's kitchen.

'So I says, "What are y' talkin' about? Sure yer cat's half fed." She stamped one of her big feet while I stood my ground and Provo had that mean look in his eyes which told me he was measuring up her ankles. I was calm and I says to her, "A mouse would break its neck before it would break its fast in your house."' The hint of a smile appeared on Jimmy's face and vanished just as quickly. 'That shut her up.'

'Maybe she didn't understand you.'

That hadn't occurred to Jimmy, and he scratched his head. 'What would you have said?'

Stephen reassured him that the reference to a mouse being more likely to have an accident than find a scrap of food in Mrs Jones's house was a clever way of dealing with her. It occurred to him that this was another gem from the writings of Bouan but he dared not ask.

'And that's not all,' said Jimmy. Stephen again shut his eyes, this time from tiredness and the after-effects of vodka.

Jimmy leaned forward, his right eye hardly visible through the grime on the spectacle lens.

'She walked away, that big arse of hers like a tin bath on springs. It's a wonder she managed to get out the gate. Provo was ready t' go after her but I kept him in hand. Anyway, she's halfway across the street and turns. "I'll get the boys for you," she shouts.'

Stephen was fast asleep, Provo at his feet and Billy lying

across his lap. Jimmy fetched a worn tablecloth and gently put it round the young man's shoulders before shovelling coal on the fire.

It was midnight when Stephen was wakened by Provo barking.

'Don't worry about him,' said Jimmy, walking over to Stephen and patting him on the shoulder. 'That dog's got a nose for trouble. He's just given Michael short shrift.'

The old man took a piece of paper from the mantelpiece, handed it to Stephen and tactfully walked towards the window.

The note read 'Meeting with our friends in two days. Be at the usual place at 6 p.m.'

Stephen folded the note and threw it into the fire while Jimmy feverishly rubbed his hands together, his body facing the window.

'Is something wrong?' Stephen asked him.

'That fella Michael couldn't walk a straight line, so you watch yerself. As for that auld bitch across the way, if she's talkin' about me, she talkin' about you. Don't underestimate anybody.'

5

The barman winked at Brendan McCann and discreetly placed a receipt beside his pint of Guinness. Brendan pulled the receipt towards the edge of the bar, shielding it from other customers, and read the written instructions on it. Rolling it into a ball, he stuffed it in his pocket, nodded at the barman and began making his way to the rear exit.

Two young men were waiting for him next to the fire door. 'The car's out the back,' said one of them. 'You're in good hands.'

He pulled aside his jacket, revealing a .357 Magnum in a makeshift holster.

As they drove through Dublin, Brendan contrasted the relaxed normality of the city with the nervous atmosphere of Belfast.

'You guys down here don't know you're living,' he told his companions. 'Up North we'd have hit a road block by now.'

This wasn't Brendan's first visit to Dublin but each time he travelled through the city it was a fleeting look at a different life: Belfast was a city at war; Dublin was one which merely remembered and honoured war.

His thoughts returned to the reason for his trip and the meeting he was about to attend with the IRA's ruling body, the Army Council.

They're armchair generals, he said to himself: a bunch of has-beens, most of whom sit down here in an unreal world while we in the North spill our blood.

'Are the leaders of the Belfast Brigade here for the meeting?' he asked the driver.

'I think so,' he replied tentatively. 'But you understand, Mr McCann, we're not allowed t' discuss that.'

The Belfast leaders, mused Brendan to himself: more has-beens who've never fought a campaign and won . . . Foley, Skillen and McKee – old men who've never known anything but defeat.

As the car pulled into a leafy driveway near Howth, it was waved down, and he got out.

'Hey . . . Brendan!'

Barry Devine, the Belfast Brigade intelligence chief, was striding towards the car, his youthful appearance comple-mented by a wide grin.

'You look like shit, Brendan.'

'So would you if you were about to meet this lot,' said Brendan, shaking his hand. 'Who the hell's here?'

Devine walked him towards a clump of trees that hid them from the house. 'The whole fucking leadership, so be careful.'

'So what's new?'

Devine's eyes kept darting in the direction of the house. 'Look, Brendan, I have to watch myself. If I'm seen talking to you, they'd say –'

Brendan interjected, 'That you're another one of these troublemakers.'

Devine laughed. 'That's exactly what they'd say. I'm here on other business, so you're on yer own in there. They've been waitin' for you for over an hour.'

'Let the fuckers wait . . . I wanted a few pints t' charge me up. Who exactly is here from the Belfast Brigade?'

'Our revered commander, Tom Foley, and his illustrious sidekicks – Digger Skillen and James McKee.'

Brendan raised his eyes skywards. 'Isn't that just neat? Old men from the North and old men from the South – a fuckin' bunch of geriatrics who can't see the wood for the trees.'

'Keep yer voice down,' cautioned Devine, taking several steps forward to make sure no one was close by. 'Brendan, they value your opinion . . . we all do. They're lookin' for your support. Don't quote me but I hear they've had overtures from the Brits and they're talkin' about doin' a deal.'

Brendan could barely contain his anger. 'The Brits will eat us,' he said, spitting out the words. 'How many fuckin' times have I told Foley and the others that this is a long war? You only negotiate from strength.'

Devine looked at his watch. 'Somebody may have heard the car arrive.'

'Well, I'll tell them I had a good piss on the lawn,' said Brendan, walking towards the house.

As the front door swung open on his approach, the Belfast Brigade Commander of the IRA, Tom Foley, glared at him from the hallway.

'The others are waiting,' snapped Skillen, opening the door to the drawing-room.

'Let's have no disharmony,' hissed McKee.

Ten minutes later Barry Devine was lounging against the entrance to the house when Brendan's voice boomed out.

'So we're going to capitulate! That's what you're telling me. The Brits are gonna give us the scraps off the table and we should open a dialogue with them.'

The meeting sounded like a bar-room brawl as members of the Army Council rounded on Brendan.

'I told you we shouldn't have invited him!' screamed Digger Skillen. 'He's always been a fucking troublemaker.'

Suddenly Brendan burst into the hallway, slamming the drawing-room door behind him.

'Take it easy,' said Devine, physically slowing his momentum.

Brendan brushed him aside. 'Sorry, Barry. I'll see you in Belfast. There's a real war goin' on up there – not that those fuckers would know it.' He pointed to the young men standing beside the car and shouted, 'Get me to Connolly Station! I want t' be in Belfast this evening.'

Brendan arrived in Belfast three hours later, bought an evening newspaper and, after brushing his hair in the gents', went to the station car park and climbed into his sleek Jaguar.

Driving through Shaftesbury Square, he straightened his

tie and lowered the driver's window as he brought the car to a halt at a roadblock. A fresh-faced soldier looked enquiringly at him and, declining to examine his driver's licence, waved him on. Glancing in his rear-view mirror, he smiled as a shabby Ford Escort was subjected to a full military search. Within five minutes he was in tree-lined Malone Park, where road ramps slowed the car to fifteen miles an hour and the noise of the city faded away. One end of Malone Park was sealed, to discourage through traffic or sightseers curious about how the wealthy created an oasis of calm in the middle of a battlefield.

Andersonstown and the other Catholic estates of West Belfast rose ominously into the hills above Malone, a reminder that life was cruel elsewhere. The park was the preserve of the affluent in South Belfast, both Catholic and Protestant, but with the balance favouring the former. From the beginning of the Troubles the district had seen an influx of the new Catholic middle class – lawyers who knew the financial benefits of a legal-aid system in which one community seemed to be at the mercy of the judicial process. It was a social curiosity of Northern Ireland that there was no upper class in the British tradition of inherited wealth, but a new middle class of upwardly mobile lawyers and businessmen.

Brendan McCann fitted into that new élite, with his Jaguar car, his pin-striped suits and his large detached house.

Once inside the house, he carefully bolted the door and was about to take off his jacket when a voice asked:

'How did it go?'

A man in his early twenties flanked by companions of a similar age appeared at the top of an imposing stairway which rose from the hall to a second floor which contained five bedrooms.

Brendan walked into the drawing-room, removed his jacket and, placing the briefcase on a table, lifted documents from it and casually put them to one side. He drew the curtains, switched on a table lamp and lit a cigarette, seemingly oblivious to the presence of the three young men.

78

'So what happened?' enquired Liam Brady, joining his companions, who were now seated opposite Brendan.

'C'mon, give us the lowdown,' said Damien Nolan, tapping his fingers on the polished oak table.

Patrick Rodgers silently angled his head to one side in an effort to read the documents, while Brendan drew on his cigarette, looking at each of the three young men with a cold and penetrating gaze. These were his constant companions and he knew every nuance of their character traits, his eyes deciphering their thoughts. Brendan had a talent for delving into the private lives of others, seeking out their faults and their fears. He had chosen these men for their intelligence, dedication and loyalty, and for certain individual qualities which matched his vision of what a small political grouping required.

Liam Brady was forceful, incisive and prone to anger, whereas Damien Nolan was cunning and quietly competent. Patrick Rodgers possessed sharp analytical skills, yet beneath his reserved exterior were ruthlessness and rage in equal quantities. Sometimes Brendan felt like a father-figure, especially when they squabbled, discussed women or listened to contemporary music. He was relieved that sex did not figure largely in their lives; sex invariably led to commitments, time away from the job and the risk that a failed relationship might compromise all of them.

'I don't demand celibacy,' he once told them, 'but just remember that women are trouble. They want to know too much about you and when they're hurt they'll savage you.'

At thirty-six, he felt he'd made his choice, believing marriage had passed him by and his objectives conflicted with the demands of a normal lifestyle.

None of his group had a criminal record, or personal attachments that might conflict with the need for total security or dilute their loyalty to the others. Liam and Damien were A-level students when they came to his attention; he snatched them from the folds of the junior IRA before they were swallowed up in the ranks of the movement where there was always a risk of being exposed by an informer. Patrick had been selected after an alert member of Sinn Fein talked to him at a protest rally and reported that he was a likely candidate for recruitment. Brendan was asked to vet him and in the process recognised he had qualities that were appropriate for his internal security unit, which was designed to root out informers in the IRA and to combat British intelligence and Special Branch.

The core of the internal security unit was formed by this group of four men. They were assisted by two-man cells which fulfilled specific tasks set by Brendan. The other cells were isolated from the core; contact with them was made by two women couriers, whose real identities were known only to Brendan. They received their orders by means of a complex arrangement whereby letters were sent to an address in Donegal and subsequently forwarded to a priest, who then passed them to the couriers in a confessional. Two separate couriers brought communications to Brendan from the cells by depositing written notes with a shopkeeper in West Belfast. In the event of an emergency the Belfast Brigade intelligence officer, appointed by Brendan, acted as a go-between. The internal security unit was feared within the IRA because it was ruthless not only in pursuing informers but in tracing anyone in authority who failed to detect them. No one was beyond its scrutiny.

It was the core group of four who carried out the major tasks of counter-intelligence, especially the detailed interrogation of top informers and analysis of the information extracted.

'Always remember', Brendan had warned his team, 'that the analysing of information is sometimes more important than the uncovering of an informer. This may give us a clearer picture of how the Brits target and run agents. Then again, the Brits may have sacrificed an agent in the hope that we blindly accept what he says.'

With a few exceptions, the execution of informers was undertaken by the hard men of the two-man cells who were often referred to as the 'clean-up teams'. They were summoned only after the core group were convinced that all the information was in place; and when a member of the Army

Council had donned the black cap, and all documents relating to the interrogation and confessions of the condemned man had been placed in a secure dump. Brendan and his team maintained a thorough written and tape-recorded archive of all confessions, which were perused at intervals to remind them of the detail.

Contrary to Brendan's policy on executions, Patrick believed the core team should 'see the job done from beginning to end', whereas Liam and Damien felt the process of interrogation was stressful and an execution a much too personalised involvement. When it came to dealing with women suspected of betrayal, no one liked the task.

On one occasion Brendan had been ordered to interrogate a husband-and-wife team, who were British military intelligence agents operating a radio link from their home in West Belfast. 'I hated that fuckin' job,' Brendan had later confided to the Brigade intelligence officer. 'I was looking at a mother pleadin' for her family.' Troops had swamped West Belfast in search of the couple and the Brigade commander had demanded their immediate execution. Patrick had had no qualms about carrying out the double killing; he had coolly shot them in an alleyway. Brendan recalled his own remarks to the Brigade intelligence officer after the killing. 'There weren't any fuckin' hoods to put over their heads,' Brendan had told him. 'What a fuckin' organisation that can't even find two pieces of cloth in an emergency.'

Now, in the elegant detached house in Malone Park, Patrick leaned towards Brendan and placed the palm of his hand on the documents.

'I suppose it's time t' beg you for information,' he said with obvious sarcasm.

'They don't know shit,' Brendan shouted, stubbing out his cigarette on the documents. 'It's a leadership of tired old men.'

Patrick slowly withdrew his hand, seemingly unmoved by the outburst.

'When I arrived in Dublin,' continued Brendan, 'the whole fuckin' Army Council was there . . . and what do y' think was in their minds?'

He looked at the other three and waited for a reply. Liam Brady raised his right hand mimicking a child in a classroom and lowered it when it was clear Brendan was in no mood for trivial gestures.

Damien Nolan tried a different approach, using a measured tone. 'They think the Brits are ready t' do a deal and we should concentrate on the Prods.'

Patrick turned away, unimpressed with Damien's theory and clearly in no mind to add anything to the proceedings.

'Well, what the fuck have you t' say?' demanded Brendan, pointing an accusing finger at him.

Patrick straightened his body and, reaching out, pushed the documents closer to Brendan. 'They told you t' fuck off.'

A stony silence descended. Then Brendan leaned back in his chair and began laughing.

'He's got it,' he said, bending forward, his hands spreading out the documents and a look of disdain creasing his face. 'They've no stomach for a long war. They're armchair generals from that great campaign of 1956 that ended an hour after it began.'

Pointing to a bottle of Black Bush, he nodded to Liam to bring it to the table and with his right thumb and index finger indicated that he wanted a large one. Liam poured the whiskey and handed the glass to Brendan. The others declined a drink and waited patiently for their boss to tell his story.

'They're doin' just what the Brits want,' said Brendan angrily, avoiding a momentary inclination to slam the glass on the table. 'We're gonna get sucked into a dirty little war with the Prods, because that's easier. The Brits will be over the moon. I can just imagine the tabloids in Britain – "gangsters", "thugs" . . . What's that gonna say to our supporters in the States?'

He paused to light a cigarette and Damien quietly interjected, 'I didn't join t' kill Prods. I thought we'd all learned by now that the Brits would love us to point the guns at the Prods and not at them.'

Patrick rose from his chair, poured himself a large whiskey and drank it in one gulp.

'I wonder is there someone in our midst who disapproves of what's been said,' remarked Brendan, emphasising each word.

As Patrick pushed the empty glass away from him, Damien turned to caution him but he waved aside the gesture. 'I don't give a fuck about our leadership. I want t' know where we're goin',' said Patrick. He pointed to the documents. 'I could write the script of the Dublin meeting.' He gestured at Brendan. 'You told them that we have t' carry the war t' Britain because the Brits are content with an acceptable level of violence here. Keep it here and not over there and nobody gives a shit.'

Brendan nodded approval.

'You told them we need a strategy using both the ballot box and the Armalite – that without the politics we can't win the political struggle and the hearts and minds of our people. And without the gun there's no real threat.'

Always the chain smoker, Brendan lit another cigarette and poured himself another whiskey, indicating to Patrick to continue.

'You said we should develop a bombing campaign in Britain so that the Brits can't isolate the problem. If all we do is kill Prods, we'll be tied into a tribal war which will again detach us from our real goals and deprive us of our ideology.'

Pushing the whiskey bottle in Patrick's direction, Brendan murmured, 'You should be lecturing at Queen's, instead of studying.'

'Our leader speaks,' replied Patrick, sensing sarcasm.

'I'm not takin' the piss. I couldn't have said it better m'self,' said Brendan with the hint of a smile.

Tension in the room eased, and the others reached for the Black Bush.

'Do you think our cover still holds?' asked Damien, changing tack.

'We've been here six months and there's been no problem,' Brendan observed. 'And people around here are only concerned about the trappings of respectability. As for me having three students sharing my house . . . well, they think that either I'm queer, that I exploit you or that I'm a generous benefactor. Remember, when I'm not around, make sure you keep to a routine of attending lectures at Queen's – not that they'll ever successfully educate you three.'

He rose from the table. 'In my briefcase you'll find documents that were passed to me by the Belfast Brigade IO. They're about a security breach – so read them, burn them and then get t' bed. We've a long day t'morrow.'

On his way out of the room he stopped and pointed at Patrick. 'Don't worry about the future. There are others who think like us. Things are gonna change.'

It was 7.30 a.m. when Brendan pulled aside the bedroom curtains and watched the mist lifting off Divis Mountain. In Malone Park a solitary dog wandered aimlessly citywards. Brendan rubbed sleep out of his eyes and cradled his head in his hands, regretting the large whiskeys of the previous evening. It was the dog's sudden change of direction which encouraged him to focus on the deserted scene before him. The scrawny mongrel approached the driveway and began barking, its back legs fixed to the ground ready for action. As Brendan studied this bizarre event there was a slight movement in the hedging which sent the dog into a frenzy. Brendan's eyes moved sideways to a high wooden fence on the left of the drive and saw a rifle barrel protruding between two of the wooden slats.

Quickly he lowered himself to the floor, crawled across the room to the landing and was on his feet running madly, hammering on the bedroom doors.

Within moments he was in a huddle with the others, his voice trembling with anxiety.

'We're about t' be hit . . . It's gotta be the Brits . . . the Prods would have come through the door in the middle of the night. Don't panic . . . Just remember the routine. Just return to your rooms.'

Brendan was about to open his bedroom door when Liam Brady rushed towards him.

'We forgot t' burn the documents.'

Brendan pushed him to one side and ran to the staircase. He was halfway down it when a sledgehammer brought the front door crashing to the floor and two soldiers in military fatigues, their faces hidden by balaclavas, burst into the hallway. Brendan lost no time in raising his hands above his head, hoping his sudden compliance would save his life. The soldiers raced towards him and unceremoniously dragged him down the remaining stairs. They spreadeagled him face down, and one held a gun barrel to the nape of his neck while the other slammed a boot into the middle of his back.

There was a sound of boots running through the house and orders being shouted. Then came a clamour as Brendan's companions were dragged along the landing and pushed down the staircase, yelling and struggling all the way down to the hall.

A breakfast of rolls and coffee, with a BBC Radio 3 recital, was the way Richard Milner liked to begin the morning.

'Sir, the major's on the secure line.' An aide was standing in the doorway, breathless from a frantic run along the corridor. 'He says there's a chopper on the way and apologises for the short notice.'

Milner casually looked at his watch, then at his aide, and sipped his coffee.

'Sir, he says it's important.' The aide was nervously waiting for a reply, his fingers scratching the palms of his hands.

'It had better be important.'

The Ops Room at Johnston's HQ was filled with collators, radio operators and people running back and forth with pieces of paper.

'Good to see you, Richard . . . Sorry about the short notice.' Tim Johnston quickly led Richard to the wall display of photographs of the central figures in IRA intelligence. Pointing to the blank outline marked 'Brendan', he slammed his right index finger in the middle of the featureless face. 'We've got our man.'

Richard stared in disbelief at the wall and failed to notice Commander Stanley Davidson seated in a dimly lit corner drinking coffee from a plastic cup.

'Richard.'

Milner turned round as the RUC Special Branch chief approached him with an outstretched hand.

'Good to see you again. I think I may have been of some help to you people this morning.'

Richard was surprised by the speed at which things were happening and he took Davidson's large hand, not knowing whether to shake it or be shaken by it.

Tim Johnston sensed annoyance and confusion in the look on Richard's face and took him to one side.

'Is anything wrong?' whispered Johnston.

'When something like this is going down, don't ever take it on without consulting me.'

'Sorry about that. We had to act quickly.'

'We'll discuss that later and not in front of our friend here.'

Johnston led Milner and Davidson into a side room.

'Stanley's done a great job,' said Johnston as they sat down. 'He acted on a tip-off and I sent some of our people to help out.'

'It was merely a hunch,' remarked Davidson. 'No great detective work on my part . . . Simply a tip-off from an alert member of the public.'

Richard gave a thin smile.

'The daughter of one of our people,' continued the commander, 'is married to a high-ranking civil servant who lives in Malone Park. She's paranoid about his security and won't even let workmen into the house unless they've been vetted by us. She was like a toothache, but her father was one of our best officers and we kept her sweet.'

Commander Davidson leaned forward. 'Anyway, she had become suspicious of four people living next door, though I think she was just annoyed that from her point of view three students were able to live in her neighbourhood. So she phones one of our collators about a dozen times, and finally she gives him the registration of a Jaguar saloon and asks him to check it out. It turns out it's registered in the name of a Brian Graham. Now this is where her paranoia and luck provide a breakthrough. One of the female staff overhears the collator talking about a Brian Graham and says, "I knew a Brian Graham but he was killed in a car crash two years ago."

'At that point I order a tight surveillance operation and put some people in her house. Some of our watchers follow the Jag while others tail the three students, but they turn out to be regularly attending lectures at Queen's University. The guy in the Jag begins to interest us, though, because our people sense that his behaviour is that of someone who expects to be followed. As you know, people trained in man-to-man surveillance soon sense if they're dealing with a pro. Each time we put people on him he lost them. Three days ago we tailed him to Newry, where he parked the Jag at a private house and took the train to Dublin. He shrugged off our people in a market near O'Connell Street . . .'

Milner was growing restless, but Davidson pressed on. 'I decided to concentrate our efforts on the house and thought what the fuck are three students doing living in the splendour of Malone Park with an older man who has an alias? We put photos of him across our people and CID and came up with zero, so I decided to ring Tim.'

Johnston opened a file marked 'Secret' and passed it to Richard.

'See that photo . . . Look closely at the face of the man to the left of the coffin and just behind the IRA colour party.'

Richard was scrutinising the swarthy features of a slightly built man. Tim Johnston leaned forward and fingered the image.

'Our people matched the Branch photos to that one.'

'He looks like a spectator,' replied Richard, pointing to other figures who were milling around in the funeral picture.

Johnston laughed. 'That's what *we* thought until Stanley came up with his name.'

Davidson was determined to force an interruption, to ingratiate himself with Richard. Bending forward, his hands outstretched, he fixed his gaze on the MI5 officer. 'I told our people to pull out all the stops and hand me an answer. John Bradford and Bill Green provided it.'

Tim Johnston jabbed at the photograph. 'This guy disappeared from view over two years ago, and when Stanley came up with the name Brendan McCann my gut feeling was that this was our man. As I told you, the name Brendan has been filtering through to us for a long time but nobody could describe him or knew his whereabouts.'

'Yes, but what have we got on him? How do we know he's our man?'

Stanley Davidson reached inside his jacket, withdrew five A4 pages and placed them in front of Richard, remarking, 'This answers your query.'

On each page the words 'Brigade Staff Report' were marked in pencil. Lists of names were headed 'Acting Suspiciously', with further headings such as 'Civilians' and 'Low-Level IRA Personnel'.

'These were found in the house in Malone Park – hardly the notes students should be studying.'

Richard raised his hands to indicate that he was being bombarded with too much information too quickly. 'Are we saying we've captured an IRA intelligence cell?' he asked, looking first at Davidson and then sternly at Johnston.

'Exactly that,' replied Davidson.

'Yes, but what kind of evidence do we have to put all of them behind bars? There's nothing I want more than having McCann where I can see him and his little team, but it seems to me that the three students might well proffer a legal argument that they knew nothing of McCann's activities.'

'Leave the legal side of it to Stanley,' said Johnston. 'He has a strategy to deal with that.'

'I can get a magistrate to remand them in custody. With the burdens on the legal system, they could be in custody for a year before they got a proper hearing. You just tell me how long you want them there.'

Richard was unhappy that he was learning so much at second hand, though he was beginning to develop a sneaking regard for the Special Branch chief.

'I take your point, Richard,' added Davidson. 'The legal issue is important because we'll get a conviction of McCann. He won't want a trial where those documents are presented in open court. He'll plead guilty to IRA membership and possession of incriminating documents, and go down for ten. The others will probably walk free because they've no history. Even if we find their fingerprints on the documents it wouldn't be enough. They'll produce more references than the Pope, and a judge will be swayed by the need for them to continue their academic careers. What I can do is keep the students in prison for as long as you want them there.'

Tim Johnston was on his feet, pacing up and down the room. 'Listen, Richard,' he began. 'This little cell is the nucleus of something bigger. These people are intelligent terrorists who know what they're about.'

'Absolutely,' said Davidson.

Richard was tiring of Davidson's sycophancy. 'I know all that,' he said, walking across the room and taking Johnston by the arm. 'We have to talk.'

The Special Branch chief got the message and left the room with a parting nod of recognition that his company was intrusive.

'I hope you haven't given him an insight into our plans.' Richard spoke crisply to the major.

'He's a wily old bird . . . he can be useful.'

'The next time he decides to be useful, you let me know about it. There are too many things at stake here for people to be going off half cock.'

Johnston was stung by the implicit criticism, and resentful that his operational freedom was in question. 'I thought it was better you continued with the planning while I sorted out matters on the ground.'

'Major, when you use your people, I want to know about it. You need me to cover your back if something goes wrong.'

Johnston was annoyed by Richard's formal and stern manner, but recognised that he had transgressed the rules which shaped their professional relationship. Holding out his hand to Richard, he apologised.

'Let's have a coffee,' replied Richard, smiling. 'I can't fault you on providing the most important ingredient in our plans.'

Johnston ushered him back into the Ops Room.

'There's something else?'

'Bradford and Green will be here this evening.'

'Whatever you do, major, make sure I'm consulted before the other pieces of our jigsaw are ready to be put in place.'

John Bradford was at his desk when Commander Davidson arrived and casually pulled up a chair. Bill Green's presence at the window went unnoticed for several seconds as Davidson eased his large body into a comfortable posture. Green was about to leave, when Davidson turned round.

'Green, I'm glad you're here, because I need to talk to you both.'

He motioned to Green to take a seat, adding, 'This is not a courtesy call. There are people who'd like a chat with you . . . Now these people are not in my jurisdiction, if you know what I mean, so you're not obliged to talk to them.'

Davidson looked uncomfortable, and Bradford came to his rescue. 'Sir, if you say it's OK, we've no objection.'

'Let's just say that this chat and whatever transpires will be a favour to me,' said Davidson quietly, his normal tough exterior transformed by a benevolent smile.

'Who are these people?' asked Bill Green.

'One of them's a major who runs one of the secret military units. The other – Milner – is one of these London-calling boys. You know the type.'

'Fuckin' wide boys,' said Green, laughing.

'Of course, as head of Special Branch, I don't have to accede to requests from outside agencies to talk to my staff.' Davidson fidgeted with a plastic cup and looked at the floor. 'So whatever happens at this meeting I expect you to keep me informed. No one else is to know . . . Is that straight?'

Davidson rarely socialised, apart from a Christmas drink with his staff, and was always gruff at meetings.

'Sir, is there anything in particular we should know about

these people?' asked Bradford, with a sideways glance at his partner, expecting him to pose some penetrating questions. Green, however, was too busy swilling his coffee round the cup and nodding agreement every time the boss spoke.

'Just don't get in over yer heads and watch out for Milner . . . He's a spook, and a clever one at that. He's got London's backing.'

'Does that mean he outranks you, sir?'

Davidson sat upright and stared angrily at Green; John Bradford was secretly pleased.

'It simply means he's got the approval of the people who matter in respect of certain operations. *I'm* the person in charge here and don't forget it.'

Bill Green was not a man to challenge his own boss openly, and the tone of the commander's reply was sufficient to silence him.

'Just remember your allegiance is here in this building,' added Davidson, glancing first at Green and then at Bradford.

'Sir, what about the military person?' asked Bradford in a deferential tone.

'He doesn't exist, if you know what I mean. I checked him out and he's been here before – the SAS type if ever I saw one. These people are in the same business as us, so if you can help them, do so. I've told them you'll be at Palace Barracks at 8 p.m.'

'What kinda help might they need?' enquired Bradford, but Davidson ignored the question, rose to his feet and left the room without a backward glance at his staff.

'What the fuck do y' make of that?'

'I don't like this,' Bradford began. 'I think he's lyin' through his teeth about somethin'.'

'I reckon that MI5's up his ass once again and he's pretendin' to be in control. Do you remember the last time? The bastards strode in here and interrogated some of us without so much as a by-your-leave . . . and all because a lot of bleedin' hearts out there were sayin' we were supplyin' the loyalists with weapons. They didn't interview any of these wide boys in the military . . . Oh, no, just blame the locals.'

Bradford sat with his elbows on the desk and his face cradled in his hands.

'What are y' thinkin' about?' asked his partner.

'When you put spooks and the SAS together, we're talkin' dirty operations. These guys leave their fingerprints on nothing but the rest of us are left to take the flak when it goes wrong. I don't fuckin' like this.'

'We're in no position to refuse,' replied Green, and began to mimic his boss: 'I would like to tell you that this has fuck all t' do with me. You don't have t' talk to them because this is my patch but you'd better fucking talk to them because Five has a big pole up my arse.'

Bradford was forced to laugh: Green was the only person on the staff who could perfectly imitate Davidson's slow rural drawl.

'Calm down, Bill, this is serious.'

Green was not going to forego an opportunity to have a laugh at his boss's expense. 'As head of Special Branch,' he began, rising to his feet, 'I would like to inform you that I am washing my hands of this, but keep me informed of something nobody knows anything about, including you pair. I'll repeat that for my own benefit.'

'You've made your point, so let's be fuckin' serious here.'

'OK, OK,' said Green, lowering himself into a chair. 'I may be takin' the piss but what I'm really sayin' is that he's lyin' through his teeth.'

'Let's just keep our heads.' Bradford motioned to his partner to keep his voice down. 'The walls have ears, even in this building. It's my hunch, knowing Five, that this guy Milner is a high-flier, otherwise the boss wouldn't be so jittery. That means we take it easy and watch our asses.'

'Well, John, you know I don't trust the Brits.'

'*You* are one,' replied Bradford with a smile.

'That's below the belt. You know what I mean . . . all this unattributable stuff.'

'And what do y' think we're about?' Bradford stood up, closing the conversation.

*

At 8 p.m. they were met by escorts at the front gates of Palace Barracks and taken to the MRF command post. On the way down the corridor to the Ops Room, Green pointed to a door marked 'Target Room' and laughed.

'Cowboys and Indians. What did I tell you?' he whispered to Bradford.

Johnston and Milner were sitting at a table in the middle of the Ops Room but only Milner rose to his feet to greet the Special Branch officers. Green was fascinated by his surroundings and had to be persuaded to sit down with the other men.

'What can we do for you?' asked Bradford, looking at Milner.

'We want two of your agents,' said Johnston dismissively.

Bradford laughed. Green did not respond; his eyes were fixed on a montage of photographs which included him and his colleague and, alongside them, Michael McDonnell and Stephen Kirkpatrick.

'What the fuck's goin' on here?' demanded Green, pointing to the photographs. 'What right have you to have us on that wall?' He gesticulated at Johnston.

'It simply illustrates how important you are to our operation,' suggested Milner with a reassuring smile.

Green placed his hands on the table and leaned towards Johnston. 'We don't work for you people and neither do our agents. I know all about you lot . . . comin' here and thinkin' you can just run the place.'

'What my partner's trying to say,' added Bradford in a more measured voice, 'is that we only take orders from the head of Special Branch – '

'They know exactly what I'm saying,' interjected Green, making a dismissive wave of his hand in Johnston's direction.

Richard Milner stood up and casually approached the wall of photos. Slowly he removed the portraits of Green and Bradford and, returning to the table, placed the relevant pictures in front of the Special Branch men.

'Your friend is right,' said Milner, addressing Bradford. 'You don't work for us, but *they* do.' He gestured to the photographs of McDonnell and Kirkpatrick. 'Tell them to pack

93

some things and have them here at this time tomorrow evening. Is that understood?'

Green pointed a finger at Johnston. 'If you people think you can walk in here and tell us what t' do you've another think coming.'

Bradford placed a restraining hand on Green and stared at Milner. 'It's your call this time round. I'd just like t' say one thing. I don't like this. We've put a lot of time and energy into those agents and if you screw it up I don't want our fingerprints on it or I'll come looking for you.' Pointing to Johnston he added: 'And also you, major.'

Milner stepped close to Bradford and when he spoke his voice was tinged with menace. 'I thought we could reach an amicable arrangement but it appears that's not possible. A word of warning . . . This operation is classified, so you and your partner must get on with some other business.'

Milner pressed a button opening the electronic doorway behind him and gestured towards it.

'This meeting is now ended. Thank you for your time, gentlemen . . . You know where the door is.'

As the door closed behind the Special Branch officers, Johnston re-entered the room, his face red with rage.

'Take it easy, Tim. There's no point making enemies of these people.'

Johnston began pacing up and down. 'It's been the same with indigenous forces in all colonial situations,' he began, looking to Milner for agreement. 'They want you here and then they shit on you.'

'We've got what we want,' observed Milner. 'I never thought it would be easy. It's my guess that Davidson behaved like Pontius Pilate and told them nothing. *He* doesn't want his fingerprints on it either, so he's probably sent them to us as though it has nothing to do with him.'

'I don't trust Green,' said Johnston. 'He's a loose cannon. And what guarantee do we have that they won't interfere with McDonnell and Kirkpatrick?'

'Bradford's the thinker in that partnership, Tim. He's the one who'd concern me. Green's personnel file shows he's merely a malcontent with a penchant for survival. Bradford's the only one who'll work with him, and Green will do what he's told out of self-interest. Bradford intrigues me. He's a family man, and he's believed to have some sort of social conscience. I have the feeling that he's a moralist, and there's no room for that type in this business. I want you to put some of your people on to both of them.'

Johnston looked reassured and sat down. 'What kind of surveillance do you want?'

'Low-key . . . man-to-man.'

'What about phones? I can organise a tap on their home phones but we'd need to put a device in their office . . . Now that's a tight one.'

'Don't worry about the latter. I've people in that building who'll do the job.'

Bradford and Green drove towards Belfast, both of them too angry to speak. On reaching the city centre, Bradford pulled over on to waste ground and turned off the engine.

'Some day, Bill, your mouth's gonna get us into serious trouble. You don't mess with these people and there's more than one way to skin a cat. These people don't exist, which means they're not accountable. If they wanted t' stick a bomb under our car, they could do it, and the papers would read "Murdered by the Provos".'

'That's all very fine, but we've been had, and that bastard Davidson knew it.'

'That should tell you something,' said Bradford, slamming his hands against the steering wheel. 'If they can get to him, then we're small fry.'

'Bollocks.'

'OK, Bill, you go and tell that to the boss.'

Green was lost for words and looked through the windscreen at passing traffic.

'It's like this, partner,' advised Bradford, his right hand forming a fist. 'They have us by the balls.'

'But *we* own Kirkpatrick and McDonnell.'

Bradford smiled and patted his partner on the back. 'Now you're thinking.'

'And *they* wouldn't shit without telling us.'

'That's right, but keep yer powder dry because Milner could have us moved to the border to sit out our days if he ever thought we were keepin' tabs on his little operation.'

'Which means we have t' get to Kirkpatrick and McDonnell.'

6

'The world and its aunt's been lookin' for you,' said Mary Kirkpatrick as her son sauntered into the kitchen. 'There's yer buddy Michael McDonnell, that nutcase next door who put a note through the letterbox, and Bernadette. She phoned about three times. You're never around and I'm fed up. Y' took yerself off at eleven this morning and now it's five. It beats me where y' go.'

'I was out looking for work,' said Stephen as he rummaged in the fridge.

'There's a pie in the oven but if y' think I'm gonna start making a big meal you've another think comin'.'

Stephen laughed and blew her a kiss before removing the pie from the oven and sitting down at the table. 'So what did Michael have to say?'

'That fella's always vague, but what can y' expect when he's never been anything different.'

'Mum, I wasn't lookin' for another one of your tirades about Michael . . . Just tell me what he said.'

'He said you've a meeting with yer friends tonight. He's always talkin' in riddles. I asked him who you were meeting and he just said you'd know. Then I asked him what time and where. It was like gettin' blood out of a stone. He said the Albert Clock at seven-thirty. Now I don't suppose you're goin' t' enlighten me any further.'

'A few of us are goin' to a party and it's better t' meet in the city centre.'

'Yeah, and I'm the Duke of Edinburgh.'

'What did Jimmy want?'

'Y' see,' said Mary sitting opposite her son. 'Bernadette,

God help her, is not very high on your agenda – now is she?'

Here we go again, thought Stephen, annoyed that his mother always measured his behaviour in terms of his relationship with Bernadette.

Mary reached into a pocket of her apron and removed a crumpled piece of paper. Stephen held out his hand for it but she drew the note closer to her and began inspecting it. 'This is like the writing on a mummy's tomb.'

'Give it to me.'

Mary continued to scan the note, much to her son's annoyance and growing irritation. Finally he reached across and snatched it from her.

'That's no way to treat yer mother,' she shouted angrily.

'I'm sorry, but I'm not goin' t' wait all day for you to decipher it.'

'If you're such a genius, what does it say?'

Stephen appeared to have difficulty reading it, then burst out laughing.

'It says, "I'd rather have le bottle in front of me than a frontal lobotomy."' Stephen giggled again.

'And what does that mean?' demanded Mary, with a vexed stare.

'He's taken to drink.' Stephen tried to explain that Jimmy had used the expression to indicate his view of Bridget Jones, his neighbour.

'This street would be a lot saner without him,' said Mary. 'I'd like t' know what he's been on before he hit the bottle.'

Mary was now in full flow, and Stephen was reduced to being a one-man audience.

'He's been there as long as I remember, runnin' around wringing his hands, talkin' like a little mouse with those bony hands of his cupped round his mouth. Sure everybody knows he's lettin' in air . . . well, everybody it seems but you. Everybody says there's somethin' dodgy about his past. Bridget Jones says she heard he was in a nuthouse for somethin' he'd done.'

'If anybody's a nut, she's certainly one,' said Stephen, raising his voice. 'That woman should be certified. She's nothin' but a busybody who spends her time spreadin' lies about other people. Anyway I'm not gonna sit here and listen to all this crap.'

He walked into the hallway and put on his coat.

'Y' treat this place like a boarding house,' shouted Mary as he opened the front door. 'Maybe you'd like t' take up residence with yer friend next door.'

He could still hear his mother's voice as he stepped through Jimmy's front door.

The old man came out of the kitchen with a bottle of Scotch and two grubby cups.

As he poured the whisky, he said, 'Y' should never spoil it with the water from whence it came. The Irish can't make whisky. The only thing they ever invented was the tyre.'

It was not a drink favoured by Stephen and without water it was much too strong for his palate.

'Do y' mind if I put some water in it?' he asked meekly.

'That's the problem with people,' said Jimmy as he went to fetch water. 'They get a good thing and then they dilute it. Doesn't matter if it's drink, politics or –'

'Sex.'

Jimmy ignored the interjection and poured a minute drop of water into Stephen's cup.

'That's the first time I've seen you hit the bottle. What's the occasion?' asked Stephen.

Jimmy paused while he gently sipped from his cup. 'I got my pension this morning and I thought to myself: What's worse – livin' in this world with a tea-bag or havin' a belt at the real thing? So I walked Provo round to the off-licence, bought myself the whisky and got him a bottle of Guinness.'

'Will Provo touch the stuff?'

'If he's any sense he will. If not, he'll just have t' learn. He needs somethin' t' build him up. Take Billy there.' He pointed to the cat, which was stretched across the window-sill. 'He'll take a drop of the hard stuff with his milk and he's a pair of arms on him like a bricklayer.'

'I never knew you drank whisky,' said Stephen, curious about this break in the old man's routine.

'When I was a lot younger I hit the bottle with a vengeance. Now don't get me wrong, I wasn't alcoholic or anything like that . . . It was just my way of copin' with life. Some people beat their wives, some become the people's heroes, a few stick their heads in the oven and the rest of the world pretends there's nothin' wrong. So last night I was sittin' here thinkin' why should I pretend there's nothing wrong.'

'What does that fella Bouan say about drinkin'?'

Jimmy stared at his guest, wondering whether the question was asked with malice. Satisfied that he appeared serious, he leaned forward, his spectacles perched on his nose and the elastic holding them stretched tightly across his ears.

'Bouan says it's a gift of our invention and as such should be treated with the respect it deserves. Could you imagine a Frenchman not havin' his wine with his bread? Sure they fought the revolution over that. And what about the marriage feast at Cana?'

By the time Stephen left, the old man was sleeping soundly by the fire, Provo at his feet, an empty bottle in his lap and Billy resting on his shoulder.

Michael McDonnell was lounging against the railings at the base of the Albert Memorial clocktower, a rucksack slung across one shoulder, when Stephen joined him.

'Where are your things?' asked Michael, pointing to his own rucksack. 'I told yer mum to tell you t' pack a few things, and that we were goin' on a wee trip.'

Stephen laughed. 'Y' know, she's smart. She never said a thing.'

'She was probably waitin' for y' t' say something so that she could trip y' up.'

'Where are we goin'?'

'Let's hope it's somewhere sunny.'

A car horn alerted them to the arrival of their handlers, who were sitting in a Ford Granada with Bradford at the wheel. Stephen and Michael climbed into the back. Then the car made its way along the Newtownards Road and into a shadowy side street in the heart of loyalist territory.

'I don't feel safe in this fuckin' area,' complained Michael as Bradford drove the car slowly into a yard at the rear of a pub.

'It's good Prod territory,' said Green, 'and if we're safe here so are you.'

Bradford unlocked a metal door and led the way into a small lounge, which was linked to the main bar by a tiny walkway.

A shabby little man arrived and shook hands with the two Special Branch officers, sparing only a glance for their companions.

'Two pints of lager for the lads,' said Green, pointing to Michael and Stephen, 'and the usual for us.'

No one spoke until the drinks arrived and the barman left the room.

'Where are y' takin' us?' asked Michael.

'All in good time,' replied Bradford, 'all in good time.'

'Well, how are you lads gettin' on these days?' enquired Green, with a friendliness that surprised the young men. 'Are you OK for funds?'

Bradford looked slightly embarrassed by his partner's effusiveness and his overplaying of the role of benefactor. 'You're gonna be working for some friends of ours,' he began, as Stephen began to feel uneasy about the cosiness of the meeting.

'Speaking of money –' Michael interjected.

Bradford ignored him. 'We'd like you to keep us informed of your progress with these people.'

'What's in it for us?' asked Michael, his right hand held out.

Bradford's voice was gentle but firm. 'You'll be well looked after by these people.'

'Does that mean two pay cheques?' Michael gave a cheeky grin.

'You see,' shouted Green, glaring at his partner, 'this ungrateful little fucker is always lookin' for an edge.'

'Calm down, Bill.' Bradford assumed the tone of a kind mediator. 'He's right to look after himself. Of course we'll continue to look after them. Their loyalty's to us – and what are friends for?'

'I just thought our generosity had been forgotten,' added Green rather grudgingly.

'In that case, Bill, I'll have a large vodka and tonic and the same for Stephen.'

Green contrived a smile, and hurried off to order the drinks. In his absence Stephen felt less inhibited and asked Bradford who were their new handlers.

'People like us on the military side.' Bradford's manner implied the matter was of little consequence.

'What's the bottom line here with these people?' Stephen's directness startled even Michael.

'Do what you're told and keep us informed,' answered Green. Stephen recognised the old pals' act as Bradford put a glass in front of him, poured tonic into it and smiled.

'We have your interests at heart,' he said, looking into Stephen's eyes, 'and we can protect you.'

'From what?' demanded Michael with an expression of concern.

'Bill's only letting you know that this is a nasty world and we'll deal with anybody who messes you about. If you're not happy workin' with these people, we'll sort it out . . . Nothing can be fairer than that – isn't that right, Bill?'

'That's exactly the point I was goin' t' make,' said Green. 'Everybody needs back-up and in your case we're it.'

Bradford gave Stephen a reassuring pat on the back and encouraged him to drink faster, but Stephen was finding that the mixture of vodka and Jimmy's whisky was making it difficult for him to concentrate.

'What you lads must remember', continued Bradford in a fatherly tone, 'is that we can only help if we keep our own counsels.'

Michael's cunning streak never allowed him to miss an opportunity to strike a financial deal. 'Does that mean we don't let these people know we're still bein' paid by you?'

Green stole a wicked glance at Michael, while Bradford reached into his pocket and withdrew a fat envelope.

'Here's a little somethin' t' keep you going.'

Michael's eyes widened with pleasure as he reached for the envelope, but Stephen was there before him and stuffed it inside his jacket.

'If I'm to get this right,' said Stephen, 'we're gonna work for these military people and they mustn't know we're still workin' for you.'

'When you've two masters, always make sure y' give your total allegiance to one of them.'

Stephen nodded agreement, even though he was still trying to understand the import of the advice.

But Michael was in no doubt about the purpose of the meeting. 'You pay us to stay quiet about our wee arrangement and to keep you informed of their wee arrangement.' He rubbed his right forefinger and thumb together to indicate loads of money.

Stephen smiled in approval: there were times when he admired his friend's lack of tact and directness.

Announcing it was time to go, Bradford raised his glass to his lips and drained it.

'What are these people gonna ask of us?' Michael persisted.

'That's what you're gonna tell us,' replied Green.

As they drove out of Belfast, Stephen looked back at the lights rising from the city on to the mountainside and wondered whether Jimmy was still sleeping by the fire and whether his mother was concerned about where he might be. In the foreground the tall cranes of Harland & Wolff shipyard stood limp, a testimony to better times for the Protestant workers of East Belfast. Michael was still exchanging banter with Green as Belfast Lough came into view. Stephen had happy memories of trips with his father to Bangor and along the coast to Donaghadee, where you could see the coast of Scotland on a clear day. Once they had travelled round the bay to Millisle and eaten dulse and icecream. 'Only the Italians make proper icecream,' his father used to say. There was something about all those places which made him feel uncomfortable. They contained images of Protestant Ulster, where Sundays were observed according to the Presbyterian sabbath tradition. Even Belfast city centre on Sundays was affected by Protestant custom; for Stephen, the dusty streets of closed shops created an eeriness exuding dejection and the suggestion that everyone was transformed into a sort of non-person. He always felt that Catholics celebrated the sabbath with games and a sense of joy, whereas Protestants seemed merely to tolerate it.

'We're almost there,' said Green, pointing to barbed wire and watchtowers.

As the car moved slowly to the entrance of Palace Barracks, Stephen stared apprehensively at the armed sentries and stole a glance backwards towards the city. One of the sentries scrutinised the car number-plate and waved to Bradford to stop the vehicle.

'This is as far as we go,' said Green.

Two soldiers opened the rear doors of the car.

'So we're about t' join the professionals,' joked Michael. He got out of the car and presented his rucksack for inspection.

As Bradford reversed the car, Green leaned out the window. 'We'll be in touch,' he shouted at Michael.

'Not if I can help it,' whispered Michael. 'All that shite about two masters. I'm no piggie in the middle.'

Stephen took his friend by the arm. 'Listen, I don't know what we're gettin' into, so let's not forget that we may need those two.'

'Bollocks! This is where the real people are. Those two are has-beens.'

As the two Special Branch men drove back towards the city, John Bradford grinned at his partner. 'That was a fucking good double act. For a moment I thought you were gonna stick one on McDonnell.'

'I wouldn't trust the two of them as far as I could throw them.' Bill Green shrugged his shoulders.

'Neither do I, so I've opened up a little file on them and

detailed two of our watchers to keep an eye on their movements. Our fingerprints are all over those two and I want t' know what they're at.'

'What did y' tell the surveillance lads?'

'I gave them a cock-and-bull story that we were worried the army might be using two agents who were dodgy and we'd been asked by the military to keep an eye on them.'

'Did they believe you?'

'Well, I told them this job had come down from MI5 and they needed our expertise and all that bullshit about it being classified etcetera.'

'I'd be fuckin'. careful about that, John. Who are the watchers?'

'Retired SB staff.'

'I don't trust Milner and Johnston . . . they're insolent bastards.'

'That's choice comin' from you, Bill.'

'You mark my words . . . Milner's a funny one – over-ambitious. Isn't he the one who did those electronic surveillance courses in London? He's a smartarse and I don't trust him.'

'You've got t' trust somebody,' said Bradford, then added, 'I'll bet you liked that explanation I gave the two lads. Wasn't it a load of shit? Anyway, I'm starvin'. What about a burger and chips?'

'What I'd like is a camera in that Ops Room and a tap on Milner's phone.'

Nothing had prepared Stephen for the fear he felt as he and Michael were driven through Palace Barracks. The roar of armoured vehicles, the shouting of orders and boots pounding the tarmac reverberated in his head, aggravating the effect of too much alcohol.

Michael, on the other hand, was fascinated by his surroundings and kept pointing to camouflaged emplacements. 'Look at that,' he said, as a soldier handed a general-purpose machine-gun to a colleague in a waiting armoured personnel carrier. 'That's what I call a persuader.'

Stephen listened in silence while his friend gleefully drew his attention to everything which excited him.

'This is the real thing, Stephen. If we need protection, it's here.'

At the steel doors of the MRF command post, Michael looked up at the overhead camera and made funny faces.

'Don't be so fuckin' childish,' warned Stephen. 'It's not a kids' playground.'

In the corridor leading to the Ops Room, one of their escorts indicated a door marked 'Mess' and told them to go in.

In the diffused lighting, Stephen blinked. It was several seconds before he realised that the room was laid out like a lounge bar. There were people in military fatigues and civilian clothes, talking loudly and drinking pints of lager.

A slightly built man approached and warmly shook Stephen's hand. 'I'm Richard Milner.'

He turned to look for Michael but the latter was already at the bar ordering a drink.

Stephen tentatively began to apologise for his friend's rudeness but Milner interrupted his explanations and led him to a corner table where a large man wearing a woollen cravat was huddled over a tiny glass of orange juice.

'This is Major Johnston,' Milner told Stephen.

'It appears your friend is at home here,' said Johnston, gesturing towards Michael, who by now was chatting to a young woman.

Stephen was uneasy at being left to make conversation and tried to excuse himself on the pretext of summoning his friend.

'Don't worry about him,' Richard reassured him. 'There will be plenty of time for formal introductions.'

The offer of a drink made Stephen feel more comfortable but he didn't relish the prospect of more alcohol. His request for a lemonade drew a laugh from Tim Johnston.

'I think the major intends you to have something a little stronger,' said Richard, smiling. He summoned a barman.

Stephen ordered a vodka and Coke. It'll kill me or cure me,

he thought, taking a gulp from the glass that was brought to him.

The vodka was sending a warm glow into Stephen's cheeks as Milner ordered another round of drinks which included an orange juice for the major and a large Scotch for himself.

'The major is still hung over from last night,' explained Richard, aware that Stephen was puzzled that Johnston was not joining in the revelry.

'Your friend seems to like the ladies,' Milner added.

Stephen turned and caught a glimpse of Michael at the back of the room with his arm round a young woman dressed in fatigues. 'He'd screw a –'

A disapproving look from the major silenced him.

'Let's talk about more interesting matters,' said Richard, engaging Stephen with an approving nod and a dismissive wave towards the bar. 'How were you and Michael treated by our friends in Special Branch?'

Stephen was unsure how to reply; he didn't know whether he was free to talk about his handlers.

'Did they pay you well?' asked the major.

'Sometimes,' replied Stephen hesitantly. 'Depending on certain things.'

'What things?'

'Depending on the information we gave them . . . or if they felt generous.'

'Well, you won't have to worry about us,' said Richard Milner, placing a hand on Stephen's arm. 'We'll open a bank account for you in England and while you're with us we'll give you fifty pounds a day in cash. At the end of your time with us we'll place twenty thousand pounds in each account.'

Stephen's mouth opened in amazement.

'And that's not all,' added the major. 'We'll give you a new identity and send you wherever you wish to settle.'

'America?'

Milner and the major laughed and spoke in unison. 'Yes.'

'Is that on the line?' asked Stephen half expecting them to say it was a joke.

'Of course,' said Johnston. 'We look after our people.'

Hoping to attract Michael's attention, and knowing his friend would be ecstatic with the new financial arrangements, Stephen turned towards the bar but the major reached over and with one hand turned him towards Richard Milner.

'Has anyone made you a better offer?' Richard enquired.

'*Any* offer?' added the major curtly.

Stephen nervously reached for the vodka, but the major gently placed a restraining hand over the glass. Slowly and anxiously, Stephen began to explain that Bradford and Green paid him only on an *ad hoc* basis when they were happy with the information they received and often withheld payments as a form of punishment.

'We're loyal to those who are loyal to us,' remarked the major, withdrawing his hand from the glass. 'We are your lifeline. If you do what you're told there'll be no problem.'

Stephen was reminded of John Bradford's advice to give allegiance to only one master. 'I'm not supposed t' tell you this,' he began. 'And Michael will probably go crackers . . . Bradford and Green –'

'They've offered to pay you if you keep them informed of our operation.'

'How did you know that?' Stephen stared at Richard Milner.

'It's my business to know these things.'

Major Johnston leaned forward and his eyes and voice were full of menace. 'Tell them nothing.'

Shocked by the brevity and directness of the advice, Stephen sat back slightly, placing his hands on his knees.

'I don't tolerate anyone messing with my people, and that includes Special Branch.'

Michael was approaching the table, trailing his rucksack along the ground.

Richard laughed, then rose and introduced himself.

Michael nodded towards him and the major. 'It's all right. Jane, your lovely lieutenant up there, told me who y' are. God, I love women in uniform.'

Tim Johnston got to his feet. Pushing back his chair, he

patted Stephen on the back and left the room without acknowledging Michael's presence.

'It's time to call it a night.' Richard summoned two soldiers to the table. 'Drive these lads to number 14.'

Michael was not ready for bed; protesting that he hadn't finished his pint, he sat down and lowered the rest of it in one gulp. With a hand on the young man's shoulder, Richard made it clear he expected him to leave. Michael truculently ignored helping hands and quietly followed his friend out of the bunker and into an open jeep.

'Shit, they've even got a housing estate here,' he exclaimed a few moments later when the jeep drew up at No. 14 Harwell Terrace.

Making an ungainly exit from the vehicle, he staggered to the door, much to the amusement of the soldiers escorting them.

'These are your quarters,' said one of the soldiers, handing Stephen a key. 'Make sure you give him the hair of the dog in the morning before he sees the major.'

The house comprised a living-room, kitchen, bathroom and two bedrooms, one of which had two beds. There was a bottle of vodka in the fridge which Michael instantly seized.

'Well, I'm hittin' the sack,' Stephen announced.

'Sit down on yer arse for a minute,' said Michael as he opened the bottle, 'and I'll tell y' about the piece of skirt I met.'

Placing his right index finger on the edge of Michael's nose, Stephen warned him that the major hadn't seemed too pleased by the attention he was paying the woman at the bar.

His friend laughed. 'Maybe he's screwin' her, and if he's not then I'm gonna give her one.'

Stephen slumped into an armchair.

'She's real foxy, that lieutenant,' Michael continued. 'There's definitely somethin' about women in uniform. You tell me any man who doesn't get turned on by a girl in uniform.'

'What about traffic wardens?'

'If they'd take those double yellow lines off their heads, they wouldn't be too bad.'

'Can we change the subject?'

It was a pointless question: Michael was determined to indulge in drunken self-examination.

'I reckon it's about schoolgirls. The first time y' ever get a hard-on is at school. And what do y' have at school? Uniforms. After that y're hooked on uniforms.'

'What a load of old bollocks,' replied Stephen, trying to remove the vodka bottle from his friend's grasp. Then he started to walk towards the hallway.

'Here, where's that money Bradford gave you?' asked Michael. 'I'm gonna ask that lieutenant out.'

'I've told Milner and the major about the money.'

'You did what?' screamed Michael, spilling his drink over his trousers. 'Now you've well and truly fucked up our financial deals.'

Reaching into his jacket, Stephen withdrew the fat envelope containing Special Branch cash and flung it into his friend's lap. 'You fuckin' keep it . . . I'm throwin' my lot in with these boys.' He paused. 'And another thing . . . you'd better start layin' off the booze. Recently we've been livin' in a fuckin' alcoholic haze and we're gonna need clear heads t' deal with this.'

He then explained the financial arrangements that Milner had offered.

Michael began calculating what he was going to do with his £20,000 bonus. 'Just think of the birds I can pull now . . . Y' know, we could've screwed more money out of Bradford and Green. I'm not convinced that we shouldn't take those bastards for a ride.'

It was half past midnight when Richard Milner arrived in the Ops Room, where Tim Johnston was engaged in a heated debate with Lieutenant Jane Horton. There was an embarrassed exchange of glances before the major dismissed the woman officer.

As Richard walked into the centre of the room his attention was drawn to a reel-to-reel tape machine which was still running. He picked up a pair of headphones and began laughing.

'McDonnell's counting his fortune,' he remarked with a wry smile as Tim Johnston approached the table and switched off the machine.

'As always, Richard, you were right about the difference in their personalities. McDonnell is conceited, devious and self-driven. No one's going to break through that exterior. Whereas Kirkpatrick's like a stricken animal. He'll crack under pressure.'

'Now it's your job to get them ready.'

'I've no difficulty with your overall strategy,' said Johnston, stopping directly in front of Richard, 'but there could be one chink in the defences.'

Slowly and deliberately he pointed a finger at a wall-marker which read 'Special Branch'.

'I'm fully aware of that problem, Tim, and it will be dealt with when the need arises and not before.'

This was Richard Milner the organiser, the man of authority, and he showed no sign of perplexity that he was gently ticking off an experienced soldier.

'There is one thing, major,' he said ruefully as he rose and began to leave the room. 'The lieutenant has her orders, and personal interest will not conflict with them.'

By one o'clock in the morning Richard was in his quarters at Stormont Castle logging the day's events on a tape recorder, detailing the minutiae of his observations and conversations with Tim Johnston. He ended his report with an assessment of the potential compromising of his plans by RUC Special Branch and also requested permission for 'Affirmative Action 1, if considered necessary'.

Tim Johnston entered his quarters with a different topic on his mind.

'It's about time,' exclaimed a female voice, as he walked

into the bedroom and began to undress. 'I was beginning to think that our spook was more important than me.'

He pretended not to notice Lieutenant Jane Horton, who was lying in bed, her blond hair spread over the pillows.

'Are we going to play hard to get?' said Jane, lowering the bedclothes to expose her nakedness.

Johnston walked into the bathroom and began to shower.

'That's what annoys me about you,' shouted Jane, feigning hurt. 'You're so bloody functional. Are you going to wash off some of those stains on your character?'

Emerging with a towel tied round his waist, he slid quickly into bed and reached for her crotch.

'Could we please have some loving? Whatever happened to foreplay?' she complained, and pushed him away.

He threw back the bedclothes and sat on the edge of the bed like a petulant schoolboy. Moving towards him, she began kissing and massaging his shoulders.

'That bastard Milner knows about us and I'm not happy about him using you for this one,' he said, spitting out the words and turning to look directly at Jane. 'We almost lost you during the shoot-out of the Four Square Laundry. If that heli hadn't picked up your radio signal you'd have been a black bag job, and not a pretty sight at that.'

Jane laughed. 'I didn't know you cared.'

'Don't get cosy. I just don't like losing good operatives.'

'At least I know where I stand with you . . . Milner's a whole different ball game. With him it's about power and control. Perhaps he wants me on this mission just to show you he's the boss.'

'Well, screw him.'

'No thank you,' she replied, and delicately ran her nails up and down his spine. 'I've always thought those spy types were asexual.'

It didn't take much encouragement to get him back into bed and he roughly climbed on top of her.

'I hope this isn't another of your one-minute exercises,' she remarked with a wicked smile. 'Relax, I can handle the McDonnell business.'

'Not like this, I hope,' he said, with a thrust of his pelvis.

Stephen awoke to the sound of footsteps on the stairs and glanced over at Michael, who was sleeping soundly face upwards on the other bed, his breathing punctuated with snoring.

The bedroom door opened and Jane Horton was framed in the doorway, dressed in a khaki skirt with a sleeveless combat jacket, shirt and brown patent shoes.

'I see lover boy needs his beauty sleep,' she remarked, straightening her jacket and casting a look at Michael. 'There are fatigues in the wardrobe, and food in the kitchen. Be ready for a pick-up in an hour.'

Stephen put on the fatigues and wakened his friend.

'Jesus, y' look like a hoodlum,' exclaimed Michael, rubbing sleep from his eyes as though making sure this was not an apparition.

Glancing at himself in the full-length mirror of the wardrobe, Stephen stepped back in amazement. The knitted woollen scarf round his neck was expertly tied, the shirt and combat jacket were correctly buttoned, but every button on his fly was open, exposing his pubic hair, and he'd forgotten to tie his bootlaces.

'I couldn't find any underpants,' he explained.

Michael ignored breakfast and spent half an hour dressing – tying and untying his combat scarf, wrapping it round his forehead, dangling it from his waist and admiring himself in the mirror.

'I think women get turned on by men in uniform,' he remarked later in the jeep taking them to the MRF compound.

They were led through the Ops Room into a tiny office where Johnston was seated behind a desk with a stern-looking Sergeant Dawson beside him.

Michael was about to speak when the major gave him a withering look and told him and Stephen to sit down.

Leaning forward, Johnston scrutinised both young men and his voice was almost a whisper.

'Alcoholics Anonymous have a motto which applies here
. . . Who you see here, what they say here, when you leave
here, let it stay here.'

Stephen sat upright as the words faded into the stillness of
the room and into his thoughts. Even Michael, who normally
found it difficult to keep his mouth shut, waited for someone
else to break the silence.

'Any questions?' Johnston asked briskly, as Michael lit a
cigarette and looked for an ashtray.

'Well, Kirkpatrick, is there anything you'd like to ask me?'
Stephen shook his head.

'I'd like t' know when we're gonna get goin',' said Michael.

Ignoring him, Johnston looked at Stephen. 'Has the cat got
your tongue, Kirkpatrick?'

'I'd like to know what we're supposed t' do here and when
we go home.' The question was delivered crisply but with a
tinge of nervousness.

Johnston nodded. 'You and your sidekick will be staying
at Palace Barracks for one week. You're here to learn new
techniques, and the sergeant here' – he pointed to Ron
Dawson – 'his job will be to train you in the use of firearms.
There'll be no letters and no phone calls. After a week you
can go but you'll be summoned here when we need you. I'm
given to understand that no one keeps tabs on you, so there
should be no problems with your security. We'll phone you,
McDonnell, and arrange a pick-up at a secure place, if and
when the need arises. Regard this as your home, and don't
talk to anyone on this base apart from those you meet in this
compound. Is that understood?'

If there was one fault which Stephen detested most it was
what he described as Michael's tendency to stick his foot in
his mouth while talking out of his arse, and that was about
to happen.

'What about Bernadette?' said Michael with a mischievous
grin.

Stephen blushed.

'That's one phone call, Kirkpatrick,' said the major, sending a dismissive glance at Michael.

'I still don't know what we're doin'.' The tone of Stephen's question was subservient; he hoped his approach would encourage a favourable response.

'That's for us to decide.' There was no rancour in the reply, but a firmness in the major's voice which implied that the question session was over.

Sergeant Dawson led the two young men outside to a waiting jeep.

A short ride brought them to a firing range, where the attractive figure of Jane Horton immediately caught Michael's attention. She was standing with binoculars in one hand, a clipboard in the other, watching five men firing rifles from a prone position.

'She's using the binocs to read off their scores,' explained the sergeant.

The matter-of-fact nature of the observation deterred Michael from his instinct to respond to the word 'scores' with a sexual quip. He remained in the jeep while Stephen followed Ron Dawson to the firing range and listened while the sergeant explained the technique of firing a 7.62 target rifle.

'That target's two hundred metres.' Dawson demonstrated how to grip the weapon and tuck it into the shoulder. 'Keep both your eyes open and look down the barrel. Breathe normally . . . don't tense your muscles . . . Keep that trigger finger loose . . . Your hands are too tight. Relax them.' The advice was given slowly, each point being made with gentleness and precision.

'Now you do it for real,' said Dawson. 'When you're ready, squeeze the trigger gently.'

Stephen felt the recoil of the gun digging into his shoulder before he heard the explosive sound of the high-velocity round leaving the barrel.

'Where did it go?' he asked.

Sergeant Dawson smiled, then knelt down beside him and adjusted the butt of the rifle into the orthodox position between the neck and shoulder.

'Lad, they could have done with you in the Battle of

Britain,' said the sergeant, pointing to the sky. 'You'd have taken out the German pilots, no bother.'

The exercise was repeated over and over but Stephen's aim did not improve and he felt sore and depressed. His ears were dulled and his shoulder felt as if someone had been hitting it with a baseball bat.

Twenty yards away, Michael was running up an impressive score with the assistance of Lieutenant Horton.

Stephen retired to a wooden bench and shared a cup of coffee with his instructor.

'I don't think you're cut out for this end of the business,' said Dawson, as the lieutenant walked towards them.

'Sorry . . . That performance was pathetic. I suppose I've never had any desire to fire guns.'

Jane Horton nodded agreement. 'You're the sensitive type.'

He was happy to leave the firing range for lunch and dismayed when it was clear he was required to spend the afternoon firing handguns in the target room of the compound. It was a repeat performance. At first he thought it would be easy. Having watched so many movies about cops and gangsters, he imagined that firing small arms was simply a case of pointing them at the target. He soon discovered that a .357 Magnum had a powerful kick and the bullets didn't go where he expected. The same applied to his attempts with a .9mm Browning pistol and a .45 Colt semi-automatic.

'This is the life,' observed Michael, firing single shots from a Mauser, a handgun favoured by the IRA.

The following morning there was another session on the rifle range, and to Stephen's amazement Sergeant Dawson produced a Thompson sub-machine-gun and an Armalite, neither of which was standard British Army issue.

The Thompson was a heavy, unwieldy gun which fired .45 ammunition. If not held properly, the barrel was inclined to jerk upwards when the gun was on automatic. Stephen found the experience of firing single bursts much too difficult and was content with the Armalite, which was lightweight and had less recoil than a 7.62.

'Why do y' train with the kinda guns only used by the IRA?' he asked.

'You'll have to ask the major that one, but my advice is: don't.'

Later that day, as the two young men relaxed in No. 14, having been served dinner in the mess, Stephen brought up the question.

'What the fuck was all that about ... firin' things like Thompsons?'

Michael simply laughed.

'I don't think any of this is very funny,' Stephen said. 'There's no fuckin' way I'm gonna shoot anybody.'

'Jesus, everything with you is a problem ... Maybe they go out and shoot people and claim it's the IRA ... How many times have y' heard the IRA sayin' that shootin's blamed on them were the work of the army?'

'Doesn't that bother you?'

'Personally I don't give a fuck, and neither should you. Aren't we gettin' paid?'

'Yes, but what if they ask us t' shoot people?'

'For twenty thousand pounds I'd do anything,' said Michael. 'Anyway, I'm goin' t' the mess for a drink. If you want to be a fuckin' manic-depressive y' can stay here on yer own.'

Stephen decided to keep his anxieties to himself, and set off with his friend. They walked through the camp to the command post and declared their identities.

As they entered the mess, Stephen recognised men he'd seen on the firing range and in the target room but there was no sign of the major or Richard Milner. Just as Michael was making for the bar and Jane Horton, Sergeant Dawson approached them.

'You go ahead,' he said, gesturing to Michael. 'Kirkpatrick, you've a phone call to make.'

Stephen accompanied him to a tiny room next to the Ops where there was a telephone on the wall next to a large glass partition which offered a view of two separate cubicles, the walls of which were covered in a foam-type material.

'Just make the call,' warned Dawson, aware that Stephen was preoccupied with the unusual and secretive appearance of the room and the adjacent cubicles.

Bernadette was at home, but she sounded angry when she heard Stephen's voice.

'Where the hell are you?' she asked, but he ignored the question and began a lengthy explanation of how he and Michael had decided to stay with friends in Dublin. Each time she tried to halt his flow, he began another monologue, expanding the lie that he was 'in need of a break'. 'I'll be home soon,' he kept repeating.

When he finally stopped to draw breath, she seized the opportunity to demand whether he was with another girl.

'Don't be daft,' he replied, hoping he sounded sincere.

'I know when you're lying, Stephen Kirkpatrick, so just give me your phone number and I'll call you back.'

He mouthed the request at Dawson, who shook his head.

'Is that what I get for ringin' you?' asked Stephen, a tinge of hurt pride in his voice.

Dawson signalled his approval of this new approach.

'Relationships are about trust,' Stephen continued, 'so I'm gonna go now and hope that you'll show me some. I love you . . . Tell Mum I'll be home in a few days.'

As Stephen replaced the receiver, Dawson said, 'You're learning, lad. Now go and get a drink.'

The mess was noisy and smoke-filled. When he spotted Michael at the bar with Jane Horton he received a look which said 'Don't disturb'. After ordering a drink, Stephen sat down at a vacant table in the corner of the room where he could watch Michael's antics. He was just taking his first sip of lager when a man in his early thirties approached, his hand extended, and smiling.

'Godfrey Phillips. Do y' mind if I join you?'

It was unmistakably a Belfast accent and Stephen momentarily paused before gesturing to a seat opposite.

'You're one of the newcomers . . . Stephen Kirkpatrick, isn't it?'

Stephen was relieved to be in the presence of a local; perhaps his sudden relaxation was so obvious that the stranger had to warn him quietly, 'Walls have ears . . . best keep yer voice down.'

'I know we're not supposed t' ask questions, but are you one of us?' asked Stephen.

'Sure,' replied Godfrey Phillips, touching him on the shoulder. 'But if y' mean republican the answer's no. I'm a loyalist . . . well, I'm in the Ulster Defence Association.'

'You're pullin' my leg,' said Stephen with an incredulous expression which drew a laugh from Phillips, who moved closer to the table and leaned towards Stephen.

'This, lad, is the élite – the MRF. Sometimes the major calls it the Military Reconnaissance Force and sometimes the Military Reaction Force . . . depends on what he's at.'

Phillips went on to explain that the MRF didn't officially exist and that it was staffed by SAS and terrorist agents.

'Do y' remember that shootin' in Andersonstown two weeks ago? We did that,' said Phillips, grinning defiantly.

Stephen had no difficulty recollecting the event, which had happened behind Bernadette's home, near Casement Park. Shots had been fired into the homes of Provisional IRA sympathisers injuring two elderly men and a baby.

'I thought that was the Stickies . . . the Official IRA,' said Stephen, puzzled.

'That's what you were meant t' think. The major reckoned it would set them at each other's throats and take the heat off the army. Sergeant Dawson was there with a Thompson . . . That guy beside him at the bar – James Feeney – he used an Armalite. We didn't intend t' kill anybody. That was the major's orders, though it's not always that way.'

Looking towards the bar, Stephen saw a squat, dark-haired man engaged in an intense conversation with the sergeant.

'Is . . . James Feeney . . . one of us as well?' he asked.

'He's a top Provo . . . Lots of different types here.' Phillips gave a reassuring wink. 'Take me . . . I set up the hit on Tommy Herron, the UDA's chief in East Belfast.'

Stephen took a long sip of his lager, wondering if sanity would ever return to his life, but content to listen to Phillips.

'The major wanted t' set the UDA in East Belfast at the throats of the leadership in the west – a kinda wipe-out . . . So it was decided t' make Herron's death look like the result of an internal feud. I knew he liked the women, so that lieutenant who's with yer friend was the bait. She's a looker but don't be fooled. That woman would cut yer balls off if the major ordered it . . . Anyway,' continued Phillips, glad to have a receptive audience, 'she lured Herron to a car and got him t' take her for a ride. I knew he carried a side-arm so we'd specially rigged the car with me in the boot. The back seat was loosened, and when he stopped to give her a quick one I pushed down the seat and put one through the back of his head . . . Neat job, eh?'

'I couldn't shoot anybody,' said Stephen, nervously rubbing his hands. 'It's just not my scene.'

'We all have different skills. You take the guy on the left of Feeney . . . he's Seamus O'Brien . . . He's a bit like yerself – he's not a shooter.'

'Why do y' do it?'

Stephen's question was met with silence by the otherwise talkative Phillips.

'Is it for money, like us?'

He sensed that his line of questioning was unexpected and resented. Phillips's friendly expression was replaced with a tight-lipped scowl and his eyes narrowed.

'No one gets int' this for the money – that's only a perk. We're all here because we've no choice, so make the best of it.'

Stephen suddenly felt uncomfortable and decided it was time for him to excuse himself. 'I reckon I need an early night.'

Phillips made no objection as Stephen left the mess, stopping momentarily to announce his departure to Michael.

No sooner was he seated in the living-room of No. 14 when

Michael arrived, swearing profusely and punching into the air.

'She's nothin' but a fuckin' tease. "I need my beauty sleep," she says. Did y' ever hear anything so fuckin' ridiculous. No, don't say a word. I know what you're gonna say – "What's new?"'

'I'll tell y' what's new.' Stephen pushed his friend into a sofa. 'This place is full of nutcases who're goin' round shootin' people. I think we should get t' fuck outa here.'

'You've an awful wild imagination.'

'I've just talked to a UDA guy who told me they've got Provos and loyalists in here who kill people for the major.'

'Holy fuck! Are they gettin' paid?'

'Yeah.'

'Then we've nothin' t' lose.'

In the Ops Room, Tim Johnston switched off the tape machine and smiled at Richard Milner.

7

It was raining heavily when Stephen arrived at Jimmy's front door. He stood there shivering while the old man peered furtively out of the window and slowly shuffled into the hallway.

'What do y' want at this time of the night?' asked Jimmy, before slowly opening the door.

Stephen explained that he'd lost his front-door key, his mother was in bed and he'd no desire to waken her. Rain was running down his neck and under his shirt collar yet Jimmy scrutinised him for several minutes before consenting to let him in.

'Provo's lost his bark,' complained Jimmy, ushering him into the hallway and casting a suspicious glance at the street. 'Some guard dog without a bark.'

The light from a blazing coal fire was the only illumination in the living-room. Stephen tentatively negotiated a path between cardboard boxes and a sleeping dog before settling into a soft chair at the fireside.

'Do y' want a cuppa?' said Jimmy, slouching towards the kitchen.

Billy was curled up, with one eye on the visitor.

'I should have trained Billy as a burglar alarm when he was younger,' shouted Jimmy. 'Now he's like a lot of people I know . . . too comfortable and won't use his faculties. If y' don't use yer faculties they become redundant like me.'

He emerged from the kitchen with a wooden mallet in his hand.

'The other day there was a mouse scratchin' away in that cupboard near the window. I sent Billy in t' sort him out. Well, Jesus, doesn't Billy fall asleep in the cupboard, and the mouse eventually peeps out and runs through Provo's legs and on to a chair.'

Jimmy began excitedly waving the mallet.

'The mouse is sittin' on the chair, mutterin' to himself, and Provo is lookin' at him. Well, I says t' myself, I'm not goin' t' stand here while these two eejits do nothin', so I took a swipe at the mouse. Didn't Provo take a buck leap at the mouse, and the mallet connected with his head. The dog's out cold, Billy's in the cupboard and the mouse runs back in there t' join him . . . I was wonderin' if that's maybe why Provo's lost his bark,' added Jimmy and returned to the kitchen.

Ten minutes later, with his customary lack of urgency, he arrived with two mugs of tea on a grubby tin tray. He retrieved the biscuit tin from the cupboard where the mouse was resident and produced milk which had apparently passed its sell-by date.

Lifting out a biscuit, Jimmy announced that Stephen's mother, Mary Kirkpatrick, had paid him a visit. 'She's worried about you, and she's not the only one.'

Stephen shrugged, explaining that she knew he was on holiday with Michael. 'Maybe she didn't know I was in Dublin.'

'It was a bad train crash, wasn't it?' said Jimmy, taking out another biscuit and staring into the fire.

Stephen didn't know whether to express surprise or pretend he knew what Jimmy was talking about.

'The one in Dublin,' added Jimmy.

Stephen still looked blank.

'I knew it, I just knew it. If you'd been in Dublin you'd have heard about the train crashin' int' Connolly Station.'

Jimmy was determined to press home his advantage. 'Lyin' is a dangerous game . . . Just don't do it around me. You're learning bad habits from the company you're keepin'.' With the hint of a smile he said, 'Y' know I've never liked trains. All y' ever see are telegraph poles and hedges.' He was now waving his arms like a windmill. 'A telegraph pole here . . . a hedge there . . . it damages yer eyesight.'

He pointed to the sleeping cat. 'I once took him t' Dublin

on the train, and those were the days when you could see the hedges and the telegraph poles. Billy was sensible, slept the whole way and then pissed over my shoes when he got into the station. Nowadays on those fast trains it's only a blur. You have t' strain yer eyes t' decide which is a hedge and which is a telegraph pole.' When is he going to get to the point? thought Stephen. All this nonsense about trains.

Like a good place kicker Jimmy was lining up the punchline. 'I've been askin' myself why the IRA keeps blowin' up the Belfast t' Dublin train and I've solved it. They're worried about the effects on people's eyesight. Now isn't that thoughtful of the Provos?'

Jimmy placed a biscuit beside the dog's nose. Opening one eye, Provo examined it briefly, then gave it a disapproving stare.

'The other day, after the mouse business, I gave him a biscuit when he regained consciousness, so maybe he thinks if he takes the biscuit I'm goin' t' beat the shite outa him again.'

Stephen bent down and tried to encourage the dog to eat the biscuit, but was advised to mind his own business.

'Dogs are like people. He'll never eat another biscuit. Bouan says a guy called Pavlov got it right about dogs and Bouan's proved it. He says dogs will do anything for a reward. He taught the first dog t' find those French mushrooms ... truffles or somethin' like that. He hid these pieces of truffle and every time the dog found them he gave it a bit of meat. Now if you're a dog, you say to yerself, "Jesus if I find something I get a pressie." So from that moment on he'd find those mushrooms in shite. That's how Bouan did it. Now if you're so minded and y've got money y' can do that with people.'

Stephen was fast asleep, the mug clenched tightly in his right hand.

When he awoke the fire was still blazing and the old man sitting opposite.

'That was some holiday. You've been sleepin' for twelve hours.'

Stephen removed a motheaten blanket from his shoulders

and a ragged jacket from his knees. 'I'd better be gettin' home.'

'I told your mother y' were asleep in my house. I thought it was better t' prepare the groundwork in case y' need t' go int' battle.'

Stephen looked terrified. 'Jesus, she'll go buck daft . . . she'll murder me.'

With a fatherly concern, Jimmy put his arm round him as he saw him to the door.

Moments later, entering his own house, Stephen was astonished when his mother greeted him with a smile.

'I was wrong about Jimmy Carson,' she began. 'He talks a lot of sense. There's no point in me tryin' t' keep tabs on a big lump like you. Just don't take Bernadette for granted.'

'He's very funny,' said Stephen, distancing himself from any issue which might lead to conflict, particularly the mention of his girlfriend.

'Not as funny as some of the people I know. He talks a lot of sense if y' can stomach the tea and biscuits. You should help clean up that house of his . . . You're in it that often you should be paying rent.'

Stephen shook his head and laughed. 'He says dust only settles on clean surfaces.'

'Like your bedroom,' said Mary, placing a bowl of cereal in front of him.

Michael rang mid-afternoon while Mary was out shopping.

'Michael, for God's sake slow down. I can't make head nor tail of what you're sayin'.'

'That bastard phoned me the minute I got home. Those fuckers must be keepin' tabs on us,' screamed Michael.

'Who are we talkin' about?' asked Stephen quietly.

'I told him t' fuck off and get somebody else t' do his dirty work,' shouted Michael, hardly pausing for breath. 'And I also told him t' shove his finger up his arse.'

'Jesus, Michael, I'm gonna hang up unless you calm down and tell me who you were talkin' to.'

There was a pause while Michael took breath.

'It was Green, but I know Bradford was listening.' Michael

continued, 'Green was all chatty when he came on the line and tried to arrange a meeting for tomorrow. So I told him I'm not workin' for Special Branch any more, and if he had any fuckin' questions he should ask the major. And do y' know what that fucker Green said to me? He said we had his money. So I told him he could go piss in the snow.'

'Michael, that wasn't very sensible. Why didn't y' just tell him we'd give him back his money?'

There was an embarrassed silence. Then Michael said, 'I spent it this mornin'. I bought meself some nice gear.' He laughed. 'When I told him to piss of, he went berserk. He started makin' threats and slammed the phone down. It's a pity I didn't tell him what I was goin' t' do with the money.'

Stephen's voice was unsteady. 'I reckon we should let the major know. Let's meet up this evenin' . . . about seven? . . . In the city centre? Then we can talk about how we deal with Green and Bradford.'

At 6.30 p.m. Stephen climbed out of a taxi in Castle Street. He made his way to the rendezvous point and found Michael lounging against the railings in front of the Bank of Ireland.

'I thought I was the one who was supposed to be obsessed with money,' said Michael McDonnell. 'Only you could choose a bank for a meet.'

A sudden screeching of tyres diverted him. Turning towards the roadway, he was just in time to see Green stepping on to the pavement and Bradford in the driving seat of a Ford Granada. As Green strode purposefully towards them, Michael grabbed Stephen by the arm, hoping to drag him from the scene.

'Shit, it's them! Run!'

Before they could move, Green blocked their path. 'Let's go,' he said, indicating the car.

'You and your partner will regret this.' Michael pointed a warning finger at Green and maintained his grip on Stephen's arm. Green moved closer and pushed Michael against the railings, almost forcing Stephen to the ground.

'You're the ones who should worry!' screamed the Special Branch officer, and shoved his right index finger into Michael's temple.

'You gonna shoot us in front of all these people?' said Michael, raising his voice and gesticulating to passers-by.

'Let's go, Bill,' warned Bradford, staying behind the wheel. 'There'll be another time.'

A small crowd was gathering. Green slowly backed towards the car, spouting threats through clenched teeth.

As the car drove away, he leaned out of the window and pointed threateningly at the two young men, raising a finger to his temple to indicate an execution.

It took Stephen several minutes to get his breath back, while the onlookers dispersed and Michael paced up and down.

'Get a taxi . . . Let's get the hell outa here . . . I need a drink.'

'No way, man. There's no way I'm going drinking,' said Stephen. 'I'll go see Jimmy . . . There's no way I can go home like this. Maybe he'll know what t' do.'

'Y' know I can't stand that house . . . It's better if you go alone.'

The old man made Stephen a hot whisky with sugar and cloves. As he pondered the problem, he began tapping his left hand on the edge of the chair, then shuffled his ragged slippers.

After a while he launched into a prolonged denunciation of armies, regular and irregular, but to Stephen none of what he said made sense. Suddenly he lunged to one side, his left hand searching out a book among a pile of old newspapers, his right hand still holding his whisky. The manoeuvre was effected with such agility and precision that the whisky remained level in the glass.

'This is it,' he announced, thumbing through the pages of *Don't Lie to the Children*. '"Uniforms are a man-I-festation . . ."'

Stephen was confused. Were the pauses in 'manifestation' deliberate, or due to the effects of alcohol?

As if he'd read Stephen's thoughts, Jimmy repeated the word with the same pronunciation and emphasis.

'They're "a man-I-festation of the non-head syndrome".'

'What's a non-head?' asked Stephen, trying to sound interested, although privately he found the statement nonsensical.

'It's just what it says,' Jimmy responded, squinting, nervously twitching his lips. 'When a man puts on a balaclava or a stocking mask, what do you have? Anonymity . . . a nobody . . . a non-person. Why do y' think the people's heroes put on balaclavas and stick hoods on people before they kill them? They want t' be non-people killin' non-heads . . . It's simple.'

It didn't appear that simple to Stephen, who excused himself and went out to the toilet in the back garden. It was a construction of concrete blocks resembling a one-man bunker in which there was restricted leg space when seated. A large poster of the lush County Down countryside was on the back of the wooden door. At eye level, squares of newspaper hung from a nail on the wall. A banner headline, yellowed with age, read: 'Hawk Takes Over As Chief of Provos'. Closer examination revealed it was a front-page headline from the British *Daily Telegraph*. I wonder what happened to the doves, thought Stephen.

The back garden was as untidy as the front, with nettles which would have made a potential burglar think twice about a forced entry.

'I hope you only shit once a day,' said Jimmy by way of a comment on the length of Stephen's absence. 'I've found something to interest you,' he added, with a contented smirk. 'This one's Bouan but I think it applies to the sons of Fianna Failure.'

Adjusting his grimy spectacles and holding the book a few centimetres from his nose, he began reading:

'"When y' take them out of their leather sandals and put them into suits, they don't want to go back to the leather sandals. When you put them into suits and limos . . . you'll never get them back to the leather sandals." That's one way of dealin' with uniforms. Mark my words, that's the way they'll deal with the Provos when the time comes.'

Stephen returned home before midnight and soaked in a hot bath for an hour.

The next morning he plucked up the courage to phone Bernadette and arranged to meet her after work. He was waiting apprehensively at the bus stop outside Casement Park when she approached from behind and tapped him on the shoulder.

He tried to kiss her but she pushed him away.

'I'm waiting for an explanation,' she said, her voice filled with anger. 'You seem to think you can treat me like a doormat.'

Producing a single red rose from inside his coat, he held it in front of her. 'I know I've been a shit, and I'm sorry.'

She grudgingly took the rose from him and walked briskly countrywards, forcing him to run after her like a naughty child seeking forgiveness. When he reached her she was smiling.

'I won't wait around for ever, you know,' she said, looking directly at him.

He kissed and hugged her and they walked hand in hand in silence until they reached the edge of Andersonstown.

'Mum's arranged to visit my auntie, so I've got t' go straight back to make Dad's supper,' Bernadette complained. 'I was hopin' we could spend the evening together.' She squeezed his hand tightly. 'We're goin' t' have to talk about the future. Everything seems to be drifting.'

Then she asked about his stay in Dublin. 'I bet you met lots of pretty girls.'

'Nobody prettier than you.'

Stephen gave what he thought was an impressive account of the sights he claimed to have visited in Dublin.

On the way back, Bernadette brought up the subject of marriage, and suggested he try to find a real job. 'Mum keeps askin' me what you do, and I say you're self-employed. I don't know what I'm supposed to say.'

'Don't I have the right to earn money without havin' t' wear a suit and work in an office? I'll soon have a big deal in place and we can take ourselves outa here.'

It was nothing new to hear him fantasising abut the large sums of money he would win on the horses or through some sort of shady dealing, and Bernadette was not impressed.

'What's it now? Another big win on the horses?'

Putting an arm round her shoulders, he said, 'Y' know this trip to Dublin . . . ? It was to set up a business deal.'

'Pull the other leg.'

'Have it your way,' he replied, hurt by her sarcasm. 'Michael and me have a big thing goin' and if it comes up we're quids in.'

Her demeanour changed to one of serious enquiry. 'Is it something dodgy?'

'No . . . it's legit., and if it goes OK we'll get married in the States.'

Suddenly he looked at her and wished he'd said nothing. He tried unsuccessfully to divert the conversation by expressing his love for her.

'I'm not stupid,' she began. Her eyes confirmed she was familiar with his ploy of avoiding an explanation of his work. 'Your buddy Michael couldn't *walk* straight, so you'd better be careful. I can't stop you doin' what you want. All I can do is pray you don't get into trouble.'

'Keep the faith,' he told her as he kissed her goodbye.

Richard Milner's small Operations Room was devoid of the starkness and noise of its MRF counterpart. An ornate walnut desk with carefully arranged files and a silver tea service on a polished oak table conveyed a luxury and order lacking in Tim Johnston's headquarters. The windows opened out on to a view of well-tended lawns stretching upwards towards the impressive parliament buildings.

A dark-suited aide arrived with a communication and deferentially waited for approval to approach the desk.

After scanning it, Richard carefully fed it into the shredding machine.

'Is that all, sir?' asked the aide, his posture erect and his hands by his sides.

Somewhat irritated, Richard lifted a pen and notepad and handed them to him. 'Try to come prepared,' he advised, and began dictating a memo: ' "Project viable, full point. Will resort to Affirmative Action One if required, full point." Encrypt that for London and then tell the major I would like to see him here for dinner this evening – eight o'clock if possible.'

Tim Johnston cut a dashing figure in dinner dress and was applauded by Jane as he straightened his bow-tie. She gave his shoes a final polish and ran her fingers up the inside of his trouser leg.

'I wish you'd get dressed up for me,' she teasingly remarked. 'I presume military men only do that sort of thing for the chaps.'

He playfully slapped her rear and walked outside to an armour-plated limousine flanked by two jeep-loads of soldiers.

'Well, well,' exclaimed Richard when the major arrived in his suite. 'I never thought I'd see you out of uniform. You'll have to excuse me because I assumed you would expect it to be casual.'

Johnston's face reddened and he muttered something about only wearing a dress-suit once in three years. As if to underscore the point he gestured to the tatty edge of one of the jacket sleeves and to places where the fabric had worn thin.

Milner himself was dressed less formally, yet elegantly, in a dark blue Savile Row suit. 'As you see,' he said, pointing to a table and trolley spread with hot plates and silver containers, 'we're slumming it and serving ourselves this evening.'

Richard spent most of the meal expounding his views on wine, explaining that he'd guided the chef in the choice of courses and personally selected the wines. He extolled the delicacy and bouquet of a 1971 Bâtard-Montrachet, but could not resist mentioning that the French sometimes chose a sweet wine like Monbazillac with *foie gras*.

'Of course, the Englishman's palate is better suited to a crisp dry white with *foie gras*,' he observed.

Tim Johnston preferred claret, and when a 1966 Château Palmer was produced for the main course he addressed it with vigour; he smiled when he was told that another bottle had been decanted.

'This is the moment when the gods are in our midst,' said Richard as he examined a Château d'Yquem to accompany the gâteau.

Much to Richard's dismay, his guest ignored what was the greatest sweet white wine in the world and unashamedly poured himself another glass of red.

'What would you do if Bradford or Green got too close?' asked Richard. It was the opening gambit of a well-prepared inquisitorial process.

Undaunted by the question and bored by the discourses on food and drink, Johnston looked happy that now they were getting down to the real business.

'I would have no hesitation in taking them out.'

He drew heavily on his cigar while Richard remained calm and studied.

'What exactly are you saying?'

'I thought I made it perfectly clear,' replied Tim Johnston mildly irritated. 'I am prepared to eliminate any obstacle to this operation. We're only going to get one chance at this. We should take positive action if required.'

'Just how would you do that?'

Stubbing out his cigar, Johnston responded by moving aside plates, cutlery and crystal glasses. Pointing to the space in front of him, he declared, 'This is OOB Zone – that means out of bounds.'

He took up the posture of a strategic planner as he moved sugar cubes into the imaginary zone.

'If I declare a civilian area OOB, it will be out of bounds

for a defined period to regular army and police. The order will be passed at ground level through military intelligence officers who will reschedule patrols. That effectively makes it my zone, free from interference. One of my teams can enter and leave that zone without fear of being impeded.'

Richard looked blankly at him as a ruse to encourage him to provide more detail, but he needn't have bothered, because Johnston was delighted to have the opportunity to explain his modus operandi.

'Once I have the area,' he went on, indicating the space on the table and moving sugar cubes inside it as though they were chess pieces, 'I can make that area viable for whoever we choose to extirpate. We can make it look like a Provo or loyalist hit depending on our choice of weapons. After that it's up to the lads in the information policy unit at Psyops to feed the press with disinformation.'

'Are there any operations of that nature ready to be activated?' Richard asked.

'We've selected part of West and North Belfast for OOB jobs. As soon as the order is given we'll make it look like sectarian stuff. It will generate the assumption that Catholics are under threat and lead to IRA retaliation against the loyalists. That's the atmosphere we need before the final piece of our plan is in place.'

Richard casually let his eyes flit from his guest to a door which led to the room where his electronic eavesdroppers kept their equipment. It was a momentary glance, not prompted by any noise or movement, yet it spurred Johnston into action. He leapt to his feet, scattering glasses and sending his chair careering across the room. In two strides he reached the door and in a menacing tone demanded, 'Is there anyone behind this door?'

Richard remained seated and lifted his wineglass as though the major's behaviour was a temporary aberration. Johnston tried the door handle and, finding it locked, retrieved his chair and returned to the table.

'I'm sorry, Richard. I don't like talking about classified

matters outside my own compound,' he said, looking shame-faced. 'I thought we had an intruder.'

The episode made conversation difficult; subsequent exchanges were punctuated with embarrassed silences. Finally, Johnston announced that it was time to leave and Richard walked him to the castle entrance. As they shook hands, Johnston bent his huge frame and whispered in Richard's ear.

'I hope we have mutual trust and there's no unofficial record of what we're doing. Second time round I will not be made a scapegoat.'

He gave Richard no time to respond, but strode to his waiting transport.

So that's what happened to him first time, thought Richard as he returned to his quarters: MI6 dumped on him and he left Northern Ireland – that's what's missing from his file.

'You can come out now,' he shouted as he walked into the dining-room. An aide in shirtsleeves appeared from behind the door to the electronic surveillance room.

'Sir, if he'd come through the door, I would have got on to the window ledge. I would have jumped and taken my chances rather than face him.'

Richard laughed and told the aide to pour himself a brandy. 'It was my fault. It was risky, and he's razor sharp. At least we have the recording, so send it to London before you go to bed.'

Richard Milner was wakened by one of his staff at 8 a.m. and told London HQ were on the secure line.

'We received the tape,' said a male voice. 'The controller wants a word . . . please hold.'

Milner waited anxiously, wondering whether London would respond favourably to his questioning of the major.

'Richard, that's just what we wanted.' The controller's voice was a refined Oxbridge accent. 'Heard about the rumpus, old boy . . . Could have been caught with your pants down . . . Must be more careful.'

It was a mild ticking-off, though Richard knew the affable tone disguised a serious observation.

'Sir, what is the life-span of that item?' asked Richard, half expecting a vague reply.

'That depends. If we were to face a problem with the Joint Chiefs or the Cabinet, it's our insurance. We might require blanket cover if things went badly wrong. Let's hope it doesn't come to that . . . he's a good officer. We're your insurance, so keep us informed.'

Putting aside the phone, Richard went to the dining-room and poured a strong black coffee. He didn't know whether he should feel satisfied or wary of those who controlled him. He was beginning to feel personally contaminated by the duplicity and seediness of the job he was doing. In quieter moments he told himself that the end justified the means; a classic moral thesis which permeated his Judaeo-Christian upbringing and was the central doctrine of his profession. Richard knew his survival depended on a thorough and clinical attachment to his work, though he enjoyed filling his time alone with music and good food and wine. His mother constantly pleaded with him to find a woman – preferably a wife – to brighten those solitary hours, yet apart from a brief love affair with a woman research student at university he had preferred to live alone. He reckoned there was little room for a caring relationship; nor would it ever be easy to find someone prepared to tolerate the introspective nature of his character and his work.

In his early years at HQ a woman colleague, a collator, had bombarded him with flirtatious notes which he regarded as frivolous, not worthy of attention. Occasionally there were sexual advances from men who mistakenly regarded him as gay because he was single and led a secretive life. But the only love in his life was his mother, and that relationship had often been one of conflicting passions. When it came to assertive women like Jane Horton, his innate conservatism made him steer clear. He believed Jane's overt sexuality had undermined Johnston's better judgement, yet understood why the major was attracted to her. There were times he fantasised about Jane, but chastised himself for what he believed were fleeting adolescent urges such as dreams in which he was aroused by the prospect of tying her to a bed and punishing her. This was a dark side of his character which occurred almost always when he was asleep; if it was reawakened in fragmentary moments of solitariness he dispelled it from his thoughts.

There was something about the sex act which disgusted him. Watching secret recordings of foreign diplomats having sex with call girls, he had been fascinated but not aroused. He told himself it was the grotesqueness of the sex act which offended his sensibilities. It generated an inner despair which tore at his belief in the purity and innocence of woman. In reality, he thought most women he encountered seemed devious, manipulative and empty-headed. Jane Horton was no exception.

'Rebecca, what about a kiss?' said John Bradford. He stood in the hallway watching his nine-year-old daughter slowly descend the staircase carrying a teddy bear and holding a piece of cloth to her mouth.

'Jesus!' he exclaimed, angrily turning to his wife. 'Is she still sucking her finger through that cloth?'

Rebecca burst into tears and ran back to her bedroom.

'John, all kids have comfort blankets.' Sandra Bradford put a restraining hand on her husband's arm. 'Your teenage nephew has one, and his mother buys him a new one when he's sucked it bare.'

He looked appalled, and fidgeted with his car keys. 'What's the world coming to?'

Sandra laughed and placed one of his hands on her breast. '*You* don't need a comfort blanket,' she joked as he squeezed her breast.

'I wish I'd more time for it,' he replied, with a kiss and a cursory glance towards the empty staircase. 'I've gotta go. See you when I see you.' He left the house and walked to his car.

'You're late,' said Bill Green when Bradford arrived at the office. 'Where've you been?'

'Talkin' about comfort blankets.'

'About what?' Green looked pained and puzzled.

'Ach, Jesus, sure you wouldn't understand.'

'Try me.'

'They're pieces of cloth, and grown kids suck their fingers through them. It's a sick world when teenagers need pieces of cloth t' make them feel secure.'

'Speaking of a sick world . . .' said Green, tiring of the discussion and pointing to a file on Bradford's desk. 'Take a good look at that.'

Green left the room; five minutes later he returned, bearing two cups of coffee.

His partner was sitting at the desk, his mouth open in amazement. As the coffee was handed to him he stared at it blankly and remained speechless.

'What did y' think of the comings and goings of known terrorists from the major's compound?' asked Green.

Bradford reopened the file and again studied a series of photographs. When he came to a picture of Michael and Stephen walking along Harwell Terrace, his partner began to perform a jig.

'How did you get this lot?' Bradford closed the file and put it through a small shredding machine.

'One of our watchers has a daughter married to a squaddie and they live in one of the houses overlooking the MRF compound. The husband's having his appendix out so our man got int' the house for a few days . . . told his daughter some bullshit story that he was on the trail of a rapist.'

'What the fuck is a loyalist hitman like Godfrey Phillips doin' in there?' asked Bradford, running his hands through his hair, desperately trying to remain calm.

'That's not the best part.' Green performed a little pirouette which resulted in him falling against the desk.

'Are you off yer head?' Bradford started to laugh.

Green was in great form and could not contain his delight at the information he'd assembled. 'The best part is yet to come,' he began. 'Where do you think we tailed Phillips to? Dublin!'

'There's somethin' big goin' down here,' said Bradford, his eyebrows furrowing. 'Can we get back into Palace Barracks?'

'Not a hope in hell. I wouldn't take the risk.' Green sat down, his expression suddenly worried. 'I thought this might be the end of it. At least we know there's something goin' on and we can always keep that in mind. In fact I was thinkin' that maybe we should have a word with Davidson and leave it at that. Then it's up to the Boss.'

Bradford laughed derisively and raised one finger in the air. 'What the fuck would he do? Can you just imagine us tryin' to explain that we've been snoopin' on Johnston? What if Davidson told Milner? Just think of the repercussions here if we blow our cover at this stage.'

Green appeared increasingly anxious and began muttering, much to his partner's annoyance.

'If you've anything t' say, let's hear it,' said Bradford, waving to Green to sit down. 'You're making me fuckin' nervous, walking up and down.'

'Maybe we should leave well alone.' Green spoke hesitantly and seemed reluctant to look directly at his partner. 'If we get in too deep, Milner could have us moved to the wilds of Crossmaglen to investigate sheep shaggin'.'

'Jesus, Bill!' shouted Bradford, rising from his chair and walking to the window. 'Do you ever think of anything but yerself? These people have treated us like shit and you're gonna lie down and take it.' Bradford kept talking, his back to the room. 'I live here, for Christ's sake, and these bastards breeze in here and take over. I'm not havin' that. I'm goin' for broke, and you're either with me or against me on this one.'

Green walked across the room and laid a hand on his shoulder. 'All right, I'm in. But if this goes wrong remember that I warned you.'

8

Two smoke-stained bulbs hung from the ceiling in the lecture-room of A Wing as daylight vaguely penetrated the thick glass panes of two barred windows high on the walls. The atmosphere was a surreal evocation of Victorian times and the sanatoria in which unfortunates never saw the real world. Crumlin Road prison was such a place within the city of Belfast, a reminder to all that incarceration meant total isolation. It sat on the rising Crumlin Road surrounded by a school, a hospital, drab housing and the columned courthouse to which it was linked by a tunnel. Its antiquated and over-crowded cell blocks were said to be escape proof. The proximity of houses made tunnelling impossible; the only way out was through the front gate or over the 25-foot-high stone walls of the exercise yard. The whole place was ringed with barbed wire and overlooked by watchtowers.

The IRA knew every inch of Crumlin Road prison. There, during several campaigns, its men had been imprisoned, interned or held on remand. The creation of an internment camp at Long Kesh outside Belfast had reduced 'the Crum' to a remand centre for hardcore gunmen and bombers. The British way of taking them out of circulation was to keep them there awaiting trial as long as possible, so as to reduce the ranks of activists and go some way to protecting the community.

When Brendan McCann and his small team arrived in the prison, they were interrogated by their own people, so that a report could be made to the IRA command on whether their arrest had been caused by a security lapse or an informer. It was customary for even a high-ranking IRA officer to lose his rank when he entered Crumlin Road; he could possibly find himself under the control of someone who would have been his junior on the outside. One exception to the rule was Brendan McCann, who was so highly regarded by the Belfast Brigade that he was immediately confirmed as officer commanding the Provisional IRA contingent in the prison.

In the lecture-room thirty men sat on wooden benches waiting for him to arrive, their conversations producing a barrier of noise which distracted from his sudden appearance.

'Hey, it's the big chief,' someone whispered.

When he reached the front of the room and turned to face his audience, the noise subsided and a butterfly's wings would have been heard in the engulfing silence.

'As some of you already know, I am your new OC.' He spoke slowly, taking time to emphasise the term OC – 'officer commanding'.

'Those who don't know me soon will.'

He gave a half-smile which only partially concealed the menace in his voice.

'There is a war going on and we're part of it, though some volunteers in A Wing seem t' have forgotten that. The prison regime is designed to break us. That's why we must never forget that as prisoners of war we're still part of the struggle.'

Brendan surveyed the rows of men, most of them aged between eighteen and thirty-five. The majority hadn't known earlier IRA campaigns; they belonged to a new generation shaped by conflict. The Provisionals had won their hearts and minds from the day the barricades went up and the British Army defined its enemy as the Catholic population.

'You', he said, pointing at each row, 'are the vanguard of a new phase of the struggle, and that requires political re-education.'

From inside his jacket he produced a torn newspaper headline and held it in the air.

'This is not what we're about,' he shouted, his face contorted with rage. '"Two More Protestants Killed in Revenge Attacks by the Provos." Is that what we're about . . . killing our fellow countrymen? Have we forgotten that the enemy is the British presence?'

He lit a match and slowly placed it under the torn-out headline. Studying the faces in front of him he let the burning paper fall to the floor and waited until it was curled into ash before stamping on it.

'If anybody disagrees, step up here and defend sectarianism.'

There was a murmur of approval and a slow handclapping which began in the front row and spread throughout the room. He let it continue for thirty seconds, then raised his hands to silence it.

'The Brits use the loyalists to kill our people t' force us into a sectarian war. Why? It's simple! They want t' make this a tribal conflict. That way, it makes it easy t' criminalise us. Their tabloid newspapers tell the world we're not freedom fighters but mindless thugs killing innocent people. By doing that they gradually try t' steer us away from our real purpose . . . and that weakens us and traps us in a religious war. We have t' send a clear message to our leadership that we don't approve of sectarian revenge killings.'

As each man present rose to his feet to applaud, Brendan called Patrick Rodgers to the front of the room and told him to begin the first lecture.

'This is where it begins,' said Brendan quietly to him. 'Don't forget that many of these guys have families out there who are vulnerable t' loyalist attack and have been brought up to hate Prods. So, take it easy . . . Develop the argument gently.'

Brendan returned to his cell in C Block, where he was joined by Liam Brady and Damien Nolan.

'How did they react?' asked Liam, hauling himself up on to the top bunk.

'Were they receptive?' asked Damien.

Brendan sat down on a wooden stool and told Damien to take the lower bunk. 'You lads selected the right people and the rest is up to us.'

'What about sendin' a signed petition to the Brigade Staff condemning sectarian attacks,' suggested Liam.

Brendan was not impressed. 'Have you learned nothin'? If we did that, at this early stage, the Brigade would be obliged t' refer the matter t' the Army Council, and those bastards in Dublin sittin' in their cosy armchairs would see it as a coup.'

Damien gestured to Brendan to be careful as a warder arrived at the open door of the cell.

'The Governor wants t' see you.' He pointed to Brendan and smirked.

'Follow me, Commander,' he said, and began striding down the cell block, where steel gates separated the area from other prison wings.

Two armed warders on the other side of the gates waited for the signal to unlock them and frisked Brendan before allowing him to continue his journey.

Brendan memorised the position of every overhead camera, the positions of guards and the number of gates he passed on his way to the rendezvous. It was the duty of each IRA prisoner to note all aspects of prison security in the expectation that any detail, no matter how insignificant it seemed, might be useful in a breakout.

Brendan looked at the warder alongside him and wondered how much hatred of the Provisionals resided in his heart. Since the majority of the prison staff were from the Protestant loyalist community, it would be virtually impossible for Brendan's men to persuade any of them to assist the prisoners of A Wing in a breakout. Yet the Governor recognised the Provisionals' right not to wear prison uniform. As officer commanding, Brendan would be allowed to ensure that his people conducted military drills in the prison yard and received weapons training by means of diagrams and guns meticulously carved from wood.

The first question an inmate was asked on arrival in the prison was 'To which group do you owe allegiance?' or 'Which group would you like to claim you?' If he replied 'The Provisionals', the Governor would send for Brendan and allow him to decide whether to admit the person to A Wing.

Brendan would be free to question the person in a separate room and determine whether he was a genuine volunteer or an informer being planted in his midst by Special Branch or military intelligence. If he refused to accept an inmate, the man would be sent to the wing for ODCs – 'Ordinary Decent Criminals'.

As he reached the door of the Governor's office Brendan wondered if he was about to be asked to consider another admission to A Wing.

'OC McCann, please take a seat.' The Governor rose from his chair behind the desk and offered a handshake.

Brendan ignored the gesture and sat in a chair in front of the desk. Heavy breathing behind him revealed that two other warders had arrived and taken up strategic positions on either side of the door. There were no rules on how to behave in the Governor's presence, but Brendan felt it best to maintain cold and merely pragmatic relations.

The office – the only part of the prison to have been modernised – was warm and colourful, with newly painted walls and comfortable seats. A portrait of the Queen hung on the wall behind the Governor's chair and a tiny Union Jack protruded from an antique inkwell on his desk.

A smile creased the Governor's reddened cheeks. 'I hope, OC McCann, that your stay here will be a positive one. It's important we have an understanding.'

He was a heavily built man, with feet that would have steadied someone twice his size. His bulbous ears were testimony to hours spent in the middle of rugby mauls.

'I recognise your authority within the wing, and I hope you in turn realise that I am in control of this prison. From all accounts, you're a secretive and persuasive personality, Mr McCann.'

Brendan detected the change of mood with the reference to 'Mr'. News travelled fast in prison, particularly if the lecture room was bugged; Brendan suspected that was the reason for the Governor's summons.

'You must know, Mr McCann, that if there is any disturbance in A Wing, or an atmosphere which conflicts with this prison's ethos, I can close the wing.'

That's what this is all about – the veiled threat, thought Brendan, gazing blankly at the ceiling.

'That would mean a lockout and your people would be kept in their cells twenty-four hours a day at my pleasure.'

'Is that all?'

Brendan rose to his feet, and two warders appeared at either side, each placing a hand on one of his shoulders.

'Take him back to his cell,' the Governor ordered. The earlier greeting was replaced with a look of controlled hostility as the warders escorted Brendan out of the room.

When the metal gates of A Wing had closed behind him, Brendan walked along the cell block, exchanging greetings with some of the younger inmates who were running a card school outside a cell. Liam and Damien were standing at his cell door.

'He's a tough son of a bitch,' said Brendan, and described his encounter. 'They've even got bars on the window in his office. Maybe they're there t' keep him in.'

Tim Johnston crossed the Ops Room and joined Sergeant Dawson, who was staring at a row of telephones and tapping his fingers on the desk.'

'Sorry I was delayed,' said Johnston.

He lifted the receiver of a secure phone which was fitted with a scrambler. Then he handed it to his junior and told him, 'Get McDonnell on the line, Ron.'

'But it's three a.m., sir. Surely McDonnell will be in bed.'

'That's exactly why I want you to phone him. At least we know where he is.'

Johnston grinned and walked away, issuing instructions. 'Lieutenant Horton will pick them up tomorrow. It's a two-day trip and they'll need their Sunday best.'

*

Jane Horton spotted Michael and Stephen at the front of Belfast City Hall but made three passes in heavy traffic before pulling the car alongside them.

Michael insisted on occupying the front passenger seat with a travelling bag on his knee.

'Throw it in the back,' she said angrily. 'Do you want someone to think it's a bomb.'

Michael was not hurt by her tone, and smiled as he tossed the bag into Stephen's lap.

Jane was smartly dressed in civilian clothes and looked at home in the BMW in which they were travelling.

Michael said, 'I like the skirt . . . you've got a good taste in clothes.' His eyes never left her legs as she changed gear or braked.

Conscious of Michael's close attention, she smiled knowingly at Stephen who was watching his friend.

'Where are we going?' asked Michael.

'Dublin, but *you* are taking the train.'

Michael was disappointed and self-consciously adjusted his seatbelt.

'I'll be joining you later . . . if that's what you'd like to know,' she added.

Michael turned and winked at Stephen as the car stopped outside Central Station.

Indicating the glove compartment, Jane said, 'Michael, there's an envelope with cash and tickets inside there. Take it out.'

He was stuffing it into his jacket when she leaned across him and opened his door. Stephen was standing by the driver's door and caught a glimpse of stocking tops and suspenders. For a second he remained there as she closed the passenger door and he wished he'd had the chance to see more of her body.

Michael led the way to the gents' toilets and began counting out the cash.

The first part of the train journey was interrupted with a one-hour delay caused by a bomb scare at Poyntz Pass outside Newry.

'This is bandit country,' said Michael, pointing to the rugged terrain of South Armagh. 'I wouldn't like to be stuck here for too long.'

Stephen was more interested in the reason for a trip to Dublin and what they were going to do when they reached the city. 'Where's that envelope?'

Michael took it out of his jacket. 'Be careful with that – my stash is in there.'

Stephen removed the money and found a small piece of paper concealed in a corner of the envelope. 'You're an awful stupid bollocks . . . Did y' not see that?'

Michael reached out and snatched it.

There was no one else in their first-class compartment. Stephen tossed the envelope and money on the floor, forcing Michael to bend down, whereupon Stephen retrieved the piece of paper from his grasp. They were squabbling like two children when an inspector arrived to examine their tickets. Michael was on the floor scooping up money and Stephen was trying to read what was written on the piece of paper.

'Can't even count your social security benefits in peace,' Michael remarked at the inspector and picked up three remaining ten-pound notes.

The interruption restored calm to the compartment, and Stephen explained that the piece of paper was a note containing a series of directions. 'It says, "Destroy this note after you've read it."'

Away from the tensions of Belfast, the two young men soon relaxed, and arrived in Dublin with the intention of enjoying the trip. Michael's proposal of a pub crawl was overruled and they went to a cinema in O'Connell Street to see a film, *The Deer Hunter*.

'It's supposed t' be a cult movie,' said Stephen.

'I'd love t' live in Dublin. The talent's classy, and there's more of it.' Michael smiled. 'I wonder would the Gardai Special Branch be interested in our services.'

They left a burger bar in Grafton Street and took a taxi to

the Burlington Hotel. Their instructions were to walk from there along Leeson Park Avenue into Appian Way.

'Shit, this is some pad,' exclaimed Michael as they walked through a small wrought-iron gate to a two-storey Georgian house.

Inside the house Tim Johnston greeted them with a smile and ushered them into a room to the right of the hallway. He was dressed in brown corduroy trousers, a hacking jacket and a shirt with a cravat tucked neatly under the collar. Stephen thought he heard the sound of women's voices as the door closed behind them and Johnston reached out and drew them conspiratorially into a huddle.

'In recognition of your loyalty, I have a little surprise for you both.'

Stephen felt uncomfortable with the sheer physical presence of Johnston's arm round his shoulders and embarrassed by his sudden familiarity, but Michael was eager to get to the 'surprise', suspecting it was the woman he'd lusted after.

'I have three beautiful ladies waiting to entertain us,' said Johnston, winking at each of them. 'Michael, you will have the gorgeous Barbara. Stephen, I have reserved something special for you – the exquisitely refined Grace.'

This sounds so much bullshit, thought Stephen, who disliked the over-gushy way Johnston was expressing himself.

'Stephen, with Grace you will not be in a state of grace.'

'Let's get at it.' Michael attempted to release himself but Johnston held him close.

The major lowered his voice and bent towards them. 'They are Jane's friends, and we wouldn't want them to know who we are, now would we?'

'Of course not,' answered Michael, visibly restless.

'Well, that calls for aliases. So that we don't get confused – you're Michael Doran and he's Stephen Curran. *I'm* just good old Tim. They think I'm in the rag trade and I'm hoping to buy a successful clothes business which you lads run from Belfast. I'm lushing you up to win you over to my plans for expansion.'

Stephen nodded, indicating that he understood the ruse.

Johnston grinned. 'You lads know about the clothes trade, working in the market on Saturdays, so that should not be a problem.'

'What if I prefer Grace to Barbara?' asked Michael, realising that Jane Horton was not part of the equation.

Johnston laughed and prodded him with an elbow. 'You're booked under your aliases into executive suites at the York five minutes from here. Put what you want on the bill, provided you spend your time there in your suites.'

'We can order anything?'

'The hotel is booked to a company account which is of no concern to you . . . The tab will be picked up. Just try and keep a low profile and do everything in your rooms. I mean *everything*,' added Johnston, resuming his jocular mood.

'What if Barbara doesn't want t' play?'

'Jane has chosen her specially for you because we know how much you like to play.'

Despite his reservations, Stephen did not hold back when Johnston motioned them towards the door. The major led them into the room across the hall, where they found Jane Horton drinking champagne with two young women. Michael pushed past Johnston, took a glass of champagne from a table and made a bee-line for Jane, who immediately drew him towards one of her companions.

'Michael, may I introduce you to Barbara?'

Barbara was vivacious. She had long blond hair and wore a tight-fitting, low-cut red dress which enhanced her curvaceous figure. Stephen stood on the edge of Jane's company, sipping champagne and laughing inwardly as Michael went to work in his inimitably brusque fashion and placed an arm around his latest 'conquest'.

'This is Grace,' said Jane, ushering forward a slender dark-haired girl.

Her glittering blue eyes caught Stephen's interest in an instant. Grace didn't have curves like Barbara's or her flashy dress style. She was demure in a soft blue skirt, a white blouse fastened with tiny pearl buttons up to her chin, and single pearl earrings rimmed with gold. Her glossy hair bounced as she walked towards him.

'You're Stephen, aren't you? I've heard so much about you.' Her voice was quiet and low, unlike that of her friend, who could be heard throughout the room.

Stephen felt scruffy in her presence and regretted not having exchanged his jeans, boots and denim jacket for the kind of tailored suit worn by Michael.

'Jane says you're a very successful young man.'

Stephen blushed, but with Johnston hovering beside him quickly assumed the mantle of his alias.

'Not as successful as Tim, but we're goin' places in the trade.' He tried not to think about Paddy O'Reilly's seconds at the Knox Corner Market.

Johnston gave him an approving nod and turned towards Jane, leading her towards the mantelpiece, at a short distance from the two couples.

'What do you do?' Stephen said quickly.

It was a ploy to steer Grace away from asking him personal questions and it succeeded. She told him she worked with Barbara in a big London advertising agency and knew Jane from college days.

'Jane gave us a call and said her boyfriend was setting up a big deal . . . She asked if we'd like to come along.' She flashed a smile, then whispered, 'I couldn't turn down a chance to spend a night in Dublin . . . and meet an interesting young man.'

'I hope Grace will handle our account,' said Johnston, approaching with a bottle of champagne. He refilled their glasses. 'And I see you two have hit it off.'

Stephen felt his face slowly redden with embarrassment.

Then the major walked into the middle of the room, and announced, 'I think it's time you young people went off and enjoyed yourselves.'

He didn't need to repeat the advice. Michael was already on his way to the door, with Barbara giggling in his wake.

'Michael,' Johnston called after him, grinning. 'We'll need

to finalise our deal in the morning. I'd be much obliged if you and Stephen could be here at eleven.'

As if on cue, Grace excused herself and went out into the hallway. 'I'll just fetch my case.'

Stephen stood in silence in the middle of the room, while Johnston lit a cigar and Jane cleared away the empty champagne bottles and glasses.

'What do I do about Grace this evening?' Stephen asked Jane as she walked past him.

'Use your imagination . . . I've told her she's staying in your suite. I'll be picking her and Barbara up at nine sharp tomorrow morning for a flight to London, so enjoy yourself while you can.'

He was about to protest when Grace returned wearing a blue jacket and carrying a leather suitcase. Quietly he took the case from her and set off into the hallway. As they reached the wrought-iron gate, Johnston came bounding up to them and gave them instructions on how to get to the hotel on foot. 'It's a pleasant walk.'

Grace seemed happy to hold his hand as they walked along Leeson Park Avenue. For his part, Stephen felt apprehensive, expecting every passer-by to be Bernadette.

'Oh, that's a lovely-looking pub . . . Can we go in? I've never been in an Irish bar.'

Stephen was relieved at the diversion and the noise inside the pub, which drowned conversation.

Grace kept whispering in his ear, her lips sometimes brushing his skin and her perfume light and exciting. When he poured tonic into her gin, she giggled and gently kissed him on the cheek. Then she unbuttoned her jacket and leaned against him. They exchanged frivolous observations about strange-looking characters in the bar, and he told her a story about Jimmy Carson which necessitated his remaining close to her face where he could see the slender curve of her neck and breasts.

'In his toilet, Jimmy has a sign which says, "If it hasn't passed through your body, don't put it down the toilet." He claims that's bein' ecologically sound.'

150

Gradually he relaxed into a playful exchange of kisses and began to feel aroused. She exuded sexuality with even the smallest gestures such as the way she laughed and shook her head until her hair cascaded over her forehead.

'Perhaps we should go to the hotel,' she breathed into his ear. 'It would be easier to talk.' The way she laughed left him in no doubt that conversation was not what she meant.

Stephen's mind was in turmoil, but he calculated that one mistake was not the precursor to damnation; and Bernadette need never know. When would he ever again have a beautiful girl with no commitments and de-luxe hotel accommodation at his disposal?

At the hotel reception he was gratified to have Grace on his arm and to be treated like a celebrity by the staff when they learned he was occupying an expensive suite. A porter was assigned to guide them to the rooms. The space and the furnishings exceeded his expectations, and he handed the porter a large tip with a flourish he'd learned from the movies.

While he examined the unfamiliar luxuries and read the room service menus, Grace went to the bathroom. After about ten minutes she emerged wearing a cream silk dressing-gown, then walked to the double bed and lay back on the ornate pillows.

'Come here.' Stephen pretended to read the wine list as she tried to persuade him to join her. Eventually she sat up and got off the bed.

'Relax,' she said.

Her dressing-gown had caught on the edge of the bed, opening to reveal a black bra and pants and suspenders, with a glimpse of bare thighs above the tops of her stockings. He couldn't take his eyes off her as she provocatively opened the gown wider, approached him and removed his jacket. He was helpless, rooted to the spot, as she knelt down and undid his laces, taking off each boot and tossing it aside.

Then her fingers searched for the zipper of his jeans. He quickly bent down and with his hands under her arms raised her to his chest level and kissed her forehead.

'Maybe we should order something before it's too late,' he

said, thinking of his next move, not certain that he wanted her to resume her search for his zipper.

'OK,' she said. 'You have a shower . . . there's a bathrobe in there . . . I'll do the ordering.'

Fifteen minutes elapsed. Grace knocked on the bathroom door just as Stephen was putting on the robe. He'd had a cold shower and his head was clearer. There wasn't the same sexual urgency in his head or his loins although he feared that if confronted with Grace under the sheets he'd yield very easily.

'*Voilà.*'

She was pointing to an elegantly laid table with champagne uncorked and a hot food trolley.

'How's this for service?' she exclaimed with a curtsy.

As the champagne flowed, they laughed and joked about Michael and Barbara, and Stephen told her that his friend fell in love with every attractive woman he met.

It was almost 2 a.m. when she took him by the hand and led him to the bed. He felt drunk and helpless as she removed his bathrobe.

'I'm sorry, I can't go through with this.'

Stephen sat upright, his hands hiding his genitals, and then ran unsteadily into the bathroom. He was kneeling on the tiled floor vomiting into the toilet bowl when she arrived and tried to support his head.

Pushing her aside, he muttered, 'I'm sorry . . . Please leave me alone . . . I'll be OK . . . It's the champagne . . . I never drink that stuff.'

Grace was sleeping diagonally across the bed when he quietly tiptoed back into the room an hour later. For several seconds he stood admiring her firm breasts and rounded bottom. Taking his bathrobe, he placed it over her and got dressed. Then he wrote two notes on the hotel's headed paper, placed each in an envelope and put one of them on top of Grace's suitcase. It read: 'Sorry it didn't work out. There's somebody else in my life.'

On the way out of the hotel he handed the other note to

the commissionaire with instructions to slip it under the door to Michael's suite.

For nearly four hours he wandered aimlessly through the deserted leafy streets of Southside as dawn crept into the sky. By the time he reached St Stephen's Green the traffic was flowing freely and Dublin was coming to life. His thoughts kept returning to Bernadette, and he could not push away his sense of guilt. At O'Connell Street he settled for a large fried breakfast, believing it was the Irish cure for everything, especially a hangover.

O'Connell Bridge was lacking space by ten o'clock. Shoppers jostled each other and fended off the beggars who lingered there as though they had a claim to it.

Michael arrived fifteen minutes late. 'I didn't get your note until half past eight anyway. I was too busy givin' Barbara a good seeing-to.'

'Jesus, y' look like shit.' Stephen indicated the creases in Michael's suit and the wine stains on his shirt and tie. 'Yer clothes stink of champagne. Have y' been pourin' it over yerself?'

'Barbara did.' Michael sighed like a man who'd lost something precious. 'What a woman! Here . . . smell that.'

He tried to persuade Stephen to smell his hair, which was sticky and tousled.

'She poured the most expensive champagne in the place over me and licked it off.'

'I don't give a shit,' Stephen said sharply, stressing his lack of interest. 'Anyway it's time we were goin' t' Johnston's house.'

'What about Grace?'

Walking to the edge of the pavement, Stephen hailed a taxi, while Michael continued to press him for details of his night with Grace.

'C'mon, I told you what *I* did,' said Michael as they got into the taxi. He pestered his friend with questions throughout the short journey to Appian Way.

'OK . . . I screwed her,' said Stephen in the hope that would end the interrogation.

'I knew it! Maybe now y' know what y're missin' with Saint Bernadette.'

Michael looked pleased, like a criminal who'd just learned that his buddy had also committed a crime.

The front door of the Appian Way house was slightly ajar. Michael marched into the hallway and opened the door to the room where they'd been drinking the previous evening. As Stephen tentatively stepped into the hall, he found himself being seized by Johnston, who slammed the front door shut and propelled him by his jacket collar into the room.

Michael was standing speechless in the middle of the room looking down at the floor, and Godfrey Phillips was standing nearby with a pistol aimed at him. The curtains were drawn and the only light came from a table lamp.

Stephen stepped back but the major blocked his path.

'What the fuck are they doin' here?' asked Phillips, pointing the pistol at Stephen.

'It's my fault,' replied Johnston. He pushed Stephen closer to his friend. 'I'd forgotten they were due here around eleven.'

Michael was still staring at the floor and nudged Stephen, who followed his gaze. There were open boxes of gelignite and alongside them detonators, timing devices, two home-made sub-machine-guns of a type they knew were used by loyalist paramilitaries and three Browning 9mm pistols.

'Get this stuff to the safe house,' said Johnston, shoving the young men aside.

Phillips tucked his pistol in the back of his trousers and began taping shut the boxes of explosives.

Then the major told Stephen and Michael to go to the room across the hall and wait there. Obediently they followed his orders. A few minutes later, to their amazement, Johnston entered the room smiling, his demeanour radically changed.

'How did it go with Barbara?'

Michael would have been only too happy to describe in graphic detail every sex position he'd been in. He profusely thanked Johnston for his generosity.

In a scene reminiscent of the previous evening, the major drew them into a huddle and lowered his voice. 'The party's over for now and it's time for you to get the train. Remember you haven't been in Dublin.'

'I know the routine,' said Michael in an effort to ingratiate himself. 'What you see here . . . what was said here and all that . . . let it stay here.'

'Good lad.'

Johnston patted Michael on the back and led them both to the door. 'I'll be in touch,' he promised as they left the house.

Neither of them talked on the way to the station – Stephen wondering about the significance of the explosives but frightened to raise the issue, Michael wrapped up in his own world of lust and self-indulgence.

It was near Drogheda, at the point where the train traverses a high bridge over the River Boyne, that Stephen finally plucked up the courage to reveal his fear on seeing what was in the house.

'I don't want to know,' said Michael, staring at the river beneath. '*That* says it all – too much water under the bridge for us to take cold feet at this stage.'

'They don't frighten me as much as the Branch,' Stephen went on, nudging his friend to pay attention to what he was saying.

'They're our only way out,' Michael responded. 'With the Branch we'd never be off the hook. At least this way there's a big pay day . . . and maybe more Barbaras.'

Michael's tendency to trivialise serious issues angered Stephen but he decided it was pointless continuing the conversation. In any case Michael was sleeping soundly, the smell of stale champagne filling their compartment.

Tim Johnston was listening to the RTE lunchtime radio news when Jane Horton arrived with a Chinese takeaway meal.

'Did you wrap up the lease on this place?' he asked as she began removing items from food cartons.

She handed him a spring roll, giggled and curtsied. 'With my best Oirish accent I paid in cash.'

He was in no mood for humour and told her to sit down. 'What about the girls?' he enquired, searching for another spring roll.

'They're happily winging their way to London. I was wrong about our dear little spook . . . He certainly knows how to choose his women.'

Jane was eager to discover more about Richard Milner, and annoyed that Johnston was too preoccupied with food and the news to satisfy her inquisitiveness. Finally he relented when she playfully removed the prawns and threatened to eat all of them if he didn't tell her how Milner found the women.

'He's a bloody expert on honeytraps. That was his forte in Five. I've a friend in Six who knows him.'

'You mean he personally chose Grace and her friend?' Jane was sitting upright, her eyes alight.

'Don't be nosey.'

'Oh, come on . . . tell me.'

'Those girls are trained by Five,' continued Johnston. 'I'm not saying he personally trained them, though he has probably employed them in other operations.'

He reached towards her and squeezed one of her breasts. 'Would you like to see him personally debrief them?'

Jane shrugged him away. 'I don't want to play games, Tim. Can't you give me a serious response? Tell me Richard hired the girls.'

'Look. He knows the type of women who'll be attractive to his targets, but sex is definitely not his thing.'

'I still can't figure out what he hopes to get out of all of this – the girls . . . and you leaving the front door open with bomb-making materials for all to see. What the hell's going on?'

Johnston laughed. 'You don't think like Milner or me.'

'Are you going to tell me or not?'

'The girls were Milner's idea. On the one hand, he wants to know the exact psychological profiles of Kirkpatrick and McDonnell . . . Pillow talk and boasting can reveal a lot . . .

Secondly, we wanted them to see the explosives with our loyalist agent, Phillips. We know the loyalists are going to hit Dublin, and when it happens the Provos will blame the loyalists and say we had a hand in it. We've got to convince Kirkpatrick and McDonnell of the extent of our operations. The explosives they saw in here were just a set-up. It's imperative these boys believe we're up to our necks in this. If we're running loyalist agents we're also capable of running Provo agents – Phillips has already told Kirkpatrick that some of the guys he saw at the base were leading Provos. That was Milner's real purpose in having them here . . . The girls were for background information on them.'

'Are you saying you know the loyalists are about to bomb Dublin?'

'Yes.'

'Aren't you going to stop them?'

'That would compromise our operation. We have bigger fish to fry.'

Grace stepped out of the lift in Curzon Street HQ and straightened her identity tag as a balding security guard waved her towards a door with no markings.

As she entered the room and closed the door behind her, Richard Milner moved out of the shadows in one corner and pointed to a wooden chair in front of a shabby mahogany desk. Grace sat down and waited patiently while he pushed aside files on his desk and lowered himself into a high-backed chair. She reached out her hand but he ignored it and removed a pen from inside his jacket.

'I've spoken to Barbara.'

Grace understood the terse comment and clipped tone to mean that he'd spoken to Barbara about her.

'I did everything you asked. He's very sensitive, sir.'

'That's no concern of yours.'

She began to outline her conversations with Stephen, accepting interruptions from Richard Milner when he asked for greater detail.

He smiled only when she recounted the story she was told about the sign in Jimmy Carson's outdoor toilet.

'Are you saying he couldn't get an erection? That's not like you.'

Blushing slightly, Grace replied that she and Stephen had drunk a lot during the evening. 'I'm sorry if I failed to entice him into having sex with me,' she added somewhat sharply.

'I want to know the real reason why he didn't do it?'

She hesitated for a moment, unsure whether to reassert that alcohol may have played a part in the outcome. 'Sir . . . I got the feeling that he was . . . frightened . . . even guilty. I sent you the note he wrote. He's different from the other targets. Maybe he has more moral scruples, or is vulnerable in some way.'

Milner appeared satisfied with the reply and began taking notes. 'Did you fancy him?'

He put the notes in a file, closed it and left the question hanging in the air.

'Well . . . did you?' Slamming his hands on the desk, he got to his feet.

'I liked him, if that's what you want to know.'

He waved to her to leave the room, but when she reached the door his tone softened. 'I'm sorry if I was rude. I was merely trying to find out what made him tick.'

Grace responded with a smile which melted away the tension between them. Then a look of genuine sadness crossed her face, and she added: 'He's not like the others we've targeted.'

9

It was a dismal evening in Dublin's O'Connell Street. Hundreds of moving feet trekked along the wet pavements towards cafés and cinemas. When the bomb exploded without warning in a parked car, it was like a massive shrapnel device sending thousands of hot metal fragments tearing through the innocent. Instantaneously, a myriad pieces of broken glass cut a swathe through the pedestrians on both sides of the busy main street. In the smoke and chaos the young and old ran like lambs in a slaughterhouse, while others lay quietly waiting to die.

Suddenly Dubliners felt the pain and loss of their fellow countrymen in Belfast. In the midst of the carnage, Members of the Irish Parliament were considering the consequences of implementing tougher legislation against the IRA. Any doubt about the need for such a move was washed away in the feelings of revulsion as news reached them that the death toll was twenty and rising.

By midnight, newspaper presses throughout the world were churning out the gruesome details of the tragedy and ritual condemnations of the IRA.

Mary Kirkpatrick was watching the television morning news when her son joined her on the settee and sat silently while the celluloid images brought home the horror in Dublin.

'The Provos have done it this time,' she observed with a tinge of regret. 'My God, why do they kill our own people?'

Stephen handed her the *Irish News*, which provided her daily diet of nationalist opinion.

'Maybe they didn't mean them to go off like that,' added Mary, putting aside the paper and concentrating on the television footage of the aftermath.

'Well, that's done it,' remarked Stephen. 'They'll have no sympathy down there, and nowhere t' run . . . Slap it into them.'

Mary looked uncomfortable and stood up. While she was considering abandoning the conversation with her son, the news presenter announced that the IRA had issued a statement denying responsibility for the explosions.

'They would!'

Stephen's assertion was shouted at the television but his mother, thinking it was intended for her, looked down at him and glared.

'You're so bloody smart,' she began. 'I've never known the IRA t' lie about somethin' they did, no matter how terrible it was. There'd be no point because if it turned out that they had done it no one would ever believe them again. Has anybody thought that maybe the loyalists did it t' force the Irish government t' clamp down on the Provos? Well, maybe the Brits did it.'

Stephen got up and put on his coat. 'I think y're showin' yer prejudice, Mum.'

A final glance in her direction confirmed that she was troubled by her inclination to defend the Provos and the overwhelming evidence pointing to their guilt.

'Have y' heard the news?'

Jimmy Carson ignored the question and began arranging cushions on his favourite chair.

'Do y' think it was the Provos?'

Jimmy's facial reaction was such as to imply that it was a foolish question.

Suddenly Stephen felt vindicated in his earlier exchanges with his mother but his interpretation of the old man's response was inaccurate. Jimmy sensed that he'd been misunderstood because of his visitor's look of satisfaction.

'The people's heroes are stupid but not that stupid.' A mischievous grin followed the comment. 'You have t' admit it was a timely one for the Brits.'

Stephen felt ill at ease, never having expected his friend to side with the IRA. 'If that's the case, why does everyone think it was the IRA?'

Jimmy didn't like being interrogated; he preferred his views to be accepted at face value.

Stephen remembered that the best way to behave was to ignore Jimmy's physical manifestations and never press him for answers at critical moments. For his part, Jimmy liked an audience that didn't question the substance of his assertions nor apply pressure when he was constructing his theories.

'OK.'

That was the signal that he was prepared to continue. It was delivered with a mixture of weariness and resignation. Stephen sensed an undercurrent of delight that the pupil was now prepared to listen to the master without interrupting.

Jimmy lifted a book from the shelf and flicked through the pages. 'This is IRA General Army Orders,' he said at last, beckoning to Stephen.

'What's that?'

'That's the IRA's bible . . . Sometimes it's called "The Green Book". It's the gospel according to the Irish Republican Army.'

'Jimmy! Havin' that's illegal.'

'That's what people said about havin' the works of Martin Luther. It's a piece of history . . . Mind you, so is Luther . . . Speakin' of Luther –'

'What? Martin Luther King?'

Jimmy looked decidedly perturbed. 'No! The German fella . . . Wasn't such a bad guy as Germans go.'

'Jimmy . . . he was a black –'

'That's what Rome said about him.'

'Hold on, Jimmy, what's this got to do with the IRA?'

'Oh, right . . . Look at that,' said Jimmy, identifying what he considered to be the most important reference. 'Read that.'

'What?'

'That bit there. Read it out loud.'

'"General Order Number 8. Volunteers are strictly forbidden to take any military action against Twenty-Six County forces under any circumstances whatsoever. The importance of this order in present circumstances, especially in the border areas, cannot be over-emphasised. Minimum arms shall be used in training in the Twenty-Six County area. In the event of a raid every effort shall be made to get the arms away safely. If this fails, the arms shall be rendered useless and abandoned. Maximum security precautions must be taken when training. Scouts must always be posted to warn of emergency. Volunteers arrested during the training or possession of arms will point out that the arms were for use against the British forces of occupation only. This statement should be repeated at all subsequent court proceedings. At all times volunteers must make it clear that the policy of the army is to drive British forces of occupation out of Ireland."'

'The IRA has had that policy from the fifties,' Jimmy declared. 'It states that they'll never operate against the armed forces or the government of the Irish Republic.' He put the book aside and leaned back in his chair. 'For Christ's sake, the South's the only safe haven they've ever had on this arsehole of an island . . . Why would they jeopardise that?'

'Are y' sayin' the Prods did it?'

Jimmy adjusted his spectacles, exposing two pressure lines where the elastic band attached to the frames had cut grooves which ran from the edges of his eyes to the tips of his ears. For a brief moment a tight little grin fanned out along the edges of those lines, highlighting the ingenious way in which the glasses were held in place. The arms of the spectacles were mere stumps, and the elastic was looped through the bridge between the lenses, across the top of the frames, and sellotaped to the stumps to allow him to stretch it over his head.

'They couldn't organise a piss-up in a brewery, never mind find their way t' Dublin,' said Jimmy.

Stephen rightly concluded that the comment referred to the Protestant loyalists, who planned most of their operations in drinking clubs and rarely left the confines of Northern Ireland.

'My mother says it was the Brits.'

If there was ever a clear signal that the old man was tired of the conversation it was when he showed a sudden desire to tidy the room.

As Stephen opened the front door, a tap on his shoulder momentarily detained him.

'Your mother has a lot more sense than you think.'

Stephen left with the feeling that perhaps there was more to what he witnessed on his visit to Dublin than he knew. He found it difficult to believe that Tim Johnston would do such a thing. He had assumed the explosives would be used against an IRA training camp or arms dump in the Republic, but certainly not against innocent people. What could possibly be gained by the British? Their job was to fight the IRA.

Michael was admiring the window display in a menswear boutique when Stephen quietly approached him from behind and put his hands over his eyes.

'OK, Stephen, cut the crap. I knew it was you, and anyway you're ten minutes late.'

Apologising, Stephen said he'd gone shopping with his mother and taken Provo for a walk. 'I was watching the evening news when I realised the time,' he added. 'That business in Dublin was terrible.'

Michael refused to discuss the events in Dublin. 'We're gonna have a good night,' he said, indicating his new jacket and Levi jeans.

Again Stephen tried to get his reaction to the bombings and was rebuffed.

'Don't want t' know about it and neither should you. We've enough t' think about without worryin' about what happens in Dublin.'

They began discussing where they should go to have a good time and were so preoccupied that they failed to notice Green and Bradford walking towards them in a pincer movement.

'Fuck this,' said Michael, as Green's hand was firmly

planted on his shoulder, forcing him to back up against the shop window.

'We're going for a little drive,' announced Bradford, and took hold of Stephen's arm.

Michael was ready to resist arrest and struggled until Green grabbed him by the lapels of his jacket and threatened him.

'If there's any nonsense, I'll kick the shit out of you here and now,' announced Green, pointing to the empty street where this time there were no passers-by to act as witnesses.

'Just leave it,' Stephen warned Michael, who was no match for his adversary but was prepared to have a go.

Walking to the car, Michael dusted down his jacket and remarked that Green was a germ carrier.

Bradford drove them to the loyalist pub in East Belfast and led them into the back room. The landlord served them drinks and with a wink at Green left the room.

'What do you think of that?' asked Bradford, producing a copy of the *Irish Times* and laying it on the table front page upwards.

Michael pulled the paper towards him and scrutinised photographs of the devastation in O'Connell Street.

'It's fuckin' terrible,' he said, and passed the paper to Stephen, who folded it up and handed it to Bradford, remarking that he'd already seen it all on television.

'But what do you think?' asked Green. 'Was it the IRA?'

'It says so on the news.'

Stephen looked away and the Special Branch men laughed.

'Now why would the IRA bomb Dublin?' Green's question was half serious, and he directed a knowing look at his partner.

'I've no idea.'

Gazing up at the ceiling, Bradford rolled his eyes in disbelief.

Then he turned to Stephen and whispered, 'We've friends in the Branch in Dublin who think the Brits had a hand in this . . . Now you lads wouldn't happen t' know anything about that, would you?'

'What the fuck . . . ?'

Michael's interjection was dismissed by Bradford, who pointed a warning finger at him.

'I want t' know what good old Stephen thinks.'

The physical distance between Stephen and Bradford was narrowing as the latter moved closer.

'Well . . . What's your theory?'

'I don't know . . . It's nothin' t' do with us.'

Green slammed a fist on the table and each of them reached to steady his glass. Michael was the slowest to react, and cursed as beer spilled off the table on to his new jeans.

'That's what I call an emphatic denial!' screamed Green. He pushed Michael back against the wall behind him with one hand and stretched across the table to shove his other fist flush against Stephen's chin. 'You boys are gettin' in too deep for your own good.'

The well-rehearsed role of peacemaker was left to Bradford, who pulled away his partner's fist and apologised to Michael for the stains on his jeans.

Bradford began in a conciliatory tone. 'You see, we know you two were in Dublin with a mutual friend, and naturally we're suspicious and worried that you're being taken for a ride by very dangerous people.'

Humour was not Green's forte, and no one knew that better than Michael.

'In Dublin with high-class hookers, no less,' he replied.

'Yeah, mine told me the last time she met you, y' couldn't get it up.'

A scuffle broke out between Green and Michael, and Bradford had to stand up and separate them.

'She probably had a social disease,' shouted Green.

'Yes, Bill, she told me she got it from you,' Michael retorted.

'Just go get another fuckin' round,' advised Bradford, exasperated, and hoping a brief absence would erode his partner's anger.

As Green got to his feet again, Michael smiled at him and it was the smile of a winner.

'There are worse things than social diseases,' said Bradford, with menace reminiscent of Green's. 'And we could make those worse things happen.'

Stephen had used the diversion caused by the scuffle to assemble his thoughts and find a way out of their present dilemma.

'Johnston . . . the major, that is . . . and Milner . . . have told us to talk to no one, not even you two.'

Embarrassed silence followed. The two young men were now convinced that their trump card had been played to grand effect. Momentarily Bradford nodded. That encouraged Stephen to reinforce what seemed to be a winning position.

'That's the truth.'

'I understand.' Bradford spoke with fatherly concern. 'But are you prepared to talk to the Brits? Listen,' he continued. 'These buddies of yours in Palace Barracks won't be here for ever.'

'Yeah, they're fly-by-night men,' added Green. 'They'd sell their mothers to the highest bidder.'

'Yeah, and I suppose you're the Sisters of Mercy,' said Michael.

He tried to move out of reach of Green but his timing failed him and a fist caught him above his left ear.

'You'd better believe we're the Sisters of Mercy.' Green laughed and pretended to hit him again.

Bradford pushed a pint of lager towards Stephen and resumed his concerned manner. 'We know what Milner and Johnston are at, and we're your only fall-back.'

'If you know so much, why torment us?' asked Michael, moving closer to Stephen. 'Just remember the motto about who you see here, etcetera,' he added, nudging his friend.

Much to the amusement of the Special Branch men, Stephen recited the Alcoholics Anonymous motto they'd been given by Johnston: 'Who you see here, what they say here, when you leave here, let it stay here.'

Bradford removed car keys from his pocket and, standing up, beckoned to Green to follow him.

'Jesus Christ, you can't leave us here,' protested Stephen.

Green laughed, and his partner pointed at Stephen before delivering a parting threat.

'When you're walking int' town, just remember that a tip-off to the loyalists would seal your fate . . . Y' know how they feel about Taigs. Not even your new friends could do anything about that.'

As they walked through the darkened streets of East Belfast, Michael was too angry to worry about the dangers facing them, and kept muttering and cursing. With each passing car Stephen's heartbeat increased as he half expected a loyalist hit-squad to pull up and open fire. His thoughts raced to newspaper headlines about the abduction, torture and murder of innocent Catholics in East Belfast, many of whom had walked these same streets. They were the unfortunates who had missed the last bus and were too drunk to appreciate the risk. Some had been burned and branded with hot pokers, others carved with knives.

'Jesus, will y' stop all that mutterin',' said Stephen. You'll only attract attention and get us killed.'

On reaching the city centre, Stephen was still shaking with fear and headed for the nearest pub, while Michael announced that he was going to ring Johnston from a call-box. 'I'll get this thing sorted out once and for all.'

Sergeant Dawson took the call and told Michael to calm down while he summoned the major.

'He sounds in a real flap,' said Dawson as Tim Johnston arrived in the Ops Room.

'Speak slowly,' said Johnston curtly, but Michael launched into a longwinded description of his meeting 'with the Branch' and laced it with a range of colourful expletives.

'Those bastards'll fuckin' kill us one of these days,' yelled Michael at the end of his story.

'Stay at home until you hear from us . . . Now get off this phone and don't ever ring me again from a call-box.' Johnston slammed down the receiver and threw his hands in the air.

'It could have been worse,' said Dawson. 'McDonnell could have phoned from the pub.'

Johnston was in no mood for jokes. 'Bradford and Green are getting too close for comfort. We'll have to speed up this operation before they fucking blow it, or put the frighteners on Kirkpatrick and McDonnell so that they run. Get hold of Milner – we need him down here. And get me our IRA agent, James Feeney.'

'Milner's no problem, I can get him straight away, but Feeney's at a meeting of the IRA's Second Battalion tonight.'

Johnston paced up and down, clearly troubled. 'Shit . . . Who have we got who could go into the Lower Falls and contact Feeney?'

'What about our other IRA agent, Seamus O'Brien, sir?' Dawson suggested. 'He could make contact, and he wouldn't be at risk in the Lower Falls.'

'Whatever you have to do, do it. Just get me Feeney.'

Stephen and Michael began to relax once they had left East Belfast behind them and reached the Falls area. It was the birthplace of the Provisional IRA and the symbol of the republican struggle for decades. The scars of conflict were there on the blackened roadways where rioting and the hijacking and burning of buses was a feature of everyday life. In darkness it was a forbidding thoroughfare of damaged streetlamps, a myriad side streets and solitary figures making their way to and from illegal drinking clubs. Walking along the Falls at the junction of Whiterock where the city cemetery rose towards the mountain, the two young men were oblivious to danger. Every house was familiar and their tribal instinct seemed to tell them they were safe.

They stopped outside the gates of the cemetery, and Michael spread out both hands to indicate the size of the place.

'Have y' ever thought it's strange that the Prods bury their dead here?'

It was unusual for Michael to be enquiring about anything

other than money and clothes, and Stephen indulged him by agreeing that it was in some ways bizarre that a Protestant cemetery should exist in the heart of Catholic territory.

'That's what I'm sayin',' Michael explained. 'I mean, we don't bury our dead in the Shankill or go to church there. Remember that Protestant church in Albert Street when we were kids? They were always well dressed and had cars.'

'They've no shame,' interjected Stephen with a smile.

His friend was unimpressed by his lack of seriousness. 'Imagine tryin' t' bury a Catholic on the Shankill, or building a Catholic church there . . . You'd be crucified.'

'That's how it's always been,' said Stephen. Michael would not be deterred. 'It's just that the Prods always have t' demonstrate they have the right t' worship and parade and bury their dead anywhere they like in "good old Ulster".'

Intrigued by his friend's seemingly new-found interest in politics, Stephen baited him. 'You're startin' to sound like a Provo, McDonnell.'

Michael looked confused, and paused to find an explanation for his outburst which wouldn't characterise him as a Provisional. 'Well, maybe I'm a wee republican like all the rest of us. That doesn't make me a Provo.'

There's no answer to that, thought Stephen, shadow-boxing and pretending to left-hook his friend in an attempt to detach him from politics. They ended up with their arms round each other, laughing and joking, but unaware of two saloon cars gliding on to the edge of the pavement.

'Run for it!'

Michael glimpsed several balaclava-clad figures about to pounce but his friend's warning came too late. Hands seized him from behind and a hood was roughly pulled over his head. As he was lifted bodily and shoved into the back seat of a car he heard Stephen's stifled cries.

Two sets of hands pushed Stephen into a wooden chair and held him down. Choking inside the hood, he was terrified and helpless, with no strength to resist. One rope was tied tightly

169

about his ankles and another round his chest to fix him to the chair back. Under his right armpit the pain was scalding, as though the skin was about to burst.

'Jesus! Who is it? What have I done?'

A fist smashed into his ribcage and he squealed in anguish.

'That's the last warning . . . Speak when you're spoken to.'

One of his captors tightened a cord round the bottom of the hood so that he could not see his feet. In the darkness he recited a Hail Mary and hoped that he was not in the hands of the Provisionals. Only one of the captors spoke, and his accent was unmistakably Belfast.

Please God, don't let them be Provos, he prayed, but the prayer didn't relieve his terror.

Cold water suddenly cascaded over his head.

'Jesus, no! Please . . . no.'

His cries were drowned by choking as the water soaked into the hood, forcing him to exhale quickly to prevent the cloth sticking to his nose and mouth.

Two sets of hands undid his shoes and pulled off his socks. The panic increased when hands began undoing his trousers and removing his underpants. There was laughter as he pushed his body to release his hands, trying to hide his nakedness.

Then the chair crashed to the floor and his head collided with concrete, leaving him dazed. Blood oozed from his nose and a sharp pain shot through the side of his head. All the turmoil he'd ever felt as an informer, the nights when his sleep had been tormented by fear of being caught by the Provos, now left him shivering with dread. His worst moment had finally arrived. He lay there for several minutes expecting to be shot.

'Who do you work for?'

It was the same Belfast voice. His chair was being lifted into an upright position.

'What do you mean?'

A fist thudded into the muscle on his upper right arm.

'You know exactly what I mean, you little shit!'

An open hand smashed into the top of his head and in its wake he felt dizzy, with a ringing in his ears.

For what seemed like eternity he was asked the same questions time and again:

'Where do you get the money t' hang around so many bars? . . . Who's payin' you? Who are your Special Branch handlers? . . . Who do you work for in British intelligence? How do your handlers contact you? . . . Do they have a go-between? . . . Who do you know in the Provisional IRA?'

Whenever he failed to answer, or made vague replies or outright denials he received punishing blows or kicks to his legs and feet.

From the nature of the questions and his interrogator's knowledge of Andersonstown it was obvious he was being held by the Provisionals. Instinct warned him that his survival depended on denial. The men appeared to have no solid information and if he could just continue to endure the torment he might persuade them to let him go. It was better to take a beating than a bullet.

Abruptly they paused and he heard lowered voices, as if they were conferring.

Has Michael talked? Stephen wondered. What new menace were they planning?

In his cold isolation there was a world of uncertainty; the hood seemed to have stolen his humanity. He was beginning to understand the terror and helplessness other victims suffered when they were tortured . . . knowing that death was the only escape. Nothing brought that home to him more than the hood. It was like the 'non-head' Jimmy Carson had talked about. In the blackness he felt reduced to nothing without his eyes; his brain was in turmoil, deprived of crucial information about the risks to his life. Every sound was accentuated and every exterior movement carried a sinister message.

Suddenly hands held his arms rigid while one of the men pulled his legs apart.

'Oh, shit! He's pissed himself.'

The urine soaked the chair and ran down his legs as he cried out in humiliation and pain.

171

'Maybe an electric current will jog his memory.'

Stephen felt something being attached to his genitals and heard his interrogator say, 'Now he's in for a shock.'

His whole body tensed as hard objects were pressed into his skin and his genitals. An icy terror coursed through him, momentarily obscuring the pain of his other injuries.

'Oh Christ, don't . . . Please don't . . . Please . . . I'll tell y' what y' want t' know.'

'You'd better tell us everything. Who's running you?'

'The Brits . . . it's the Brits at Palace Barracks.'

'You mean the British Army?'

'I don't know who they are but they have a compound in Palace Barracks.'

'Names . . . we want names.'

'Major Johnston and a guy called Milner.'

In an instant the electrodes were removed from his genitals, ropes were untied and the hood was loosened.

'Give him a large Scotch.'

The hood was pulled off. Keeping his eyes closed, he put his head in his lap and, with his hands, covered his genitals.

'You did well.'

Looking up he saw a smiling Tim Johnston, who threw him a blanket. In a corner of the room were the two men Godfrey Phillips had pointed out to him in the bar at the barracks, James Feeney and Seamus O'Brien; they were grinning at him. Close by, Sergeant Dawson gave him a thumbs-up.

Stephen experienced both revulsion and disbelief that people he thought were his protectors should have done this to him. He was so confused, he couldn't express his anger or any sense of relief. A quick glance at his surroundings revealed he was in one of the cubicles he'd seen the night Dawson took him to the telephone room. It was there he'd noticed what he now realised was a two-way mirror giving a view of two sound-proofed cubicles.

'You'll be fine after the medic has attended to the bruises,' Johnston said cheerfully. 'They didn't do any serious damage and your clothes will hide it.'

Holding a glass of whisky, Richard Milner appeared in the

doorway. Walking up to Stephen he handed him the glass.

'Fuck you,' Stephen spat out, sending the glass crashing against the wall. 'You're all a pack of bastards.'

'That was your introduction to interrogation,' Milner remarked calmly. 'You have to know what it feels like in the unlikely event you are ever taken captive by the IRA. You now know you are capable of withstanding a lot more.'

'Make sure Kirkpatrick sees the medic, Ron, and then take him to the mess,' Johnston told Sergeant Dawson. 'Treat him well . . . He deserves it.' Then he left the room with Milner.

Announcing that he was going to find the medic and would return in five minutes, Dawson strode out of the room, accompanied by Feeney and O'Brien, who were conversing quietly with each other.

Stephen was relieved to be left alone. He pulled the blanket round him and sat back in the chair, anger and resentment churning in his stomach. Rage had disguised his pain; now he closed his eyes and began to cry.

Draped in a blanket, Michael entered the room and tiptoed towards his friend.

'Did you get the treatment?' he whispered. 'Here, look at this.'

Michael threw off the blanket and, standing in his underpants, pointed to bruising on his legs, chest and arms.

'Did you crack?' he asked, wrapping the blanket round his shoulders.

Stephen looked searchingly at his friend and wondered how he should reply.

'No.'

The denial was unconvincing.

'C'mon, tell the truth.'

'Of course I fuckin' did!' yelled Stephen, unable to hide his misery and embarrassment. 'What did y' expect faced with that?'

With every appearance of concern, Michael laid a hand on his friend's shoulder, then said with conspicuous pride, 'I suppose I'm just a hard bastard.' There was a stalling emphasis on the words 'hard' and 'bastard'.

173

He crouched down and looked into Stephen's eyes. 'Milner says I'm a real survivor, and Johnston couldn't believe it when I told them t' get on with it.'

In a corner of the Ops Room, Johnston and Milner were sitting discussing the episode while Dawson lounged against a desk.

'Do you think they're ready?' the major asked Milner and beckoned to Dawson to join them.

Milner invited Dawson to comment.

'They reacted exactly in the way you predicted, sir. Kirk-patrick clearly doesn't have the stomach for it. He'll crack like a nut when the Provos get to him.'

'Good, that's all I wanted to hear.' Milner indicated to the sergeant that his presence was no longer required.

Johnston leaned forward. 'There's a problem called Brad-ford,' he whispered, and flicked his right hand as if he was swatting a fly.

'Put it in place,' said Milner, getting up and leaving the room with the air of a man who'd just played a winning game of chess.

Johnston stood up, summoned Dawson and led him to a side room.

'Milner's just given us the go-ahead,' he announced.

He pointed to a map of Catholic West Belfast and with his finger traced a circle encompassing the Kennedy Way roundabout, Falls Road and the motorway route to the city.

'That area will be OOB for one hour. The insert team will be Feeney and O'Brien – Mallon will do the driving. They'll be in an unmarked car. Your job, Ron, will be to go in and extract them once they've done the hit and dumped the car.'

Johnston sat down behind a desk and waited for Dawson's reaction. They'd been together a long time and Johnston expected his junior to make an instinctive assessment of any plan with speed and cunning.

'One thing, sir. What if they fail?'

'Pick them up and get them out of there.'

'What if Green is with Bradford? Do they take them both out?'

'Yes!'

'Just one other thing, sir. Why Bradford in particular?'

'Because he's the thinker. If anybody's going to discover what we're up to and pre-empt our strategy it will be him. He'd told Green he's not happy with the situation. But Green's only motivated by self-interest. He'd never dare go up against us.'

'We'll need a Thompson and a .357 Magnum. Feeney with the Thompson and O'Brien with the Magnum – he's a better eye.'

'Good . . . Test-fire the weapons – we want no hiccups.'

'I'll need a Ford Transit for the extraction, sir.'

'That's not a problem, but there's one thing you haven't identified.'

As if to emphasise his superiority, Johnston got up, walked to the wall map and placed his hand in the zone he'd designated as out of bounds.

'The unexpected is what you must also put into your calculations. If for some reason the zone is compromised by a police or military patrol who ignore the OOB code, take out the insert team and radio base. Then sit tight until we get in and we'll choose another time.'

Early-morning mist was lifting over Lisburn, and Sandra Bradford was happier than she'd been for a long time. Standing in the kitchen she felt a sudden rush of love for her husband and a desire to hug him as she watched him fill a flask with coffee and wrap up sandwiches.

It had taken a long time to persuade him to devote Sundays to his family and here he was like a little boy contentedly preparing food for a picnic.

It was a bright summer morning as they drove through the countryside, stopping at Strangford Lough to admire the flocks of birds feeding in the muddy flats at the water's edge. At Portaferry they drove on to the ferry, which ploughed through the fast tides of the lough and travelled the twenty-minute crossing to Ardglass, a tiny fishing village famous for its herrings.

John Bradford walked hand in hand with Rebecca along the harbour wall, answering questions about the machinery on the fishing boats.

'Look at that one . . . It surely needs its ass painted.' He laughed, and gestured at an old boat half buried in the mud at the edge of the tide. 'That was probably used to transport stones from the Mourne Mountains to Liverpool.'

His daughter looked at him in amazement. 'Why would they have needed stones in Liverpool?'

He bent down and looked into her eyes, happy that she had an enquiring little mind.

'There was a time', he explained, pointing towards the Mourne range with its majestic peaks, 'when the granite from there was the best. So it was used to pave the streets of Liverpool and Birkenhead.'

'Just think,' he added, stroking her hair, 'even to this very day, people in Liverpool are walking on part of Ireland.'

She put a small hand in his pocket and snuggled against his body. A cool wind wrapped itself around them.

Sitting in the car, Sandra felt complete, watching her husband and daughter on the harbour wall. It was a scene she'd longed for but rarely had the opportunity to experience, and it made her feel like a wife and mother again.

At midday they were in the picturesque town of Newcastle, encircled by the sea and the Mournes, which seemed to rise from the main street. It held memories of John's childhood, when summers were spent with his family in a boarding-house there. It was a four-storey building with only basic amenities but it was cheap and the food wholesome. Every morning the lady of the house waited for everyone to arrive at eight-thirty for fried breakfast and the sound of all those feet was like soldiers coming down the stairs. He'd always hoped to return in winter when the sea took umbrage with the rocks along the peninsula, the icecream parlours and amusement arcades were closed, and there was no distraction from the relentless roar of the waves.

'I know where we're goin',' said Sandra gleefully as they drove out of Newcastle.

'And so do I,' Rebecca called from the back seat.

She hugged her teddy bear, which was wrapped in her comfort blanket. She'd been apprehensive about taking the blanket on the journey and it was her father who had encouraged her, saying, 'What about that old thing . . . ?'

Bradford drove on over the hills towards Coney Island and Sandra smiled when Rebecca clapped her hands.

'Only the best for my two girls.'

They parked on the edge of the beach and Sandra laid out the picnic on an old red tartan rug. John Bradford added whiskey from a hip flask to his coffee – 'I'll need some strength to run the beach.'

An elderly couple were barely visible at the edge of the water at the far end of the beach, she with her arm looped in his, and their gait a testament to their familiarity with the speed of the tide as they tracked the wake of the sea. He was no longer able to skim stones on the water yet the preoccupations of his youth were evident to Bradford. Occasionally the old man stopped and with the tip of his walking-stick lifted a shell and propelled it into the sea.

Rebecca was thrilled to have her father's undivided attention and persuaded him to take off his socks and shoes and roll up his trousers. With youthful exuberance he flung aside his jacket and made an ungainly rush to the sea, his belly straining his shirt until it broke its moorings and four buttons were left in his trail. Sandra and Rebecca laughed as he turned and undid the remaining buttons and splashed water on his chest.

For the next hour Sandra sat on the rug while he and Rebecca walked up and down the beach, tracing out their footsteps in little circles, kicking sand at each other and skimming pebbles off the waves.

'Where do shells come from, Daddy? . . . What is seaweed? . . . How can crabs walk sideways?'

These were some of the many questions he couldn't answer and others he answered without a straight bat.

'You were asking about that crater on the mountain,' he said, pointing to what was once a quarry. 'Well, that was caused by a meteorite.'

He told her sheep were sheared using a razor and shaving foam, and that telephone interference was caused by the rows of starlings sitting on the cables.

'Daddy, why do birds always sit looking into the wind?'

Solemnly he bent over, his rear facing the wind coming off the sea.

'The tender part of a bird is its bum. Now, you just put your bum towards the wind and feel how cold it is. Birds have no feathers on their bums, so they have t' protect them from the cold and rain . . . Anyway, if all birds sat with their bums into the wind they wouldn't be able t' shit on us.'

'Could we go up the mountains?' asked Rebecca, and began to cry when he replied that he had an appointment at five.

'There, there.' He took her in his arms and kissed her. 'We'll have plenty of days like this from now on, and next Sunday I'll take you up and show you where the meteorite landed.'

'You always say things like that.'

She was sobbing as he gently put her down. She grabbed hold of his waistband and refused to let go, hanging on to him when he made his way back to Sandra.

On the journey home they listened to the new Van Morrison tape Sandra had bought for his birthday, and he joked with Rebecca that he was a deprived child because he'd never had a teddy bear.

When they arrived back, Bradford changed his shirt before going out to Special Branch HQ.

'This meeting will be the shortest one ever,' he announced.

'Is that a solemn promise, Daddy?'

Sandra smiled at Rebecca. 'Yes, love, it's true.' Then she prodded her husband, and joked, 'Is this St Paul on the road to Damascus? Is there anything in particular that's brought this about? You know it says in women's magazines that when husbands begin to behave in a peculiar way it's because of another woman.'

He grabbed her and playfully ran his hands down her thighs. 'Why eat a burger when you've got prime steak at home?'

She gently scolded him. 'Don't talk that way in front of Rebecca.'

As he got into the car he blew her a kiss and winked. 'I'll have the steak later.'

When John Bradford arrived in the office, Bill Green laughed and pointed at the sand on his shoes.

'I've just taken the family on a picnic.'

'Aye, well, this is some picnic we've got here.'

Bradford ignored his partner's comment and bolted the office door. Then they sat by the window talking in whispers.

'What else have you got?' asked Bradford.

'The Branch in Dublin say it wasn't the Provos, but they'll not say that publicly. I reckon they're under orders to leave this one alone. It's my feelin' that the Irish government couldn't risk accusin' the Brits – international incident and all that – and without the proof. Everybody's happy to let the Provos take the rap . . . You can see the sense in that politically.'

'Why not blame the loyalists?'

'Because everybody knows they couldn't do it on their own and if you begin followin' that line y' might come up with the same dilemma – Brit involvement. Christ, we all know the loyalist groups are one big sieve, but what puzzles everyone is that there's not a cheep from the UDA or UVF. That leaves us as the only ones with the real answer.'

As though he feared his words might reach the outside corridor, he stood up and faced Bradford.

'What I'm tryin' to say,' he whispered, 'is it had to be Johnston's crowd using the loyalists . . . We know Phillips was there, don't we?'

Bradford also stood up and placed his hands on his partner's shoulders, inclining his mouth towards his ear. 'I hope you didn't say that to our pals in Dublin.'

Green backed away, hurt by the accusation. 'Do y' think after all this time I'd be so fuckin' daft? This is dangerous water . . . pal.'

Bradford sat down and pensively stared at the Ards Hills, while Green hung back, waiting for an apology which did not materialise.

'For Christ's sake, sit down, Bill . . . You're makin' me nervous.'

Green petulantly took a seat and inspected the view.

Emerging from his reverie, Bradford had a tortured look and when he spoke there was fear in his eyes.

'I've been thinkin' of a scenario that scares the life out of me. Say the shit hits the fan and the Brits have their finger-prints on the Dublin operation. If, as we suspect, our two young friends are up to their necks in that with them, and if they were picked up and were offered a deal, who would they finger?'

Green shrugged off the idea. 'There's no way they could get at us. Don't worry . . . I'll see those little bastards in hell.'

'But the Brits could do a deal with them to cover their own asses. Who's got the clout? Milner! Anything's possible . . . They could dump on us and say we were runnin' a rogue operation. Our boss in Special Branch . . . good old Stanley Davidson . . . would cover his own ass because he'd be stood on by Five. So who would they dump on? It just leaves you and me, partner!'

'The sea and the sand's got to your head, John. There's no way the Brits would want a set to with the local Branch.'

'Christ, Bill, y' still don't see it! We're the fuckin' people with nowhere t' run on this one. We can't go to Davidson . . . and, as for Milner and Johnston, they don't exist . . . That's why I keep saying we've got t' cover our own asses. If you don't want to do it, I'll do it alone, whatever it takes.'

Bradford paused momentarily, then walked to the door and checked there was no one in the corridor.

'There were moments when I considered talkin' to Davidson but that's like pissin' into the wind. It's better we step up the surveillance on Kirkpatrick and Co. We know they were in Dublin with Johnston and Phillips. They weren't down there to watch the fuckin' rugby, that's for sure.'

'I'm not gettin' in any deeper than we are already, John. If you're right, and we do anything that blows the fuckin' lid off it, nobody will thank us. You can do what you want, but keep me out of it. Milner has made it clear that Kirkpatrick and McDonnell are no longer our territory . . . and that bastard could make anything happen.'

'Well, Bill, while you're decidin' how t' cover your ass, I'm off home for dinner.'

'You're not yerself,' shouted Green, as Bradford stormed out of the office.

Overjoyed to see her father come home on time, Rebecca ran to his car and discovered he'd bought her sweets. He had also arrived with a bottle of Beaujolais and a bunch of red carnations for Sandra. His favourite meal of Irish roast beef and roast potatoes accompanied by a thick gravy sauce was on the table within five minutes. Afterwards the three of them sat in front of the television devouring the sweets. When it came to her bedtime, Rebecca insisted on an extra ten minutes sitting between her parents, her teddy bear still wrapped in its blanket.

'Did you notice she never sucked the blanket?' observed Sandra when she and her husband got into bed. 'It shows how much she needs you around her life. She needs more days like this with the two of us beside her. They grow up so quickly. It's true what they say – you don't own your kids, you only have them on loan.'

Whether it was the sea air or the wine, Sandra contentedly lapsed into a deep sleep, while John lay on his back, his thoughts troubled by his conversation with his partner.

*

Sandra was first up and, without wakening her husband, dressed Rebecca for school.

Bradford was still in bed when his daughter arrived to say goodbye. 'See you later, Daddy.'

She grinned cheekily and planted a kiss on his cheek while he tried to rub the sleep out of his eyes.

Breakfast was a cup of black coffee with a scolding from his wife: it wasn't, in her view, the way to start his day.

'I'm in a hurry, love. I've a meeting with the boss, and y' know what he's like . . . A second late and he thinks you've jilted him.'

After checking the underside of the car for explosives, he blew her a kiss and promised to be home in good time.

Suddenly Sandra rushed towards him as the engine was running. 'There's been a problem with the school.'

She went on to explain that three days earlier she'd been summoned by the headteacher, who had given her a dressing-down and complained that Rebecca's school-work had deteriorated.

'Fuck her!'

Sandra cast an embarrassed look at one of their neighbours who was walking her dog just across the road. 'Keep your voice down.'

Aware of prying eyes that might conclude he was shouting at his wife, he turned off the engine and lovingly held her hand. He spoke quietly, as though he was sharing an intimate moment with her, but his tone was still angry.

'If there's one group of people I detest, it's teachers . . . They're always in control when they're talkin' to kids . . . They believe their own bullshit so much they think they can treat adults in the same way. I'll bet this headmistress has never had kids. That type's the worst – they think everybody's a pupil.'

'You're on your hobby horse again,' she admonished, refer-ring to his frequent condemnation of the teachers at his daugh-ter's school.

'*Their* fuckin' problem . . .'

Sandra glared at him.

'Sorry . . . Their problem is ignorance. It's bad enough at Special Branch meetings. Can you just imagine a staffroom where all those bastards are outdoing each other? The whole bunch are riddled with one-upmanship and snobbery . . . little Hitlers, that's what Bill calls them.'

Sandra regretted she'd ever raised the topic. 'Look, I'll deal with it myself,' she said, kissing him goodbye.

The M1 motorway was quiet, and rainclouds hung over the Divis Mountain stretching towards North Belfast and obscuring the contours of Cave Hill.

'That's the car!'

The voice from the back seat was hard Belfast.

'Keep yer distance until I tell y' t' pull alongside . . . Just don't get too fuckin' close.'

A hand patted the driver on the shoulder and a magazine was slammed into a Thompson sub-machine-gun.

'When you aim, keep it steady.'

The same voice with measured menace produced a reaction from the passenger in front.

'Keep it steady when it's aimed . . . Two hands.'

The front-seat passenger gripped the .357 Magnum in his lap and cocked it.

The front and rear windows were open on the passenger side and cold air fanned the cigarette in the driver's mouth.

The rear-seat passenger moved closer to the open window. 'Outer lane now . . . We need to hit him before the Kennedy Way exit . . .'

For thirty seconds the driver kept his eyes on the car in front, measuring his speed until the exit came into view.

'Go.'

The driver pulled the car slightly to the right in line with the target.

The other driver had a fraction of a second to realise his fate. Then his eyes opened wide in disbelief.

A bullet from the .357 Magnum smashed into the side of his head before he could take evasive action. Spinning sideways, he was jolted upright by the seatbelt as the .45 calibre bullets from the Thompson ripped into the door and almost cut him in two.

The hit was over in four seconds. The gunmen sped into the exit towards Andersonstown, leaving the other car spinning out of control on its roof and sending sparks into the air. As it struck the metal barrier of the central reservation, the driver's door was torn off and the dying body of John Bradford was flung on to the tarmac.

10

The door to the Ops Room was open. Richard Milner held back, expecting someone to detect his arrival. A movement caused him to turn and see Jane Horton standing in the corridor near the Target Room.

'He'll be out in a minute. Perhaps you'd like to wait in Ops.'

A large pile of folders lay on the oak table in the centre of the room and he sat down, his eyes straying to one marked 'Loyalist Connection'. Picking it up, he scrutinised the front page which began: 'Penetration levels are complete . . .' As he glanced through it, his eyes fell on the name 'Godfrey Phillips', which was followed by an outline of his career with Johnston's MRF; it ended with the words '*Must be kept in place*'.

Milner looked up just as Johnston walked in and approached the table, holstering his 9mm Browning pistol.

'Do you need to practise?' asked Richard, closing the file.

'It relieves stress.'

Indicating the file, Richard said, 'Why is so much importance attached to Phillips?'

'He could be a future UDA leader.'

'Does that imply you think we may some day have to face down the loyalists?' Once again Richard was probing the major's politics.

Johnston appeared to relish the question. 'Of course. History is not on our side. Some day there'll be an island solution here. If we succeed now, we'll have removed only one enemy. Wouldn't it be better to face the future dealing with a single enemy and not being piggy in the middle?'

Not having considered British disengagement from Ireland, Richard was speechless – much to Johnston's delight.

'You must surely recognise by now, Richard, that I am a realist. One cannot be introspective about these matters.'

'Surely our present objective is to strengthen the Union?'

Johnston walked towards the wall map of West Belfast and slowly identified the Catholic districts coloured in green ink.

'We cannot eradicate all of these people,' he began. 'Their instinct is to rebel . . . Remember civil rights and all that . . . ? We'll only put off the evil hour.'

Richard looked flustered.

'This was never my plan,' said Johnston, returning to a seat at the table. 'Your people put it together – surely you know that?'

Sifting through the folders, he pulled out one and extracted a three-page memorandum.

'That was my reply to your people.' He handed the document to Richard. 'Note that I said their objectives were attainable. I did not say they were politically desirable or politically correct.'

Richard glanced through the memo, his eyes narrowing in anger as he turned each page. 'Are you saying we should not proceed?'

Johnston sat down and moved aside the files as though they were of no importance. 'Paperwork . . . paperwork.' His voice was tired. 'I was asked to make a military judgement of the viability of this plan. They knew my personal feelings about the need to deal with the serpent. However, I am a soldier and as such my job is to enable the military to hold the ring. I was asked to proceed and I take orders.'

Richard had a sneaking admiration for the way the major narrowed the terms of reference of their exchanges. 'You cannot have your cake and eat it.'

Johnston smiled; it was clear he was not going to be drawn unless Richard clarified what he meant by that remark.

'You cannot say, on the one hand, that you placed your military imprimatur on this, yet, on the other hand, you are unsure of its desirability or correctness.'

Lifting the memo, Johnston held it in his right hand as he began to speak. 'I was asked if it was possible to kill the serpent in its infancy, and I told them how I thought that could be achieved. It's not for me to comment on the moral or political desirability of that strategy. That is for your people and government.'

It was apparent that he did not like politicians or MI5. In fact his experience in Northern Ireland and other colonial emergencies had convinced him that the British Army was always the fall-guy for the politically inept.

'Is our strategy politically desirable?' Richard was not going to let this slip.

'The plan is feasible. It's for your masters in London and the relevant people in government to answer your question.'

'Let us put our cards on the table,' said Richard, taking the memo from him and tossing it to one side.

'Let's do just that,' replied Johnston, frustrated by the cross-questioning.

'Is there a risk,' Richard began, 'or . . . let me put it another way . . . what is the likelihood the serpent will grow another head and prove unstoppable?'

Looking at the montage of photos of the IRA intelligence hierarchy, Johnston walked across the room and put his finger on the name 'Brendan McCann'.

'I'm not a gambling man,' he said, closing his eyes as if he were a psychic searching for a way into the future. 'If we don't get it right there will be no military solution to the IRA problem. The McCanns of this place have families . . . There's another generation waiting in the wings. Even if we succeed, all we're doing is buying time for your people to find a political solution and maybe a different enemy.'

'The loyalists?'

The question shook him out of his introspection. Opening his eyes, he smiled. 'Maybe,' he said, indicating that he was fed up with the line of questioning.

'Excuse me, sir.'

Jane Horton was walking towards the table and Johnston went to meet her. Her eyes settled on Richard, who self-

consciously looked away. An outsider would have noticed that
Johnston was excited by her arrival because his gaze took in
her body from head to toe.

'Yes, lieutenant, what is it?'

'Stanley Davidson is in the corridor . . . sorry . . . *Commander*
Davidson. He would like a word, sir.'

Puffing and panting, Davidson reached the table and complained that he'd never liked helicopter rides. 'They frighten
the daylights out of me,' he added, taking a seat and then
apologising for forgetting to shake hands.

He looked worried, and fidgeted with his tie. 'I've got CID
breathing down my neck looking for suspects and a motive
for Bradford's death. I've kept Green away from them but
they're demanding to know the names of the agents run by
him and Bradford.'

Richard took a piece of paper from inside his jacket and
handed it to Davidson. 'Give that to CID.'

Davidson stared at him in disbelief.

'Just do it,' said Johnston, 'and leave the rest to us.'

'CID will smell a rat. And what about Green?'

Placing a hand on his shoulder, Richard first looked at
Johnston before speaking. 'I will talk to you later about Green.
You can always lean on CID if there's a problem.'

Davidson scratched his head and got up. 'I hope you guys
know what you're doin'.'

It was after midday when Stephen finally gave in to his
mother's pleading to get out of bed and sit down to lunch.

'You mightn't like those,' she said, pointing to the carrots
on his plate, 'but they're good for you.'

With the edge of his fork he moved the carrots aside and
began eating the hamburger and chips.

'When I was a kid,' he remarked, 'you used t' say they
were good for my eyesight, and it hasn't made a damn bit of
difference.'

Mary Kirkpatrick reproached him for swearing and criti-
cised his love of junk food.

'Yer friend Jimmy was here . . . he left some money you'd dropped.' She grinned. 'He looked at that burger and said that somebody had probably knitted it.'

'Yeah . . . and look what carrots did for him.'

The next few seconds passed in a blur.

The kitchen door was kicked open and two soldiers rushed towards Stephen, their rifles levelled at his head. Mary screamed as two uniformed policemen burst through the front door and pulled her son out of the chair. Trying to go to his aid, she found her path blocked by the tip of a rifle barrel which was pressed against her stomach.

'Leave her alone.'

Stephen's plea went unnoticed but Mary pushed aside the rifle and threw her arms round him.

'You're not takin' him. He's a good boy.'

The policemen pulled them apart and dragged him from the room while the soldiers formed a human barrier to keep her penned against the cooker. Stephen was led to an armoured personnel carrier and roughly pushed into the arms of waiting soldiers.

Jimmy was at his front gate, and Provo barked and bared his teeth at the men.

'What's goin' on? Where are you taking that young fella?'

The army vehicle drove away to screams of abuse from neighbours, and Jimmy rushed to comfort Mary, who was kneeling on the kitchen floor sobbing. With his arms round her shoulders, he coaxed her into an armchair. Then he began making a pot of tea. Her other neighbours gathered around her in support.

She kept screaming, 'They've lifted my wee son without a warrant! They've taken my wee fella! My God, they've taken my wee fella!'

As he made the tea, Jimmy launched into a tirade against the police and army. 'That's yer Special Powers Act again . . . The whites in South Africa would love to have our special powers . . . draconian, that's what I call it . . .'

'I suppose I'd better get him a solicitor . . . How do I do

that? I don't know any solicitors . . . What'll I do?' Mary began crying again.

'I'll ring one for you,' said Jimmy. 'The law here – if you can call it a law – allows them to interrogate anybody for seven days.'

There was a single cell waiting for Stephen at the police and army interrogation centre, where he quickly discovered that he'd no rights.

'We'll sort you out,' said a burly sergeant, locking the cell door and walking away.

Remembering his interrogation experience at Palace Barracks he resolved to say nothing until he had talked to a solicitor. Secretly he hoped that word of this would reach Johnston and Milner; he suspected that Green and Bradford had something to do with his arrest.

When his cell door opened he began to learn that there was a fine distinction between torture and ill-treatment. Two detectives dragged him from the cell. One of them, a large, heavily built man, pulled his hair until his head was snapped backwards.

'Leave me alone, you bastards . . . You can't do that – I've got rights . . . Where's my solicitor?'

A fist slammed into his kidneys. 'Fuck your rights. You'll only have rights when you give us the right answers to the right questions.'

Stephen slumped to the floor and curled up in pain. His back felt as if it had been hit by a sledgehammer. Yet he was immediately hauled to his feet by the detectives, dragged along a corridor where some doors had small spyholes in them and marched into a tiny room containing a table and two chairs.

'Against the wall, Kirkpatrick.'

He was forced to stand with his fingertips supporting his body while his feet were kicked into a spread position.

'You're gonna get to know us well. In fact you might say we could become great buddies . . . that is, if you co-operate.'

Slightly turning in an attempt to face them, Stephen

received a blow to the base of his skull and was warned that he'd get similar treatment if he moved.

'My friend rarely leaves any bruises with this.' A rubber truncheon was waved under his nose. 'He might just beat the livin' shit outa y' and say you resisted arrest.'

He heard the detectives walking away towards the table, where they sat down and lit cigarettes.

Slowly pain surged along his wrists into his arms and shoulders, causing a tightness in his chest. His legs felt rubbery and the muscles of his calves ached. Momentarily he lost concentration and control, slipping and steadying himself with his palms.

At that moment, one of his interrogators ran towards him brandishing the truncheon and delivered a blow to the base of his spine, sending him sprawling to the floor.

The pain in his back was excruciating and he temporarily lost consciousness. As he came round, he opened his eyes and the room began to spin as he tried to focus on his interrogators.

'Give him a break,' said one of them, helping Stephen to his feet and holding him steady before returning him to a standing position. 'You can use the palms of your hands to support yerself.'

The intervention was timely: Stephen was beginning to despair of his ability to maintain silence.

Leaving him propped facing the wall, the detectives returned to the table and sat in discussion. As the minutes passed, the heat of the room made Stephen dizzy, and sweat dripped from his forehead on to the floor. No attempt was made to question him, and this increased his fear and sense of isolation. His thoughts raced back to the interrogation at Palace Barracks. Was this another ploy? Frantically he tried to work out why he was being detained, and what he should say to these men.

Suddenly his heart began pounding. The detective who appeared to be the more reasonable of the pair, a shorter, stocky man, announced, 'I'm going for a piss.'

Two minutes after he left, the other detective began pacing

up and down the room, hitting the truncheon against the palm of his hand. Occasionally he edged close to Stephen.

Then he screamed in his ear, 'If it was up to me, I'd kick the shit outa ya . . . I know how to deal with cop-killers.'

Cop-killers, thought Stephen. What the fuck is going on? I'm no cop-killer.

The urge to react was overwhelming, yet Stephen cautioned himself that it might be a trick to get him to talk.

Slowly and menacingly, the big man circled him, rhythmically beating the truncheon against the wall. Twice Stephen winced as the rubber caught the edges of his face.

A key turned in the door.

'I needed that piss.'

Slamming the door shut, the other interrogator walked over to Stephen.

'Yer pal, McDonnell, is down the corridor, and he's cryin' like a baby . . . Before the day's out he'll be singin' like a bird.'

That was what Stephen needed to hear, and it renewed his determination to say nothing. Michael was not the type to cry like a baby – physical punishment would only strengthen his resolve.

'He says he was the driver and that you and another Provo shot Special Branch Officer Bradford.'

'Bradford? I know nothing about that! Why would I want t' shoot him? I don't even know how to fire a gun . . . I'm no Provo.'

But the mention of Bradford had made Stephen shudder and almost lose his balance. Bradford dead – Jesus, somebody's shot Bradford, he thought.

'That got his fuckin' attention!' yelled the bigger detective. 'I'm goin' out for a minute and when I come back I'll sort you out once and for all.'

The other detective, standing inches from Stephen, placed a comforting hand on his shoulder.

'If I were you,' he whispered, 'I'd get it off yer chest before he comes back. He's a bad bastard when he gets started.'

'I never killed anybody,' said Stephen, and turned towards

the other man, only to find his face being pushed against the wall.

'My partner has had guys tougher than you bawlin' their eyes out after he's finished with them. Now, if you put yer trust in me, I'll protect you, and we'll get this over with . . . And who knows? Maybe you'll be able to go home.'

Trust and protection were words which sounded hollow. Stephen decided not to be drawn.

'Did somebody set up the hit?'

Silence.

'Did you and Michael know Bradford?'

Stephen ignored the question.

'Look here,' whispered the detective, 'I'm gonna do you a favour. I'm gonna take you back to your cell and give you time to think about it, but remember I can't protect you for too long. I'll have to spin my partner a line that you were sick . . . and I don't like lyin' for anybody.'

The cell was painted white with a fluorescent strip on the ceiling and a camera mounted high in one corner. Beside a single bed a bare toilet bowl gave off a sickly stench and a tiny piece of toilet paper lay on the floor.

Left alone, Stephen began to feel disorientated; his watch had been removed the moment he entered the interrogation centre.

Is Bradford really dead? he asked himself. Or could this be another of Johnston's ploys? If he *is* dead, why are we being accused of it? Is it that fucker Green who's nailed us out of spite?

Nothing made sense: time and again he examined all the possibilities.

Why wasn't Milner here to sort this out?

That was the one hope which kept him sane. With luck, Milner and Johnston would arrive and demand their release.

Every time he closed his eyes to rest, someone scraped on the cell door with a metal object, reminding him of the sounds in a dental surgery.

Suddenly the door opened, and the two detectives ushered

him out into the corridor. He was returned to the same interrogation room.

'Come over here and sit down.'

He walked towards the table where the detectives were seated and was pressed into a chair.

'Your friend McDonnell thought he was tough, but my partner here sorted him out.'

'He says you were one of the shooters.'

'That's bullshit. I don't know what you guys are after. I don't even know if Bradford's really dead or what should make you think I'm connected with anything.'

Stephen was trying hard not to react, or look at his interrogators, who reminded him of Green.

'McDonnell's gonna cut a deal and you're goin' down for life.'

Stephen remained expressionless. Inwardly he was praying, or thinking of Bernadette, in an effort to distance himself from events around him.

'If you're wise,' suggested the other, 'you could say you were the driver . . . That's maybe ten years at most.'

'C'mon, if Kirkpatrick helped us, we could do better than that.'

'OK. If you give us McDonnell, your other accomplice and the people who set this up . . . and you're willing to turn Crown evidence . . . we'll put you into a witness programme, get you immunity and move you out of the country. You'll have a new identity and plenty of money for a new start.'

When he got no reply, the large detective grabbed Stephen by the hair and ran him towards the wall, stopping inches from it. Stephen stood with his face and mouth against the concrete while the detectives talked in agitated whispers.

Individually the two men left the room and returned with coffee and sandwiches. They smoked cigarettes, shared jokes and laughed at Stephen's predicament.

'We can do it the easy way or the hard way.'

'I've killed nobody, and I don't even know a John Bradford,' Stephen burst out.

'Did we say he was called John?' asked the shorter man.

194

'Did *you* say he was called John?' asked the other.

'*I* never mentioned that his name was John.'

'Let's take this piece of shit to his cell.'

No sooner was Stephen on his bunk than sleep closed in on him. Ten minutes later he was woken by a banging on the door which ceased after ten seconds. Each time he drifted into sleep the noise began. Sometimes it was a rhythmic tapping, sometimes it was so loud he felt the door would be kicked in; occasionally it was the metal scraping sound that he hated most.

The interrogation sessions continued, with roles alternating between the two detectives. The same tactics were applied until Stephen was sleeping on his feet and collapsing to the floor, only to be returned to his cell where the noise disturbed his desire to sleep and dream.

'Get up!'

A kick in the groin induced him to open his eyes, whereupon he discovered he was asleep on the floor of his cell. He was crudely lifted into a sitting position on the bunk.

'Don't you fuckin' dare sleep.'

Kneeling down, one of them grabbed Stephen's face and shook it. 'We'll let you sleep if you stop holding back. Just tell us what we want to know.'

'Ask . . .' stammered Stephen, as he drifted back to sleep.

They had to shake him to keep him awake.

'Ask who?'

'Bill Green. He knows about the major and Milner.'

There was nothing to be gained from further questioning: Stephen could not keep his eyes open. They pushed him back on the bunk and left the cell. He was fast asleep by the time his head touched the pillow.

'Who the fuck are the major and Milner?'

'Yeah, but what's that he said about asking Bill Green?'

'Green was Bradford's partner.'

'This stinks.'

'I think we should talk to the head of Special Branch.'

'No. I think we should pay Green a visit first . . . Never go to the top unless you've scraped the bottom. Sometimes that's where the dirt settles.'

'It's four in the morning . . . How can we go to see Green at this ungodly hour?'

'Maybe he needs his sleep interrupted.'

'I've a friend in HQ works nights . . . He'll get us Green's address.'

Twenty minutes later they were out of the building on their way to an armoured Ford Granada.

'I smell a rat here.'

'Me too.'

'Kirkpatrick's no shooter. McDonnell – he's a different kettle of fish, but even so he doesn't strike me as a trigger man. Even the Provos couldn't teach him to play with interrogators the way he does . . . All that shite about the women he's screwed, the places he's been. He's so full of bullshit, yet there's somethin' about him . . . I can't put a finger on it.'

'You mean he's too clever to be a nobody.'

'Exactly . . . There's somethin' about this pair that doesn't fit the bill we've been given. I mean we get it from on high to pick these guys up. If our boss is so fuckin' clever . . . so sure they're the shooters . . . why doesn't he know the name of the third member of the hit team? It doesn't make any fuckin' sense – none of it. If they're not the shooters, they're takin' the fall because somebody else is being protected.'

'Let's not get paranoid. Let's just concentrate on what we've got. If it's dirty we'll have to make a decision about where we go with it, even if that means going to the chief, or dumping it.'

Green lived overlooking the sea at Bangor on the County Down coast. The front garden and surrounding privet hedge were immaculately trimmed and the door and windows newly painted. Unlike his neighbours, he tolerated the cost and work of redecorating every year to counteract the ravages of the heavy salt air of the Irish Sea.

As the detectives approached the front door, a voice shouted, 'Get yer fuckin' hands in the air.'

The request was made again, so one of the detectives announced their identities: 'Detectives Laing and Nixon – CID.'

Standing with their identity passes in their hands, they waited, a cold sea breeze biting the tips of their ears. Green took his time opening a metal door which reinforced the front door, and reminded them through the intercom to stay put.

'Christ, he looks like Wee Willie Winkie,' said Nixon, as Green emerged in a white silk dressing-gown and slippers. In his hand was a Walther PPK, which he put into the pocket of his gown when he was satisfied with their CID passes.

For a second, Laing half expected him to force them to stand in the cold, but that did not happen because Nixon brazenly walked into the hallway.

'This had better be important,' remarked Green, and reluctantly invited them into a spacious living-room. 'Excuse the mess.'

Laing was surprised by the apology. There wasn't a speck of dust on the deep-pile beige carpet or on the beige sofas with their matching cushions. The heavy furniture was old pine, with antique Irish linen covering some of the surfaces. An oil painting of male bathers was prominently displayed above the fireplace, and watercolour seascapes hung on the other walls.

'We'll go straight to the point. Who are Milner and the major?'

Laing sensed that his question rattled Green, who turned towards the fireplace and began winding a Victorian clock.

'Do you know these people?'

Green ignored Laing and sat down on one of the sofas, placing a cushion at his back and adjusting it until he felt comfortable.

Meanwhile Nixon was indulging his curiosity, looking through a pile of magazines on a side table.

'Are you here to read or to speak?'

Green's point hit home, and Nixon sat down.

Treading carefully in an effort to trap Green, Laing briefly described meeting Michael and Stephen and explained that the latter had mentioned people called 'the major and Milner'.

'We thought you might be able t' help us,' said Laing. 'Who ordered the arrest of Kirkpatrick and McDonnell?'

Green was giving nothing away and Laing pointed an accusing finger at him.

'The order came from our boss,' he said. 'But that kind of information could only come from *your* people or . . .'

He let his statement hang in the air, hoping Green would complete it, but Green was an old hand and didn't take the bait.

Green stood up. 'Why the fuck don't you go and waken up my boss and ask him what you want t' know?'

Laing closed in on him physically and smirked. 'We're here because Kirkpatrick said we should ask *you*.'

Their dislike was mutual. Green glared at him.

'Maybe you and your partner Bradford knew these lads,' Laing suggested.

Green was not going to let the screw be further tightened. 'You've no fuckin' jurisdiction over me, so get t' fuck outa here.'

His hand went to his pocket and he moved threateningly close to the detective.

Nixon, sensing danger, moved between the two men. With his eyes he indicated to his partner that they should back off and leave the room.

Calmly Laing apologised for arriving in the early hours and explained that he and Nixon were only seeking his assistance. 'Maybe it would be better all round if the matter could be settled amicably. Nobody wants t' open up a can of worms.'

Green laughed derisively. 'If CID aren't careful, you'll find yourselves goin' up your own asses. I don't give a fiddler's fuck about McDonnell . . . or, for that matter, Kirkpatrick. Stick the little bastards away if y' like.'

'What if they're not guilty?' Laing laughed.

'That's *your* fuckin' problem.'

It was clear that Green was not going to play ball.

Laing walked to the door. 'There's just one thing . . .' He placed a hand on the front door to stop Green closing it. 'Where would we find the major and Milner?'

'In Cloud-cuckoo-land.'

Green slammed the door; the rattle of metal bolts confirmed that he'd retired to his bullet-proofed refuge.

Laing cursed Green as his partner drove the car along the seafront.

'He's weird,' said Nixon. 'See all those magazines? They were all porno. I was goin' to ask him if I could borrow them.'

Laing laughed. 'That fella's so mean he wouldn't give you the smell of yesterday's shite.'

Nixon stopped the car opposite the Royal Hotel and turned off the engine. 'Let's calm down,' he said, 'and concentrate on the facts. It seems to me that, from what we know so far, somebody's lyin' to us . . . and I'm not talkin' about Kirkpatrick or McDonnell. I think we're being turned over on this one. The Branch tells our boss they know the guilty men. "Put them away," says our boss . . . And I'm beginnin' to think: for what?'

'We're gonna have t' charge them.'

'With what?'

'With murder.'

'How?'

'We remand them in custody on a murder charge . . . That gets them out of our hair for a long time. If no evidence is produced by the deposition stage, they'll be freed. If you ask me, there's something dirty about this one. We need to do a bit of digging. The next stop is Davidson, head of Special Branch.'

'I suppose you're right . . . A period on remand won't do them any harm. Some fuckin' lawyer will make a lot of money out of the system gettin' them off.'

'Sounds fine to me . . . We'll have to be careful, though . . . I don't like fuckin' with the Branch, and when it comes to the Brits, particularly the long-haired lot who are runnin' around like fuckin' cowboys, they'd shoot us as quick as anyone else if we trespassed on one of their operations. I want an easy life. We're dealin' with the system here unless I'm wrong, and it's not worth it to fuck with the system . . . In the long run nobody will care if we expose somethin' here and end up dead or out of a job.'

'Well said, pal.'

After catching a few hours' sleep, Laing and Nixon telephoned Commander Davidson and arranged a meeting with him.

'I've spoken to your chief in CID,' said Stanley Davidson as soon as they entered his office. 'You men are very hard-worked, and he agrees that in recognition of your services you need a break.'

Nixon was about to protest when Laing nudged him.

'That's fine, sir,' said Laing, 'but what about this case involving Kirkpatrick and McDonnell?'

'Just charge them today. Your boss will have someone else take over the case in your absence.'

As Laing ushered his partner into the corridor, Richard Milner entered Davidson's office through another door.

'Well done, Stanley. We'll have them in prison by mid-afternoon.'

'If you want to see them, they're in Room 12C down the corridor. Try and make it fast,' said Davidson. 'Even this place leaks at times.'

'What about Green?'

Davidson smiled. 'Just as you said . . . When I told him I was recommending him for promotion, he calmed down. He'll play ball.'

'And CID?'

'They've too much on their plates to worry about this one. The chief is my buddy – he'll talk to the detectives. Everybody wants to survive.'

Stephen was relieved to see Richard Milner, and walked towards him with a hand extended in greeting.

'Some friend you are,' shouted Michael, refusing to leave his chair. 'Does the major know about this?'

Richard waited patiently while the young man vented his anger.

'How many fuckin' days have we been here?' Michael demanded.

'Six,' replied Richard. 'You've both done well. You can thank your training for that.'

Michael interpreted that as praise; finally he calmed down and shook Richard's hand.

'Listen carefully to what I am about to say,' advised Richard. 'Green has it in for you but he'll never make it stick. That's why I am here. Once the police and the courts are involved, matters become complex, but in the end you will both be cleared and receive your rewards.'

Michael pulled away from him. 'In the end? That's a fuckin' joke! What are we talkin' about here . . . a week . . . a month?'

Richard pointed a warning finger at him. 'We're talking about your lives. Now would you prefer that I left you to deal with this on your own?'

There was silence. Michael continued to look angry and it was clear what he was going to say.

'Don't say it, Michael. Nobody would believe your story. You need me to survive.'

'Excuse me a moment,' said Stephen.

He took his friend to one side and reproached him for jeopardising their only hope of combating Green and the law. Richard sat at a small wooden table waiting for them to finish their private conversation.

Then Michael turned back to Milner, subdued. 'OK. Sorry. Tell us what's goin' to happen.'

'They are going to charge you,' said Richard. 'That's only a formality, and it should not concern you. I suggest you anticipate that event by making a statement of your innocence later this morning. Your families have appointed a lawyer. Tell him nothing. Let him enter your "Not guilty" plea at the court hearing which will take place after midday. Only if the major and I remain anonymous can we effectively and in secret clear this up.'

'In this neck of the woods they can keep y' in custody for years without a trial,' said Michael.

Richard assured him that would not happen; that the case would never come to trial but they would have to spend 'a little time' in Crumlin Road prison.

The prospect of incarceration infuriated Michael, and again Stephen had to defuse his friend's urge to confront Milner.

'Look, Michael,' he pleaded. 'Bradford's dead: D–E–D. Somebody set us up, and whoever they are they have clout, so they'll make it stick. Our only hope now is Mr Milner here, and the major . . . We'll be out soon. Isn't that right, Mr Milner?'

'It's Richard to you, lads.'

Impressed by the intimacy he was suddenly being afforded, Michael listened earnestly as Richard told them what to expect when they arrived at the prison.

'It's like this,' he began. 'The prison is divided up into blocks controlled by different paramilitary factions. When you enter the prison, the Governor or his assistant will ask you which group you wish to give your allegiance to. For your own safety I recommend you choose the Provos. You'll be interviewed by one of their representatives and you'll say you have both been framed. They will question you about your time in police custody but that should not prove a problem.'

'Why would they question us?' asked Stephen.

Michael laughed. 'Don't worry. It's no big deal. We're Catholics from Andytown and everybody knows the cops frame people. You know, like in the song.' He began to sing:

> 'If you're Catholic, come into the jailhouse,
> There's a welcome there for you.
> And if your name is Seamus, Pat or Mick
> We'll cook some dodgy evidence
> And then we'll make it stick.'

Richard smiled. 'I doubt if it will ever make the Top Ten, McDonnell.'

When they were alone, Stephen expressed his concern about spending time with the IRA. 'Everything we do seems t' go wrong . . . And the Provos are not people you fuck with.'

Michael said he was sure Milner and Johnston would sort out the problem. 'Anyway, this is the best cover we could ever have – the cops beatin' up on us . . . We'll be fuckin' heroes when we get out.'

The magistrate's court was packed with armed policemen, journalists and interested members of the public.

'All this security for us!' Michael laughed as they were led into the dock. 'Do you think we should give them the Black Power salute?'

He smiled at a woman court clerk and waved to his mother, who was sitting at the rear of the courtroom.

Stephen kept his head bowed, not wanting to face his mother or sisters, but he needn't have bothered.

'Hey, there's that wacko who lives next door,' said Michael, pointing to Jimmy Carson, who was desperately trying to be invisible by sitting on the edge of the bench closest to the entrance. 'Yer mother and sisters aren't here.'

Looking up, Stephen spotted Jimmy and saw he was clean-shaven and wearing a trenchcoat. He slightly raised his right hand to indicate his support, then looked away.

One of the guards nudged Stephen and gestured towards Jimmy. 'Did y' ever see *Casablanca*, the film with Humphrey Bogart? Well that old boy down there reminds me of it. In the last scene somebody says, "Round up the usual suspects." I think they missed him.'

Revelling in his notoriety, Michael insisted on standing, while Stephen sat down, his face below the level of the dock.

'Didn't I tell you we'd end up as heroes?'

Stephen ignored his friend. Then abruptly he was hauled to his feet by the guards as the magistrate entered.

The hearing lasted fifteen minutes. After a reading of the charge, pleas of 'Not guilty' were entered by their solicitor, who looked at them and shrugged with resignation when the magistrate rejected his request for bail.

As they were led handcuffed from the dock, Bill Green brandished his identity pass and forged a path towards them, singling out Michael.

'I told you fuckers to trust us,' he whispered. 'Now look where your new friends have put you.'

Michael tried to head-butt him but was dragged swearing to the doors of the courtroom by two burly policemen, one of whom was wielding a truncheon.

Stephen stole a glance round the courtroom, hoping to see Jimmy, but he was gone, and there was no sign of his family.

11

Mary Kirkpatrick was sitting in the living-room saying the rosary when Jimmy Carson arrived with news of her son. He was agitated and his habitual hand-wringing worsened as he described the court hearing. She was grateful for the old man's help: she'd felt unable to cope emotionally with seeing her son in the dock.

'It was no holiday for me,' said Jimmy, anxiously looking towards the kitchen where a kettle was boiling and hoping it was for tea.

After two cups of tea and a biscuit his nervousness eased and he immediately launched an attack. 'That eejit McDonnell was standin' up there as if he was waitin' for somebody to ask him t' hum a tune . . . "Mockingbird Hill" would've been my choice.'

His unconscious humour made Mary understand her son's fascination with her neighbour and his eccentric speech and mannerisms.

'He's a star turn,' continued Jimmy, extending his cup towards the teapot. 'He doesn't know he's a victim, and I'd say that makes him dangerous.'

After consuming most of the tea he said he'd like to spare her the humiliation of a prison visit. 'I don't like prisons or the people who inhabit them . . . That includes the screws . . . I think it's better you stay away from the Crum until we find out how things are goin'.'

He stood up and scratched his head as if a thought were lurking there and refusing to be articulated.

'Do y' think they'd let Provo in? With a name like that he could take up residence.'

There was not even a hint of a smile as he slouched out of the house and down the pathway. Bridget Jones, arms folded and legs apart, stood at her favourite vantage-point – her front door. Her look of defiance was intended to let him know she disapproved of his visiting the Kirkpatricks.

Crumlin Road prison was not a place for the faint-hearted, and Stephen's spirits sank as he looked up at the thick stone walls and watchtowers. He and Michael were led handcuffed to separate interview rooms normally used by solicitors for consultations with inmates.

'Stand up, Kirkpatrick.'

Pushing himself off an oak bench, he stood to attention as a warder approached.

'This is the Assistant Governor, Mr Wainwright,' announced the warder.

A man in civilian clothes was standing in the doorway.

'Our rules are simple.'

Wainwright's tone and swagger matched the arrogance in his eyes and the curl of his lips. Closing in, he prodded Stephen's chest.

'This is one of Her Majesty's finest hotels, and you will treat it as such.'

The warder was enjoying the performance and moved from side to side to watch Stephen's reaction. He stifled a laugh and leaned against the door.

'In here as in any hotel we have different floors for different types of guests. Do you get my drift?'

Stephen nodded.

'We have –'

'My solicitor has told me about the arrangements. If it's OK, Mr Wainwright, I would like to go to the Provo wing.'

Whether he had learned the habit at school or at home, Stephen tended to be excessively polite when faced with authority. Generally this worked to his advantage, but he didn't know Wainwright.

'So we've a smartarse.' Wainwright looked round at the

warder and winked. 'We don't like smartarses in here.'

With that he pushed Stephen, making him topple off the bench, his right trouser leg tearing against a ragged piece of wood. As he struggled to his feet, the handcuffs inhibiting his movement, he backed slowly towards the wall.

'That's my boy.'

The warder smiled at Stephen's discomfort.

'You see?' Wainwright pointed to the warder. 'He has a sense of humour . . . We all have in here . . . and the humour is much more serious if you step out of line.'

Stephen raised his cuffed hands, holding the palms outward to indicate that he didn't wish to make any trouble. Blood was running down his leg and he realised the jagged edge of the bench had gashed the flesh of his calf.

Wainwright smiled. 'The next thing you'll want is a doctor . . . You'll be crying "Torture". Isn't that right?' He moved towards Stephen.

'No way,' said Stephen, again raising his hands, this time defensively.

'That's what I like to hear.'

Wainwright backed towards the door. 'The Provos may not want you, but there again they like cop killers, don't they?' He turned on his heel, leaving the warder to close the door.

Stephen sat down on the bench and tried to stem the flow of blood from the wound to his leg. He was in the process of trying to dress the wound with a handkerchief when the warder opened the door and stood to one side to let Brendan McCann enter.

'This is the Provo commander,' shouted the warder.

Brendan glared at him. 'Shut the door on your way out.'

The warder sheepishly complied.

Stephen tried to get to his feet but Brendan waved to him to remain seated.

'Quiet.' Brendan put a finger to his lips to indicate the need for silence and tiptoed to the door. Placing his right ear against it, he remained there for several minutes. Suddenly he stepped back and then launched himself at the wooden door, causing it to vibrate. 'That'll teach that bastard t' be sneaky.'

Smiling, he joined Stephen on the bench. 'The screws in here are the eyes and ears of the Governor and the Brits . . . Never forget that.'

Then Brendan noticed the blood soaking through Stephen's trouser leg and the bloody handkerchief he was holding.

'Shit!' he exclaimed, attempting to tie the makeshift bandage. 'I see you've had the Wainwright treatment. He does that with kids like you. He doesn't fuck with *us* – he knows better. Once you're with us he won't touch you. You see, he's as vulnerable as anybody else outside these walls and in the future there'll be scores settled . . . He doesn't want to be one of them.'

Stephen slowly warmed to his new protector and began to explain that he'd been framed.

'What I want t' know is why you've asked to be accepted by us,' said Brendan. 'Quietly.' He pointed to the door. 'You never know who might be listening.'

'I'm not a member of the IRA,' Stephen began, but got no further.

'I didn't ask that question, and it's not one for this room.' Brendan placed a hand on Stephen's shoulder in a fatherly fashion and spoke slowly. 'There are things we can get to later. For now, all I want to know is why you've chosen us.'

Swallowing hard, Stephen realised that he'd miscalculated the ease with which he could justify his request. Milner had told him that all he had to do was ask to be housed with the Provos, and that was it.

'I'm a Catholic from Andersonstown.'

It was the first response which came to mind; but it didn't satisfy Brendan, who stood up and aggressively paced up and down the room.

'You could have named the Stickies – the Official IRA,' he said, stopping momentarily in front of Stephen.

Stephen felt betrayed by Milner, who had not advised him how to construct answers to these questions.

'If all you want is protection . . . you could have chosen any of us.'

'But the Provos are the strongest grouping.'

Brendan shook his head in dismay. 'You'll have to come up with a better reason than that.'

Thank God for Jimmy Carson, thought Stephen as he started to formulate a suitable explanation. 'The Provos are . . .'

Brendan shook him. Gone was the fatherly expression. 'Irish Republican Army.'

He spoke the words with reverence and Stephen hastily apologised.

'We are not Provos or Provisionals – that's Brit language.'

The point was not lost on Stephen, who'd grown accustomed to the military and media descriptions of the IRA and what was essentially common usage among his contemporaries. Brendan sensed that he'd frightened the young man and with a contrived smile encouraged him to speak.

'I chose the IRA because they're the people's heroes.'

Brendan laughed. 'Where the hell did y' learn that phrase?'

Stephen looked away embarrassed. 'That's what people think, isn't it? I mean, in Andytown . . .'

A key was turned in the door and, with no hint of a swagger or the sarcasm which had characterised his earlier visit, Wainwright took several paces into the room.

'We'll take him.' Grabbing Stephen by the handcuffs, Brendan pulled him upright. 'From here on, he's under our protection.'

Then Brendan released his grip on the handcuffs and strode towards the door, where two warders blocked his exit. He stopped in front of Wainwright and pointed at the wound on Stephen's leg.

'Get that cleaned up, and don't ever let it happen again.'

Wainwright's mouth twitched in anger.

'Now get t' fuck outa my way.'

One of the warders stepped aside and the other followed Brendan as he walked out of sight.

When the doctor arrived, Wainwright quickly explained that the wound had been accidentally caused by a nail protruding from a bench in the interview room.

While the doctor attended to the wound, Stephen was left to

reflect on the antagonism between Brendan and the Assistant Governor. Brendan was a contradiction. On the one hand he could be considerate, yet there was something disturbing, even sinister, lurking behind his pale blue eyes. Stephen could not decide whether to admire him or reserve judgement. One thing was certain: he carried considerable authority in the prison and, in that respect at least, Milner was right to advise that the Provos were the best protectors.

After the medical attention he was taken to be fingerprinted and photographed. A prison clerk described the daily routine for inmates and explained that terrorists on remand were entitled to wear their own clothes and not required to work.

'In here,' said the clerk with a wry smile, 'we've the biggest bunch of maniacs anywhere in the world. It's a cross between a nuthouse and a parade ground.'

Relief shone out on Stephen's face when he was led to the block housing the Provisionals in A Wing and allocated a single cell. When he discovered that Michael had been placed next door in similar accommodation, his spirits lifted.

'Not bad, eh?' Michael was leaning against the door frame. 'At least I don't have t' watch any of these fruitcakes havin' a piss or a crap.'

A metal bed and hard mattress took up most of the cell. There was also a makeshift lavatory comprising a toilet seat over a large metal bucket.

'At least y' can wash yer hands,' said Michael. 'And if it isn't a basin made by Twyfords of Byford and Lynas! Makes y' feel at home, doesn't it?'

Brendan swiftly shoved a paperback under his pillow as Liam Brady entered the cell and stubbed out a cigarette on the metal door.

'They're on the block. What do y' want us t' do?'

Brendan rose to his feet and shook Patrick Rodgers, who was sleeping on the upper bunk.

'Let them settle in,' said Brendan.

Patrick slowly lowered himself to the floor. They all

described him as an insomniac because he lay awake at night and snatched sleep during brief moments in the day. According to Brendan, however, it was not so much insomnia as a penchant for reading at night when the block was quiet. He'd stolen a torch from the surgery and developed what the others called 'night owl sickness'. Replacement batteries were provided by Jimmy Duffin, an 'ordinary decent criminal' who worked in the kitchens. Patrick had discovered that Duffin was due for a beating by the IRA on his release because of a misdemeanour involving a schoolgirl. He had promised Duffin he would intervene to spare him punishment if he supplied him with batteries for the torch. According to Patrick, it was an offer he couldn't refuse.

'I want a meeting here in one hour.'

Patrick hadn't finished his nap and a meeting was the last thing he wanted. He was about to return to bed when Brendan pointed at him.

'You.'

'What, me?' asked Patrick, meekly placing his hands on his chest.

'Yes, you. Get some air. You look like you've just come out of hibernation.'

Among the young men who were his constant companions, Brendan considered Patrick the most politically astute and ruthless. He was pleased by the way he'd bonded them together within his internal security cell: through their months in prison they'd learned to support each other and form a strong team with varying intellectual skills. He had no doubts that when released they would set about building the groundwork for a new command structure in the republican movement and provide a political dynamic that would enhance the military campaign.

Before leaving the cell, Patrick asked if their lawyers had confirmed that he, Liam and Damien were unlikely to face trial.

Brendan nodded. 'Yes, the legal view is that none of the specific evidence found at the scene could be linked directly to you three. You have no previous convictions, and they've no intelligence to tag you to the IRA.'

In prison he'd used the time to guide them politically, making sure they knew how to develop the strategy of the Armalite and the ballot box. 'The smoking gun is not enough to win a war,' he had stressed time and again. 'The odds are in favour of the Brits, and international opinion will support that. It's essential to develop a dual strategy and win the hearts and minds of the young and the next generation.'

Although he was resigned to serving a prison term, he was glad that his influence would continue to be exerted through the three core members of the team on their release.

'The lawyer I spoke to today says the authorities will not waste time on you guys. Ostensibly you're students renting property. The evidence is circumstantial and your student status will weigh heavily in your favour. Me . . . that's a different ball game.'

'How long does the lawyer think you'll get?' asked Damien Nolan, who was standing in the doorway of the cell.

'Christ knows. He feels I'm the one they're really after. They want me to go down no matter what it takes. Apparently the cops are sayin' that if they could forensically tag that gun they found in the house to a few murders they'd put me away for life.'

'But you never used that gun,' said Damien.

'No way . . . That weapon was clean as far as this place is concerned.'

'What do y' mean?' asked Liam.

Brendan grinned. 'That gun was from a new batch which was smuggled out of New York on the *QE2*. One of our Noraid people – in the New York Police Department, no less – put together a consignment of pistols and rifles taken in raids in the city.'

'You're joking.' Liam started to laugh and the others joined in. 'If they connect that gun to a Mafia hit, can you just see the headlines? . . . "Top Provo is a Mafia Hitman".'

'The bastards will have t' extradite me to New York,' said Brendan gleefully.

'When you guys get out,' he continued, 'just remember you'll be marked men because of your time in here and your connection to me. Every army patrol will be supplied with your photographs, and British intelligence will be waiting for you to step out of line. From here on, you don't undertake active service of any kind. Get involved with Sinn Fein. You won't have the cloak of anonymity, so be up front politically. Secretly, you must use the contacts from internal security and from the ranks of the younger element who think like us to prepare for a takeover of the movement. When the time comes, don't pussy-foot around with any of the armchair generals in Dublin. The people who should control this war are the people who are fightin' it – not a bunch of has-beens sittin' in the security of the Republic and spoutin' off to the foreign media. Fuck them, they'll lead us into another decline. It's the people in the North who've given their lives for this struggle and we're not goin' to be sold down the river ever again.'

Patrick was first to arrive for the meeting, complaining that he'd walked up and down the block until his feet were sore. Brendan hastily closed his paperback and was hiding it under the bedclothes when the others arrived.

'What's he reading?' asked Liam, looking at Patrick.

'Yeah . . . What's so special he needs t' hide it?' said Damien, intrigued by the secrecy surrounding the book.

'OK . . . if you're so fuckin' nosy.' Brendan retrieved the book and held it aloft.

'I got that for him,' announced Patrick, and gestured at the title: *Selected Poems of T. S. Eliot*. 'I reckoned "The Waste Land" would make good reading for him when we're gone, but all he does is recite "The Love Song of J. Alfred Prufrock". Maybe he thinks he's the patient etherised upon a table.'

Brendan self-consciously slid the book under the pillow again. 'Well, fuck you lot.'

His anger only fuelled their amusement.

' "I grow old . . . I grow old . . ." ' Patrick recited from the poem while looking pitifully at Brendan: ' "I shall wear the bottoms of my trousers rolled. Shall I part my hair behind? Do I dare –"''

'That's enough.' Brendan angrily pushed him aside. 'It's my turn for a walk. Just be in the right frame of mind when I return.'

Damien stared accusingly at Patrick. 'You shouldn't take the piss. He's self-conscious about his lack of formal education.'

Liam agreed, but added, 'Our learning days have been well and truly fucked.'

They were seated when Brendan returned, hardly glancing at them as he retreated to a corner of the cell, his hands dug firmly into his trouser pockets.

'I've been thinkin' about the arrivals.'

He lowered himself to the floor, staring up at the other three men.

'These guys say they were framed . . . Knowing the RUC and the Brits, that's not difficult to accept . . . but why these two?'

He scratched his head and unexpectedly a smile crept across the corners of his eyes.

'Kirkpatrick says we're the people's heroes.'

'Where the fuck's he been living?' said Patrick as the others started to giggle. 'Is he all there?'

Brendan calmed them with a wave of his hand. 'He's no shooter, that's for sure. I know because I've been one and –'

'And it takes one to know one,' Patrick interjected.

'Is this a fuckin' cabaret act?' Brendan angrily got to his feet. 'What are you guys on? Maybe the rest of the prison could do with some of it.'

'OK. Sorry, Brendan,' said Patrick.

Brendan began to recount his meeting with Michael McDonnell. 'He's a cheeky little fucker.'

'Maybe they're just two screwballs.'

Damien's comment was greeted with derision by Brendan, who held his head in his hands.

'There's something about McDonnell.' Brendan crouched down as if he couldn't find words to express what he felt and had resigned himself to an ongoing comedy act from the others.

214

'All right . . . You guys want a laugh?'

Brendan swaggered into the corridor and back into the cell, mimicking McDonnell's performance in the interview room.

'You know what he said to Wainwright when the bastard pushed him? He told him he'd get the Provos t' sort him out. He told him his uncle was on the Army Council. Wainwright nearly shit himself. When I arrived he held out the handcuffs and told me to unlock them.'

'Was he not scared when y' told him who you were?' Patrick asked.

Brendan doubled up laughing. 'He fucked the RUC up and down, and the screw thought he was a raving lunatic. When I asked him why he'd chosen us he said we were the kind of boys he got on well with . . . and anyway we were younger than that bunch of played-out Stickies, and the INLA had something to do with the PLO and he didn't like Arabs.'

'Why didn't you tell him t' fuck off?' Damien sniggered.

Brendan wagged his finger in a threatening fashion. 'I want t' know why they're in here. I also want t' know why a scared kid like Kirkpatrick merits a frame-up. The RUC could have lifted any of our people . . . Christ, there are plenty of them they'd like t' put away. Maybe this is a Trojan Horse . . . Never trust the obvious.'

Patrick looked away, a smile on his face, and Brendan unsuccessfully tried not to react.

'All right, it's a fuckin' literary reference!'

'First Eliot, now Homer?'

'If this is what readin' this stuff does,' said Brendan, waving at Patrick, 'I'll stick t' politics.' Then he paused.

'Just a minute.'

The other men's wisecracks stopped in their tracks.

'We handle this carefully . . . Two teams, just like the Special Branch. If they can learn from our methods, we can learn from theirs. Tomorrow after slop-out.'

Stephen spent a sleepless night praying that everything would be OK and he would soon be reunited with Bernadette.

Why the hell couldn't she visit me? Why couldn't she write? he asked himself. A few lines would be enough.

He was confused by his feelings of anger laced with longing to see her and hear her voice; but in more lucid moments he recognised that a possible compulsory strip-search by prison staff was not something she could endure, nor did he wish her to be subjected to it. Since she worked for a law firm in central Belfast, any obvious connection with him, even through a letter, could, if discovered by her employers or conveyed to them, put her job in jeopardy. Stephen understood her predicament, and had to hope that their love for each other would survive the present crisis.

Reciting a decade of the rosary reminded him of his boyhood and left him feeling like a fraud. The gulf between those early years and what he'd become seemed so vast in the darkness of his cell.

Maybe my life just spiralled out of control, he thought.

It was a comforting explanation and his conscience told him it was a convenient lie.

'You are responsible for your own soul': his mother's words were coming back to haunt him in these anguished moments of isolation.

Stephen's internal debate went on for hours; his need for survival always prevailed over his desire to confront the morality of his actions. There was nothing he wouldn't do to avoid a long prison sentence and he hoped Milner would be true to his word.

Raw instinct warned him that behind Brendan's smiling façade was a well-honed mind and a ruthlessness which was the stock-in-trade of the Provisional IRA. Self-control and an insistence on his innocence in the face of prolonged questioning were the only means of countering the Brendans of this world.

In the back of his mind was a nagging doubt about Richard Milner's knowledge of the IRA. Milner had warned they'd be questioned by the IRA but there was never any suggestion it would be a protracted affair.

As the dawn's light broke across the edge of the barred

cell window, he consoled himself that he was innocent of the Bradford murder and whatever transpired the IRA would not torture or kill him in prison.

Slopping out brought home the sordidness of his situation. A breakfast consisting only of strong tea with bread and jam was a powerful contrast to his mother's cooking.

After a brief inspection by warders, the wing was sealed, leaving its blocks in the control of the Provisionals. Prison surveillance was maintained by cameras and warders placed strategically at the gates which confined individual paramilitary zones.

Stephen was folding clothes which Jimmy had left for him at the courthouse when Brendan McCann and Patrick Rodgers entered his cell, the latter with a pen and notepad.

Brendan smiled and sat on the bed, making room for Stephen to join him, while Rodgers took up a position cross-legged on the floor.

Then Brendan began to outline the purpose of the visit, speaking in a tone that conveyed formality.

'It's our practice to establish that you are who you say you are. We question everyone who arrives in this wing. We need t' know about the interrogation methods of the occupation forces and we have t' be sure that you aren't a plant.'

He opened out his hands, as though making an offering.

'That's my position. Now what's yours?'

Stephen responded by sketching out his family history, the schools he'd attended and how he had met Michael. Anticipating a question about his financial status, he explained that he did the 'double'.

The fact that the young man was claiming social security benefit while working appealed to Brendan and Patrick, and the atmosphere in the cell lightened a little.

Sensing advantage, and happy to have an appreciative audience, he extolled the benefits of conning the state, foolishly believing he was sidetracking Brendan.

'Why do you think they framed you? You're only an ordinary guy.'

217

The question brought him down to earth because it came from Rodgers, who had been taking copious notes.

'Maybe an informer did it t' keep himself in business . . . just looked up in a phone directory and picked us out.'

He had given a quick answer without considering its import, but he immediately realised it was a foolish move.

'Do informers work like that?' Brendan's eyes were drilling into his.

'I think I saw somethin' like that in a gangster film.'

His heart missed a beat as he delivered the reply but the speed at which it was produced appeared to have the effect of easing the tension between them.

Brendan laughed. 'The informers I knew certainly weren't like that.'

Putting aside the notepad, Rodgers stared up at Stephen as Brendan continued, his pupils dilated and his concentration intense.

'Somebody set you up . . . That seems clear . . . But who? Could *our* people have done it to throw the RUC off the scent? No! That's not our form. If we did that each time there was an operation, we'd have no support. That leaves your theory, which we'll discount, or the Brits and the RUC. Now why would they choose you when there are plenty of people like us they'd like t' frame?'

Brendan further asserted his control with a glance at Rodgers, who buried his head and took a verbatim note of the question.

'Let's look at it this way . . . Either you and Michael have a very dangerous enemy, or the Brits and the RUC fucked up.' 'RUC' was pronounced 'ruck' with as much venom as he could supply.

'But the Ruck are always framing people.'

Brendan nodded his approval of the answer and nonchalantly inclined his head towards the ceiling as he spoke.

'Have you ever had any dealings with the Ruck or the Brits?'

'No!'

'That's it for the moment.' Brendan got up and Rodgers closed the notebook.

They were in the corridor when Brendan abruptly turned on his heel and walked back into the cell followed seconds later by his companion.

'There's just one small point,' he remarked, motioning to Stephen to remain seated. 'What was the name of that film about the informer? I'd like t' watch it some time.' His eyes glittered with humour as he emphasised 'some time'.

'I'm not sure, but I think it was a Humphrey Bogart film.'

'The one with "Round up all the usual suspects" at the end?'

Stephen shook his head. With a flourish of his hand Brendan said it didn't matter and left.

'Easy as piss,' said Michael, standing in the doorway while Stephen was deep in thought, wondering if he'd made a mistake by talking about a film.

Michael entered the cell and pretended to urinate. His cavalier manner angered his friend.

'These guys aren't dummies, Michael.'

'You could've fooled me.'

'So how did *you* explain why anyone should want to frame you?'

Michael sat down on the bed and laughed. 'I said if I knew the name of the fucker I'd tell them, and they could sort him out. They thought that was a cracker.'

Stephen suggested they plan their responses to possible questions but Michael vigorously resisted the proposal, arguing that it would only complicate matters.

'If we answer everythin' in the same way, they'll know we've somethin' t' hide.'

Stephen reluctantly agreed, although it made him feel vulnerable not knowing if Michael's effusiveness might also put them at risk.

Lunch was an ear-bending event; numerous conversations collided across the long tables of the canteen. Everything was up for debate – from family matters, to who masturbated most, and the state of the war. Michael took an active part in the discussion on masturbation.

'I've never done it,' he claimed, much to everyone's amusement. 'There's never been a need.'

That was the catalyst for a heated debate about the merits of masturbation, whether it made you blind, and if it was contrary to biblical teaching.

'It made him deaf,' bellowed one prisoner, pointing at Michael. 'That's why he's never heard of it!' yelled another.

Michael was not perturbed by the jibes and shouted back, 'Yeah, that's why you two are jerk-offs.'

One of his critics had to be forcibly restrained from clambering across the table with the express intention of throttling him.

Brendan and his trio sat silently observing the proceedings as Michael prattled on with hilarious tales about his drinking and sex exploits.

Turning to a prisoner on his other side, Stephen commented on the repulsive quality of the prison food in an effort to distance himself from his flamboyant friend.

It was mid-afternoon when Brendan and Patrick resumed their questioning.

Stephen felt he was on good ground as he described his arrest and the battering he received during interrogation. He made much of the rough way his mother was treated and the sneering, cynical tactics of the detectives. There were no probing questions from Brendan, merely appreciative glances, particularly when the word 'torture' was used to define police interrogation techniques.

'We've made good progress.'

That was a welcome compliment from Brendan. As they left the cell Rodgers signalled his agreement.

'What have we got?'

Brendan looked at his team, who were standing in his cell examining notes of the interview sessions.

Patrick Rodgers took the lead, and replied that Kirkpatrick appeared to be telling the truth.

'I'm a naturally suspicious bastard,' he added, flicking through the notes, 'and the only thing that bothered me was the reference to a film. It was a strange explanation.'

Brendan wagged his finger. 'A film never convicted anyone.'

Rodgers didn't appreciate the succinct put-down. 'I just don't know of a film with that kind of scenario.'

'Because you're too busy doin' other things to watch films,' said Brendan, laughing and indicating that this was a closed issue. 'So that's what we've got on Kirkpatrick . . . What have you lads got on McDonnell?'

Liam Brady was the meticulous type and everyone waited while he patiently conferred with Damien Nolan about their notes on Michael.

'There's fuck-all here,' announced Brady, putting the notes in his back pocket.

'That's fuckin' great. You spend a day with somebody and you've nothin'!'

Brendan was not amused, but Damien Nolan was not about to let the matter rest.

'What's being said here is that we've nothin' to pin on him.'

'Well, why didn't you say that?'

Nolan shook his head in disbelief. 'I thought we did say that.'

There was little point in challenging the boss: Brendan made that clear.

'You said there was fuck-all. I've always told you to be precise when it comes to interrogation. Now tell me what you *don't* have to pin on him.'

Nolan backed off as Brady removed the notebook from his pocket and scanned the pages again.

'It was a case of don't interrupt me while I'm interrupting you.'

'You mean this guy's been learnin' interview techniques from Ian Paisley and John Hume,' said Brendan with a smile.

Nolan started to explain. 'He goes off at tangents about everything. He doesn't give a fuck what we ask him. Y' could say he's not scared of us.'

Brendan glared at Nolan. 'Now you're fuckin' tellin' me

somethin' I need t' know.' He turned to Rodgers. 'Did you get the message out?'

Rodgers replied that his torch battery source, Duffin, the ODC in A Wing, had managed to get out a coded message in return for clemency from the IRA. 'We'll have an answer by visiting-time tomorrow – the usual method of communication.'

Brady sniggered at the mention of 'usual method of communication'. 'We live in a world of advanced telecommunications and we're still using rubbers and tampons.'

'Don't know it,' muttered Rodgers. 'Without them we'd never be able to talk to the outside world.'

The second session had left Stephen confident about his handling of the IRA and he slept soundly. He awoke to hear news that he was getting a visit from Jimmy Carson.

The visiting-room was a dirty-brown colour and the smell of disinfectant hung in the air. Rows of high-backed wooden cubicles permitted inmates a degree of intimacy with visitors under the watchful eyes of warders. Some of the warders strode up and down; others lounged at the entrance to the room. There was always the risk that loyalist or republican prisoners or visitors would take the law into their own hands, or that weapons or messages would be passed between people in the cubicles.

Prison life tended to militate against the possibility of inmates attacking each other because all sides felt vulnerable and an assault would lead to revenge. It was an uneasy truce, which appeared to work, but there was still the danger that a relative of someone murdered by the paramilitaries would use a visit to exact a personal justice.

Jimmy Carson, his face covered by his hands, was in one of the cubicles when Stephen arrived. He looked tired and frightened when Stephen sat down opposite, their hands almost touching across a narrow table.

'How's Mum?'

Jimmy muttered, 'She's bearin' up well. The sisters send

their love.' It was apparent the old man was apprehensive about saying too much or raising his voice.

'What about Provo?'

Jimmy cast a furtive glance at the warders when the name 'Provo' was spoken but Stephen assured him they couldn't be heard.

'No harm will come to you in here.'

This advice was met with a raising of the eyebrows and a disdainful shrug of the shoulders.

'I know all about the Crum,' he whispered, leaning across the table and wringing his hands. 'I was in here.'

Stephen was dumbfounded.

'During the war.'

'You were a visitor . . . ?'

Jimmy shook his head. 'It nearly finished me.'

Stephen's curiosity overcame his temptation to interrupt, and he sat back and listened, his eyes wide with shock.

'We all have regrets. My father died, on a Normandy beach, and here was me wantin' the Germans t' win the war. How do y' live with that?'

The hand-wringing frantically gained pace. Stephen tried to contain it with a gesture but the old man pulled back, placing his hands under the table.

'My mother died never forgivin' me.' He was desperately trying to hold back tears. 'I hate m'self . . . I hate all of them.'

Suddenly a steeliness invaded his stare and he spoke slowly and quietly. 'That's why I get at you about life.' He was like a schoolmaster with a truculent child. 'Dangers lurk in conflict for everybody. Hitler was a bigger menace than the Brits, but I couldn't see it. I believed the prejudice of my own people. They weren't wrong t' hate the Brits but the cost was too high.'

His hands returned to the table and appeared to relax as his thoughts flowed.

'My father was republican . . . not IRA . . . and he fought Hitler. My grandfather fought in the Great War. Now there was a man . . . He once told a loyalist t' shove the Union Jack up his arse. He could afford t' do that because he fought for it and Orangemen were usin' it t' beat our people.'

Like a hare expecting a fox to pounce he inclined his head towards the other cubicles for a brief moment.

'The people's heroes don't understand there's a bit of the Brit in us in the North . . . Some day they'll have t' accept it when Britain pulls out . . . That's if they want peace.'

The conversation was not suitable for the visiting-room, and Stephen rapidly diverted it to another topic.

'You still haven't told me how Provo's gettin' on.'

Jimmy clearly resented being sidetracked but it was not the time or place to raise an objection.

'I was thinkin' of gettin' rid of him.'

The announcement took Stephen by surprise, and Jimmy reacted with a typically obtuse retort.

'I was thinkin' about givin' him to the Irish Guards for their St Patrick's Day parades. I'm fed up lookin' at them with that Irish wolfhound. The Queen Mother . . . well, she can't be happy havin' that big mutt around her corgis. Provo is just right for the occasion.'

Stephen put a hand over his mouth to suppress laughter as Jimmy, straight-faced, continued to develop the theme.

'The only problem with Provo is that he mightn't take t' royalty. Just imagine him parading along when the Guards get their shamrocks from the Queen Mother. He sees her ankle, takes a lump out of it. "Mad Dog Provo Attack on Queen Mother," says the British tabloids . . .'

A bell sounded the end of the visiting period. Stephen quickly leaned across and took the old man's arm.

'Tell Mum I didn't do it.'

'That's better comin' from you.'

'Tell her I'll be out soon, and not to come here.'

Jimmy agreed to do just that and scurried from the room without a backward glance.

True to his word, Jimmy conveyed the plea of innocence to Mary Kirkpatrick and her son's wish that she did not visit him in prison.

Minutes after he had left the house, Deirdre and Sheila arrived unexpectedly and demanded to know if she'd been to visit their brother.

'What's it to you?' she replied, looking from one to the other. 'You didn't even take the time t' come up here and y' knew the state I was in.'

Sheila assumed the role of elder sister by speaking for them both. 'We thought it'd be better t' stay away until things have blown over.'

Mary turned her back on them and began cleaning the cooker. 'I suppose yer husbands don't want people t' know where y' come from and that yer brother's in trouble.'

Hurt by the accusation, both women tried to reply at once, their comments colliding with the sound of a heavy jet of water filling the kettle.

'Maybe you've come for the tea,' remarked Mary, putting a match to the cooker. 'You've hardly mine or your brother's interests at heart.'

'*Have* you visited him?' asked Sheila with a contemptuous grin.

Mary slammed an open palm on the table. 'For your information, Jimmy Carson did.'

Her daughters laughed.

'That'll do Stephen a lot of good,' said Sheila, playfully nudging her sister.

'Maybe he cares a lot more than most of us . . .' Mary's voice tailed off and she put her hand to her mouth to stifle a sob. 'Jimmy did it t' save me the pain, and I feel ashamed that my poor son's in there and not one member of his family has given him support.'

'Well, we have children t' think about,' said Deirdre.

Sheila again assumed the role of spokeswoman. 'Our husbands are in good jobs . . . and every Catholic knows that if y' visit the prison y' go down on file as a republican sympathiser . . . To the loyalists that means you're IRA. Look how many Catholics are killed because the police have given files t' the UDA and UVF.'

Mary didn't disagree with the logic of the argument. Her

only grievance was the lack of concern shown by her daughters. She began to cry.

'I'm not askin' either of you t' visit him. But you could visit *me*. This house is like a mausoleum without him. I even miss fallin' over his big boots and pickin' up after him. Has one of y' even asked if he's innocent?'

She turned off the cooker and reached for her coat, which was draped over a chair.

'At least I've Jimmy t' talk to.'

'We supported him . . .' Sheila's voice died away as Mary left the room.

'Go back to yer nice husbands in yer nice houses in yer nice neighbourhoods!'

The front door was slammed shut.

Sheila turned to her sister. 'That's what I get for comin' up here, and you can be sure some British Army patrol will have taken my car number. She just doesn't realise that every time we visit her my car goes on to army files . . . I live in a mixed area and I'm taking risks . . . None of the people my Peter works with knows I'm Stephen Kirkpatrick's sister. His cousin's married to a policewoman.'

Deirdre put her head in her hands as she spoke. 'It's the same with me. I'm not goin' up to the prison t' be strip-searched and humiliated, and put on file. I warned our Stephen years ago that he'd bring this family into disrepute . . . He's been livin' in this area like the rest of the world doesn't exist! Didn't we warn him after he was in the Fianna and got into trouble with the IRA? He doesn't care enough about the rest of us . . . C'mon, let's get out of here.'

Next door, Jimmy listened intently while Mary raged about her daughters' reluctance to support her son.

'Don't be too hard on them . . . They're your children too.'

It wasn't exactly what she wanted to hear and it wasn't exactly the end of his observations.

'Of course y' have t' understand that when y' give Catholics nice houses, nice jobs and social acceptance they behave like

226

Protestants . . . Now y' don't have t' take my word for that . . .
Terence O'Neill, the Unionist Prime Minister in the sixties, he
said just that. He knew that if you show a victim any respect
he'll give himself t' your way of thinkin' . . . Look at the new
Catholic middle class . . . They give their children Protestant
names, send them t' Protestant schools where they'll play
rugby or hockey . . . and why?'

Jimmy waited for a reply, knowing none would be forthcoming. It was a ploy to allow him time to construct his thesis
carefully.

'Because . . .'

He adjusted his spectacles and scratched his head.

'Because . . . they're the underdogs, at the bottom of the
heap . . . and the only way up is t' pander to a Protestant
way of life. Bouan says the middle class are called the middle
class because they're neither one thing nor the other – they're
the confused class. They like t' boast about their working-class
roots like some kind of measurin' stick t' show how successful
they've become . . . but they resent their background. They'd
like t' be upper class but know they'd never fit in. The middle
class is a hybrid.'

Complex political thought was way over Mary's head,
though she was glad that someone was explaining her daughters' behaviour in political rather than emotional terms.

Getting up to leave, she asked if he thought Stephen would
soon be released.

Jimmy looked perplexed and Mary, not wishing to press
him for an answer, walked to the front door.

He swiftly joined her. 'It all depends on who put him in
there.'

She half hoped he would clarify his comment but he pointed
to Provo, who was looking at them with a mean and hungry
look.

Edging her outside, he said, 'He's due a feed.'

12

Stephen stood in line with the other prisoners while warders searched the cubicles of the visiting area to ensure there were no stragglers.

'McCann, get in line.'

Brendan emerged from a cubicle with a young woman, who kissed him on the cheek and hurried to the exit.

'He likes them fresh.'

Stephen recognised the voice of a prisoner from his block.

'There are always young ones here to see him.'

The commentary abruptly ended as Brendan made his way to the line-up and stood alongside Stephen, making no effort to speak or engage him in eye contact.

'You'd think that as remand prisoners we'd get more visitin' time.'

Stephen's remark was designed to please the IRA chief, who remained tight-lipped. After a sideways glance from Stephen he bowed his head, remaining in that position as they were escorted to A Wing.

Rodgers, Nolan and Brady were waiting in Brendan's cell. When he arrived he hurried to a washbasin and spat into it.

'Rather you than me,' remarked Rodgers with a grin, as Brendan filled his mouth with water and gargled.

'Here, you open it.' Brendan threw an object at him. 'Be careful . . . We may have t' use it again.'

Removing a razor blade from under his mattress, Rodgers went towards the basin and meticulously sliced open a tampon. With the precision of a watchmaker, he removed a tiny role of paper.

'Get the eye-glass,' he told Nolan.

It was left to Brendan to decipher the tiny lettering on the note while the others physically blocked the cell entrance and exchanged pleasantries with other inmates.

The minuscule lettering consisted of Gaelic words and phrases which would have been meaningless if found by prison staff.

Rodgers hid the tampon in a large fountain pen and waited patiently while Brendan read and re-read the note, stopping occasionally to gasp in amazement. When he'd finished, he rolled the note in a tiny ball and told Rodgers to swallow it.

'It was from the Belfast Brigade intelligence officer,' said Brendan, motioning to the others to join him. 'Kirkpatrick and McDonnell omitted a vital detail about their lives.'

Rodgers was about to interrupt but Brady placed a restraining hand on his shoulder, determined to hear the revelation.

'Oh, it's not about a film,' said Brendan, noticing Brady's gesture. 'This is something you'll all love.'

All eyes were on him but he was slow to satisfy their curiosity.

'I wonder what else they're hiding from us.'

He seemed to be in a world of his own. This was the Brendan they'd come to know. When he was intense there was trouble brewing.

Frustrated with his boss's vagueness, Rodgers muttered that he didn't like riddles.

'Just the note takers.' Brendan told Rodgers and Brady to remain. To Nolan he said, 'Keep an eye out. I want to know who our young friends talk to.' He indicated the lower end of the cell block where Michael and Stephen were housed.

It was the kind of morning only Belfast can provide, when clouds roll off Divis Mountain, reducing the light and leaving the dark-slated roofs awash with rain. Stephen was listening to the downpour as Brady and Nolan arrived. They began an impromptu weather forecast.

'Today it will be sunny,' announced Nolan.

'Everywhere but Belfast,' added Brady.

It was the brightest start to an interrogation session and Stephen stood up and shook their hands. They joked about prison food and made little attempt to conceal their distaste at having to question him.

'Is there anything you'd like t' tell us? It would cut out all the crap in these sessions.'

Brady's voice had a nasal tone and it was difficult to discern if his question concealed malice or was a genuine expression of how he felt.

Stephen looked like a witness who required clarification of the question.

'Is there anything in yer past, for instance, that you might have forgotten?'

Nolan recorded the question as well as Stephen's facial reactions.

'I'll ask that again.'

'No,' said Stephen in the belief that denial might lead Brady to unveil the background to the enquiry.

'You're sure there's nothing you've forgotten?' said Nolan, scribbling down his question.

Stephen pondered his recollection of the sessions with Brendan, hoping that something would lead him to grasp what they were getting at.

'You're lying to us.'

Brady pointed an accusing finger, then the palm of his hand smacked into Stephen's shoulder, sending him reeling against the wall.

'You're a fuckin' liar!'

Stephen sat upright and moved out of range of his adversary.

'I've told you everything I know.'

He looked at Nolan to ensure that his denial was included in the record.

'Is that so?' replied Brady sarcastically.

He began pacing up and down the cell like a barrister in a courtroom, his hands clasped behind his back.

'What about that little episode when you and McDonnell were sixteen?'

Shock spread from Stephen's dilated pupils into the growing redness of his cheeks, and his mouth fell open.

'You didn't tell us about that.' Brady stopped in front of him, his upper torso inclined forward.

'I'd forgotten about it.' Stephen tried desperately to be apologetic, keeping his voice lowered. 'I didn't really think it was important to you guys.'

Brady was clearly thrilled with the breakthrough and patted Nolan, alerting him to prepare for an important delivery.

'It wasn't important!' Brady was ready to press home what he saw as his advantage, his mouth tightly set. 'It wasn't important? Where the fuck have you been? I suppose it was just a distant memory, then, that you two were in the Fianna, that you used the cause to steal money from a shopkeeper . . . That one of you two fuckers hit that shopkeeper with a bottle, causin' him to need three stitches and nearly losin' an eye in the process . . . That you used your involvement in the IRA to threaten him, bringing our organisation into disrepute . . . not to mention, of course, the very unimportant little fact that the shopkeeper was sixty-four years old and the father of one of our operators . . . If it hadn't been for your age, the fact that both your mothers were widows and you two fuckwits were their only sons, we might not even be havin' this conversation today. You two boys were publicly tarred and feathered and expelled in disgrace from the republican movement. I would have thought that was something very important.'

'We were only kids.'

The explanation was not challenged. Brady motioned to him to continue talking.

'I know we were wrong and I've regretted it ever since. My mother paid back the money. I just wanted t' put it out of my mind and I didn't even think t' mention it.'

Brady derisively threw his hands in the air. 'That's not somethin' anybody can forget.' He looked at Nolan. 'Would you forget that?'

231

Nolan's expression said it all: he wasn't prepared to grace the question with an answer.

'What else have you forgotten?' Brady closed in on Stephen until their foreheads were touching.

'Nothing. '

'Now where have we heard that before?'

Stephen's hands tightened in a prayerful position and his bottom lip quivered as Brady's stale breath filled his nostrils.

'Were you ever interviewed by the RUC?'

Stephen sat back against the wall, fearing that at any moment he was going to be punched.

'I asked you about the RUC,' said Brady, with one knee on the bed and his right hand on Stephen's chest.

'Michael and me never told them who did the tarring.'

Brady backed off and winked at Nolan, his body obscuring the gesture.

'Who in the RUC talked to you?'

'I can't remember.'

Brady leapt across the cell and put his hands round Stephen's throat.

'You'd better remember . . . Your fuckin' ass is on the line.' He spat out the words. 'Don't for a minute think we can't deal with people in here.'

He released his grip, leaving his saliva on Stephen's face.

'I think he was called Green,' said Stephen, massaging the soreness in his neck. 'It was such a long time ago.'

Brady tapped Nolan on the shoulder and they left, each of them delivering a backward stare. Stephen looked a pitiful figure, clutching his neck while tears filled the corners of his eyes.

That's it; I'm fucked, he thought, wiping away the tears.

He was lying on his back, his face to the wall, when Michael arrived five minutes later.

'What the fuck did they do t' you?'

He turned Stephen over and looked directly into his eyes. 'Fuck them!'

Stephen mumbled that the cat was out of the bag.

Michael laughed. 'I paid the price for that.'

He playfully patted Stephen on the head.

'I told McCann about that this morning. For Christ's sake, everybody in the RA was at it in those days, but we got caught. I told him I didn't feel guilty about anythin'. Their hands aren't clean . . . What about Bloody Friday? I didn't kill innocent shoppers. Fuck them. Tell them nothin'.'

Stephen asked Michael if he had named the cops who'd interviewed them after they were punished by the IRA.

'I said it was some fat bastard with a moustache and if I could remember his name I'd tell them so that they could blow his fuckin' brains out.'

'Oh, shit.' Stephen cradled his head in his hands. 'I told Brady that one of the cops was called Green.'

'Fuck me.' Michael jumped off the bed. 'You stupid bastard.'

Stephen tried to calm him. 'Someone might hear you.'

For the first time in their shared history, Michael acted menacingly towards his friend.

'You'd better keep yer fuckin' mouth shut. If those bastards ever begin t' put two and two together, they'll get ten, and we'll be no more. Just tell me the warder in here who's gonna stop the Provos murdering two cop-killers . . . eh?'

'That's the whole fuckin' point. We're *not* cop-killers, so what the fuck are we doin' in here?'

'Talk about the fuckin' weather,' advised Michael, waving his hands in the air. 'If you tell them nothin', they know nothin'. If they'd anythin' on us we'd have known about it on day one. Your problem . . .' He poked a finger into Stephen's chest. 'Your problem is that y' feel guilty about things. I don't give a shit. I intend t' survive.'

'Who's put us in here? . . . Can't be Bradford – he's dead. Green? Knowing that fucker, that's a possibility . . . but he knows we're not shooters and we wouldn't have had the clout to pull off a job like that.'

'So what's your fuckin' problem, Einstein? Sure, didn't Milner tell us it was Green?'

Stephen muttered, 'Our problem, dickhead, is that we have to figure out who's pullin' the strings here. Why would Milner

233

and Johnston take the risk of puttin' us in here with the Provos and risk blowin' our cover just to allow Green to screw us out of spite? Let's just say it's not Green, and this is not another of Johnston's fuckin' dress rehearsals for somethin', then who's put us in here, and why?'

'OK, just to satisfy you . . . Let's say it's Johnston . . . Then maybe he wants to know about the Provo organisation in the prison.'

'Don't be fuckin' stupid,' said Stephen. 'It's the guys on the outside they want to know about . . . What the fuck can these guys in here do? They're no threat. Like us they're behind bars.'

'In the meantime – and until such time as your wonderful brain figures it out – I suggest you just keep yer mouth shut,' hissed Michael.

Twenty yards along the block, Brendan McCann and his team analysed the session notes and reached a unanimous conclusion that the interrogation should continue.

'Leave Kirkpatrick to sweat,' recommended Rodgers.

Brendan expressed the view that there was a tiny aperture in the boys' armour. 'They lied,' he added, 'and that's enough for me to think they may be lyin' about other things. McDonnell's the prime mover, and you have to ask: why is he not frightened of us?'

He waited for a reaction.

'Because he's got backers.' The other three spoke in unison, and laughed.

Brendan sat silently composing his thoughts. When he spoke, his voice was controlled and malevolent. 'We're gonna get nothin' from McDonnell, so turn up the pressure on Kirkpatrick. Maybe they were framed or maybe they're a plant. My gut instinct is that we're on to somethin'.'

Putting his right forefinger to his temple, Brendan grinned as if a brilliant idea had suddenly struck him.

'Get me old man Quinn . . . He was in the visiting-room

the other day ... And check with some of the lads in the wing to see if they know of Green.'

Forty-eight hours passed. Stephen was just beginning to think his troubles were over when Rodgers, Brady and Nolan arrived and frogmarched him to Brendan's cell.

'Take it easy.' Brendan gestured to Rodgers's tight grip on Stephen's jacket collar.

Stephen accepted an invitation to sit on the lower bunk, while Nolan and Brady stood in the doorway to cloak the proceedings.

'We know a lot about you,' said Brendan in a quiet and less threatening manner. 'Take that old man who visited you ... He was once like us but now I hear he's a turncoat. That's not the company you should be keepin'.'

Springing to Jimmy's defence, Stephen exclaimed, 'He's just an eccentric ... He's never harmed anyone ... He's an innocent.'

Brendan dismissed the explanation with a wave of his hand. 'I might have said that about you, Kirkpatrick. Maybe we'll have t' find out more about Carson and also your girlfriend.'

In an instant Stephen was on his feet but found himself blocked by Rodgers.

'Think carefully about that,' said Brendan.

Stephen backed out of the cell, and Brady and Nolan stood aside to let him pass.

'You wouldn't touch the old man ... would you?' Brady enquired.

Brendan smiled. 'Of course not. Quinn says he's a nutter.'

'And what about his girlfriend?' asked Nolan.

'Jesus, what do you think I am?' Brendan was annoyed by the questions.

'What's the line on Carson?'

At first, Brendan stared at Rodgers and appeared reluctant to answer.

'He was involved in the late thirties campaign,' Brendan began. A sadness crept into his voice. 'Some people in the movement say he was the guy who planted the bomb in Coventry in '39 and that he was never the same after that.'

'Was that the bicycle bomb that killed shoppers?'

Brendan nodded. 'According to Quinn, Carson was interned here in the Crum during the war, and his mother died when he was inside, and his old man was killed on D-Day. There's no way I'd harm that old fella. Quinn says he was one of the best operators. As for the Coventry thing . . . nobody knows the truth.'

Stephen considered telling Michael about his ordeal but rejected the notion, believing his friend would not be concerned about the welfare of either Jimmy or Bernadette. For two days he sat in his cell racked with worry and a growing fear that his actions could lead to violence against those he loved most in the world.

Michael paid him three brief visits and spent the rest of the time parading along the block, searching for people willing to listen to his fanciful yarns. Occasionally, members of Brendan's team walked by, staring into the cell and thus increasing his sense of fear and isolation.

Hour by hour he examined the options open to him; during the night he cried, his head buried in his pillow to hide the sounds of his distress. The prospect of telling the Governor about his plight was not appealing, since it was unlikely anyone would have sympathy for someone charged with the murder of a policeman or believe that he was an agent for Special Branch and British intelligence. Michael's advice to say nothing was sensible but it had worked only for him.

If he was going to protect Jimmy and Bernadette, the only course open was to strike a deal with the IRA. He'd seen them grant immunity to informers and parade them before the press and television cameras. Maybe he could bring off a deal that would also grant him and Michael immunity. The raging inner debate inexorably moved towards a belief that Milner had abandoned them and that a deal with the IRA was the best – even only – option. Without Milner, he faced the possibility of life in prison with the IRA waiting for him to make one mistake: that would be fatal. Working with Special Branch and the British, he'd learned that wheeling and dealing was part of the game. He knew something the IRA wanted. He knew about Milner and Johnston and the bombs in Dublin that had been blamed on the Provos. That information, he concluded, had to be worth a lot and despite Michael's wishes it might just save their lives.

It was mid-morning when he nervously peered round the entrance to Brendan's cell. Putting aside a book, the IRA commander swung his legs off the bed and patted the top bunk to alert Rodgers that they had company.

'Come in.'

The invitation was friendly, and Stephen took two paces into the cell, waiting to be told where to sit.

Brendan got up and, taking him by the arm, led him to a wooden chair in the corner of the cell. Rodgers jumped off his bunk and took up position in the doorway, his eyes trained on the block.

'I need t' talk t' you,' Stephen began. 'I don't know where t' start . . . If I tell you the truth, will you promise me y' won't do anythin' to Bernadette or Jimmy?'

'People on the outside won't be touched if they're not involved . . . Depending on what you have t' say . . . if it's of value to the republican movement, you won't be harmed.'

'What about Michael?'

'McDonnell's a separate issue . . . We'll deal with that later.'

There was an embarrassed silence while Rodgers went to fetch Nolan and Brady, who were given the task of taking notes. They all huddled round Stephen, who found himself centre stage as he began retracing his steps to the day he was tarred and feathered.

His voice cracked and his hands shook when he recalled the humiliation of being tied to a lamp-post and doused with hot tar and a bag of feathers. He had been a bizarre spectacle for a crowd of teenagers who had spat on him and jeered. It had taken three days of medical care to remove the tar from his hair and skin before he was released into police custody. In Andersonstown police station he had been confronted by Green and Bradford.

As the story unfolded, Brendan shielded his face with his hands and the others breathed quietly, each of them intrigued.

'Green and Bradford told us that sooner or later the IRA would kill us, and Green threatened t' leak it that we were Special Branch informers, and that would surely get us killed.'

Stephen paused.

'Go on.'

' "Work for us or you're fucked" – that's what Bradford said. "We're the only people who can protect you." We . . . Michael and me . . . were scared shitless and decided t' go along with them. It wasn't just the money . . . They said they'd keep us protected. Sometimes Michael would feed them bogus information by pickin' names from the phone directory.'

Brendan looked up and smirked. 'Now I know how you came across the directory idea . . . Continue.'

Stephen described how the initial contact developed into meetings; the more they responded to demands for information, the deeper they were entrenched in a dirty world. 'They started having meetings with us . . . sometimes on the edge of Andytown, sometimes in East Belfast. At one of them Green threatened t' circulate photos of us with him and Bradford if we didn't come up with better information. We had nowhere to run.'

'What kind of information did you give them?' asked Brendan.

'Not much. They asked us t' watch out for people. They'd show us photos of people and we had to make notes on when they were seen in the area, or who they were seen talking to, or what bars they drank in. Sometimes we'd sit in bars and listen t' conversations and report back t' Green and Bradford.'

'Name some of the people.'

Stephen reeled off a list of names.

'Who the fuck are those guys?' Nolan asked Brendan.

'McConville was an operator in the late fifties . . . The others are nobodys – republican sympathisers and Gaelic footballers . . . That's how fuckin' good their intelligence is.'

As Stephen began to describe the shooting at Hannastown on the day of the Gaelic football match, Brendan sat upright and kicked Nolan, who was so captivated by the story that he'd neglected to record it in his notes.

The revelations were gradually leading to the handover of the two young agents to Johnston and Milner, but suddenly Brendan called a halt to the proceedings and recommended that they begin again the following morning.

'You've done well.'

Rodgers was ordered to accompany Stephen to his cell.

'Remember,' said Brendan, as Stephen was about to leave. 'Don't discuss this with your pal if you value your life and those of your friends on the outside.'

Brady and Nolan sat in silence, unable to come to terms with what they'd heard, and it was left to Rodgers to speak for them.

He strode into the cell like a man possessed. 'You can't be serious about giving him immunity.'

That was met with a typical reaction. Brendan scratched his chin in irritation before replying, 'You know the procedure. If they're guilty . . . they're goin' down.'

Brady asked why he had cut short the interrogation. Brendan looked exasperated. He didn't resent his team asking questions provided they weren't confrontational or accusatory.

'This is only the tip of the iceberg.'

'Why didn't you raise the issue of Bradford's death?'

'All in good time.'

Brendan looked tired, as if the quiet concentration he'd applied to Stephen's revelations had mentally exhausted him.

'I don't want t' panic Kirkpatrick . . . My instinct tells me to be careful . . . There's somethin' about all of this I don't understand . . . Ah, fuck it! You guys know what I mean. In one sense it all seems too easy and in another . . . I feel we may be on the edge of somethin'.'

239

He ambled out of the cell, knowing that at such moments he preferred to be alone. He stored the details of interrogations in his head: on some other occasion he might need them to help him understand or trap an informer agent. This enabled him to construct a portrait of his enemy – how he operated, how he ran agents and what ploys he used to target the IRA.

Stephen lay on his bunk, debating with himself whether he should ignore Brendan's advice and confide in Michael. Experience warned him it was not a wise course of action. His friend was headstrong and rarely deviated from an exclusive belief that everyone could be duped. Perhaps in the future he would be grateful that his life had been saved. Whatever the outcome, Bernadette and Jimmy would be spared, and they were more important to him than anyone, even Michael, his long-time friend. He and Michael had taken the risks, and he was increasingly of the opinion that it was their responsibility to face the consequences.

The next morning Michael was in a quarrelsome mood. He stood at the entrance to the cell and glared at Stephen.

'You keep yer mouth shut,' he said, and strode off.

Five minutes later he repeated his warning, and Stephen, not wishing to alarm him, nodded agreement.

'They're concentrating on you because they think you're weak.'

As Michael's footsteps echoed along the block, Stephen realised that for the first time in their relationship he was taking the initiative. He'd always allowed Michael to determine the course and pace of events but now this was his personal stand, and it would protect them both.

'Did you sleep well?'

Brendan's unshaven face appeared round the cell door, his eyelids heavy with lack of sleep.

'Is McDonnell giving you a hard time?'

Stephen replied, 'Oh, Michael's a regular complainer . . . He's been soundin' off about the prison regime, particularly the food.'

Brendan appeared satisfied with the explanation and summoned Rodgers, who took Stephen to Nolan's cell. The change of venue made Stephen apprehensive but after five minutes everyone was present and the previous day's session was resumed.

For two hours, the interview took the form of a question-and-answer routine, reviewing the disclosures about the Special Branch recruitment of the young men.

'When they took us t' Palace Barracks I smelled a rat.'

'Just relax, we're in no hurry . . . One thing we all have in here is time.' Brendan laughed. 'What happened when they took you to Palace Barracks?'

'They took us to this concrete building in the middle of the camp . . . There was no windows or anything . . . and it was called "the compound". When we went in through these big steel doors, we were taken down a corridor to the mess, where we met these two guys, Johnston and Milner. It was all very sociable and they were –'

'Wait a minute . . . wait a minute . . . Did you say Johnston?' asked Brendan, crouching forward.

'Yeah . . . Johnston and a guy called Milner.'

'What do you know about Johnston?'

'All I know is that he's a major . . . big guy . . . dresses in uniform. He seems t' run the show in the compound. The other one, Milner, he looks like a bank manager or somethin'. Doesn't say too much . . . very polite . . . Talks a bit like the Duke of Edinburgh. Johnston gave us a house on the base in a place called Harwell Terrace . . . even taught us t' fire guns. Michael thought it was great – the weapons, that is. I was useless at it . . . couldn't fire my way out of a wet paper bag.'

He went on to explain everything that had occurred with Milner and Johnston, including the meeting in the mess with Godfrey Phillips.

'Phillips pointed out IRA men in the mess and said they were top people.'

Brendan broke his silence. 'Names, Kirkpatrick, names.'

Stephen was pleased that there was a growing reliance on the quality of the information he was providing. He no longer felt threatened by those around him; they were absorbed with what he was saying. Occasionally he received an approving glance from Rodgers, who normally looked sombre and menacing.

'James Feeney, Seamus O'Brien . . . Danny McGovern, Davey Burke . . . Brian McAteer . . . Joe Casey.'

'Holy fuck!' Nolan jumped up. 'That's battalion staff.'

Brendan glared at him. 'Shut up!' Then he turned back to Stephen. 'Are you tellin' me you saw these guys in there . . . in that compound . . . you saw them with your own eyes?'

'Not all of them.'

'Who, then?'

'Feeney and O'Brien.'

'Where did you see them?'

'They were in the mess at the bar.'

'Did McDonnell see them?'

'Yeah . . . he was at the bar drinking with them but he doesn't know them.'

'Well, how do *you* know them?'

'Phillips told me who they were, but I recognised Feeney because he lives round the corner from me.'

'Did you speak to him?'

'No, I was sittin' in the corner with Phillips. He pointed Feeney and O'Brien out to me.'

'Did they see you there?'

'I'm sure they did . . . but there was no way I was gonna talk to those boys . . . I didn't know what I was into at that stage. As far as I was concerned the less I said the better. I wasn't that happy talkin' to Phillips. If he hadn't talked to me I wouldn't have talked to him.'

Patrick turned to Brendan. 'How do we know these really were Feeney and O'Brien?'

Brendan looked back at Stephen. 'Describe them!'

'Well, O'Brien's a small stocky fella with black hair, and Feeney's a bit taller and has a beard and glasses. Oh aye,

O'Brien has a stammer because Michael was takin' the piss out of him later on.'

Patrick nudged Brendan. 'Is that right?'

Brendan simply stared at him but his eyes confirmed the information was accurate. 'What about the other guys you mentioned?'

'I never saw them . . . It was Phillips who told me about them.'

'What was Phillips's role in all this?' asked Nolan. 'Is he British Army too?'

'Sorry, I thought I'd already told you . . . He's a leading UDA man.'

The team exchanged glances.

'You're telling us all this information was given to you by a UDA man?' said Rodgers, eyeing Stephen suspiciously.

'That's what he said he was . . . In fact he told me he was involved in the killin' of the UDA leader, Tommy Herron, and he was the guy in Dublin with Johnston when we saw them with the explosives.'

'Hold on!' shouted Nolan and Brendan in unison. 'What explosives?'

'I was about t' come t' that. It was when we were in Dublin with Johnston, and Phillips was there . . . and they had guns and explosives.'

'Where?'

'In a house at Appian Way.'

'What were they doing showin' them to you?'

'They weren't showin' them to us . . . We walked in on them. In fact Johnston nearly strangled me when I walked into the room and saw them.'

'When was that?'

'The day before the bombs went off in Dublin.'

'Shit! Jesus, I knew it! I fuckin' knew it!' yelled Rodgers.

'For Christ's sake, shut your mouth,' said Brendan, raising his hands to silence the others, who were also agitated.

The IRA commander's face reddened and his breathing quickened. 'Wait here. Rodgers! Come with me. You two stay put.' He got to his feet and left the cell with Rodgers.

'What's wrong?' asked Stephen.

'Don't worry about the boss,' Nolan assured him. 'He needs space to think.'

Brendan returned to his own cell.

'Have you any fuckin' idea how important this is?'

Rodgers shook his head.

'Christ, the things that come back t' haunt you . . . Remember the Four Square?'

It was beginning to dawn on Rodgers that Brendan had hidden part of his past from the team.

'The MRF . . . Johnston . . . McKee and Wright.'

Rodgers looked puzzled. 'I don't understand what you're gettin' at. I knew about the Four Square – everybody does . . . But what's the connection with this one?'

Brendan took a long deep breath. 'Just listen,' he advised, with a seriousness conveyed by a darkness in his eyes. 'Kevin McKee and Seamus Wright were two of our volunteers from West Belfast. Unknown to us, they were recruited by the MRF, just like Kirkpatrick and McDonnell. McKee was an arrogant little bugger and Wright was a Kirkpatrick type. I put tabs on Wright when one of our intelligence staff reported that he'd taken a holiday. I hauled him in and put on the pressure, and what did I get? He gave me McKee and the whole MRF set-up, Major Tim Johnston and the Four Square Laundry. Everything Kirkpatrick's told us, even the fact he was billeted in Harwell Terrace, fits with what I got from Seamus Wright. It's the same fuckin' Major Johnston.'

He lowered his voice. 'I had a problem, because McKee's family helped found this movement and Wright was well connected. I said, fuck it . . . this is too big to allow any interference . . . I had to act quickly because the military would realise I was holdin' two of their agents. McKee was hard t' crack but I did it . . . He asked for a deal and I said "Maybe". He told me how he strode around Palace Barracks with a pistol Johnston gave him. He loved the role . . . It made him feel important. I had McKee and Wright taken to South Armagh with orders to kill them. We moved against the Four Square Laundry. We wiped them out. We hit the MRF and we hit them hard within forty-eight hours . . . before they even knew what was happenin' or that we'd lifted their agents.'

Rodgers stood up, disturbing Brendan's concentration.

'What is it now?' said Brendan irritably.

'I just want t' know what happened to Wright and McKee.'

Brendan sighed. 'They were sent to two separate locations in the wilds of South Armagh. Wright was shot and buried, but the guys sent to do McKee chickened out. The bastards got t' like him – can you believe that? They couldn't pull the trigger. I sent two others, who finished him off.'

'So what are we sayin' here?'

'It all tallies . . . the way Kirkpatrick was recruited, the Dublin bombings, the whole MRF set-up. There's no way Kirkpatrick's lyin' . . . right down to the detail about where he was billeted in Palace Barracks . . . It all matches with McKee and Wright. As for Milner, he's probably Five or Six – it doesn't matter which . . . These fuckers are back with a vengeance. Jesus, they may as well be runnin' the Belfast Brigade! Just look at the names we've got . . . Feeney, O'Brien, and a lot of names of other guys Phillips gave him. That's serious penetration.'

'Could those two . . . Milner and Johnston . . . have ordered Kirkpatrick and McDonnell to do the hit on Bradford t' keep the Branch from meddling?'

'I don't think so . . . It doesn't measure up. Anyway Kirkpatrick told us he was no shooter and he said that without thinkin' about it.'

'So why are they in here? What would Milner and Johnston have to gain from lettin' them burn on this one?'

'Wait a minute,' said Brendan, turning his back on Rodgers. 'Let me think!'

The pair remained silent for several minutes while Brendan paced the cell.

'Right,' said Brendan. 'I think I've got it. Either the Branch have got it wrong and genuinely believed these guys did it, or Milner and Johnston have set them up to take the heat off them. If you ask me, these guys will never face trial.'

'Hold on a minute,' said Rodgers. 'Let's go back to Kirkpatrick and ask him if Milner or Johnston have made contact with them since their arrest. If they have, and Kirkpatrick gives us any indication that they're gonna get them out, then we'll know that your scenario about the MRF setting them up is the right one.'

Brendan smiled. 'Let's get back to our friend Kirkpatrick.'

Stephen looked up apprehensively as McCann and Rodgers returned.

'Tell us a bit more about your friends, Milner and Johnston,' said Brendan.

'What do you want t' know?'

'What kind of things did they ask you to do for them?'

'Nothin', really. I think we were still bein' trained. We didn't get a chance to get doin' anything before we were lifted and arrested for Bradford's killing.'

'What do you mean by training?' asked Brady. 'You mean with weapons?'

'Some chance . . . Those bastards Johnston and Milner could have trained the SS in Germany. They picked us up, hooded us and pretended they were IRA. They took us to the compound but I didn't know where I was. They beat the shit out of me and threatened to use electrodes on my balls. Then they took the hoods off and were all pallsy-wallsy, as if I should be grateful to the fuckers for doin' it. Those two bastards, Feeney and O'Brien, were there too. Feeney must have been the one askin' me questions because the rest of them are English and it was someone with a Belfast accent interrogating me. That's why I thought it was the IRA. It couldn't have been O'Brien 'cause, like I told you, he has a stammer. Milner said it was for our own good and that we had t' learn anti-interrogation techniques in case you guys ever lifted us.'

'How did McDonnell react to that?'

'You know him . . . He thought he was a fuckin' hard man after it. That's why you guys don't put the frighteners on him.'

'Have you heard from Milner and Johnston since your arrest?' asked Nolan, still taking notes.

'Not Johnston, but we saw Milner.'

'Where did you see him?'

'In the interrogation centre at Castlereagh.'

'What did he say?'

'He told us that Green had set us up out of spite because of our involvement with them . . . that things were complicated when the law became involved but to bide our time on remand here, and he and Johnston would get us out.'

Rodgers winked at Brendan. 'Did he say how or when?' he asked.

'No . . . only that he would get us out.'

'Hang on, Brendan, I've a cramp in my hand tryin' to get all this down,' said Nolan.

'OK, let's call it a day,' replied Brendan. 'We're gonna need time to analyse all this anyway. Take Stephen back to his cell.'

He turned to Stephen. 'For your own safety, say nothing about any of this to McDonnell . . . and I mean for your own safety.'

Back in Brendan's cell, his companions were clearly animated.

'You were right,' said Rodgers, patting him on the back.

'Yeah . . . maybe . . . but I need time to digest this. The big issue here is not just these guys but the Irish Republican Army. It's the level of penetration that worries me. We have t' get this information out to the Belfast Brigade. We know Kirkpatrick saw O'Brien and Feeney in there . . . and he knows them and who they are . . . So the other names have to be right.'

'Surely they could have fed him that,' argued Nolan. 'They could have given Kirkpatrick that description of those two guys. That wouldn't be hard to do.'

'I understand what you're sayin', Damien, but there are elements you don't know,' said Rodgers. 'I didn't know either until Brendan explained them to me earlier. A lot of what Kirkpatrick says matches up with what Brendan knows about the MRF.'

Rodgers described to Nolan and Brady how Brendan

cracked the Four Square Laundry operation, how McKee and Wright's experiences tallied with Kirkpatrick's account, and how Johnston was central to both episodes.

'Why not give Phillips to the UDA?' he suggested. 'That fucker was involved in the Dublin bombings.'

'That's hardly gonna turn the UDA against him.' Brady smirked.

'Knowing the loyalists,' said Rodgers, 'they're so close to the Brits, they might well have known about his involvement with the MRF.'

'No way!' shouted Brendan. 'The UDA think the Brits are on their side but they'd never tolerate their own people bein' run by them. Do you think the UDA would be happy that someone like Phillips is in the pocket of British military intelligence? We've a line to their commander in here. That's your job, Patrick. Don't tell them why . . . Let's hope they hit the bastard.'

Brendan was already preparing a report for the Belfast Brigade; considering the seriousness of Stephen's revelations, he decided to use a contact who had handled the previous message. Patrick Rodgers wanted them to focus on the connection between Bradford's death and the two young agents, but Brendan thought it would divert their attention from the central issue of the MRF penetration of the IRA.

'Anyway,' said Brendan cheekily, 'you've better things to think about . . . The chaplain, Father O'Hagan, has been askin' about you.'

Rodgers shifted uncomfortably and looked away.

'It seems we all like the confessional,' Brendan observed with a grin.

Formal worship was not part of Jimmy Carson's life, although each Sunday morning he listened to Mass on Radio Eireann while preparing his breakfast of tea and toast. Just as the priest was delivering a sermon on the importance of penance, Bernadette arrived to talk to him about Stephen.

'That's what gets me.' Jimmy pointed in desperation to the

radio and switched it off. 'Where in the Scriptures do you find Christ makin' people do penance?'

Bernadette was surprised by his preoccupation with religion but smiled sympathetically. According to Stephen, the old man was critical of the church and had chased priests from his door.

'You see, the problem is we complicate things. Christ never told these men in dog collars t' punish us when we ask forgiveness . . . The whole bloody thing's artificial.'

Knowing she might be rebuked, Bernadette asked why he bothered to listen to the service.

He cleared his throat and fingered the frayed edges of his shirt collar; she suspected it was a question he'd rather not answer.

'Maybe there's a wee bit of God somewhere in me.'

He paused, and she seized the opportunity to reveal the purpose of her visit.

'Stephen's sister Deirdre told me you'd been to the prison and I felt awful. I should have phoned Mrs Kirkpatrick but I've been havin' a terrible time at home. It's my mother . . . she doesn't want me to visit Stephen. It's not that she doesn't like him, you understand . . . It's just that she's worried that if I go there it'll draw attention to our family.'

Jimmy understood her dilemma and told her that Stephen didn't expect her or any member of his family to visit him. 'He'll be out soon, so don't worry yer little head.'

Abruptly he left the room and went upstairs, where he shuffled across bare floorboards, leaving her wondering if this was just another facet of his eccentricity.

Soon afterwards he returned carrying a small cardboard box, and sat opposite her with the box in his lap.

'When he gets out, you'll both have to leave here . . . Memories are long in Ireland . . . memories kill people, y' know.' He reached out and handed her the box. 'That'll help you make a new start.'

She slowly lifted the lid and stared in amazement at the contents.

'Saved it from my pension . . . There's close to five hundred quid in there.'

Closing the lid, she handed it to him. 'I can't take this.'

Angrily he pushed the box towards her. 'I knew some day he'd need it.'

Her eyes filled with tears, and she cradled the box, while Jimmy looked distressed and fumbled with the buttons of his cardigan. For several minutes they tried not to look at each other.

'Do y' think he's guilty?'

With a swift upward movement, his hands reached for the back of his head and the elastic band which kept his spectacles in place. Ponderously he began wiping the lenses against his knees, and by the time he had adjusted them on his face the lenses were so smudged his eyes were hardly visible.

'He's not the killin' type . . . and even if he was it wouldn't matter to me.'

Bernadette made a hurried apology for daring to question Stephen's innocence but Jimmy ignored it.

'He's got enemies – that's his problem. Somebody put him in there and that somebody has clout.'

In a faltering tone she revealed her worries about her boyfriend. 'Even before Stephen went to prison, I'd been frightened t' question him about his life . . . all those stories about business scams and gambling.'

The cat came to her rescue just as she was about to cry. Billy strolled out of the kitchen, his tail erect, and sniffed the box. She laughed, and Jimmy sat back in the chair, his eyes on the ceiling.

'Gambling.'

He paused, and reached for his favourite book.

'Page 89.'

Bernadette was stroking Billy and failed to notice the old man shutting the book with a sigh of finality.

'Our society is all about gambling . . . games of chance. It's *ludique*, that's what it surely is . . . Everybody wants to win. Just listen to the wireless – quizzes, quizzes, quizzes . . . people screamin' like idiots. And the postman, he's shovin'

all that shite through my door about this offer and that offer
. . . it's shite . . .'

He apologised for using strong language but needn't have
bothered. Provo and Billy were competing for Bernadette's
affections. The dog's nose was in her lap and Billy was perched
on the back of the chair with his paws on her shoulder.

'People are obsessed . . . everybody wants to win. The
whole world's at it. The society's *ludique* but the English don't
have that word . . . I call it American soup and we're all
eatin' it.'

Concerned that he had no audience he slammed the book
down.

'I'm awfully sorry,' said Bernadette, smiling and indicating
the dog and cat. 'You were talking about ludo . . .'

Her smile melted his anger. Jimmy's thoughts moved on
and he began talking about his trip to the prison.

'There was neither sight nor sound of Michael.'

Bernadette blurted out, 'I blame Michael for all of this . . .
Stephen wound never have got into trouble if it wasn't for
him. Forgive me for sayin' it but he's a bad bastard. My dad
says they should put him where the crows won't shit on him.'

Jimmy was visibly shocked by the stark contrast with her
normally placid demeanour, suddenly transformed by her
furious use of coarse language.

Equally surprised and embarrassed, she looked away, giving him the opportunity to take to his imaginary pulpit.

'There are no bastards in these islands . . . In Europe everybody has rights, even the village idiot. Bouan says each of us
brings our little stone t' the edifice. Each of us has somethin'
the others don't have. Y' see, we all contribute in some way
t' society, and that makes us equal . . . but it also means we
have responsibility. He calls it complementarity.'

'Is that like flatterin' somebody? Like telling them they're
the greatest thing since sliced bread?'

Clearly upset by her failure to grasp the concept, he sighed
and scratched his head. 'Complementarity means equality
with responsibility, and the hard men don't understand that.
They think *their* stones are more important than *ours*. They

just don't get it ... When y' put yer stone at the edifice y' have a responsibility. All these joyriders and people demandin' money at my door, they're not puttin' stones at the edifice, they're takin' stones out of it ... the whole bloody world's crumblin' because people are too concerned with their individual rights. They don't give a shite about their responsibility to me and everybody else in society.'

Bernadette argued, 'But the young lads in our neighbourhood live in a war zone ... It's only to be expected that they'll take to crime.'

'That's no excuse,' said Jimmy with a gesture of annoyance. 'Those young lads have a lot more than I had when I grew up in this city. People are always at war ... fightin' the bureaucrats or each other ... Violence has always been in the air and it's not an excuse.'

Bernadette was tiring of a debate she couldn't win and got to her feet, announcing that she was expected home after midday to make lunch for her parents. It was welcome news for Jimmy, who felt uncomfortable in the presence of women.

At the door he told her to wait while he went in search of a plastic bag to conceal the cardboard box.

'Don't want people t' think we've a bomb factory in here.'

She was walking towards the garden gate when he shouted a warning:

'Mind the nettles.'

Bernadette looked at the path but there were no nettles.

Turning towards the house, she half expected him to explain the warning but the front door was shut.

13

'Get that operator in here . . . now.'

'And keep that OOB in place for twenty-four hours.'

Sergeant Dawson and several other soldiers watched as Jim Johnston traced the OOB zone on the map with his right index finger to indicate the Falls and Andersonstown areas.

'I want the Provos to feel comfortable. Alert our people on the ground to maintain low-key surveillance on the club near Casement Park. I want no compromise of the OOB. Is that understood?'

The major walked across to where Richard Milner was studying a batch of telex messages. A telex operator came up to him, to complain that he had stomach-ache and had been to see the doctor.

'I don't care if you need surgery . . . Stay at that machine.'

The operator nodded, and nervously edged his way past Richard, who handed Johnston a message.

Johnston read it and grabbed Richard's arm.

'It's begun . . . McCann has finally taken the bait.' He could scarcely contain his excitement.

Both men retired to the anteroom.

'As we anticipated,' said Richard, 'Kirkpatrick has cracked and gone running to the Provos for cover.'

'If anyone was going to break him it was McCann.'

Richard sat down on a chair and, leaning back, uncharacteristically rested his feet on top of Johnston's desk. 'That set-up in Dublin with the explosives was a good ploy. Kirkpatrick would have told Brendan McCann that he saw you and Phillips with the explosives. Whether or not Kirkpatrick believed you were up to something, it would serve to convince

McCann that the MRF is back in business, and that you were running loyalist agents for the Dublin bombing. McCann should also conclude that if Phillips is genuinely an MRF agent so are Feeney and O'Brien. I think it was a good idea to ensure that Kirkpatrick saw Feeney and O'Brien in the mess . . . he should be able to describe them accurately to McCann, who knows them personally.'

'I must admit, Richard, I was concerned about your choice of Kirkpatrick and McDonnell but you were absolutely right – your judgement was exact . . . Kirkpatrick's allegiance was always to his own life, his own identity – and he was going to crack. The fact that McDonnell has given them nothing has reinforced McCann's view that he's on to something big . . . Christ, we're finally on track.'

Richard tried to curb Johnston's enthusiasm by handing him a communiqué from MRF agents on the ground in West Belfast.

Johnston read it and nodded. 'Don't worry about that: they abducted Feeney and O'Brien during the night. That's not a problem . . . They were well briefed, and they can take punishment – their lives depend on it. What's more important here, and what lets me know they've taken the bait, is that – on the basis of what Phillips said to Stephen in the mess that night – McCann has got word out to pick up all the so-called agents Kirkpatrick named. They've been lifting and interrogating their own people all over the city.' Johnston laughed. 'And all on the word of McCann and a nonentity called Stephen Kirkpatrick. Give it time.'

'What about Phillips?' Richard asked him.

Johnston took a telex message from his desk and pointed to a reference to the UDA agent. 'Like Feeney and O'Brien, I've put him out in the open just in case the loyalists take the bait, but it's unlikely they would lift him on McCann's say-so.'

'Are you absolutely sure that it's wise to declare part of West Belfast out of bounds to the regular army? You don't think it could lead the IRA to believe the army are planning a covert operation? Surely the IRA will suspect we're up to something if we're not seen to be maintaining a presence on the ground in that area?'

'No, Richard . . . They'll be happy to have the area to themselves – and too busy to recognise the subtlety of our plans. I want them to feel they can tear themselves apart and have their brigade meetings without fear of discovery. It's the only way to ensure the momentum builds nicely.'

Richard cautioned against euphoria at such an early stage in the operation. 'Look, Tim . . . We must not prolong this. Irrespective of your confidence in Feeney and O'Brien, they are human and have a breaking-point. I know you've trained them well in anti-interrogation techniques but we should leave nothing to chance. The next phase must begin tonight. If you need me, I'll be in the prison from mid-afternoon – in Wainwright's office.'

Ross Place was a cul-de-sac of local-authority housing in the shadow of the main stand of Casement Park. It was the kind of street where a strange dog was likely to be scrutinised from behind lace curtains; but there were no prying eyes when residents quietly left their homes under the watchful eyes of two groups of armed IRA men. A short time later a funereal procession of black London-type taxis deposited the Belfast Brigade staff outside number 7. In the event of the arrival of a military patrol, there was sufficient firepower to create a diversion that would enable the leadership to flee to safety.

The brigade officers, men hardened and shaped by warfare, filed silently into the living-room of the house. The youngest was Barry Devine, a man of twenty-eight who had joined the organisation when the barricades shut out the external world in the early 1970s, causing the genesis of a new IRA. Republicanism had become his way of life when the British Army smashed the barricades and curfewed the Lower Falls in July of 1970. 'If we're all the enemy,' he had told his mother, 'then I need something to help me fight back.'

His role as senior intelligence co-ordinator in the Belfast Brigade brought him into close contact with Brendan

McCann and they had developed a mutual respect. Unlike his older colleagues in the leadership, Devine supported McCann's contention that the struggle would never be won by military means alone; there had to be a blending of politics and the gun. Devine recalled McCann's meeting with the Army Council in Dublin shortly before his arrest and remembered the enmity between Brendan and those members of the Council who were also leaders of the Belfast Brigade. His anticipation of an attack on McCann had been quickly realised.

'McCann had better be right.'

The Brigade Commander, Tom Foley, had spoken, and the room fell silent.

Foley was known as a man of few words, yet no one dared speak until he had made it clear that he had nothing else to say. Devine regarded him as crude, and capable only of promoting orthodox republican doctrine.

His deputy, 'Digger' Skillen, was a thuggish former book-maker's assistant, who was often heard to say that 'The Prods should be taught a lesson.' The war would be over, he argued, if the Brits offered what he called 'reasonable concessions'.

It was Foley and Skillen who were detested by Brendan McCann as 'armchair generals'. These were the men who had lost the 1950s border campaign; all they had ever known was defeat. According to Brendan, they believed that the Prot-estants were the softer target, and therefore would capitulate to the British.

Barry Devine rarely contradicted his superiors, reckoning that if he kept his own counsel he would eventually see them off.

'We're beatin' confessions out of our best people on McCann's say-so . . . I think it's fuckin' madness,' bellowed Skillen.

Skillen regarded McCann as a dangerous upstart but was unable to undermine him because of his success in the under-cover war, particularly his flushing out of British agents within the IRA. 'Digger' Skillen had been nicknamed for his skill in driving heavy digging machinery on building sites; much to his annoyance, McCann claimed Skillen had been given the nickname because he was a gravedigger.

'The battalions will be demoralised if this continues,' screamed Digger.

Devine cautioned against rushing to judgement. 'We all know that Brendan's an experienced interrogator. He's hardly given to flights of fancy.'

Foley didn't seem impressed, and that spurred Digger to continue his tirade.

'There are too many Young Turks around McCann . . . and they think they know more than us.'

There were murmurs of approval. Devine felt he had little choice but to defend Brendan.

'This isn't about personalities. We all know how the MRF recruits guys like Kirkpatrick. Just look back at Wright and –'

He swallowed hard and paused, realising that if he mentioned McKee, the other MRF agent executed on Brendan's orders, he would be raising a subject that would lead to a clash with the dead informer's uncle.

James McKee was the Brigade Quartermaster, a veteran of the campaigns of the 1940s and 1950s. The execution of his nephew as a British Army agent was a topic never raised in his company.

McKee stared at Devine as if the damage were already done. 'What if McCann is wrong? What are we going to say to all our people who are now being treated as agents and informers?'

He glared at Devine, who decided it was unwise to reply. It was obvious McKee was looking for a quarrel.

'If McCann has got it wrong, we'll have beaten the shit out of some of our best people . . . if not executed them. Most of them are denying treason . . . The others are saying what they think we want to hear to save themselves punishment. What the fuck is this going t' do for morale if McCann's been conned? For Christ's sake, Kirkpatrick and McDonnell are nobodies . . . You put the screws on kids like that and they'll tell you what y' want t' hear.'

Foley unbuttoned his tweed jacket and removed a pipe and

tobacco pouch from an inside pocket. No one spoke as he rolled tobacco in the palm of one hand and meticulously packed it into the bowl of the pipe. Three deep draws, and smoke curled upwards along the cracks in the ceiling.

'Digger and James are right.'

Smoke came from both ends of the pipe as he held it between his teeth, his lips curling inwards.

'McCann likes conspiracies.'

In his effort to keep the pipe steady, the words sounded like an elongated 'S'.

Why the fuck doesn't he just hold the pipe in his hand like any normal person? thought Devine. But Foley was busy rubbing his hands up and down his thighs which pained him with arthritis.

'Of course he cracked the Four Square, but he thinks the Brits have a hand in everything.'

'Give it another twenty-four hours,' said McKee begrudgingly. 'If he's got it wrong we court-martial him.' This was McKee's *quid pro quo* for his offer of extra time.

Devine argued that demotion was the only defensible punishment considering Brendan's contribution to the struggle.

That pleased Digger, who preferred to see Brendan suffer the indignity of being reduced to volunteer status rather than a quick death.

'That'll be a lesson to all these young hotheads who think he's God's gift to the movement,' said Digger, looking to Foley for support.

'It's done.' Foley removed the pipe from his mouth, displaying two rows of teeth chipped and stained by the pipe stem. 'As usual the Prods are havin' a go at us and everybody's askin', "Where are the IRA?" Remember what happened in '69? We didn't have the guns to defend our own people. Women and children were being burned out of their houses around here and everybody wanted to know where the IRA was. There were no fuckin' guns, because people were too interested in politics. Well, we now have the guns, so let's use them. We can't fall into the '69 trap . . . and as I see it we're bein' sidetracked by this McCann business.'

'Surely the real enemy is the Brits.'

Devine was playing with fire, and he knew it as Foley angrily pointed the pipe stem in his direction.

'The Brits want a deal, and that makes the Prods the real target.' Foley stood up and with an authoritative wave of his hand ended the meeting. 'Twenty-four hours . . . same venue.'

Watched attentively by the armed men positioned in the adjoining houses, the brigade leaders filed into the street towards waiting transport.

Five hours later, Devine was summoned to a meeting in the back room of a pub in the Lower Falls and found himself in the company of the Belfast Brigade leaders, Tom Foley, James McKee and Digger Skillen. Three armed men stood at the entrance to the room.

'These guys' – Skillen indicated the men – 'are from the three battalions in the city. They say the situation is gettin' out of control. There's fuckin' paranoia in the ranks . . . people bein' picked up and interrogated, just because they've had a loose connection with all these people mentioned by McCann.'

McKee banged his pint of Guinness on the table, spilling some of the contents. 'People are making confessions and blaming half the fucking staff . . . It's a wonder *we* haven't been named as agents.' He looked hard at Devine. 'You're our brigade intelligence co-ordinator . . . At brigade level that makes you senior to McCann, who was head of internal security – so it's up to you to sort out this mess.'

'Given Brendan's history and expertise,' said Devine, 'it's difficult to make a judgement until all the facts are clear. He's not the kind of guy to make snap judgements – he always assesses the facts.'

Foley's face was red with anger. 'I'll give you some fucking facts. We started with a list of names supplied by McCann, and now we've an interrogation craze. It's a fucking wonder they haven't named the whole Army Council as a bunch of touts. Get word to McCann that this stops in twenty-four hours unless he's got something more to back it up.'

The Assistant Governor's office in Crumlin Road prison was a small communications centre with radio equipment linking it to the MRF Ops Room and MI5 headquarters in London. Richard Milner was sitting behind the desk drinking coffee while Assistant Governor Wainwright briefed a senior warder.

'Create an altercation with McDonnell,' advised Wainwright, laying a hand on the warder's shoulder. 'That shouldn't be too difficult! Make it look good, and have him here within the hour. Insult his mother . . . and if that doesn't work give him a good kick in the balls.' The last few words were whispered to the warder as he left the office.

Wainwright walked towards the desk and sat down opposite Milner. 'You realise what you're asking me to do could backfire?'

Richard Milner sensed that Wainwright wanted him to compliment him on his co-operation. 'Within twelve months you'll be sitting comfortably in the Home Office and this will be forgotten.'

The promise of a desk job in London spurred Wainwright to congratulate Richard on his astute knowledge of the workings of the prison and to promise that everything would be done to ensure their plan worked smoothly.

'As you know,' said Wainwright, impressed by Richard's willingness to involve him in the operation, 'I was confident you and I could work this out. My only concern was that your man on the inside might leave us with a corpse, and none of us wants an inquiry.'

Wiping his mouth with a pocket handkerchief, Richard thanked him for the coffee. 'You have no need to be concerned. It's been taken care of. Our man has been well briefed. In the event that he slices too deeply . . . it will simply highlight the daily risks faced by your prison staff.'

'What's in it for him?'

'His son is on a drugs charge, and we will have it dropped.

As for him, he can serve out his time here and you will ensure that he is protected, though I doubt if anyone will connect him with us when this is over.'

There were sounds of a scuffle outside the door and they both got to their feet. True to form, Michael had attacked the warder for describing his mother as a whore and it had taken two other prison staff to remove him, kicking and screaming, from his cell to Wainwright's office. The door flew open and Michael was flung into the room, tumbling on to the carpet.

Richard extended a hand towards him.

'Fuck you,' said Michael, refusing the handshake and scrambling to his feet. 'You're some fuckin' friend!'

With a sideways glance, Richard made it clear that he wanted Wainwright to leave. Michael walked to a sofa, sat down and flourished two fingers at the Assistant Governor, who glared at him as he left.

Richard paced up and down, allowing Michael's temper to cool. 'I can have you out of here in forty-eight hours with all charges dropped, but that will depend on you.' He sat down beside Michael.

'Name yer price . . . We're dead meat! . . . Stephen's singin' like a bird. He can't hold his own water. That fucker McCann has it in for us. As sure as fate he'll have us if you don't get us out.'

'I pull the strings, not the IRA – is that clear?' His tone was crisp and severe.

Michael lowered his eyes, afraid the offer of help might be withdrawn. 'Whatever you say.' The resignation in his voice betrayed the strain he was under.

'It's like this, Michael.' Richard spoke gently. 'I can only help if you do as I advise. You must get to Stephen first thing tomorrow morning . . . not before. Do you understand? Not before. He must go to Brendan McCann and deny everything.'

'Deny what?'

'Deny everything he's told them . . . and I mean *everything*.'

'But he's only told them about us bein' tarred and feathered, and McCann knew that anyway.'

'Don't ask questions at this stage. It's in your interests to do exactly as I tell you and *only* as I tell you. Your life is on the line. If Stephen does what he's told, you will both be released and have nothing to fear.'

Michael laughed derisively. 'I'm gettin' the impression that Stephen's been squealin'.'

'That's of no consequence. What he's said to McCann doesn't compromise you.'

'He's supposed to be my mate.'

'If you want to see the outside world, stop asking questions ... Just do as you're told. If not, I won't be able to help either of you and you'll both be left to deal with McCann. You must emphasise that to Stephen, and stress the fact that we know McCann is planning to have you both killed in here.'

Richard made to leave.

'Hold on.' Michael grabbed at him. 'Whatever you say. But what about the Provos on the outside? I suppose they're gonna give us the Nobel Peace Prize?'

'*We* will deal with McCann and his cronies. It's really up to you. Your choice is to rot or die in here, or to trust me. I gave you my word, and I'm here for you. McCann is planning to kill you both and we have that on the best authority. You have my guarantee that once outside the prison you will be safe.'

Michael smiled for the first time since he had entered the room, and Richard knew he was getting through to him.

'So all he has t' do is deny everything he's told them – it's that simple?'

Richard nodded, and Michael leapt to his feet.

'There's no catch? He just does that?'

Richard stood up and placed a hand on his shoulder. 'When he goes to see McCann, he must say the following – remember this carefully: "I've told you a pack of lies. I was told to tell you all those things. I don't know if they're true." He must not elaborate.'

Confusion was written all over Michael's face. 'Jesus, what did he tell them?'

'Listen carefully, Michael. We have our own means of protecting you both. Don't question what I say, just do it ...

It's for your own good. What you don't know you can't be hurt by. Remember one thing: the only way you two will get out of here alive is with our help. Take it or leave it.'

'I'm with you all the way.'

'Just one other thing.' Richard gripped his arm. 'When Stephen goes to see McCann, you go to the end of the block. The warder who gave you a hard time today will be there. Tell him Stephen is doing what's he told. When Stephen returns from the meeting with McCann, let the warder know. Just say, "He's done it" or "He hasn't done it".'

It was the following morning, and Michael watched Brendan pacing in and out of his cell.

Choosing an opportune moment, Michael slipped unnoticed into his friend's cell, motioning to him to be quiet and to listen carefully. Taking care not to leave out any detail, he described the fight with the warders and explained how that was a ruse to enable him to be taken to Wainwright's office, where Milner was waiting for him.

'Even Wainwright's in Milner's pocket, and so are all the fuckin' screws. Milner says he knows for a fact that McCann's plannin' t' kill us. He's just playin' cat and mouse with you. Those bastards can't be trusted. After what we did in the Fianna, they'll never trust us . . . that's the way they are. Milner's our only way out of here . . . Please believe me.' He looked dejected, most unlike his usual arrogant self.

'Please, Stephen . . . it's our only chance. We've got very little time. Milner says McCann is plannin' t' kill us.'

Stephen buried his head in his hands and Michael sat beside him. They remained like that for several minutes while Stephen reflected on the risks to Bernadette and Jimmy if he accepted Milner's offer.

'What about other people around our lives? The IRA might target them.'

Michael retorted, 'Now you're bein' selfish.'

'That's choice, comin' from you.' Stephen looked into his eyes. 'You've only ever considered yourself.'

Michael chose not to retaliate, and continued his attempt at calm persuasion. 'If Milner says he'll deal with McCann, I'm willin' t' believe him. For Christ's sake, look at the people he and Johnston control within the Provos . . . They're runnin' some of their top brass on the outside like Feeney and O'Brien, so that's probably how Milner knows McCann is plannin' t' kill us. McCann's in here t' stay.'

It was difficult to challenge that argument. Stephen silently listened to his friend and tried to work out a response. The prospect of freedom and no retaliation was hard to ignore. Michael repeated Richard's warning that they'd rot or die if they refused his help. Fear of Brendan and the IRA surfaced, as Michael continued to chip away at Stephen's resolve. He was weak and terrified, and Michael knew it.

'We've nowhere to run in this place . . . nowhere t' hide . . . Milner is offerin' t' change all of that . . . Our lives are in your hands.' Michael knew it was blackmail and that his friend was easily swayed by emotional argument. 'If you walk away from this and I'm killed, it's somethin' you'll have t' live with. My blood will be on your hands, and God knows who else will suffer. In McCann's clutches we're his. He can kill us and brand us as touts. With Milner we've a real chance.'

Placing his hands over his ears, Stephen tried to shut out his friend's entreaties, to allow himself time to clarify his own troubled thoughts.

'You want t' see Bernadette again, don't you?' added Michael. Then he sat back to watch his friend's reaction.

'OK.' Stephen got to his feet. 'This is the last time I'll listen to you. It's a question of the devil y' know . . . I'll go with the Milner plan, but may God look down on both of us if I'm wrong.'

Michael sprang from the bunk and threw his arms round him, then just as quickly withdrew when he'd established physical contact.

'What does Milner want us t' do?'

Michael repeated Milner's instructions.

'What if McCann doesn't believe me?' said Stephen after a short silence.

'Milner's the guy with all the answers. He must know what he's doin'. I don't know what you said to McCann and I don't want t' know, but Milner must know because he told me it was none of my fuckin' business.'

Stephen looked shocked.

'Maybe that'll convince you that somebody on the outside is feedin' Milner information about what's goin' on in here . . . and that could only have come from somebody high up in the IRA, close to McCann.'

Stephen sat down on his bunk, shocked by the terrible logic that his secret discussions with McCann were known to Milner. 'Right . . . I'll do it.'

Michael propelled him towards the cell door. 'Remember,' he stressed. 'Don't complicate things. Just say only what Milner said t' tell them. That everythin' was a pack of lies and you were told t' tell them all those things. He said, whatever you do, don't elaborate or you'll tie yerself up in knots . . . Keep it simple. Don't be scared of these fuckers. Just remember Milner is in control and he's gonna get us out of here.'

As he made his way to Brendan's cell, Stephen felt as if his brain would explode. His mouth was dry with fear and his body was telling him that it was unable to continue the short journey. Then Rodgers saw him and walked to meet him, guiding him to his boss.

Behind him, Michael was at the entrance to the block, talking in hushed tones to the warder who'd staged the fight with him the previous day. Their exchange lasted thirty seconds, after which Michael returned purposefully to Stephen's cell.

Meanwhile Stephen was standing in the lion's den, nervously waiting for Brendan to finish shaving.

'What is it, Kirkpatrick?' He sat on the bed wiping a residue of shaving foam from the base of his neck.

'I've a confession to make.'

Rodgers placed a chair behind Stephen, while Brendan sat poker-faced.

'Another one?'

'I've told you a pack of lies,' said Stephen, ignoring the offer to be seated.

Brendan's lower jaw dropped. Rodgers punched Stephen in the kidneys, sending him sprawling across the tiled floor with his head coming to rest against the toilet bowl.

'Hold it.'

Brendan placed himself between the victim and the attacker.

'What are you saying?'

Brendan stretched out his hand to assist him to his feet but Stephen decided it was safer to remain where he was.

'Johnston and Milner told me t' tell you all those things. I don't know if they're true.'

Brendan looked as if someone had smacked him in the face with a shovel. 'You mean all that stuff about Feeney and O'Brien is bullshit?'

Remembering Michael's advice, Stephen merely repeated: 'A pack of lies.'

Brendan appeared dumbfounded but there was no explosion of violence. Slowly, like a man in a trance, he backed towards the lower bunk and sat down.

'Don't fuckin' leave your cell, Kirkpatrick. Get him outa here.'

Stephen scrambled to his feet, and Rodgers grabbed him by the hair and pushed him out of the cell, finally giving him a kick in the rear as he left.

'You're a fuckin' dead man!'

Stephen hurried along the corridor, relieved to think that the solitude of his cell would give him the opportunity to get rid of the vomit that was rising in his throat.

As he entered his cell he found Michael sitting on his bunk.

'Did you do it?' whispered Michael.

Stephen just got out the word 'Yes', and Michael scurried out of the cell towards the entrance to the block, where the same warder stood watching his approach. Michael winked at him and nodded before retracing his steps to his own cell.

Minutes later a klaxon sounded. Inmates began running to

and fro along the block and the noise of rioting echoed through A Wing.

Stephen put a blanket over his shoulders and crawled into a corner of his cell.

'What the fuck's going on?' demanded Brendan, grabbing a fleeing prisoner and pinning him against the cell door.

'A warder's been attacked and all hell's broke loose.'

Rodgers emerged from a highly agitated group of inmates, out of breath and anxiously looking towards the entrance to the block where a fierce battle was in progress.

'Some fucker let a criminal from another wing on to our block. There's something afoot here . . . Criminals are not allowed in paramilitary wings like ours . . . Somebody's deliberately let him in. He sliced a warder's neck with the sharpened edge of a tin plate – nearly severed his jugular.'

'What the fuck is an ODC doing in our wing?' screamed Brendan.

'Lock down! . . . Lock down . . . Lock down . . .'

The unmistakable voice of the Assistant Governor signalled the arrival of lines of warders in riot gear with orders to lock down A Wing.

Within ten minutes every IRA prisoner was locked in his cell and Brendan was like a trapped animal, banging his hands against the metal surrounds of the upper bunk, where Rodgers lay with his head cradled in his hands.

'We'll have to find out who let the ODC in here . . . and his identity. Did anybody recognise him?' Brendan asked Rodgers.

'One of the boys said they thought he was a Catholic from Ardoyne doin' time for theft and burglary.' Rodgers added, 'Apparently he's a fuckin' nutter. There's no way he could have got in here without the help of a screw – unless he managed to get on to a cleaning detail, and even that would take connections.'

'I want the bastard when this is over. Why isn't the Governor here t' talk to me . . . It's standard procedure to talk to the commander of this wing in the event of a lock-down.'

'He's on leave. Wainwright's in charge. It's his patch now

and we all know what he's like. It could be like this for days.'

'I'll give Wainwright a fuckin' riot to remember,' said Brendan, kicking the cell door. 'And as for those two bastards down the way ... they're dead when this lock-down is lifted.'

Richard was pouring a Scotch when Wainwright peered round the office door and announced the arrival of Michael and Stephen.

'Nobody saw them leave the block. I'll lift the lock-down tomorrow morning. You lads,' he said, pointing at the young men, 'will be in solitary until the paperwork is completed.'

Shaking his hand, Richard thanked him and then courteously asked him to leave the room.

The drinks cabinet was open and Michael couldn't resist the temptation. By the time Wainwright had closed the door, Michael was in possession of a large whisky, while Stephen stood in the middle of the room ashen-faced.

Ignoring Michael, Richard took Stephen to a corner of the room. 'Stephen, you have done the right thing. In forty-eight hours you will be a free man. The charges against you both have been dropped . . . insufficient evidence, that sort of thing. No need to bother you with the detail now. Come and have a drink. You look as though you could use one.'

Michael was sitting behind the desk rotating in Wainwright's swivel-chair, glass in hand. 'Don't ya love it when a plan comes together?' He laughed, and raised the glass to his lips.

Handing Stephen a drink, Richard glared at Michael. 'You have your life. Consider yourself lucky.'

Michael almost choked, and some of the whisky spluttered over his chin. Then, with unaccustomed meekness, he slowly crossed the room and sat beside his friend.

*

In A Wing, Brendan spent the lock-down period analysing everything Stephen had told him. With a tedious revisiting of events, he asked Rodgers for his recollections of all the interrogation sessions.

They pored over the notes taken by Brady and Nolan, remarking on inconsistencies and moments when Stephen appeared to deliver unchallengeable truths.

'We can't hide this latest development from the brigade staff,' warned Rodgers. 'We'd be disobeying the rules.'

'It's that little fucker McDonnell,' yelled Brendan, tossing a notebook across the cell. 'He's got to Kirkpatrick, and somebody's got to McDonnell. When they lift this lock-down, we'll really put the screws on Kirkpatrick and we'll get the rest from McDonnell if we have to kill him doing it.'

'It's simple,' argued Rodgers. 'The brigade gave us twenty-four hours, and that's runnin' out while we sit here mullin' this over. The latest word from the Kesh is that they're turnin' people over . . . anybody ever connected with the names we gave them. It's not a question of what we know but what other people are willing t' believe. Like it or not, we have t' tell them that Kirkpatrick's retracted his confession.'

When the lock-down ended at seven the following morning, Nolan and Brady rushed into Brendan's cell.

'The bastards are nowhere to be found . . . The birds have flown!' they shouted.

Brendan brushed them aside and ran down the block, looking first in Stephen's cell, then in Michael's.

'It's a fuckin' nightmare.'

Brendan's voice could be heard halfway down the block. Other prisoners peered round the doors of their cells as he ran towards the three members of his team.

'We've been had.'

He turned to each of them, his face red with anger.

'Whatever way it cuts,' he added, walking towards the corner of his cell and staring at the wall, 'this is too big to hide.'

He continued to talk with his back to them. 'If it ever got out that we deliberately concealed Kirkpatrick's denial, we'd all be executed. Get the message out. If our courier refuses to take it, tell him I'll choke him with my bare hands.'

Turning towards Rodgers, he poked a finger at him. 'I want it out before morning. If the brigade thinks we've been stalling that'll fuck up everything we've worked for.'

He slumped on to his bunk and buried his face in his hands. 'Never underestimate the Brits . . . When they're on form, they're fuckin' brilliant . . . We've been well and truly stung.'

'What are you saying?' asked Nolan, visibly shocked and confused.

'He's sayin' we've been stitched up,' replied Rodgers, pushing Nolan and Brady out of the cell. 'Leave him alone. He needs time t' think.'

At 7 Ross Place a Belfast Brigade staff meeting was becoming a furious altercation, with Digger Skillen and James McKee hurling abuse at Barry Devine.

Tom Foley's calls for calm were ignored. In desperation, he pulled a pistol from a shoulder holster and slammed the butt against the edge of his chair. 'Shut the fuck up!'

That did the trick: silence descended on the room, though some of his staff shifted uneasily in their chairs as the pistol remained unholstered.

'It's simple. McCann was looking for conspiracies where there were none. We got a communication from him saying that Kirkpatrick has retracted his confession and has said he told him a pack of lies. McCann could have blown a deal we're planning with the Brits. We're on the verge of a ceasefire . . . and McCann's been causing all this fuckin' mayhem with this Kirkpatrick and McDonnell business. There's chaos in the ranks. His fuckin' reign's over. I've replaced him as commander at the Crum, and the interrogations are to be stopped immediately.'

Foley took out his pipe and pointed the stem at Barry Devine. 'You make the apologies to Feeney and the others.'

Devine nodded, and then asked what they intended to do about Kirkpatrick and McDonnell, adding, 'One of our people in the court service says they're gonna be released with all charges dropped. We should haul them in. Somebody's set up McCann . . . It's as obvious as hell.'

'Are you in McCann's pocket?' shouted Digger Skillen.

'Aye, what's your problem?' added James McKee.

Devine looked at Foley, hoping he'd resolve the issue, but McKee seized the opportunity to vent his hatred of Brendan.

'I lost a nephew, and I have t' live with that.' The bitterness in his voice was obvious to everyone in the room. 'But this time McCann is off the fucking wall. McDonnell and Kirkpatrick are nobodies. You have it from the horse's mouth . . . Kirkpatrick says he told a pack of lies – that he was told to say all those things. Now, if you want my opinion, McCann probably got him to say what he wanted t' hear.'

'Are you telling me those two wee bastards are clean?' exploded Devine. 'Somebody had to be pulling their strings.'

McKee punched the air in anger. 'Even if the Branch or the Brits got to them, they're not responsible for all the shit that's happened. We've beaten the crap out of some of our best people, and for what?'

Devine crossed the room and faced down McKee. 'For the fact that somebody, somewhere, used Kirkpatrick and McDonnell to stitch up McCann and discredit this organisation.'

'Bollocks!' shouted McKee. 'Weren't you the one who told us how brilliant McCann was, and –'

'Quiet!' Foley reasserted his authority as Brigade Commander. 'This isn't the time for more bloody argument. The fact is, if we shoot Kirkpatrick and McDonnell, we're saying McCann was right, and that means we should shoot Feeney, O'Brien and all the others. There are more important things to deal with here . . . like the Prods, and these talks with the Brits. Leave Kirkpatrick and McDonnell alone. They're not to be touched – and let that be known at battalion level. Sooner or later we'll find out who was running them, but now's not the time. Let's get on with the real business.'

Foley gestured towards Devine. 'I suggest you go and make your peace with Feeney, O'Brien, McConville and the other lads who were caught up in all this, and don't expect them to treat you like the prodigal son.'

As soon as Devine left the room, McKee turned to Foley. 'I've no love for McCann, as everybody knows, but there's no way I'm gonna convince my battalion commanders that Kirkpatrick and McDonnell can walk away scot-free. Somebody had to be running them. There's no way they were operating on their own initiative.'

'Do you think I'm bloody stupid?' said Foley, drawing on his pipe. 'McCann and his Merry Men would have challenged this leadership if they hadn't been put inside. If I know that, the Brits know it. They're currently negotiating a ceasefire with us. They want it and we want it. They know they can do business with us. There's no way McCann and his crowd would ever have accepted that. They'll never give up until there's a united Ireland, and we're all in our graves and there's damn-all left worth fightin' for.'

Foley lowered his voice. 'If you want my opinion, Kirkpatrick and McDonnell were put in there by the Brits to destroy McCann's power-base and clear the pitch for us to do business with them. That's done us all a favour. Like I said to Devine, if we shoot Kirkpatrick and McDonnell, that's tantamount to saying that McCann was right, and that would give him back his power-base. So let it be known down the line that Kirkpatrick and McDonnell are to be left alone.'

It was a frosty December morning, and one of Richard's aides was cheerful as he approached the breakfast table in his private suite at Stormont Castle. The two Belfast morning papers dangled from his hand, the headlines prominently displayed for his boss.

The *Irish News* read: 'IRA Ceasefire From Midnight: Prelude To A Lasting Peace?' The *Newsletter* took a more belligerent stance, with a headline that asked 'Ceasefire . . . At What Cost?'

Both papers also carried stories in smaller type describing the overnight murders of four people, two from each community, Catholic and Protestant. 'Sectarian killers strike again' was the gist of the coverage of the murders in the two papers.

Richard smiled as he laid the newspapers on the table. 'Get me Major Johnston.'

Tim Johnston arrived at Stormont Castle at midday and strode confidently across the courtyard like a man ready to do battle.

'It's only a snack,' said Richard, leading him into the dining-room where the table was laid for lunch.

'You've been working hard,' observed Johnston, glancing at the table and grinning.

Richard looked mischievous. 'Beware the saying that it's the condemned man who is given a good meal.'

After drinks they sat at the table and reminisced about their time together and the moments when they had both doubted that their plan would succeed.

'The IRA leadership were clamouring for a deal, and now they've got one,' said Richard, raising his glass to the major. 'We've sucked them into a process in which they will choke politically, and then the rest will crumble. We've given them incident centres, and what do you think the foot soldiers are going to do? They will kill Protestants, the Protestants will kill Catholics, and we can sit back and watch it happen.'

He laughed, and helped himself to a cold buffet from a side table.

'The more sectarian killings the better. When we've criminalised them in the headlines across the world, we will say enough is enough and close the centres. There will be no concessions. London HQ is awash with praise for us. It's like killing two birds with the one stone . . . The loyalists will suffer the same fate. We have not restricted either side's right to retaliate – and that's where your people come in, Tim. If they don't get on with it, you will need to help them or –

to use your military terminology – apply counter-insurgency measures.'

Johnston spoke quietly and deliberately, as if he were making a personal confession. 'Some people might say I'm a misinformed pessimist, but perhaps I'm the cautious optimist. Nothing ever seems real in this country. I keep asking myself if all we've done is to wound the serpent and leave the head intact.'

'The post-mortem confirms that we have cut off the head and the corpse is about to decay.'

Wineglass in hand, Johnston walked to the window and pointed towards Belfast. 'Maybe we're killing the wrong serpent.'

Richard joined him and nudged him playfully. 'You are truly the misinformed pessimist.'

Ignoring the comment, Johnston strode back to the table and slumped into his chair. 'I've been reading Tim Pat Coogan's book on the IRA, and I'm beginning to suspect that the IRA is a Hydra . . . We cut off the head and another one forms. I am not Heracles . . . All I can do is buy time for the politicians and, if that's the case, God help us all.'

Richard reached for the decanter.

'You don't get it,' Johnston went on, pushing the wine to one side. 'We should have killed McCann and his cronies before all this began. Time is on their side, and they can await the resurrection.'

Richard smiled at him. 'Don't be silly, man. The history of the IRA is one of internal disputes, failed campaigns and long periods of inactivity. My prediction is that the IRA have been destroyed for at least another twenty-five years, by which time Europe and the world will have moved on politically, leaving little room for that kind of nationalism in Ireland.'

'Perhaps you're right, Richard. Only time will tell.' Johnston got up to leave, clearly preoccupied with his own thoughts.

'What about our young friends?' asked Richard, hoping to detain him.

As Johnston reached the door, he paused. 'You know my views on that, but if you like I'll see them this evening.'

Richard remained seated, wondering about this complex soldier who had been so enthusiastic about their plan at the outset and was now doubting its eventual outcome. It was an aspect of Johnston's character he'd never grasped: the soldier who took orders and tried to fulfil them to the best of his ability, never wishing to declare victory; the soldier who didn't trust the politicians and bureaucrats to protect him from failure.

After two days in solitary confinement, during which they shouted at each other through the locks in the cell doors, Michael and Stephen were relieved when Wainwright arrived and took them to an interview room to fill out their release forms. On the way to the prison courtyard Michael was busy announcing his plans for a long holiday.

'Jesus, Michael . . . You never shut up. I've had two days of this and I'm reaching breaking-point.'

Unmoved by the criticism, Michael shook hands with Wainwright, with two prison warders and an official who handed him his belongings. Lieutenant Jane Horton was standing beside a car, watching the performance and smiling.

As she drove them towards Holywood, Stephen lowered a window and breathed deeply, while Michael hummed a tune.

Johnston and Milner were waiting in the Ops Room, and Michael lost no time in shaking Richard's hand. Stephen stood in the background, wilting under Johnston's stern gaze.

'You're both free to go.'

'Go where?' asked Michael.

Richard pointed to the door.

'And what about the IRA?' asked Stephen.

'You have nothing to fear from the IRA.'

'How do you know?'

'Our agents in the IRA have told us that word has gone out from the top that you're not to be touched. McCann has been stood down. There's a new commander in the IRA wing in the prison.'

'Why? What did McCann do?' asked Stephen, confused.

'Who knows?' replied Milner. 'It appears he botched some operation. Anyway, right now the IRA's Army Council are committed to a ceasefire, and they don't want to draw attention to you young men and McCann.'

Stephen turned towards the door, where Jane Horton was jangling a set of car keys.

Michael was motionless, his mouth open, but Stephen knew his anger was burning like a cortex fuse.

'What about our fuckin' deal . . . the passport and the money?' His legs were slightly apart and his hands were rolled into fists held tightly by his side.

'You've got your lives back . . . Leave it at that.'

Michael's gaze followed Richard, who walked slowly towards Stephen and stood in front of him.

'If we give you a lot of money or send you abroad, you'll both be marked down as our agents. As it stands, you have nothing to worry about . . . The alternative is to give you a new identity in a foreign country. Is that what you want?'

'I want nothing from you,' replied Stephen. He didn't blink under Richard Milner's piercing stare and he answered without hesitation. 'I'm just glad it's over.'

Michael ran towards him and grabbed him by the lapels of his jacket.

'Fuck you. This is a sell-out . . . Don't you get it?'

In three strides Johnston reached the pair and with one hand dragged Michael to one side, holding him at arm's length.

'You're not here to negotiate,' he told Michael. 'You've just been told you've got your lives back and you're free to go.'

Stephen looked first at Milner, then at Johnston. 'When you say it's over and we're free to go . . . does that mean from all of you? You . . . Special Branch . . . Green . . . everybody?'

'You're of no further use to us,' replied Milner.

Stephen dragged Michael towards the doorway.

'Don't think this is the end!' screamed Michael, gesticulating at Milner. 'I'll sort you bastards out! You'll be reading about yourselves in the *Daily Mirror*!'

Johnston laughed. 'There's nowhere to take your story,' he said. 'Who do you think would believe you?'

Jane Horton drove them towards Belfast. Turning into Oxford Street, she glanced in the rear-view mirror and smiled at Stephen. Outside the Europa Hotel, she stopped the car and reaching into the glove compartment removed an envelope and passed it to him.

'This should keep you going for a time.'

'Thanks a lot,' said Michael sarcastically. 'It's been nice knowin' you . . . real nice. Give yer boss one for me.'

'Get out!'

When the car drove off, Stephen pushed the envelope towards Michael, who seized it and began tearing it open.

'It's over,' said Stephen, walking towards the Grosvenor Road, which led to the Falls.

Busily opening the envelope and counting the money, Michael was oblivious to his friend's parting comment. 'Hey, hold it! . . . Don't you want your share?'

Stephen didn't look back.

'Fuck him,' said Michael. He stuffed the money into his pocket and tossed the torn envelope on to the pavement.

14

Walking along the Falls Road, Stephen felt both fear and exhilaration. His gaze never strayed from the groups of young men standing idly at street corners; he expected to be abducted at any moment. Yet the sense of freedom and joy as he passed familiar landmarks helped dispel a gnawing doubt that this was merely a dream.

At the gates of Milltown Cemetery he stopped briefly, staring at the marble statues resembling skeletal images on a ravaged landscape. In the fading light, the headstones were like blank paving slabs and uncoordinated lines merging into the darkness, falling towards the motorway. The cemetery reminded him of the sheer terror he experienced in his prison cell, wondering if another day would lead to Milltown. Would he lie with his father among the dead, carved into stone, so close to the monuments to the dead of the IRA, the organisation which held his life in the balance?

As he entered Pearse Row, sweat formed on his brow, his heart pounded and his steps slowed. How would his mother react? He had put her through so much torment while she was living in her private misery without a husband to help her tame a troublesome son. What was it that terrified him most? Was it his mother or his inner sadness at the way he'd led his life?

The questions, not the answers, filled his eyes with tears. The sudden tightening in his chest reminded him of the weeks after his father had died when, as a little boy not knowing how to articulate his grief, he told his mother the pain was like a toothache that hurt all over.

Could he ever convince her that he'd changed and that his

life would never be the same? During moments of despair, he had prayed for her, using the simple prayers she'd read to him in childhood. Something had entered his life and cast off the shadows of his past; but he might not be able to explain it to her. Maybe Jimmy could help him to articulate his feelings.

Unaccustomed to displays of physical affection from anyone but Bernadette, he was shocked when his old friend threw his arms round him and offered him his favourite seat by the dying embers of the fire.

Provo was standing on his hind legs, yelping and listing at a forty-five-degree angle to the ground, his spindly legs unable to keep him upright. Billy observed the performance with one eye partly open and with the detachment only a cat can muster. Jimmy's hands were flapping wildly, his body rotating as he vacillated between making tea and staring at Stephen, whose eyes still glistened with tears.

'Tea's the answer.'

Jimmy steadied himself and with an unusual burst of speed went headlong into the kitchen, tripping on the frayed tops of his slippers.

'Are you all right?' Stephen helped him off the floor.

'As long as you're home, that's what matters. Throw some coal on that fire and rest yer weary limbs.'

An unfinished letter stained by grubby fingers caught Stephen's eye, and he began reading it as Jimmy chattered incessantly. It began:

Dear Friend

A prison cell is like life. When you hide within yourself you're doomed. It's too small a space to contain fear, anger and feelings of rejection. Human beings need other human beings to share their trauma. Interrogators know that so they increase a person's fear and isolation knowing it will spill out into a collapse so that there'll be no resistance. People say no man is an island – that's rubbish – an island is a whole lot bigger than a cell. Just unzip your head and vacuum-clean it. I try to hoover mine but it's just an empty space nowadays.

You'll hear all these people in your block talking about Ireland. Don't listen to the bastards. Ireland is only Ireland when Ireland

is the world. It's like Bouan says about history. It's only important if you remember it creatively. Those bastards only want a
part of it and then they shove it down other people's throats.
Some people choke on silence but the people you're with in there
are choking on history. Thank God Provo can't eat history. Mind
you, he was choking on something the other day and for the life
of me I couldn't get him to open his mouth. I lifted him up the
way they do in hospitals when kids choke on sweets and squeezed
his chest. Well would you believe it? He pissed all over me – and
Billy, who was at my feet, looked like a drowned rat.

I put him down and gave him a good wallop with one of my
slippers and he shit himself so I thinks to myself is this dog
mental? Well, there on the floor in the middle of this steaming
turd that looked like an Egyptian mummy's head is a lump of
coal. I gave him a good talking to because I can't afford to feed
the fire and the dog. Coal is expensive. There I was thinking that
he was grinding his teeth all the time and wondering why the
coal supply was going down. Anyway he's come to his senses and
is back chewing my slippers.

I was losing track there. What I really meant to say was about
fuel. Yes, the incest of history fuels our little squabbles. Jesus,
they're not earth-shattering. We're still fighting over mental
boundaries and arguing about who owns God. The Brits don't
care much about who owns God and they think we're all nuts
over here so the sooner they get their finger out of the pie the
better. I am not saying the Prods have no rights. They suffer
from the same disease as the rest of us but they just won't admit
it. This is a little piece of rock and the Brits aren't the only ones
with the inclination to buy a lot of barbed wire.

The IRA in there will tell you they're looking for a consensus
and if you take away the con you're left with their form of majority
rule. The days are long past when I'll march to the tunes of the
glory boys. My father marched to other tunes and he's lying in
French soil, and who gives a shit? Those boys in there will tell
you about the Republic. Some Republic. The Taoiseach should
be called the Tea Shop. They don't give a tinker's curse down
there.

When my mother used to light the fire she built it like a sky-
scraper and it smoked, but it never flamed. My father used to
point at it and say, 'There's one thing that bloody woman can't
do, light a good fire,' and she'd say, 'There's nothing wrong with

that – it'll be a good fire when it lights.' He'd reply, 'Aye, that's what the fox said when he pissed in the snow. It'll smoke but it won't light.' When I hear the Tea Shops talking about what they're going to do for the North I think of the fox pissing in the snow. Lots of smoke but no fire.

Jimmy was on his way with the tea. Stephen hastily dropped the letter on the floor and pushed it under the chair with his feet.

'You need a little stiffener,' said Jimmy, indicating the tray and a half-bottle of John Powers Gold Label whisky strategically placed in front of the cups of tea.

Jimmy's concept of pouring a 'stiffener' was to fill half the cup with strong black tea and apply the whisky until the cup almost overflowed.

Three 'stiffeners' each and their conversation flowed smoothly, without Jimmy rambling off at a tangent.

'There's a lot been goin' on,' Jimmy explained with delight. 'We've all been plannin' yer future. Yer mother phoned her brother in the States and he's offered to look after y' and find y' work.'

He was proceeding too fast for Stephen, who was disturbed that he'd made no mention of Bernadette. Jimmy detected his look of dismay and smiled.

'Don't worry . . . You know who is included. Yer sister Deirdre talked to the Kanes. We all knew you were innocent and yer lawyer said they'd never get a conviction.'

Stephen helped himself to another 'stiffener', expecting more information, but true to form Jimmy's thoughts moved in reverse and the rewind brought him back to a word he'd just used.

'Parasites.'

'Who?'

'Lawyers – who do y' think?'

He contrived to look mean, squinting until his bushy eyebrows hung over his spectacle frames.

'They'll defend the indefensible for money and glory. If Provo took a lump out of Bridget Jones's arse, and I had the money, there'd be no problem gettin' a stay of execution. The lawyer would argue that Provo was provoked beyond a reasonable endurance. Lookin' at her arse, even the most hard-hearted juror would have t' say it was not without provocation. If you've got money y' can commit blue murder because y' can buy the best legal advice. All this shite that lawyers don't want t' know if their client is guilty . . . they don't care . . . They want t' know if you've got the money and, if y' haven't got it, if the government's goin' t' foot the bill. Jesus, when they put me away lawyers were nowhere t' be seen. Nowadays, if I stabbed Bridget Jones and got blood on me, and left a blood trail t' my garden, my lawyer would say it was contaminated by dogs pissin' in the streets and army vehicles runnin' over it . . . He'd argue that somebody else stabbed her but that in her death throes she tried t' cross the street to tell me what a bastard I was before she croaked it. Don't tell me about justice . . . Money buys anything.'

Stephen was sound asleep, a calm expression on his face.

'So you've decided to leave yer prison cell and take up home here!'

Stephen rubbed sleep from his eyes.

His mother was standing in front of him with his sisters and Bernadette in the background. Jimmy was wedged into a corner of the tiny room, a smile creasing the lines on his cheeks.

'Come here you, and give yer mummy a big kiss.'

Mary flung her arms round her son.

'Don't you ever hide from me again.'

As she smothered his face and forehead with kisses, Mary's tears mingled with his. Stephen hugged his mother with an affection he hadn't shown her since boyhood. Then he kissed both his sisters. Finally he moved towards Bernadette and, wrapping his arms around her, held her tightly, whispering that he'd talk to her later, when they could be alone.

In all the excitement Provo sported a huge erection and mounted Deirdre's leg with a grip like a lobster.

Losing no time in coming to her rescue, Jimmy hit him with a ragged slipper but the prospect of a sudden orgasm increased the dog's determination to maintain his hold on her leg. Jimmy rushed into the kitchen, returning with a wooden spoon, and delivered a crisp blow.

Billy raced out of the door in a blur of fur, while Provo, his ears pinned back, crawled to safety. The taming of the dog was akin to a theatrical interlude, and everyone broke into laughter while Jimmy continued to brandish the weapon.

Like a typical Irish mother, Mary reckoned the priority was to stuff her son with food. Patting his stomach she remarked that he looked half fed, and invited everyone to her house for a good fry.

Not unexpectedly, Jimmy declined.

'He gets beyond himself,' he remarked, as Provo cowered under the table. 'A good dose of bromide would sort him out.'

At the gate, Stephen thanked him.

'By the way,' said Jimmy, with a look on his face Stephen hadn't seen before, and a nod in the direction of the garden. 'If you've time, y' can cut those nettles.'

When the family meal ended, Bernadette took Stephen to one side and removed from a plastic bag a cardboard box containing money.

'Jimmy told me to give this to you. He's been savin' it for you in case you needed it.'

'There's no way I could take that. I'll give it back t' him t'morrow. There's no way I could take his money.'

'If you do that,' said Bernadette, 'he'll be hurt. He loves you like the son he's never had.'

'OK . . . Wait here for me, while I go next door and speak t' the old fella.'

As soon as he turned up at Jimmy's front door, the old man told him to sit down by the fire.

'I think the time has come for you and Bernadette t' leave.' Jimmy was unable to hide his sadness, and tears formed at the edges of his eyes. 'In Ireland, memories kill people . . .

even the dead have a voice. You won't be able t' erase the hatred of yer enemies.'

'Jimmy, you've no idea how much I regret what I've been doin',' Stephen tried to explain. 'It's like I was caught up in somethin' that got out of control.'

He stood up to leave, and Jimmy followed him to the front door.

'I'm not blind, y' know. There's still one person who shared a cell with me in the dark days who talks to me – and *he* knows when a bird farts in this city. You have to get out – not next month, but next week. In Ireland, time is not on your side.'

Stephen returned to his mother's house. Putting his head round the door, he asked Bernadette if she'd like to go for a walk.

'Are you mad?' said Bernadette. 'Wouldn't it be safer if you stayed at home for a while.'

'I just want t' talk to you.'

Deirdre glanced at her mother and Sheila. 'Look, why don't the three of us go to my house,' she said, 'and leave Stephen and Bernadette to talk.'

When they had left, he crossed the room in a couple of strides, took Bernadette in his arms and kissed her.

'God, I missed you . . . I know you've been through hell. I'm sure there must have been times when you wished you'd never met me.'

Bernadette squeezed him close. 'All that's important is that you're here. I never believed you killed that policeman.'

'I blame myself . . . What do your mum and dad have t' say about it?'

She looked up at him. 'They understand. You're not the first guy around here t' be framed. They're good people . . . and they have my interests at heart. As Jimmy says, we mustn't have regrets . . . It's the future that's important.'

'I don't know what I'd do without you. I've always loved you. I'm hopeless with words and things. I don't deserve you . . . now do I?'

Bernadette smiled. 'I hope you'll still be sayin' that when I'm old and grey.'

He clasped her shoulders. 'In prison the only thing I wanted was to see your face.'

'I wanted t' visit you, Stephen . . . you know that . . . but my parents didn't want me t' go.'

He placed a finger against her lips. 'I understand . . . I didn't want y' in that awful place, but y' were in my thoughts every minute of every day.'

'Stephen! You have t' listen to me.'

She stood back; his hands fell on to her shoulders.

'There's somethin' I must tell you. If you stay here we can't be together . . . it would kill my parents with worry.'

'It'll be all right, love . . . They've got nothin' on me.'

'No, it won't . . . Just listen . . . We have t' leave here if we're ever goin' t' have a future. At work, people stare at me . . . it's so hard for me too. I don't care what's happened in the past – I want us t' have a new start. There are too many bad memories here that'll haunt us. Your mum's brother, your Uncle Gerry in America, says he can help us. He can sponsor us until we can get work permits . . . and he says he can get us citizenship.'

'I thought y' had t' be born there for that.'

'No, y' can still do it if you have a relative but it must be a blood relative. I checked with one of the guys in our firm. I can get a visitor's visa for a while . . . but there's one small problem.'

'What's the problem?'

'I'm not a blood relative of your Uncle Gerry.'

'So?'

'So, Stephen Kirkpatrick, the only way I can stay there is if we get married.'

Stephen laughed. 'I'm beginning t' think I was better off in the Crum.' He held out his arms. 'Come here,' he whispered. 'If that's the only problem we have, then there is no problem.'

*

The following seven days were devoted to making arrangements for a new life in the United States. Stephen's Uncle Gerry was a successful builder who owned two apartments in Philadelphia. A bachelor in his mid-sixties, Gerry Downes was a considerate man who loved his sister Mary and kept in regular contact with her, sending money in the years after her husband's death. On learning of his nephew's problems, he had insisted on offering one of his apartments for the young couple and finding them suitable employment.

Three days after their release, Michael phoned, asking for Stephen, and received a verbal barrage from Deirdre, who happened to be there when the phone rang.

'Stephen doesn't want to talk to you, so get t' hell out of his life.'

Stephen was not told about the call.

'If he arrives at this door,' warned Mary, 'I'll kill him with my bare hands.'

Jimmy's concern was that Stephen should steer clear of Irish republican groupings in the States. 'Most of them are OK,' he said, 'but some might make yer life difficult.'

On the morning of his departure, Stephen visited his old friend, to thank him for his help and to promise to keep in touch. He found him holding three betting slips.

'I didn't know y' were interested in gambling.'

Jimmy pointed to his frayed little book. 'Bouan calls it votin'. He says you've a better chance winnin' on the horses than you have when you elect politicians, so I thought I'd do a little votin' meself. Here, take this.' He handed the book to Stephen. 'Y' should know it off by heart by now.' Turning his head away he placed Bouan's book in Stephen's hands.

'I can't take this, Jimmy. It's your bible, for God's sake.'

'Never refuse a gift.'

Jimmy rubbed the front cover as if a genie was captive within its pages and placed it in Stephen's jacket pocket.

'I hope y' don't come back like those Yanks who used t' visit our house when I was a kid . . . throwin' money at everybody and askin' why we all don't have all the mod cons. Mind you, it's a great country . . . and I like the Yanks – they're straight. Y' know the worst mistake the Brits made was losin' America . . . They haven't forgotten that . . . That was the end of the empire days. America's a big rock. I tell ya . . . if you were t' cut through it you'd find Ireland carved into it.'

Bernadette made a brief visit; Jimmy's arms hung limply by his side as she hugged him and kissed both his cheeks and forehead. Provo behaved impeccably, the memory of the wooden spoon scratched indelibly in his head.

At Dublin airport, the goodbyes were emotional, with both families anxiously proffering advice and clutching the young couple as if America were a world away where telephones and postal services did not exist.

After a brief stopover at Shannon, the plane rose over the west, with the landscape opening up like a multicoloured quilt. Tiny fields encased in rocky walls merged into a kaleidoscopic canvas with the Atlantic riding against the coastline of County Clare. This was the land containing the simplicity and barrenness of Stephen's childhood holidays – the land where the rocky soil held back the creeping industrialisation of Europe and the grinding machinery of mass farming. His heart was heavy as the plane banked over the sea and the coastline was tugged from sight as if by an invisible hand.

Burying his head between Bernadette's shoulder and her cascading black hair, he cried with the passing of one life and the uncertainty of a new beginning.

In Crumlin Road prison, Brendan McCann rarely left his cell; he preferred to receive visits from those who supported his theories. The new IRA commander in the prison was an elderly veteran, unable to impose his authority on the younger elements. Not once did he make an effort to communicate with his predecessor, whom he feared, knowing he was a man with a short temper.

When newspapers circulated around the wing, Brendan went into fits of rage, pointing to headlines which screamed out news of sectarian murders and branded the IRA as gangsters and killers.

'The Brits are fillin' the prisons with young lads who are caught up in all this sectarian stuff,' he yelled. 'And they're sittin' back laughin'. They've got us just where they want us . . . an organisation of criminals. Jez' Christ, what's happening to republican ideals?'

One morning, in a frenzy of hatred for the IRA leadership, he burned a pile of newspapers declaring that the ceasefire was the IRA's darkest hour.

'Why can't these fuckers see and admit that the Brits can outmanoeuvre these boys? They've been at it a lot longer than us. They've lured us into a trap.'

As smoke wafted along the block from the pile of burning paper, the Governor announced a lock-down and Brendan was taken to solitary. Five days later, he emerged unrepentant and was cheered to his cell by most of the IRA prisoners.

While the ceasefire dragged on for months, with no major concessions from the British government, Brendan gradually reduced his circle of confidants to a small group of young men who were to be his spearhead for a new organisation. They planned a strategic takeover of the IRA, with the emphasis on transferring power from Dublin to the North and getting rid of Foley, Skillen and McKee, the leaders of the Belfast Brigade. Every candidate earmarked for a role in the new, transformed organisation was a Northerner.

'It's us who're fightin' the fuckin' war . . . it's our blood that's on the streets and in the ditches . . . so it's us who should make the decisions. We'll need young men like Gerry Adams, Danny Morrison and Martin McGuinness to help us give equal status to the Armalite and the ballot box. We have to win the hearts and minds of the young people to sustain a struggle.'

One evening alone with Rodgers he began to brood about the episode with Kirkpatrick and McDonnell. 'You know I was beginnin' to like Kirkpatrick. I reckoned he'd been conned by devious people . . . we all know what the Brits are like. I stupidly put that down to Kirkpatrick being honest, and in a way it encouraged me to trust his word. It's that sort of personal thing . . . you're under threat . . . you feel grateful and you become careless. I was careless . . . I was taken in. Lookin' back, it was a brilliant ploy. You know, British intelligence is like a scorpion – the sting's in the tail. They knew what was in my head because I cracked the laundry operation, so they had to give me real facts to get me to accept the lies. It's taken me a long time but I'm beginnin' to separate the fact from the fiction. Just think of what they got with this sting.'

'What did they get?' Rodgers stared at him intently.

'They got me out of the way so they could broker a deal with the armchair generals like Foley. But having me out of the way wasn't enough . . . They needed t' discredit me because they saw me as a future threat to the leadership. They created paranoia within the ranks with the interrogations . . . and those rifts will take years to mend. They also split the leadership between those people who agreed with my policies and the Foleys of this world who are tired old men that will accept even an improvement of the status quo – whereas they know people like us will never settle for anything less than British withdrawal. And they managed to do the whole fuckin' lot in one fell swoop. Let that be a warnin' t' you boys . . . We've a lot t' learn here.'

'Like what?' asked Nolan.

'Like never lettin' down yer guard . . . Check and recheck . . . Trust nobody. Work on the basis that people are guilty until proven innocent.'

Brady seemed unimpressed.

'What's wrong with you?' asked Brendan.

'I still don't know how we were taken in by Kirkpatrick.'

'That was my fault. I have t' take the rap for that. Never let arrogance get in the way of yer judgement. Johnston gave Kirkpatrick things he knew I would recognise, right down to his own name: Johnston. By letting Kirkpatrick inside the MRF compound and billeting him in the same place as Wright and McKee, he knew I would fall for it. The bastard was prepared to give me O'Brien and Feeney to get me set up for the bigger sting.'

'What about the Dublin bombings?' asked Rodgers.

Brendan smiled. 'You've got to hand it to Johnston and this guy Milner. That was probably another set-up – just look at its timin' . . . We'll never know the answer to that one. One thing's for sure, O'Brien and Feeney were in that compound. McDonnell's involvement I still haven't figured out yet, but my gut feeling is that Kirkpatrick wasn't lyin' when he described O'Brien and Feeney. Their day of reckoning will come when I get out of here.'

On a November afternoon in 1975, Brendan was in the prison yard when news reached him that his companions were about to be released. The British government were closing what they called 'incident centres', a concession made to the paramilitaries at the outset of the ceasefire. The incident centres had allowed the IRA and the loyalist groups to monitor the ceasefire and to be seen carrying weapons for their personal protection.

'That's it,' declared Brendan. 'The Brits have them by the balls and now they can squeeze them. There's no need for concessions when your enemy is on his knees. The ceasefire's finished.'

As they exchanged goodbyes, Brendan warned his closest friends, 'Watch yer asses on the outside. The ceasefire will soon be over but it's difficult to get an army back on its feet. Remember, though – time is on your side.'

To everyone's astonishment, Brendan received a reduced sentence of two and a half years because of a legal technicality. As he had already served almost two years on remand in custody, he was released from Crumlin Road prison a few months after his companions.

On the Crumlin Road, a small number of well-wishers waited to greet him. At the side of the imposing gates of the prison a doorway opened and Brendan appeared carrying his belongings in a brown parcel. Rodgers broke from the group and embraced him, while Nolan and Brady waited nearby, grinning from the windows of a battered Ford Escort.

'Sorry about the transport,' said Rodgers, pointing to a dent in one of the doors. 'The war chest is almost empty.'

They drove towards the city centre and into the Falls, stopping at the rear of an illegal drinking club.

Rodgers led the way and opened the door to a large room. At first sight, the room, which was in darkness, appeared to be empty, but as Brendan crossed the threshold lights went on and applause broke out. He saw familiar faces in lines of men stretched along three walls. A tricolour was pinned to the back wall and under it stood four masked men in military fatigues, each carrying an automatic rifle held across the chest. In front of them was a long wooden table and seven chairs.

Three young men broke ranks and warmly shook his hands.

'This is Gerry Adams,' said Rodgers, indicating a man in a tweed jacket and spectacles who looked like a schoolteacher. 'And this is Martin McGuinness . . . and Danny Morrison.'

Brendan laughed. 'To hear him,' he said, playfully nudging Rodgers, 'you'd think I'd never met you three.'

Brendan took Adams aside and beckoned to Morrison and McGuinness to follow.

'It's time for you guys to leave . . . Your job is politics . . . Just make sure that Sinn Fein develops a ballot box strategy which gives us the political cutting edge we need. I'll look after the rest.'

Once the three Sinn Fein members had left the room, Brendan walked to the table flanked by Rodgers, Nolan and Brady. Studying the faces in the throng of men, he reckoned that every battalion area in the country was represented. The majority were young men like Barry Devine. There were also veterans, most of whom were from the North, and to Brendan's astonishment James McKee was present.

'He knows what side his bread is buttered on,' said Rodgers

as McKee strolled towards the table to shake hands.

'We need people like him,' replied Brendan. 'We can't run this organisation with nothing but youngsters.'

He walked forward and put his arm round McKee, guiding him out of earshot of the others.

'I'm sorry about what happened,' said McKee. 'We all learn.'

'The past's forgotten,' Brendan declared, patting him on the back. 'Now what's important is where we're going.'

McKee politely drew back. 'I still owe you an apology, Brendan.'

Brendan nodded.

'I was wrong about you. I let personal issues get in the way. And you were right about the Brits – the ceasefire was a fucking disaster. I'm here because I care about the movement.'

Brendan shook his hand. 'As I said . . . the past's behind us.'

'I've units on standby ready to act if you give the word,' declared McKee, his arms by his side. 'We shouldn't have any problem convincing the leadership to stand down.'

'I want no bloodshed,' Brendan warned him. 'There's been enough shed in fighting. Foley and Skillen have no choice. Send some of our battalion staff to tell them it's over.'

McKee retired to the back of the room and summoned four senior battalion officers. 'Pay Foley and Skillen a visit,' he told them. 'Take some armed volunteers and make it look official. Tell them they've been stood down.'

'What if they resist?' asked one of the battalion staff officers.

'Tell them they can live in peace or rest in peace . . . McCann's our new Brigade Commander and there's a new leadership. Tell them I've passed on the order.'

Brendan walked from the table into the centre of the room.

'Wherever we've been,' he shouted, 'we're never goin' back.'

Clapping and stamping feet beat out applause.

'The struggle begins here,' he continued. 'There'll be no deals with the Brits until we hold the aces. If they think they can contain it here, they're in for a shock. It's about time the British people got their share of the war. We'll hit the Brits where it hurts . . . on their own turf.'

Handclapping rang out for several minutes until Brendan raised his hands to calm them.

'Time is on our side.'

When the meeting broke up, he beckoned to his three closest friends. 'There's unfinished business.'

Rodgers looked at Nolan and Brady and they nodded: they knew what was on his mind.

'It will be handled in accordance with Republican Army regulations,' he told them. 'I want a record of this to show what we're up against and to put the past to rest. It will be our vindication.'

15

News of Stephen's departure reached the IRA through Bridget Jones, who had seen the young couple putting their luggage in a car. She had mentioned it to a well-known republican but it had not been passed to Patrick Rodgers and his colleagues until weeks before Brendan's release.

'Why the fuck wasn't I told?' Brendan demanded.

'By the time I heard about it,' he explained, 'it was too late. I didn't want to bother you about it in the Crum. I reckoned you had enough to worry about and we didn't know that you were gettin' out until the last moment.'

'Do you even know where the fuck he's holed up?'

'The woman who saw him leave says he's got an uncle in America. He even took his girlfriend with him. Some fucking romeo he is.'

'Forget the jokes . . . where is he?'

Damien Nolan tried to come to Rodgers's defence.

'Stay out of this,' warned Brendan. 'I want to know from him.'

When Brendan was angry, his companions knew to tread carefully.

Rodgers began slowly, looking to Nolan and Brady for support. 'Well, we . . . I mean I . . . heard from a contact that some busybody called Bridget Jones . . .'

Brendan glared at him, infuriated by the ponderous way he was explaining things.

'Right!' Rodgers had a fiery temper and embarrassment was fuelling it. 'Fuck you, Brendan . . . You told us to do nothin' about them and now you're standin' here large as life . . .'

Brendan began laughing. 'Jesus, you're in one hell of a mood . . . Will you just get on with it.'

The others tried to hide their amusement but that only served to increase Rodgers's annoyance.

'There's a fuckin' busybody who lives opposite the Kirk-patricks, and she says the old guy, Jimmy Carson, will know where he is. If you want, we'll put the screws on him. But by all accounts Kirkpatrick's flown the nest – probably to the States.'

Brendan suddenly looked dejected. 'Fuck it,' he said slowly. 'That's all I need. General Army Orders forbids operations in the US. It's neutral territory . . . We mess with Kirkpatrick over there and the Brits would love it. They'd use it to put pressure on the Yanks to close down our fund-raising.'

'We could seize a member of his family,' suggested Liam Brady, drawn to the prospect of luring Stephen out of America. 'Why not one of his sisters?'

Trying to outdo his colleague and impress the boss, Nolan speculated that abducting Jimmy Carson might be a better idea. 'We wouldn't have to kill Carson,' he declared. 'Just get word to Kirkpatrick that if he returns quietly we'll release the old man.'

Brendan put paid to their ideas with an elongated 'No', adding: 'Sooner or later there'll be a death in the Kirkpatrick family, or he or the girlfriend will get bored and return home for a holiday and we'll be waiting. It's always the same . . . the lure of Mother Ireland is not easy to resist. She'll miss her mummy and he'll miss his mummy and sooner or later they'll be back. As for Carson, leave him out of this . . . I don't want him touched . . . There are older people in the movement who have fond memories of him.'

'What about McDonnell?' asked Brady. 'When we heard Kirkpatrick had gone we put surveillance on McDonnell.'

'He's unemployed but doin' the double,' said Nolan.

Rodgers wanted action; he was now determined to obscure his failure to act on the information about Stephen.

'Maybe we should just haul in McDonnell and get it over with,' he suggested. 'He's at a loose end . . . Worked in a bar until the owner discovered he was being robbed blind . . . hasn't worked since. We know his haunts, so just give the word and we'll pick him up.'

'Hold on,' said Brendan. 'You seem to have forgotten about Feeney and O'Brien. The Brits may have fed us too many names . . . got us confused . . . But Kirkpatrick said he saw O'Brien and Feeney in the MRF compound, and I'd already had my suspicions about those two. Now I know enough to be sure they're touts.'

He paced up and down for several moments, then stopped and took a deep breath. 'There'll be one swoop, and I want all three of them snatched, so that fucker Johnston doesn't have time to tip them off and get them out of the country. Carefully select volunteers from the First Battalion and put them on standby. This will be a snatch operation. Tell them to be ready at short notice, but for Christ's sake don't tell them what's in store. I want no leaks. Names of the targets will be withheld including how and when the operation will take place.'

He turned to Rodgers and Nolan. 'You will be the spearhead of interrogation teams. Select your own people. When the targets are lifted be prepared. Remember everything that happened in the prison, so brief your associates.'

Rodgers remarked, 'There's a risk of Feeney and O'Brien learning about the snatch operation, of course.'

'At all costs,' warned Brendan, 'this must be kept tight. If they find out we'll never see them again. Nobody is to be told the nature of what we're about to do or when it's going to take place. But we've got to move quickly.'

'How quickly?' Rodgers didn't bother to hide his irritation.

'It must start tomorrow,' said Brendan. 'There's enough information on these guys. The longer we leave it the greater the risk of failure.'

'Shit! You could have told us this before,' complained Rodgers.

'Do you not trust us any more?' asked Nolan.

'I want the units to go in twenty-four hours,' said Brendan.

*

James Feeney was at home when the quartermaster of the 1st Battalion arrived looking edgy. They'd known each other since school and the quartermaster had nurtured the friendship because Feeney was operating at a higher level and was always available to provide advice.

'There's something afoot,' he told Feeney. 'I've been told not t' tell anybody, so I thought you might know what's goin' on.'

Feeney was intrigued, and listened.

'An hour ago, I was ordered to open one of the special dumps . . . A lot of gear was removed, mostly small arms . . . It was all hush-hush stuff.'

Feeney was now all ears. He'd been told nothing of a special operation. The special dumps that were kept for emergencies were only opened on the orders of the Belfast Brigade.

'What do you mean, hush-hush?'

It was obvious Feeney knew nothing of this, and the quartermaster began to fear he'd said too much. 'If this was authorised from on high, I could be liable to a court martial for talkin' to you.'

'Don't look so worried,' said Feeney nonchalantly. 'You're talking to a senior officer here . . . We're buddies, aren't we?'

'Well, OK . . . All I know is that it came from the top . . . At my house there was yer man, Cahill, and one of that crowd who used to be in internal security – '

'You mean McCann?'

'No . . . He was sittin' outside in a car . . . One of his sidekicks – Rodgers, that's him . . . He spoke to me. There's something special going down . . . I know it.'

Feeney got up and walked into the hallway, while his friend explained that another group of men had met him at the dump and removed weapons.

The front door slammed shut.

The quartermaster got to his feet and out of the window saw Feeney running to his car.

'Hey!'

By the time he reached the door, the car was speeding towards the Falls Road en route to the city centre and Holywood.

Seamus O'Brien was not as fortunate. Three armed men strode into a bar in the Clonard area, pulled him off a bar stool and dragged him to a waiting car while customers pretended to ignore what was happening. No one wanted to interfere with what was clearly IRA business.

'A fucking simple operation and we get it wrong,' screamed Brendan, pacing the living-room of the tiny terraced house which was his temporary base.

Barry Devine tried to calm him down, promising that Feeney would be tracked down and explaining how the quartermaster had blown their cover. 'The quartermaster's a good man,' he pleaded. 'He didn't know Feeney was a tout.'

'I don't give a shit,' shouted Brendan. 'He broke the rules. He was told to keep his mouth shut and he blabbed . . . Who's he gonna talk to next? Haul him in and put him on a charge. Make an example of him. He could have blown the whole fuckin' operation.'

He turned to Rodgers. 'What about McDonnell? I suppose you're gonna tell me he's the fuckin' Scarlet Pimpernel.'

No one dared to laugh.

'We tagged him in a bar at lunchtime,' replied Rodgers. 'He wasn't there when the lads arrived, and he's not in any of his usual haunts. I've put out word on the ground. He'll be spotted. Oh yeah . . . I've sent three of the lads to his house.'

'Why hasn't the house already been hit?'

'We all know he's never at home during the day . . . but, like a bad penny, he'll turn up somewhere in the area.'

Devine wanted to know what they should do to O'Brien, who was being held in North Belfast.

'Concentrate on him,' commanded Brendan. 'You know the routine. When we've got his confession – especially the names of the people runnin' him and whether he's recruited anybody in the ranks – read him his rights as a volunteer. He'll know the score. Do it according to General Army Orders. I don't want some fucker coming back to me at a future date sayin' we did it out of vindictiveness or revenge. I want a record of his testimony . . . When you get it, execute him.'

Michael was slowly recovering from a serious bout of drinking which had begun before midday. He'd received his unemployment benefit and by mid-afternoon was in bed resting himself before a further session in the evening. At 4.30 p.m. he awoke when his mother returned from work and switched on the television. He was getting dressed after a quick wash, thinking of the next pub he would visit, when he heard a car screeching to a halt. Looking through the window, he saw three men fling open the car doors.

'Christ!'

There was no mistaking the hardness and determination or the bulges in their jackets as they began scrutinising the numbers on front doors. A sure sign that they were about to smash down a door was the sledgehammer slung over a shoulder.

Downstairs, the television was at full volume because of his mother's impaired hearing. She didn't hear the doorbell but she screamed when the sledgehammer ploughed into the front door, ripping it off its hinges. Michael was two feet off the ground, gripping the downpipe from the guttering, when the IRA men rushed into the living-room. By the time they arrived upstairs, he was over the garden fence running towards the Andersonstown Road like a hare expecting the dogs to pounce.

At Casement Park he backed against the gates to draw breath and find the inspiration to make his next move. Stopping a local taxi, he asked to be taken to the city centre. From there he took a bus to the police and military base at Ladis Drive. By this time it was growing dark.

Throughout the bus journey he rehearsed what he was going to say to Special Branch, believing that, since they were the first people to recruit him, they would be the most likely to help him. A trip to Holywood was out of the question after his last experience with Johnston and Milner, and Green was his only hope.

After all, he told himself, Green was a policeman; he might even like to know all about Johnston's operations.

'There's someone here to see you, sir.' The uniformed constable stood in the doorway of Bill Green's plush office waiting for an invitation to enter but it was not forthcoming. 'He says he's a friend of yours . . . Michael McDonnell's the name.'

Green dismissed him and immediately got out of his chair. As Green walked into the foyer of the interrogation centre carrying a leather briefcase, Michael ran to greet him.

'Stop blabbering.'

He quickly ushered Michael out of the door towards the car park.

'Get in the car and don't open yer mouth until we're well out of here.'

On the approach to Edenderry where the river Lagan flows gently under Shaw's Bridge, the car turned towards a quiet beauty spot known locally as the Giant's Ring.

'Look at the state of yer shoes . . . I've just cleaned the fuckin' car.'

Michael looked down at his shoes and the rest of his lower half: mud and debris from his garden were splattered across his trousers and flaking off the soles of his shoes.

'Sorry.'

Green ignored the apology.

This was not the Special Branch officer Michael remembered. He was a slimmer version, with tailored clothes and a spanking new 3 series BMW.

'Sorry,' repeated Michael, bending his knees and drawing his feet up under the car seat so that his stained shoes were out of sight.

Green grunted.

At the Giant's Ring, he stopped the car, leaving the engine running.

'All right . . . what the fuck is this about?'

'Really like the car,' replied Michael, hoping praise would ease the tension that always existed between them.

'Fuck you.'

Unknown to Michael, Green had moved up in the world since the death of his partner, John Bradford. Promotion had been swift and he was sensitive about his unexpected rise to prominence, particularly among fellow officers in Special Branch. Any reference to it by Michael was naturally going to be interpreted as a barbed comment.

'What is it you want from me . . . smartarse?'

In different circumstances, Michael would have delivered a caustic reply but he was here to plead for his life.

'The IRA are gonna kill me, and you're the only one who can help . . . You've gotta help me.'

'What about your friends, Johnston and Milner . . . ? Why don't you run to them?'

Green clearly enjoyed Michael's distress. His face bore an expression of self-satisfaction tinged with arrogance.

'They shafted us,' said Michael, pitifully. 'The bastards sold us out.'

Green laughed, and Michael nervously rubbed the edges of his tie.

'Look, Bill, I could tell you all about their operation . . . I could go Crown witness.'

Green reached across, undid the front passenger seatbelt and laughed as it snapped back against Michael's chin.

'You see that door handle?'

Michael nodded.

'Get t' fuck out of my car . . . The walk to Belfast will do you the world of good.'

'Jesus Christ . . . Are y' not listenin' t' me? The IRA will blow my head off. The Provos were in my fuckin' house this evenin' . . . You can't just leave me here. It was you guys who got us into this.' Michael refused to move.

'Get out.' Reaching inside his jacket, Green exposed his holstered pistol.

Michael shivered with emotion. 'Jesus, y' can't do this t' me.'

'Watch me.'

Green looked around the car park to ensure no one was in sight, then drawing the pistol he stuck it into Michael's rib-cage. Michael reached for the handle, edging his body out of the car.

'Remember what you once said to me, you little fucker . . . "Who you see here, what you say here, when you leave here, let it stay here." That's now my motto, so close the fuckin' door.'

As the car drove away in the darkness, Michael ambled aimlessly towards the Lagan river, a dejected figure, his hands held against cheeks wet with tears.

Moonlight penetrated the trees and hedges, casting uneven images on the water. Standing where horses had once towed coal barges, he cried, remembering summer days when his father had walked him along this towpath, describing its history, and how the river used to contain salmon as big as a baby shark. In his father's youth, the poor in Belfast couldn't afford the beaches of Benidorm but they could picnic along the river, fish for trout and marvel at its gentle beauty.

Michael wished he could remain there, encased in memories of a childhood when the simplest of things made life worth living. It was an incalculable distance between that world and the world where the river flowed into a city imprisoned in memories of hostility. The salmon no longer came to the Lagan and no one wondered why they had left.

Two lovers passed him, their eyes straying briefly to the solitary figure hunched over the bank as if he knew there was something concealed in the river's depths. They clutched each other, huddled over as though the ground would grant them immortality by preserving their whispers.

It was an hour before he decided there was only one place left to run. Taking a route which bypassed the city, he made his way to Andersonstown, quickening his step as he reached

Pearse Row. He stopped beside Stephen's house, staring upwards at the room where they'd spent so many happy and sad moments. He'd known for some time that his boyhood friend had left the country. Bridget Jones had told everyone willing to listen and the news had reached him one evening in a bar in Andersonstown.

'Hey, you there.'

Jimmy Carson was peering round his front door, signalling to him to get off the street.

Michael rushed towards him.

'What the hell are you doin'?' Jimmy reached out, pulled him into the hallway and closed the door.

Provo bared his teeth and growled, slinking off when Jimmy pretended to kick him.

'Sit down there.' He pointed to the chair where Stephen had often sat.

'I'm in real trouble.'

Jimmy barred the door and pulled tight the curtains.

'The IRA are after me.'

It didn't come as a shock to Jimmy. 'Make yerself useful and stick some coal on that fire.'

Michael offered his hands to the flames while Jimmy shuffled into the kitchen.

Thirty seconds passed and he returned with a cup of whisky. 'Get that down ya . . . it'll calm yer nerves.'

Michael took a gulp of the Scotch.

'It's for medicinal purposes,' said Jimmy sternly, 'not for pleasure.'

'I've nowhere t' run.'

A noise of water filling a kettle followed Michael's remark. Jimmy quickly reappeared and stoked the fire.

'Y' wouldn't get far with the money I have,' observed Jimmy.

'I wouldn't ask you for money,' said Michael politely.

Jimmy didn't appear to hear him. 'Money is no use,' he said. 'They talk about the long arm of the law . . . The IRA's like a bloody octopus . . . If you're on this island it'll get you.'

Michael didn't want to reveal the terror he felt but it surged into his throat and he began to whimper, holding his hands to his mouth to stifle a cry.

'Pull yerself t'gether.'

Jimmy hurried to the kitchen and this time came back with a cup of tea which he handed to Michael. Then he sat opposite, trying not to look at him.

'I suppose y' can stay here until we sort somethin' out.'

Like a child reassured, Michael smiled through his tears. 'I thought y' didn't like me,' he mumbled.

'Your problem is that you've never liked yerself.' The observation was brutal yet not spoken with malice.

Michael nodded in agreement and sipped his tea, though his hands were finding it difficult to steady the cup.

'I never meant my life to be like this.'

'You're twenty-one . . . I'd say you've reached the age of reason . . . Take me . . . I've never wanted t' learn the facts of life. Could never understand all this stuff from St Paul about the growin' man puttin' away the ways of the child. Bouan says that he'd like to be one of those disinherited hippies left behind at the end of the Roman Empire. He says if we find the lost Chronicles of Cassiodorus . . . some Roman thinker or whatever . . . we'd find the real hippie types . . . people like you and me.'

Michael gasped at the seemingly incongruous nature of the old man's thoughts and failed to detect the glint of humour behind the thick lenses of his spectacles.

'Oh, that's right . . . you don't know about Bouan, do ya? . . . We won't go into that.'

Michael was relieved by this assurance. 'I know I've done wrong –'

Jimmy interjected, 'Look, son, it's not for me t' judge you. The past holds terror for all of us, especially if y' continue to live in it. Let it go . . . just like the wind. I used to tell a friend that the one who goes t' bed at night is not the one who gets up in the morning. You can be such a person if y' choose. Some people want t' sit between two chairs – the past and the future – and they never know where they are. You're here . . . in that one chair . . . Sit on that.'

The advice did not help Michael, who wanted to know what he should do. 'I can't stay here for ever . . . I've no money and I can't go home. Jesus, I hope my mother's OK.'

Jimmy looked piercingly at him. This was not the Michael who strutted his arrogance and treated him like an outcast. Dishevelled clothes, exhaustion and terror had transformed the young man into a vulnerable figure.

'I've got it,' said Jimmy, clapping his hands and rubbing them together.

Michael leaned forward.

'I'll go to Father O'Reilly.' He hesitated, apparently unconvinced by his own proposal. 'The only problem', he continued, 'is that some of the people's heroes think they're closer t' God than the church.'

Dejected, Michael slumped back into his chair. He didn't realise that Jimmy had a penchant for internal debate, even when he'd made up his mind about something.

'Yes, that's it. I'll tackle the priest. The church can't deny you sanctuary.'

Billy sidled up to Michael and leapt into his lap, rotating three times before curling into a ball. Michael stroked him with the cautiousness of an amateur, slowly lengthening the caresses as the cat purred. That was the signal for Provo to make his entry, with an awkward gait, his tail between his legs. Cautiously he approached Michael and lay across his feet.

Jimmy was impressed, and murmured his approval, squinting as Provo peered up at him as if to say 'Is this OK?'

'Animals are a good judge of character,' said Jimmy, adjusting his spectacles. 'Y' can now tell yerself that you're not as bad as y' thought.'

As the flames of the fire died away, they sat in a silence punctuated only by Provo's snoring. It was an opportunity for Jimmy to plan what he would say to the priest.

If the priest gives me any nonsense, thought Jimmy, I'll tell him why he was ordained. Too many of these fellas think all they have to do is preach from the pulpit. It's their duty to protect their flock.

305

'Jimmy, do y' believe in heaven?'

The old man blinked. 'Here, don't be gettin' morbid,' he said, with a chastising look. 'I'm not in the ground yet and you're talkin' about heaven.'

'I've often wondered about what happens . . . like with my dad after they put him in the grave. I used to visit Milltown and wonder where he was.'

'I'd like t' be recycled.'

'What do y' mean?'

Jimmy didn't appear to hear him. 'I'd like my body t' be placed on a big rock and left for the birds . . . Now, since that's unlikely, I'd prefer them t' stick me in the ground . . . none of this coffin business . . . we should go back into the earth the way we came out of it . . . as atoms.'

Michael appeared disturbed, and let his gaze drift round the room. Jimmy watched him, waiting for his response. Finally Michael looked at him as if he were trying to make sense of what had been said.

'Yes, Jimmy . . . But is there a heaven and a hell? . . . Like when we die where do we go?'

'I see what you're gettin' at.' Jimmy was more relaxed. 'We all go through the same door into the same tunnel of light. That's what happens.'

'And are we then judged?'

'We are our own judges.'

'That doesn't bode well for me,' said Michael sadly, dropping his gaze.

'There y' go again. You're too hard on yerself. There are no bastards. Our failings are our humanity. Y' see, there are people who want to be bastards . . . Look at Hitler . . . Now that's not you. Anyway we all go through the same door – the high and the mighty. All we take with us is what's in our heads. Every time I look at the graves of the rich, I think t' m'self: They couldn't take it with them. There's the Pope . . . When he dies he goes through the same door. Can y' just imagine him tryin' to get the Vatican through that door? . . . There comes a moment when we must all put the clock back to our beginnings in the natural world. The problem in this country is they're spending too much money on the dead and not enough on the living. If they left all that marble in the Slieve Donard Mountain where it came from and used the money for somethin' useful, I'd be a lot happier.'

Listening intently, Michael was gradually starting to feel guilty that he'd dismissed the old man as a 'nutter' and failed to recognise his kind if eccentric ways.

'I'm sorry the way I behaved towards you.'

The confession stirred Jimmy from his reverie. 'Stephen was right about you.'

Apologies made Jimmy nervous, and he fidgeted with a button of his cardigan. 'What matters here', he said, hoping to fend off more apologies, 'is to keep you out of the clutches of the IRA.'

The very mention of the IRA made Michael tremble and he began to describe his fear of the organisation. Then, without warning, he lapsed into a denigration of himself. 'They're bastards . . . but I'm no better, so why should anybody worry about a bastard like me?' He sighed, then continued, 'Y' know, I really loved my dad, and when he died the house was so empty. Mum was very good, but look at her . . . she just let herself go. I could never really explain things to her. That's why I took m'self out and about. Dad used t' say it was better t' keep women mean and keen . . . don't give them too much or they'll want more . . . keep them on their toes. I was a bastard to everybody . . . even Stephen.'

'I never heard him say a bad word about you.'

Michael looked thoughtful and was silent for a while, then looked up at Jimmy.

'Y' know, Jimmy, it was me who talked him int' doin' that job on the shopkeeper. I told him it would be easy . . . We just go in there . . . say we're IRA, and he'll give us the money. The auld fella in the shop started roarin' and yellin' at us . . . tellin' us t' get t' fuck out of his shop. He made a grab for Stephen and I lifted the nearest thing, a big bottle of lemonade, and whacked him with it. Jesus, I didn't mean t' hurt him. I just panicked, I suppose.'

He began to cry. 'I miss Stephen, y' know . . . I really miss him. He was the only real friend I ever had. Thank God he's in the States. The fuckers will never touch him there.'

Jimmy got up, put three pieces of coal on the fire and eased himself back into the armchair, taking care not to look at Michael for fear it might inhibit his confession.

'Y' know, Jimmy, months after the IRA punished us for that, all I could see every night was Stephen's face covered in tar. It nearly killed him . . . the whole business. He started goin' t' pieces, wouldn't leave the house, wouldn't talk t' anybody, and wouldn't eat. When they cut off all his hair to get rid of the tar, he looked like somethin' out of Belsen, dead skinny and sad-lookin'. I thought, Fuck it . . . what's wrong with a bald head? So I painted a face on mine and arrived at his door. Y' know what his mother's like – she's so fuckin' big. Well, all she saw was the face on my head and she hit me a terrible swipe. I said to her: "For Chrissake, Mrs Kirkpatrick, it's me." Do y' know what she said to me? She said: "It would look better on yer arse." Well, I'm standin' there and Stephen comes down the stairs. He bursts into a fit of laughin' . . . me with the face on my head and his mother givin' me abuse for being at her door in daylight. Well, that was it. Stephen stuck on a cap and we ran round to my house. Jesus, I must have looked a right dickhead . . . That was it . . . From there on, I played the eejit. I thought I was protectin' him but all I did was get him deeper int' trouble.'

Getting to his feet, Jimmy switched off the overhead light. 'Try to get some sleep.'

They watched each other in silence, Michael stroking the cat until his eyes became heavy with sleep, and tiredness finally making its mark on Jimmy. He closed his eyes, still wondering if an appeal to the church would save the young man whose features were now childlike in sleep.

They were woken by Provo growling, his back arched and his eyes fixed on the window. Baring his teeth, he ran into the hallway.

Jimmy was getting to his feet when a sledgehammer smashed against the door, splintering the wooden panels, but the door held firm. Michael dropped to the floor and crawled under the table by the window as a second blow sent the door crashing to the hallway floor. The bare light-bulb hanging from the kitchen ceiling hardly relieved the darkness as Jimmy, trying to shield Michael, positioned himself against the table, with Provo cowering in front of him. Two young men, one armed with a .357 Magnum, rushed into the room; a third, carrying an automatic rifle, ran upstairs.

Jimmy stood his ground, telling them they'd no right to be in his home. 'This isn't South America!' he shouted.

'Fuck you, old man,' said a bulky intruder who was carrying the sledgehammer. 'We're looking for McDonnell. He was seen coming in here.'

'He's not upstairs,' announced the man with the rifle.

The rifle barrel was poked into Jimmy's chest.

Provo whimpered and crept under the table and the gunman's eyes followed him. Michael panicked. In his haste to escape, he jumped up, pushing Jimmy into the rifle. The gunman's trigger finger snapped back and a loud explosion reverberated through the room.

A 7.62 round ripped into Jimmy's chest, propelling him over the table into a corner. Blood spurted over the window as the bullet tore through tissue and ripped a hole in his back.

'Jesus Christ!' yelled the gunman with the pistol. 'You didn't have t' shoot the old man. McCann will go mad.'

The gunshot had stopped Michael in his tracks and now he crawled towards Jimmy, screaming, 'Jesus, Jimmy . . . oh Jesus, Jimmy! . . . Don't die . . . Oh no . . . No!'

One of the gunmen kicked him in the side of the head, his boot connecting in a terrible crunching sound.

'The old boy's dead,' said the man with the rifle as Michael fought the pain and scrambled back towards Jimmy.

The other men tried to drag Michael away but he held on to Jimmy's cardigan.

'Let's get t' fuck out of here!' shouted the man with the pistol. 'The whole fuckin' neighbourhood will have heard that shot. We'll get McDonnell later.' Cursing under their breath, the three men ran out of the house.

Michael put his hand over the wound on Jimmy's chest but the old man pulled his hand away.

'It's no use, son,' said Jimmy, struggling to breathe, his voice a whisper.

Michael inclined his face towards Jimmy's mouth, his tears falling on to Jimmy's cheeks.

'I'm so sorry,' cried Michael. 'It's all my fault. Oh God, what have I done? I'll get an ambulance.'

'No,' said Jimmy, his right hand gripping Michael's hand. 'It's too late.'

Michael's face was almost against his mouth, his ears straining to hear him.

'It's time t' bring my stone t' the edifice. They can take your life but not what's in yer head. It's time t' put back the clock.'

For a moment Michael thought the old man was dead and rose slightly, his eyes fixed on Jimmy's face.

There was a slight smile, as though his pain were forgotten. 'Michael.' Jimmy's voice was almost lost in the rattle in his throat, as blood oozed over his lips. Momentarily his face brightened and his eyes opened wide. His hand tightened on Michael, drawing him closer.

'Don't be frightened . . . The light is there . . . I'll be waitin' for you . . . Bouan didn't lie.'

Then his grip loosened and his mouth opened wide.

Michael put his hand under Jimmy's head and pulled him towards him, staring into the lifeless eyes.

'Hey, who's in there?'

There were voices at the front door.

Immediately Michael panicked, and scrambled across the floor, getting to his feet as he reached the kitchen. Like a drunk he stumbled out of the back door and through the garden, running frenziedly towards the end of Pearse Row.

Smash! A rifle butt caught him full in the stomach.

'We've got the little bastard.'

Two sets of hands began dragging him towards a car.

'I told you he'd come out the back door.'
Looking up, Michael recognised Jimmy's killer.

Mary Kirkpatrick was woken by the shot and rushed next door to find Provo lying across the body, howling and pawing the blood-spattered chest. Billy was on the edge of the table staring at the corpse of his master, oblivious to Mary's presence.

In the back room of a social club, Jimmy's killer was flanked by two armed volunteers wearing balaclavas. He snapped to attention when Brendan McCann and Patrick Rodgers entered the room.

'I didn't mean t' kill the old man . . . It was McDonnell – he caused it.'

'How the fuck do you think this is gonna look in the media?' screamed Brendan. '"Inoffensive old man murdered by the IRA" . . . I warned you he was not to be harmed.'

'Jesus, I'd only a split second –'

'Why did you have the safety catch off?'

'McDonnell could have been armed.'

Brendan poked a finger in his chest. 'You disobeyed an order.'

'Couldn't we say it was loyalists? After all, he was an old republican.'

Brendan stepped back and landed a blow flush on the young man's chin, sending him crashing to the floor.

'He's dead, and you'll never walk again . . . Take him away.'

The killer was dragged screaming from the room. He had been condemned to the punishment of kneecapping: bullets would be fired through the backs of his legs.

In the meantime two masked volunteers had arrived with a hooded man, who was made to sit on a chair in the centre of the room and then tied to the chair with rope. The masked men took up positions on either side of him, their hands clasped behind their backs.

Brendan addressed Rodgers. 'I want an apology in the media. Draft a statement to the effect that the old man was accidentally shot while one of our units was pursuing a criminal. The Brits will make a lot of it but the local people will believe us. It's always better t' tell the truth. We should be represented at the funeral and send a wreath from the Belfast Brigade.'

While he was speaking Liam Brady and Damien Nolan arrived, and sat at a table facing the hooded figure.

Brendan sat down on the edge of the table.

'McDonnell, you know why you're here?'

The hood billowed outwards as Michael quickly exhaled air, inclining his head to one side to identify a voice that sounded familiar.

'You're here t' be judged for your crimes against the Irish Republican Army.' Brendan preferred to give the IRA its full title, never referring to it as the Provisionals and rarely, if ever, by its initials.

Michael's chest heaved against the ropes and two sets of hands slammed downwards on his shoulders.

'I know who you are . . . You're McCann.' Michael's voice was muffled beneath the hood.

'Now that we know each other, let's hear your side of the story.'

'What's the point? . . . You're gonna kill me anyway.' The words were delivered slowly and painfully and the tone was thick as though he were trying to swallow during the gaps between each word.

Standing up and leaning across the table, Brendan picked up a chair, walked to within three feet of Michael and sat down again.

'I want t' know everything, McDonnell.'

'What's in it for me?'

Brendan laughed. 'So you still think you can broker a deal?'

Blood was seeping under the hood and trickling down

Michael's neck. 'Your people kicked the shit outa me . . . Is that not enough?'

Dried blood on his battered lips made speech difficult. His words were slurred and almost inaudible.

'Take the hood off him and clean him up,' said Brendan, motioning towards the volunteers guarding him.

Still bound to the chair, Michael was dragged from the room.

Nolan grunted his displeasure that the hood was going to be removed. 'It's against orders to let an accused see his interrogators.'

Brendan laughed. 'For Christ's sake, he recognised my voice. If you want to leave, leave. I want to look in his eyes when he speaks. I want him to fear me. For some people, the hood is enough to make people talk, but this guy was always too cocky for my liking.'

The cleaned-up version of Michael was a distressing sight. One of his eyes was half closed with swelling, and bruises covered his forehead, cheeks and lips. He tried to force a smile.

'Thanks a lot,' he said to Brendan.

He flinched as Brendan walked towards him and touched a wound on his forehead.

'That's only a taste of what's to come, McDonnell. We can do it the hard way or the easy way. We've let you sleep . . . you've been fed.'

'And you've beaten the shit outa me in between times.'

For almost an hour, Brendan, Nolan and Brady took turns to pose questions, but Michael stared blankly at the wall. Brendan's patience was wearing thin.

'What about yer friend, Kirkpatrick?' he yelled, his face inches from Michael's. 'He fucked off and left you . . . you may as well come clean.'

'There's nothin' you guys don't know . . . Stephen told you everything in the Crum.'

Brendan looked pleased with Michael's sudden willingness to speak and, patting him on the back, offered him a lit cigarette.

Michael refused it, keeping his teeth clenched as Brendan tried to thrust it into his mouth.

'Maybe you're the fall-guy and Kirkpatrick was the brains behind the Brit scam?' said Brendan.

'Stephen was my friend, and I've no intention –'

'Some friend . . . he fucked off and left you,' Nolan interjected.

Ignoring him, Michael directed his reply at Brendan. 'Leave Stephen out of this . . . I should've fucked off if I'd any sense . . . He was just an innocent in all of it.'

The interrogation developed into a mixture of verbal abuse and threatening gestures. Michael responded by closing his eyes and sighing, as though his mind could not take much more. There was a respite when Rodgers arrived.

'Could I have a quiet word?' Rodgers asked Brendan.

They stood in the doorway, talking in hushed tones.

'We've got what we need from O'Brien,' said Rodgers. 'What about McDonnell?'

Brendan looked perplexed.

'Jesus!' explained Rodgers. 'A hard nut like O'Brien's cracked and that squirt hasn't.'

'I don't understand it,' whispered Brendan. 'I've seen tough men open up even when they knew they were doomed, but McDonnell . . . I don't understand him.'

'Give him the full works.'

Brendan shook his head.

'Maybe you're too near to this one,' said Rodgers. 'Why not leave it to me?'

He was about to brush past Brendan when he found himself pushed out of the room. Brendan followed and closed the door behind them.

'I have t' see this through,' said Brendan, running his hands through his hair. 'There's one thing that occurs to me and it's about that old man. Maybe he said something that changed McDonnell's attitude. I don't know how to explain it . . . McDonnell's not behavin' as I expected.'

Rodgers laughed, but quickly regained a solemn composure under Brendan's gaze.

'OK, boss . . . It's your call, but I can tell you that there's no way McDonnell could ever change. Remember in prison . . . he was the one who gave us nothing.'

'Maybe he'd nothing to give.'

'Bollocks. He was there with Kirkpatrick.'

'Yeah, but Kirkpatrick was the one they used because he had something to say.'

'Maybe they used Kirkpatrick because they knew he was the one who would crack . . . Maybe it was part of their ploy.'

'No. It doesn't match up. And even if you're right he has nothing to gain now. He might as well tell us about his role with Johnston and Milner.'

'Maybe he knows he's gonna die, so what's the point.'

'Nobody knows they're gonna die until the bullet leaves the barrel.'

'Then why don't you give him the full treatment?'

Brendan paused, as though searching for an answer.

'Don't tell me you feel sorry for that little bastard.'

Brendan grabbed Rodgers by the lapels. 'If I'd done what was right,' he hissed, still holding Rodgers, 'I wouldn't be begging McDonnell to provide answers.'

Then he relaxed his grip, dusted off Rodgers's jacket and apologised.

'Look, boss, just kill him and get it over with . . . We know what happened . . . there's no point torturing yourself.'

Brendan snapped his fingers. 'You see to it that O'Brien's executed. I'll finish here.'

'Where do y' want the body dumped?'

'Wherever's convenient . . . South Armagh.'

As Brendan re-entered the room, Michael turned towards him and was struck on the back of the head.

'*You* were responsible for the death of that old man,' screamed Brendan, bending over him.

Michael swallowed hard and tears filled his bloodshot eyes. 'I didn't mean t' get him killed.'

His sobbing intensified and his chest strained against the ropes holding him to the chair.

'Well, he's fucking dead!' shouted Nolan from behind the table. 'And that's what *you're* gonna be before long.'

Urine trickled down Michael's legs. 'I want a priest,' he pleaded.

315

'Get Father O'Reilly.'

Brendan motioned to the others, including the two volunteers, to leave the room.

'Why did you do it?' he asked when he and Michael were alone.

'I don't know . . . I just don't know . . . Why can't you let me go? I can't do you any harm.'

'I know that.' Brendan pulled up a chair and sat down facing him. 'Everybody has t' pay a price. What I want t' know is why you won't tell us about it. Are you protecting Kirkpatrick, or did the old man say something to you?'

Michael flinched with pain as he tried to smile. 'Stephen was a patsy in it all. And Jimmy was a real friend and I never knew it. He said the man who goes t' bed at night isn't the one who gets up in the morning, and he was right. I'm not stupid. I know where I'll be tomorrow. You're no different from the others.'

Brendan rose quickly, grunted and returned to the table, turning to face his victim.

Michael closed his eyes for several seconds. 'At least you won't get yer hands on Stephen, and Jimmy's better off where he is . . . he never liked you lot. I just want t' write a note t' my mother.'

'*He'll* do that.'

Brendan pointed to a worried-looking priest, standing in the doorway wearing a stole. In his hand was a small silver box containing oils for administering the last rites.

'This is a travesty –'

'Get on with it, Father.' Brendan interrupted Father O'Reilly's protest with a raised hand. 'Don't interfere. You're here for one purpose – and one purpose only.'

'This is God's time and he would like you to leave.'

Brendan sauntered past the priest and closed the door behind him as he left the room.

Michael turned to the priest. 'Father, before you hear my confession will you promise t' tell my mother I'm sorry and I love her.'

Father O'Reilly stroked his hair.

'And will y' tell Mrs Kirkpatrick in Pearse Row t' let Stephen know I'm sorry about Jimmy Carson. I was in his house when they came for me.'

Ten minutes later there was a thud, as someone kicked open the door.

'Are you finished?' It was Nolan's voice.

Father O'Reilly left the room without acknowledging Nolan's presence or glancing at Brendan, who was leaning against the door-frame.

A black hood was put over Michael's head and tied at the neck. His arms were roughly pulled backwards and bound at the wrists. A length of rope encircled his ankles as he was lifted bodily from the ground and carried from the room like a roll of carpet.

'Hold it.'

Brendan walked across the room and bent over Michael.

'What did that old man say to you before he died?'

There was a moment's silence before Michael's voice came slowly through the blackness of the hood. 'He said he'd be waitin' for me. He said y' could take my life but not what's in my head, and it was time to turn back the clock. He was happy. He said Bouan hadn't lied.'

'Who the fuck's Bouan?'

'I don't know.'

Brendan stepped back. 'More fuckin' riddles. Get him outa here.'

As Michael was pushed into the boot of a waiting car he crouched into a foetal position and the lid was slammed shut; the car drove away. He kept thinking of Jimmy and how the old man reminded him of his father. Over and over he recited prayers he had learned in childhood when his mother knelt at his bedside: 'Infant Jesus, come to me . . . in my heart abide . . .'

The car screeched to a halt sending him crashing against the metal sides of the boot.

'Get him out.'

The lid was open and two sets of hands were lifting him into a standing position. The smell of decaying leaves found

317

its way through the thin cloth of the hood covering his face and head.

'Kneel down, McDonnell.'

Fear gripped him and he struggled against the hands holding him.

'Just let me see where I am before I die,' he pleaded. 'Let me say a prayer.'

'We're wastin' time.'

'That's you, isn't it?' said Michael quietly.

Rodgers recoiled.

'I told you to keep yer mouth shut,' said Nolan.

'Please.'

'It can't do any harm,' said Nolan to Rodgers. 'We can always put the hood back on. What's a minute?'

As the hood was pulled from his head, Michael collapsed to his knees.

Brandishing a pistol, Rodgers walked behind him and Nolan placed a hand on his shoulder. A gentle breeze caught the edges of the leaves on the trees surrounding them and the moonlight picked out a clearing.

'I know where this is,' said Michael, staring towards the entrance to Colin Glen.

'So fucking what?' Rodgers pulled back the carriage of the pistol sending a run into the chamber.

'Stephen and I used to play here as kids. This is where he used t' take Bernadette.'

Nolan shook Michael. 'You've a minute, McDonnell.'

Michael closed his eyes, remembering the dusty summer days when he and Stephen sneaked away from home and carved their names on trees in Colin Glen, sometimes swimming in the deeper pools of the river and sharing sandwiches. As the hood was pulled down over his head and face, he murmured a prayer, cut short by a sharp explosion.

His body slumped forward. Rodgers fired two more shots.

Mary Kirkpatrick was watching television when news broke about the discovery of a hooded body in a ditch near Colin Glen.

'The latest update on the body found in Colin Glen', said the reporter, 'is that it's the body of twenty-one-year-old Michael McDonnell, a Catholic from Andersonstown in West Belfast.'

'Oh my God . . . my good God!'

Mary would have fainted if Deirdre hadn't been there to put a comforting arm around her.

'That could have been my Stephen.'

At the MRF compound, staff were running to and fro, packing documents in box files and unplugging technical equipment.

Richard Milner arrived in the midst of the chaos and found Tim Johnston in the ante-room.

'You've heard the news?' said Richard. 'They've disposed of McDonnell and O'Brien.'

Hardly sparing him a glance, the major continued packing his personal belongings and putting to one side certain files for the shredding machine.

'We should have closed up shop before now,' he muttered, looking briefly at Richard. 'Even the UDA jumped on the bandwagon and lifted Phillips . . . scared that the Provos may have been right all along. He'll be found with one in the head – that you can be sure of. It's anybody's guess what O'Brien's given them. It's somebody's else's responsibility from here onwards. When you get to London, my advice would be to stay there. These people mean business . . . You can't say I didn't warn you.'

Stephen and Bernadette had settled into the apartment in Philadelphia, though their first months in the States had been difficult. For weeks Stephen had wallowed in guilt, blaming himself for taking Bernadette out of Ireland. She had found it hard coping with his paranoia: every time a stranger looked at him or he heard an Irish accent he panicked.

Stephen's uncle had helped him find work, mainly casual employment in bars and restaurants. By the time a baby daughter was born, a year after their marriage, the couple were beginning to enjoy their new life.

Returning home one Saturday morning from shopping, Bernadette found the front door open and instinctively knew something was wrong. In the dining-room the television was on and the telephone handset dangled from the receiver.

'Stephen . . . Stephen!' she called, running round the apartment, the baby in her arms.

Stephen's uncle, Gerry Downes, arrived just as she had collapsed into a chair and begun crying.

'What's going on?'

'Stephen's gone . . . Something's happened.'

'Take it easy, love,' he said, lifting the baby from her.

'Maybe the IRA's got him.'

'Don't be silly,' he said, rocking the baby in his arms. 'He's probably gone for a walk.'

'It's not like my Stephen to leave the door open and the phone –'

'C'mon, Bernadette . . . Calm down.' He handed her the baby. 'You take care of little Siobhan . . . I'll go and look for Stephen.'

'Maybe we should phone the police.'

'Don't worry.' Gerry backed out of the apartment. 'He'll be close by.'

Gerry Downes found Stephen sitting on a bench, clutching the little book that Jimmy had given him. His face was wet with tears and he was gazing skywards. Gerry put an arm around him.

Raising the book to his lips, Stephen heaved with emotion. Gently his uncle took the book from him and looked at the inscription on the inside of the cover: 'To my dearest friend, Stephen, in memory of all our times together. From Jimmy, Provo and Billy.'

Gerry didn't need to ask why he was sad. His nephew never stopped talking about Jimmy Carson.

'They killed Jimmy and Michael . . . poor Jimmy . . . It's all my fault.'

'You mustn't blame yourself, Stephen . . . Just thank God you're here.'

Stephen's mind was suddenly filled with sharp fragments of memory – of cold Sundays watching Gaelic football with his father in Casement Park, Michael smoking old cigarette butts in the cottage in Donegal, getting drunk together on vodka and Coke, pushing through the nettles to sit by Jimmy's fireside with strong tea and whisky, falling asleep while the old man read from *Don't Lie to the Children* and rambled on about the soldiers of someone else's destiny . . .

Then he recalled the marble headstones in Milltown Cemetery, and how, despite the grim monuments to the IRA dead, the encircling mountains never failed to astonish him with their beauty.

As they began to walk back home, Stephen turned towards his uncle. 'Jimmy used t' say: in Ireland the memories kill people. And even the dead have a voice.'

Epilogue: 1994

Philadelphia, September

Bernadette was watching *Good Morning, America* when news of the ceasefire broke.

'Stephen . . . Stephen!'

He rushed out of the bathroom and remained in front of the television until the Ireland report ended.

'Maybe it's over,' said Bernadette, tears sparkling in her eyes.

Stephen paused. 'It changes nothing. We're happy here.'

That evening, while he was serving behind the bar near Washington Square, a middle-aged customer with a hard Belfast accent tried to engage him in conversation. Stephen waited for a leading question from the stranger and it wasn't long in coming.

'Where are you from in Belfast?'

Stephen hesitated. Seeing another customer, he rushed along the bar to serve him. Any hopes that the stranger would leave were dashed when he moved his bar stool, bringing him closer to Stephen.

'One of the staff says you're called Stephen . . . I heard yer accent when I was having a meal . . . Stephen . . . is that right?'

'Yeah.'

'I didn't get yer surname.'

Stephen looked around the bar, hoping to find a distraction which would require his attention.

The stranger was persistent. 'Stephen, I'm Seamus. I hope I'm not bein' a nuisance. I didn't get yer surname.'

'Kirkpatrick.'

'You wouldn't by any chance be related to the Kirkpatricks from the Ardoyne up there in North Belfast?'

'No.'

With a name like Seamus he was Catholic, and so was the Ardoyne. It was only a matter of time before the questioning followed a Belfast pattern Stephen knew only too well.

Suddenly he found a way out. 'I'm from Holywood.'

That seemed to work, and the stranger toyed with his car keys. Holywood was a mixed-religion town, and the implication might prevent further enquiries.

'Oh, I see.' He was confused and tried to smile. 'Don't really know much about Holywood. Passed through it once or twice.'

Stephen began to turn away.

'Fine name, Kirkpatrick . . . That was on yer father's side?'

Here we go, thought Stephen; like a gambler he wants better odds before he decides if I'm Prod or not.

It was the Northern Ireland game of 'Get the name and you get the religion.' Stephen's mother's maiden name would be the decider, so he opted for a traditional Protestant one.

'Actually my mother was a Stewart.' Work that one out, he mused. Stewart implied a link between Scots Presbyterians and Northern Ireland Unionists.

'Stewart! Fine name, Stewart. Now you take me. I'm a McAteer from the Ardoyne, but over here it doesn't matter. I've a healthy respect for the Protestant tradition. In fact, I've a friend from down Holywood way . . . lives near me at Port Washington outside NYC. We play golf together. I must bring him down here for the crack and we can all get together.'

On his way out of the door he stopped and smiled.

'If you tell people over here that you're from Holywood, they'll think you're a film star.'

The episode upset Stephen. He went home before closing, complaining of a stomach virus.

'Jesus, that's it!'

Bernadette told him to calm down.

'That's it . . . Christ, I can't even get peace in America

without some fucker from New York asking me where I'm from and wantin' t' know if I'm a Prod or a Taig.'

He began pacing up and down the dining-room with a bottle of bourbon.

'I'm done for,' he ranted. 'We'll have t' leave.'

'He's probably a chancer,' said Bernadette, putting an arm round him. 'Did he even look like the golfing type?'

'Well, he wasn't particularly well dressed, but that's no guide, and he didn't mention the PGA Masters and it was on television behind the bar.'

'You see?'

'Yeah, but maybe he does live at Port Washington, and say he has a friend from Holywood . . . I'm up shit creek.'

Stephen put down the bottle. 'I always knew we'd have to go back some day.'

London, October
Richard Milner gazed through the window of his third-floor office in Whitehall. The falling rain against the grey buildings did nothing to improve his mood. Returning to his desk, he began putting his belongings into a cardboard box.

'Could they not stretch to a courier service?'

Tim Johnston walked towards him, his hand extended.

'Tim! How good to see you. What in God's name are you doing here?'

'I heard you had returned from your posting in Washington. How was it?'

'I did what I was asked . . . you know the score . . . I was recalled with an offer of promotion. I suspect it's Belfast again, God help me.'

'No rest for the wicked.' Johnston smiled.

'What about this insistence on the decommissioning of IRA weapons?' Richard asked with his customary inquisitiveness and, leaning forward, added mischievously, 'Are we talking about another stalling procedure to get the Prime Minister through the next election?'

Johnston laughed and sat on the edge of the desk. Richard was happy to find him in good humour, and teased him.

'I suppose you personally know the quality, quantity and whereabouts of the IRA arsenal.'

'Is the Pope a Catholic?'

Richard grinned. Reaching into his desk, he produced a bottle of Cognac and two paper cups.

'I was going to leave this for the next poor incumbent but . . . what the hell! I think we are in need of it.'

Richard poured two large brandies. 'Let's drink to changing times,' he said, handing one to the major. '*Slainte!*'

There was a glint in Johnston's eye as he raised his paper cup. 'As they say in Cork, Richard, "May the wind be always at your back." *Slainte!*'

Belfast, November

It was a clear frosty morning as Mary Kirkpatrick slowly made her way into St Peter's for the early Mass.

Father O'Connor was the celebrant. Old age had slowed him down but had not corrected his habit of scolding altar boys who didn't dispense enough wine and water into the chalice.

After the service, Mary lingered on the steps outside and looked up into the twin spires, wondering whether Stephen really did plan to return.

'I remember your young fella was always intrigued with the spires,' said Father O'Connor, shuffling towards her.

'Father, does the hawk still come here?'

The old priest looked upwards and then glanced at the children's play park and the neat rows of new houses surrounding the church.

'Sure, what would a hawk want around here?' There was a hint of sardonic humour.

'Sure, it's all changed. There's nothing here for the hawks any more.' Tears came into her eyes.

'Strange bird, the hawk,' continued the priest. 'Have you ever heard of Bouan? He says that hawks . . .'

Mary was on her way down the street, smiling, perplexed.